About the author

Alai is an ethnic Tibetan who now lives in Sichuan, China. He is the author of a number of prize-winning short story collections. *Red Poppies*, his first novel, was given China's highest literary award, the Mao Dun Prize. It is the first book of a projected trilogy about Tibet.

Howard Goldblatt and Sylvia Li-chun Lin's translations include Chu Tien-Wen's *Notes of a Desolate Man*, which was named the 1999 Translation of the Year by the American Literary Translators' Association.

Red Poppies ~

Red Poppies ~

Alai

Translated from the Chinese by
Howard Goldblatt and Sylvia Li-chun Lin

Methuen

This paperback edition published in 2003 by Methuen

10 9 8 7 6 5 4 3 2 1

Copyright © 1998 by Alai

The right of Alai to be identified as author of this work has been asserted by him in accordance with the Copyright, Designs and Patents Act 1988

Translation copyright © 2000 by Howard Goldblatt and Sylvia Li-chun Lin

First published in the USA in 2002 by Houghton Mifflin

First published in Great Britain in 2002 by Methuen

Methuen Publishing Ltd
215 Vauxhall Bridge Road
London SW1V 1EJ

Methuen Publishing Limited Reg. No. 3543167

A CIP catalogue record for this book is available from the British Library

ISBN 0 413 77183 0

Printed and bound in Great Britain by
Cox and Wyman Ltd, Reading, Berkshire

Translators' Note ∽

Alai was born in a tiny hamlet in Maerkang county, in what is now western Sichuan; at the time of the story, however, his hometown was in the western part of the Tibetan Autonomous Region. Settled centuries earlier by Tibetan nomads, the region's power and legitimacy came largely from the Chinese to the east, who ennobled the strongest and richest families. Religious ties to the Buddhist centres of Lhasa and Shigatse to the west were tenuous at best; political ties were equally difficult, with encroachments from all directions always a threat. During the War of Resistance against Japan (1937–1945), Tibet was spared fighting the foreign aggressors, although power struggles among the various clans and chieftains continued. At the conclusion of the Chinese Civil War (1945–1949), territorial lines were redrawn, autonomy for all Tibet was lost, and the age of the chieftains came to an end.

In the 1980s, Alai published a story about a legendary wise man, Agu Dunba, who, in the author's words, "represents the Tibetans' aspirations and oral traditions." But, rather than focus on the sagacity so often extolled by others, he "preferred the wisdom masked by stupidity." A decade later, Agu Dunba would become the model for Alai's narrator in *Red Poppies*, feeling that "the intelligence of Agu Dunba epitomises raw and uncultured folk wisdom."

Red Poppies ～

One ～

1 Wild Thrushes ～

It snowed that morning. I was in bed when I heard wild thrushes singing outside my window.

Mother was washing up in a brass basin, panting softly as she immersed her fair, slender hands in warm milk, as if keeping them lovely were a wearisome chore. She flicked her finger against the edge of the basin, sending tiny ripples skittering across the surface of the milk and a loud rap echoing through the room.

Then she sent for the maid, Sangye Dolma.

Acknowledging the summons, Sangye Dolma walked in carrying another brass basin. She placed the milk basin on the floor, and Mother called out softly, "Come here, Dordor."

A puppy yelped its way out from under a cupboard. It rolled around on the floor and wagged its tail at its mistress before burying its head in the basin and lapping up the milk, nearly choking on it. The chieftain's wife, that is, my mother, loved the sound of someone choking on the little bit of love she dispensed. Amid the noise of the puppy greedily lapping up the milk, she rinsed her hands in fresh water and told Dolma to check on me, to see if I was awake. I'd had a low-grade fever the day before, so Mother had slept in my room.

"Ah-ma," I said, "I'm awake."

She came up and felt my forehead with her wet hand. "The fever's gone," she said.

Then she left my bedside to examine her fair hands, which could no longer hide the signs of aging. She inspected them every time she completed her morning grooming. Now that she'd finished, she scrutinized those hands, which were looking older by the day, and waited to hear the sound of the maid dumping the water onto the

1

ground. This waiting was always accompanied by fearful anxiety. The cascading water splashing on the flagstones four stories below made her quaver, since it produced the shuddering sensation of a body splattering on the hard ground.

But today, a thick blanket of snow swallowed up the sound.

Still, she shuddered at the moment that the splash should have sounded, and I heard a soft muttering from Dolma's lovely mouth: "It's not the mistress hitting the ground."

"What did you say?" I asked.

Mother asked me, "What did the little tramp say?"

"She said she has a bellyache."

"Do you really?" Mother asked her.

I answered for her. "It's okay now."

Mother opened a jar and scooped out a dab of lotion with her pinkie to rub on the back of her hand. Then another pinkie brought out lotion for the other hand. A spicy, pungent odor spread through the room. The lotion was made of marmot oil and lard, mixed with mysterious Indian aromatic oils presented to her by the monastery. The chieftain's wife had a natural talent for looking disgusted. She displayed one of those looks now, and said, "This stuff actually smells terrible."

Sangye Dolma offered up an exquisite box containing a jade bracelet for her mistress's left arm and an ivory bracelet for the right. Mother put on the bracelets and twirled them around her wrists. "I've lost more weight."

The maid said, "Yes."

"Is that all you know how to say?"

"Yes, Mistress."

I assumed the chieftain's wife would slap her, as others might do, but she didn't. Still, fear turned the maid's face red.

After the chieftain's wife started downstairs for breakfast, Dolma stood by my bed and listened to the descending steps of her mistress. Then she stuck her hand under my bedding and pinched me savagely. "When did I say I had a bellyache? When did I ever have one of those?"

"You didn't," I said. "But you'd like to fling the water with even more force next time."

That stopped her. I puffed up my cheek, which meant she had to kiss me. "Don't you dare tell the mistress," she said, as my hands slipped under her clothes and grabbed her breasts, a pair of frightened little rabbits. A passionate quiver erupted somewhere deep inside me, or maybe only in my head. Dolma freed herself from my hands and repeated, "Don't you dare tell the mistress."

That morning, for the first time in my life, I experienced the tantalizing sensation of pleasure from a woman's body.

Sangye Dolma cursed, "Idiot!"

Rubbing my sleepy eyes, I asked her, "Tell me the truth, who's the real id— idiot?"

"I mean it, a perfect idiot."

Then, without helping me dress, she walked off after giving me a nice red welt on my arm, like a bird's peck. The pain was absolutely new and electrifying.

Snow sparkled brightly outside the window, where the family servants' brats were whooping it up, throwing rocks at thrushes. But I was still in bed, wrapped snugly in a bearskin quilt and layers of silk, listening to the maid's footsteps echo down the long hallway. Apparently, she had no intention of coming back to wait on me, so I kicked off the quilt and screamed.

Within the territory governed by Chieftain Maichi, everybody knew that the son born to the chieftain's second woman was an idiot.

That idiot was me.

Except for my mother, just about everybody liked me the way I was. If I'd been born smart, I might have long since departed this world for the Yellow Springs instead of sitting here and thinking wild thoughts over a cup of tea. The chieftain's first wife had taken ill and died. My mother was bought by a fur and medicinal herb merchant as a gift to the chieftain, who got drunk and then got her pregnant. So I might as well be happy going through life as an idiot.

Still, within the vast area of our estate, there wasn't a single person who didn't know me. That's because I was the chieftain's son. If you don't believe me, become a slave or the brilliant son of a commoner and see if people know who you are.

I am an idiot.

My father was a chieftain ordained by the Chinese emperor to govern tens of thousands of people.

So if the maid didn't come to help me dress, I'd scream for her.

Anytime servants were late in responding, I'd send my silk coverlets cascading to the floor like water. Those Chinese silks, which came from far beyond the mountains, are much slicker than you might think. Since earliest childhood, I never understood why the land of the Chinese was not only the source of our much needed silk, tea, and salt, but also the source of power for chieftain clans. Someone once told me that it was because of weather. I said, "Oh, because of weather." But deep down I was thinking, Maybe so, but weather can't be the only reason. If so, why didn't the weather change me into something else? As far as I know, every place has weather. There's fog, and the wind blows. When the wind is hot, the snow becomes rain. Then the wind turns cold, and the rain freezes into snow. Weather causes changes in everything. You stare wide-eyed at something, and just when it's about to change into something else, you have to blink. And in that instant, everything returns to its original form. Who can go without blinking? It's like offering sacrifices. Behind the curling smoke, the bright red lips of golden-faced deities enjoying the sacrifice are about to open up to smile or cry, when suddenly a pounding of drums in the temple hall makes you tremble with fear. And in that instant, the deities resume their former expressions and return to a somber, emotionless state.

It snowed that morning, the first snow of spring. Only spring snows are moist and firm, able to resist the wind. Only spring snows blanket the earth so densely that they gather up all the light in the world.

Now all the light in the world was gathered on my silk coverlet. Worried that the silk and the light would slip away, I felt pangs of sorrow flow warily through my mind. As beams of light pierced my heart like awls, I began to sob, which brought my wet nurse, Dechen Motso, hobbling in. She wasn't all that old but liked to act like an old woman. She'd become my wet nurse after giving birth to her first child, who had died almost at once. I was three months old at the time, and Mother was anxiously waiting for a sign from me that I knew I'd arrived in this world.

I was firm about not smiling during the first month.

During the second month, no one was able to elicit a flickering of understanding from my eyes.

My father, the chieftain, said to his son in the same tone of voice he used to give orders, "Give me a smile, will you?"

He changed his gentle tone when he got no reaction. "Give me a smile," he said sternly. "Smile! Do you hear me?"

He looked so funny that I opened my mouth, but only to drool. My mother looked away, tears wetting her face as she was reminded that my father looked just like that on the night I was conceived. This memory so rankled her that her milk dried up on the spot. "A baby like this is better off starving to death."

Not terribly concerned, my father told the steward to take ten silver dollars and a packet of tea to Dechen Motso, whose illegitimate son had just died, so she could pay for a vegetarian meal and tea for the monks to perform rites for the dead. The steward, of course, knew what the master had in mind. He left in the morning and returned that afternoon with the wet nurse in tow. When they reached the estate entrance, a pack of fierce dogs barked and snarled at them. The steward said, "Let them get to know your smell." So the wet nurse took out a steamed bun, broke it apart, and spat on each piece before tossing it at them. The barking stopped immediately. After snapping the food out of the air, the dogs ran up and circled her, lifting her long skirt with their snouts to sniff her feet and legs. They were wagging their tails and chewing their food by the time the steward led the now familiar wet nurse inside.

The chieftain was immensely pleased. Although a trace of sadness clung to Dechen's face, her blouse was damp from the flowing milk.

At the time, I was bawling at the top of my lungs. Even though she had no milk, the chieftain's wife tried to stuff her idiot son's mouth up with one of those withered things. Father thumped his cane loudly on the floor, and said, "Stop crying. The wet nurse is here." I stopped, as if I'd understood him, and I was soon introduced to her abundant breasts. The milk was like gushing spring water, sweet and satisfying, though it carried the taste of sorrow and of wildflowers and grass. My mother's meager milk, on the other hand, tasted more like the colorful thoughts that filled up my little brain until it buzzed.

My tiny stomach was quickly gorged. To show my gratitude, I peed on the wet nurse, who turned her head to cry when I let go of her nipple. Not long before, her newborn son had been wrapped in a cowhide rug and buried at the bottom of a deep pond after the lamas had recited the "Reincarnation Sutra" for him.

Upon seeing the wet nurse's tears, my mother spat, and said,

"Bad karma!"

"Mistress," the wet nurse said, "please forgive me this one time. I couldn't help myself." My mother ordered her to slap her own face.

Now I'd grown to the age of thirteen. After all those years, my wet nurse, like other servants who were privy to so many of the chieftain's family secrets, no longer behaved herself. Also thinking I was an idiot, she often said in front of me, "Master? Hah! Servants? Hah!" All the while she'd be stuffing things like the lamb's-wool batting of my quilt or a piece of thread from her clothes into her mouth, mixing them with saliva, then spitting them savagely onto the wall. Except that over the past year or two, she didn't seem able to spit as high as she had before. And so she'd decided to become an old woman.

I was crying and making a scene when she hobbled into my room. "Please, Young Master, don't let the mistress hear you."

But I was crying because it felt so good.

"Young Master," she said, "it's snowing."

What did the fact that it was snowing have to do with me? But I stopped crying anyway and looked out from my bed onto a patch of terrifyingly blue sky framed by the small window. I couldn't see how the heavy snow weighed down the branches until she propped me up. I opened my mouth to cry, but she stopped me. "Look," she said, "the thrushes have flown down from the mountain."

"Really?"

"Really. They're down from the mountain. Listen, they're calling you children to go out and play with them."

So I stopped fussing and let her dress me.

Finally, I've come to the spot where I can talk about the thrushes. Would you look at the sweat on my forehead!

Thrushes are wild around here. No one knows where they go when the sky is overcast, but on clear days they come out to sing, their voices sweet and clear. Not much good at flying, they prefer to glide down from the heights. They don't normally come to low places, except on snowy days, when it's difficult to find food in their usual habitat. The snow forces the thrushes to come down from the mountain, where people live.

People kept coming in for instructions while Mother and I were eating breakfast.

First it was the crippled steward, who came to inquire whether the young master wanted to change into warm boots before going out to play in the snow. He said that if the master were home, he'd want me to. "Get lost, you cripple," my mother said. "Hang that pair of worn-out boots around your neck and get lost."

The steward left, of course, but didn't hang the boots around his neck, nor did he "get lost."

A while later he limped in to report that the leper who'd been chased up the mountain from the Kaba fortress had come down looking for food.

"Where is she now?" Mother asked anxiously.

"She fell into a wild boar trap on the way."

"She can crawl out."

"She can't. She's crying for help."

"Then why don't you bury her?"

"Bury her alive?"

"I don't care. We can't have a leper storming onto our estate."

Then came the matter of giving alms to the monastery, followed by a discussion of sending seeds to the people who tilled our land. Charcoal burned bright in a brass brazier, and before long, I was dripping with sweat.

After Mother spent some time tackling business, her usual look of fatigue disappeared, replaced by a dazzling glow, as if a lamp had been lit inside her face. I was looking at that lustrous face so intently that I didn't hear her question. She raised her voice, and said angrily, "What did you say you want?"

I said, "The thrushes are calling me."

The chieftain's wife immediately lost patience with me and stormed out in a rage. I sipped my tea, with the air of an aristocrat, something I was very good at. When I was into my second cup, bells rang and drums pounded in the sutra hall upstairs, and I knew that the chieftain's wife had now moved on to the business of the monks' livelihood.

If I hadn't been an idiot, I wouldn't have disappointed her at moments like that. She'd been enjoying the prerogatives of a chieftain's power over the past few days, ever since Father had taken my brother, Tamding Gonpo, to the provincial capital to file a complaint against our neighbor, Chieftain Wangpo. It had all started with one of Father's dreams, in which Chieftain Wangpo had taken a coral ornament that had fallen from Father's ring. The lama said that was a bad omen. Sure enough, shortly afterward, a border headman betrayed us by taking a dozen servants with him over to Chieftain Wangpo. Father sent a messenger with lavish gifts to buy them back, but his request was turned down. A second messenger was sent with bars of gold in exchange for the traitor's head; Wangpo could keep the remaining servants and the land. The gold was returned, with a message that if Chieftain Wangpo killed someone who increased his wealth, his own people would run off like Chieftain Maichi's servants.

Left with no choice, Chieftain Maichi opened a case inlaid with silver and beads and took out a seal representing the highest official title conferred by the Qing emperor. With the seal and a map, he went to the provincial capital to file a complaint with the military government of Sichuan, under the control of the Republic of China.

Besides Mother and me, the Maichi family included Father and a half brother from Father's first wife, plus a half sister who'd gone off to India with an uncle, a businessman. She later went to England, even more distant, which everyone said was a huge place, known as the empire where the sun never sets. I once asked Father, "Is it always daytime in big countries?"

He just smiled, and said, "You're such a little idiot."

Now they were all away somewhere, and I was lonely.

So I said, "Thrushes," got up, and went downstairs. As soon as I reached the bottom of the stairs, I was surrounded by servants' children. "See them?" my parents often reminded me. "They're your livestock." No sooner had my feet stepped on the courtyard flagstones than my future livestock came up to me. They weren't wearing boots or fur coats, but they didn't seem to be any more bothered by the cold than I was. They stood there waiting for me to give an order. My order was: "Let's go catch some thrushes."

Their faces glowed with excitement.

With a wave of my hand and a shout, I made for the estate entrance with the servants' brats, a pack of young slaves. We stormed out, alarming the gate dogs, which began barking like crazy, a racket that lent the morning an air of happiness. And what a snowfall! It had turned the world outside vast and bright. My slaves shouted excitedly, kicking the packed snow with their bare feet and stuffing their pockets with ice-cold stones. The thrushes, their dark yellow tails sticking straight up, hopped around looking for food at the base of the wall, where there was less snow.

"Go!" I shouted.

My little slaves and I ran after the thrushes. Unable to fly to a higher place, the birds flocked toward the orchard by the river as we slogged through the ankle-deep snow in hot pursuit. With no escape, the thrushes were pelted by rocks and, one by one, their heads burrowed into the fluffy snow as their bodies went limp. The lucky survivors, sacrificing their tails for their heads, stuck their tiny heads between rocks and tree roots before they too fell into our clutches.

That was the battle I commanded in my youth, a successful, very satisfactory one.

I sent some of the slaves back to the estate house for kindling and told others to gather dry branches from our apple and pear trees. The bravest and quickest among them was sent back to steal salt from the kitchen, while the rest stayed behind to make a clearing in the orchard big enough for a dozen people and a bonfire. The salt thief was my right-hand man, Sonam Tserang, who returned in no time. Taking the salt, I told him to help the others clear the snow. Which he did, breathing hard and kicking it away with his feet. Even at that he was more adept than the others. So I didn't say anything when he kicked snow in my face, though I knew he'd done it on purpose. Even with slaves, some are entitled to favoritism. This is a hard and fast principle, a useful rule of thumb for a ruler. And that was why I tolerated his insubordination and giggled as snow slid down my neck.

A fire was quickly built, and we began plucking the birds' feathers. Sonam Tserang didn't kill his thrushes before he began plucking their feathers, drawing horrible cries from the flapping birds. Everyone had goose bumps, everyone but he. Sonam Tserang didn't seem at all troubled. Fortunately, the aroma of roasted bird quickly rose from the fire to soothe our feelings. And before long, each of our stomachs was stuffed with four or five wild thrushes.

2 Shari ~

At the time, the chieftain's wife was looking everywhere for me.

If he'd been home, Father wouldn't have stopped me from playing this sort of game. But Mother had been in charge of the household for the past few days, and things were different. In the end, the servants found me in the orchard. The sun was high overhead, and the snow was blindingly white. My hands were covered in blood as I gnawed on the birds' tiny bones. Together with the slaves' children, whose faces and hands were likewise bloodspattered, I returned to the estate house. The smell of fresh blood threw the watchdogs into a frenzy. At the gateway I looked up to see my mother standing at the top of the stairs, staring down sternly. The little slaves wilted under that gaze.

I was sent directly to the upstairs fireplace to dry my clothes.

Soon after, the cracks of a leather whip reverberated in the courtyard, like the sound of a hawk racing across the sky. At that moment, I think, I must have hated my mother, hated the wife of Chieftain Maichi. Resting her cheek on her hand, as if she had a toothache, she said, "Those aren't low-class bones in your body."

Bone, a very important word here, as is another, *root*, which means about the same thing.

But the word *root* in Tibetan is short and abrupt: *nyi*. *Bone*, on the other hand, has a proud sound: *shari*. The natural world is made up of water, fire, wind, and air, while the human world is made up of bones, or roots. As I listened to Mother and soaked up the warmth of dry clothes, I started to ponder the issue of bone but got nowhere. Instead, I heard the thrushes trying to spread their wings in my stomach and the whips lashing my future livestock; tears began to flow from my young eyes. The chieftain's wife took that as a sign of self-reproach, so she rubbed my head, and said, "Son, you must remember that you can ride them like horses or beat them like dogs, but you must never treat them like humans." She thought she was pretty smart, but I think even smart people can be stupid sometimes. I may be an idiot, but I'm better at some things than other people. As I mulled this idea over, I started to laugh even though my face was still damp with tears. I heard the steward, my wet nurse, and the maidservants asking what was wrong with the young master, but I didn't see them. I thought I'd closed my eyes, but in fact they were wide open. So I cried out, "My eyes are gone!"

By which I meant I couldn't see anything.

The eyes of the chieftain's son were all red and puffy, and even the tiniest light stung like needles.

Monpa Lama, a specialist in healing arts, said it was snow blindness. Kindling a spruce branch and some herbs, he smothered my eyes with pungent smoke, as if avenging the thrushes. Then the lama respectfully hung a portrait of Bhaisajya-raja, bodhisattva of healing, in front of my bed. I soon stopped screaming, quieted down, and fell asleep.

When I woke up, Monpa Lama brought me a bowl of clean water and, after closing the windows, told me to open my eyes and describe what was inside the bowl. I saw flickers of light, like stars in the sky, emerge from bubbles on the surface. Then I saw plump kernels of barley at the bottom of the bowl releasing the glittering bubbles. Before long, my eyes felt much cooler.

Monpa Lama kowtowed to the bodhisattva of healing to express his gratitude before gathering his things and returning to the sutra hall to pray for me.

I slept for a while but was awakened by the thuds of someone kowtowing outside. It turned out to be Sonam Tserang's mother, who was kneeling before the mistress to beg forgiveness for her wretched son.

"Can you see now?" Mother asked me.

"Yes."

"Are you sure?"

"Yes."

With this affirmation, the chieftain's wife said, "Take the little bastard down and give him twenty lashes."

One mother thanked another, then went downstairs. Her sobs reminded me of bees buzzing among flowers, and made me wonder if summer was here.

Oh, well, let me continue with my thoughts on bone, since I'm stuck here for a while.

In the place where our religion came from, bone was called "caste." Sakyamuni, the Buddha, came from a high noble caste in India. On the other hand, in the place where our power came from – China – bone was considered to be something related to thresholds, a difficult word to translate accurately, but which probably refers to the height of one's door. If that's the case, the door of the chieftain's family should have been very high. My mother came from a lower-class family, but cared a lot about such things after entering the Maichi household. She was always trying to cram them into her idiot son's head.

I asked her once, "If our threshold is so high, does that mean we can go in and out of the clouds?"

She gave me a wry smile.

"Then we'd be fairies and gods, not chieftains."

With a comment like that from her idiot son, she smiled even more wryly, obviously disappointed. The look on her face was meant to make me feel guilty over my failure to amount to anything.

Actually, Chieftain Maichi's estate house was nearly a hundred feet high, with seven stories, a roof, plus a basement dungeon. The many rooms and doors were connected by a series of staircases and hallways, as intricate as the affairs of the world and as complex as the human heart. Built atop a winding mountain range where two streams converged, the house occupied a commanding position overlooking dozens of stone fortresses on the riverbank below; the *feng shui* was perfect.

The families living in those stone fortresses were called Kabas, and all belonged to the same bone, or *shari*. In addition to tilling the land, they answered to the chieftain whenever they were needed for work around the estate. The Kabas were also messengers for the Maichi chieftain's territory, some 360 li from east to west and 410 li from north to south, with more than two thousand families residing in three hundred fortresses. The Kabas have a saying: "The feather on a letter from the chieftain will set your buttocks on fire." When the gong sounded at the estate, summoning someone to deliver a message, a Kaba was required to get on the road immediately, even if his mother were on her deathbed.

Looking far off down the river valley, you could see fortresses nestled in the valley and on the mountains. The people there farmed the land and tended their herds. Every fortress had its own head-man, with varying ranks. These fortresses were controlled by the headmen, who were in turn governed by my family. The people controlled by the headmen were serfs, a class with many people who shared the same bone. They could move up and increase the weight of their bones with aristocratic blood, but mostly they went down. And once that happened, it was hard to turn things around, for the chieftain liked as many serfs to become bonded servants as possible. The family slaves were livestock, which could be bought and sold or put to use at will. It's not difficult to turn free people into slaves; setting up a rule targeting the most common human frailties will do. It's more foolproof than a seasoned hunter springing a trap.

That's exactly what had happened to Sonam Tserang's mother.

She was the daughter of serfs, which meant that she was a serf as well, and the chieftain could extract tribute and labor from her only through a headman. But she became pregnant out of wedlock, thus violating the law against illegitimate children, and turned her son and herself into bonded slaves.

Someone once wrote in a book somewhere that the chieftains had no laws. True, we didn't put everything down on paper, but a rule was a rule, and it was fixed in the people's minds. It was more effective than a lot of things that are written down. I ask, "Isn't that so?" And a booming voice comes to me from a distant place, deep in time: "Yes, it is so."

In any case, the rules in those days were set up to move people down, from freemen to slaves, not the other way around. The nobility, with their heavy bones, were the artists who created these standards.

The bone separates people into high and low.

Chieftain.

Beneath the chieftain are the headmen.

The headmen control the serfs.

Then come the Kabas (messengers, not couriers). At the bottom are the family slaves. In addition, there's a class of people who can change their status any time they want. They are the monks, the artisans, the shamans, and the performers. The chieftain is more lenient with them than with the others; all they need to avoid is making the chieftain feel that he doesn't know what to do with them.

A lama once said to me, "When facing evil, the Tibetans who live in the Land of the Snows cannot tell good from bad, like the quiet Han Chinese. When there is nothing to be happy about, the Tibetans revel in joy, like the Indians."

China is called Gyanak in our language, meaning "Land of Black Robes."

India is called Gyaghar, Land of White Robes.

That lama was later punished by Chieftain Maichi because he was always pondering questions that no one wanted to think about. He died after his tongue was cut out and he suffered the anguish of being unable to speak. As far as I'm concerned, the time before Sakyamuni was an age of prophets; after him, we no longer needed our brains to think. If you believe you're someone special, but weren't born an aristocrat, then you need to become a lama and paint pictures of the future for people. But you must hurry if you have something you feel you must say about the present, or about the future, because you won't be able to say it after you lose your tongue.

Can't you see all those rotting tongues that once wanted to say something?

Sometimes the serfs have something to say, but they hold back until they're about to die. Here are some good deathbed expressions:

"Give me a drink of mead."
"Please place a small piece of jade in my mouth."
"The day is breaking."
"Ah-ma, they're here."
"I can't find my feet."
"Heaven, ah, heaven."
"Spirits, oh, spirits!"

And so on.

3 Sangye Dolma ∼

My earliest memory dates from that snowy morning when I was thirteen.

The first spring snow had blinded me.

The sounds of the family guards whipping Sonam Tserang cooled my red, puffy eyes. Mother told the wet nurse, "Take good care of the young master."

The mistress got up to leave, and so did the beautiful maidservant Dolma. I threw off the towel covering my eyes, and screamed, "I want Dolma!"

I didn't ask my mother to stay, but she said, "All right, we'll keep you company." Of course, my little brain couldn't comprehend all that was happening, so I held Dolma's soft, warm hand tightly and quickly fell asleep.

It was nighttime when I woke up again.

From the bridge under the fortress came a woman's long, dismal wails. Somebody's child had left his soul at a place frequented by spirits, and his mother was calling for him to return home. I said to the maidservant as she leaned against the head of my bed, "Dolma, I want you, Dolma."

She giggled.

Then she pinched me before sliding her naked body under the covers.

There's a song that goes:

A sinful girl
Flowing into my arms like water.
What kind of fish
Swims into a dream?
But don't disturb them,
The sinful monk and the beautiful girl!

In our creation myth, a god living somewhere says, "Ha!" and a void appears. The god says to the void, "Ha!" and there is water, fire, and dust. The magical "ha" is uttered again to make wind spin the world in the void. That day, I held Dolma's breasts in the dark, and said "Ha" in happy astonishment.

But Dolma just muttered something. She was saying, "Hmm, hmm, hmm …"

A world made of fire and water, of light and dust, began to twirl. I was thirteen and Dolma was eighteen.

The eighteen-year-old Dolma picked me up and put me on top of her.

Something blazed inside my thirteen-year-old body.

She said, "Go in, get inside," as if there were some sort of door in her body. I did feel a strong desire to enter somewhere.

She said, "Idiot, you idiot," before grabbing hold of me down there and pushing me in.

The thirteen-year-old me let out a cry and exploded. The world vanished.

15

My eyes, which had been getting better, were swollen shut again the next morning. Blushing bright red, Dolma whispered something to Mother. The chieftain's wife glanced at her son and smiled despite herself as she slapped the maidservant's pretty face.

Monpa Lama returned.

Mother said, "The master will be home soon. Look what you did to the young master's eyes."

"The young master must have seen something unclean," the lama replied.

The chieftain's wife asked, "Was it a ghost? A handful of sad ghosts you failed to exorcise must still be hanging around."

The lama shook his head. "Some puppies were born downstairs. Did the young master look at them?"

So my eyes were smoked once more with spruce. The lama had me take some medicine made of herbal powder, which made me want to pee. He said it would hurt a little. He was right. The place that had made me feel so good the night before felt as if it were being pricked by needles.

The lama said, "That's it. I was right. The young master is now a man."

When everyone but my wet nurse left my room, she asked, "What did that little demon do to you?"

Covering my swollen eyes, I started to laugh.

My wet nurse said with bitter hatred, "You fool. I was hoping life would be easier for me once you grew up, but now you've got this little she-devil to lord it over me." She banged a pair of fire tongs against the brass brazier. I ignored her, thinking it was good to be the son of a chieftain. The world started to spin as soon as I uttered "Ha!" like a god. Then the laxative from the lama made my stomach sing.

In a singsong voice, my wet nurse later asked the lama, "What did you do to our young master's stomach?"

The lama stared her down before walking off. I felt like laughing, but as soon I did, watery shit spewed out of me. I spent the morning sitting on a chamber pot. Mother wanted to punish the lama for what he'd done, but he'd already left to see other patients. We took care of his room and board, but he liked to earn some loose change. By the afternoon, my eyes and stomach were both fine, and people were once again praising the lama's skills.

It was a bright, sunny afternoon. The sound of horse hooves racing like the wind perked everyone up as rays of sunlight turned into taut bowstrings.

My father, Chieftain Maichi, who'd been off filing his complaint with the provincial government, was returning from the land of the Han. He and his entourage pitched a tent a dozen li from the estate to spend the night while a messenger on horseback brought news that the chieftain was bringing with him a high official from the military government, someone who was to be given a grand reception.

In short order, several speedy horses tore out of the estate on their way to nearby fortresses. Standing on the balcony of a cavalry platform, Mother and I watched clouds of dust rising over the fields. The three-story platform faced the southeastern gate, which opened onto a broad valley. The other three sides of the estate house, as I've said, were seven stories high. A blockhouse was connected to the house and faced a wide road to the northwest leading down from the mountain pass. Spring was on its way, for the rammed-earth cover of the platform was getting soft. The upper level beneath the balcony served as a residence for guards and a defensive position for repelling attacks. Slaves lived in the two lower levels. The river valley gradually opened out to the southwest, from where Father and my brother would return tomorrow. That day, the scenery before me was the same as always: the mountains to the rear rose higher and higher, waiting for the sun to set. A river raged down from the mountains heading east, carving an ever widening swath through the valley. As the saying goes, the Han emperor rules beneath the morning sun, the Dalai Lama governs beneath the afternoon sun.

We were located slightly to the east under the noonday sun, a very significant location. It determined that we would have more contact with the Han emperor to the east than with our religious leader, the Dalai Lama. Geographical factors had decided our political alliance.

You see, the reason we had been able to exist for so long was that we had an accurate reckoning of our position. But Chieftain Wangpo, who'd set his mind on becoming our enemy, always went on pilgrimages to Lhasa. Wise people under his rule said to him, "We should also visit the Han people." But he replied, "Which is bigger, Wangpo or China?" He'd completely forgotten that one of his ancestors had received his chieftain's seal from Beijing. On the other hand, there's a book that says that we, the black-haired Tibetans, slid down a strand of wool from heaven to this lofty, clean, and craggy land. Therefore, Chieftain Wangpo had every reason to believe that, since people can come down from heaven, seals of authority, silver, and weapons can also descend on streaks of blue lightning.

Mother said to me, "The people who can handle Chieftain Wangpo are on their way. We'll go out to welcome them tomorrow. They've come from my homeland. Will I be able to speak with them in Chinese? Heaven, ah, heaven. My son, listen to my Chinese. Does it sound right to you?"

How would I know if you're speaking Chinese? I thought, as I slapped my head. But by then she was already chattering away. After a while, she said happily, "Dear Bodhisattva, I haven't forgotten, I haven't forgotten a thing!" Tears streamed down her face. Holding my head tightly, she shook it, and said, "I'm going to teach you Chinese. In all these years, why didn't I ever think to teach you Chinese?"

But I wasn't much interested in stuff like that and wound up disappointing her once again, just when she was in such high spirits. "Look, the lama's yellow umbrella is coming this way," I said like an idiot.

Our family kept two groups of monks. One of them stayed in a sutra hall on the estate, while the other group lived in the Mondron Ling Monastery, just across the river. At that moment, the monastery's Living Buddha, Jeeka, was rushing over after hearing news of tomorrow's ceremony. But while he and his disciples were on the wooden bridge, a sudden whirlwind picked up the Living Buddha's yellow umbrella and flung the novice holding it into the river. The chieftain's wife giggled as the little monk climbed back onto the bridge, soaked to the skin. Just listen to her, how young she sounds!

As the procession made its way up the flagstone steps, Mother ordered the gate shut.

Things had not been going well between the chieftain and the monastery.

It had all started soon after my grandfather died. Something entered the head of Living Buddha Jeeka, who declared that only my uncle, my father's younger brother, was qualified to succeed as chieftain. But as it turned out, it was my father, and not my uncle, who became the Maichi chieftain, and so the monastery fell out of favor. After my father assumed the title of chieftain, he expanded the sutra hall in the estate house and invited some renowned monks from elsewhere, ignoring the monastery, as Jeeka had forgotten his station.

Flanked by a small group of people, Mother stood on the platform balcony, facing east toward the site of imperial grandeur.

The Living Buddha was banging the brass ring on the lion's head on our gate.

Our crippled steward kept trying to send someone to open the gate, but Mother stopped him each time. "Should we open the door?" Mother asked me.

"Let them wait awhile. They shouldn't be so anxious to get our silver," I said.

The steward, the maidservant, and the other servants laughed, all except my wet nurse. I knew she must have confused the monks with the monastery's Buddha.

Dolma said, "The young master is so clever."

Mother silenced her with a piercing look, then said to me reproachfully, "How can you be so rude to a Living Buddha?" Hiking up her pleated skirt, she walked grandly downstairs to open the gate.

The lama bowed respectfully, but instead of returning the bow, the chieftain's wife said sweetly, "I saw the Living Buddha's yellow umbrella blow into the river."

"Amita Buddha, Mistress, that was because I have yet to perfect my discipline."

The wind rose in the river valley, whistling across the deep sky.

Rather than invite the Living Buddha inside, Mother said, "The wind's coming up. I want you to bring your musicians from the monastery to welcome a guest tomorrow."

The Living Buddha, so excited that he could barely talk, kept bowing to the chieftain's wife, an action that flew in the face of custom. For once he put on his yellow shirt and purple cassock, he was no longer a man, but the representative of all the gods and Buddhas on this land. But he forgot all that.

The next morning, I awoke as soon as the signal shots were fired

19

from the blockhouse. I even dressed myself. The wet nurse rushed up with a chamber pot, but I had no use for it, since I'd gotten rid of everything the day before.

Drums sounded in the sutra hall as incense smoke rose above the estate. The yard and the square outside were filled with sweat-lathered horses. Headmen had come from all over with their servants. After Mother and I went downstairs, our entourage set out on horseback. The chieftain's wife rode a white horse amid a contingent of chestnut ponies. She was wearing a silver belt as wide as her hand, with strings of beads around her neck. Her freshly braided hair shone like a mirror.

I spurred my horse to catch up with her. She smiled. My well-fed, powerful chestnut pony was faster and stronger than the others, and when I caught up with Mother, the people cheered at the sight of two such beautiful horses. Amid their cheers, I rode alongside Mother on the broad road under a bright sun. I'd thought she might not want to ride next to her little idiot, but she didn't mind. Riding side by side with her son, she waved her red-tasseled whip at the cheering crowd. At that moment my heart was filled with boundless love for her.

Tugging at the reins in my hands, I shot ahead of her.

I felt like saying, like most normal kids, "I love you, Ah-ma."

But all I said when she caught up was, "Ah-ma, look, a bird."

My mother said, "Silly, it's a hawk." Her free hand curled into a talon in the air. "Like this," she said, "they can catch rabbits and lambs."

"They can also catch dead fish floating in the river."

"They also swoop down to catch poisonous snakes."

I knew she was talking about the headman who'd betrayed us, not to mention Chieftain Wangpo, who'd chosen to be our enemy.

After saying what she wanted to say, she was escorted forward by the headmen. I reined in my horse and stopped by the side of the road, where I spotted Sangye Dolma, in beautiful clothes, walking among other servants who were all dressed in their finest. But their faces, like their clothes, lacked luster; Dolma deserved better than to be among those people.

Sadness filled her eyes as she looked at me.

When she walked up, I put the reins in her hands. By doing that, a mental midget of noble birth astride a proud steed separated her

20

from those behind her, people who could only hope for a better life the next time around. The chieftain's wife and her awesome, fleet-footed attendants disappeared around a bend in the mountain road. A bright, sunny field opened up in front – above, the golden forests; below, a shining river. Cold, green winter barley fields surrounded the fortresses. As we passed such places, our entourage swelled. But this ever expanding procession progressed on my heels, for the people dared not move ahead of their master. Each time I turned back to look, strong men removed their hats respectfully and pretty girls smiled brightly. Ah, how wonderful to be a chieftain, the ruler of a small piece of land. If I hadn't been conceived when my father was drunk, the idea of patricide might have entered my head at a moment like this.

Instead, I said, "Dolma, stop. I'm thirsty."

She turned and shouted to the people behind her. Several men ran up, dust rising in their wake, and knelt by my horse before taking out a variety of liquor flasks. Dolma pushed away the unclean ones, whose owners looked as sad as if someone in their family had died. After taking a drink from a flask shaped like a little bird, I wiped my lips. "Who are you?" I asked.

Bending low from his long, slender waist, the man replied, "I'm silversmith Choedak."

"Are you a skilled silversmith?"

"I am an unskilled silversmith," the man answered in a leisurely manner.

I knew I should give him something as a reward, but I simply said coldly, "You may go."

"Young Master should have given him something," Dolma said.

"I would have if he hadn't looked at you the whole time."

Now I understood the fragile nature of a ruler's feelings. My mood improved only after Dolma pinched me. I glanced down at her, and saw that she was openly returning my glance, which made me tumble into her eyes, unable to pull myself out.

"Why not sing a song?" I asked.

Ah, please look up.
What nice scenery is there to see?
There is a pagoda.
Ah, please look straight ahead.

21

What nice scenery is there to see?
There's a valiant young man shouldering a musket.
Ah, please look down.
What nice scenery is there to see?
There's a beautiful girl in silk and brocade.

Dolma joined in. She had such a soulful voice, so sweet and melodic. But I didn't think she was singing for me. I wasn't the youth in the song, in which she, a servant girl, got to wear silk and brocade because of our favors. When she finished, I said, "Sing it again."

She assumed the song had made me happy, so she sang it one more time.

I told her to sing it yet again, and when she finished, I told her to sing it again. This time her voice began to lose its pleasant quality, but I said, "Again."

Her tears flowed. As I said before, on that day I experienced how good it was to be a ruler and how fragile a ruler's feelings were. The pain in my heart slowly evaporated as she began to cry.

4 Honored Guest ∽

After leaving hat morning, we pitched tents to welcome our guests ten li distant from the estate.

The men were to display their riding skills and marksmanship.

It was also time for the lamas from the estate and those from the monastery to perform drum music and spirit dances. These were keenly contested competitions. To be honest, we enjoyed the rivalry, since it kept the lamas from considering themselves too lofty. Without these contests, they could have joined forces to tell us that the Buddha had said this or the Buddha had said that, and the chieftains would have had no choice but to let them do anything they wanted. But when there was friction between them, they came to us offering to pray for the prosperity of the chieftain's family. They also gave us guarantees that their prayers were more effective than those of others.

We had just dumped an entire goat into the pot, and a fragrant aroma had begun to waft from the tea. Ear-shaped pastries were barely out of the frying pan when we saw one, two, then three columns of dark green smoke rise from the mountain ridges. That signaled the arrival of our honored guest. Carpets were quickly laid inside and outside the tents, and low tables in front of the carpets were piled high with all kinds of food, including the pastries straight from the frying pan. Listen, can you hear them sizzle?

At the sound of the horn, our contingent of horses galloped off amid clouds of yellow dust.

They were followed by a procession of serfs holding *khatag*, the Tibetan silk offering. This group included singers with loud, booming voices.

After them came a group of monks carrying giant conch shells and the woodwind *suonas*.

Along the way, my father and the honored guest would be greeted by these separate groups.

We heard a volley of musket fire from the horse team as a salute. Then came the serfs' songs. By the time the distant conch shells and the *suonas* sounded happily, the entourage and honored guest were there in our midst.

Chieftain Maichi reined in his horse. We could see how happy and pleased with himself he was. On the other hand, the provincial official beside him wasn't nearly as impressive as we'd expected. He was a scrawny fellow, but when he took off his hat to wave at the crowd, the barbarians knelt in unison on the yellowed grass. Family slaves rolled a carpet up to the horses, and two young men got down on their hands and knees to serve as dismounting stools. One of them was my favorite companion, Sonam Tserang.

The scrawny Han Chinese replaced his hat and adjusted his black-rimmed glasses before dismounting on Sonam Tserang's back. He waved again to summon dozens of uniformed soldiers. When the chieftain walked over to his wife, the soldiers snapped off a neat salute. Then special emissary Huang Chumin presented silks and brocades, precious stones and gold, to the chieftain's wife, who in turn offered him a bowl of wine and a piece of yellow *khatag*. Young girls presented the same gifts to the Han soldiers. Meanwhile, the lamas started up again with their drums and *suonas*.

After Special Emissary Huang took a seat inside the tent, Father asked a man in his entourage if he should send for the dancers.

"Not yet. The special emissary hasn't composed his poem yet."

So our honored guest from the Han government was a poet! In our land, poets would not be entrusted with such an important task. When I first saw his half-closed eyes, I'd thought he was intoxicated by the aroma of food and the beauty of the girls.

After sitting there awhile with his eyes shut, he opened them wide and said he'd finished composing his poem. Then he watched the girls singing and dancing in high spirits. But he started yawning when the lamas came out to perform their long, tedious spirit dance. So he was helped outside by his soldiers for a smoke. That's what they said: the special emissary needs to go outside for a smoke to clear the cobwebs. Their enthusiasm dampened, the lamas slowed their dance steps. The Living Buddha from the Mondron Ling Monastery, who had so few opportunities to show off, waved his hand, and an embroidered painting of Sakyamuni was carried in. The people prostrated themselves, which revived the spirits of the dancing lamas.

The chieftain said to his wife, "The Living Buddha's letting out all the stops."

"Yes," Mother said. "He'd have saved himself a lot of trouble if he hadn't said your younger brother should be the chieftain back then."

Father laughed merrily. "Too bad so few people understand things like this."

"Maybe. And by the time they do, it's usually too late."

The Living Buddha, wearing crystal spectacles, came up to pay his respects. He wore an awkward look. Father took his slack, pudgy hands in his own, and said, "We're going to settle accounts with Chieftain Wangpo soon. You'll have to recite the proper sutras to ask for a sweeping victory." The face of the Living Buddha, who had been given the cold shoulder for years, perked up.

Father added, "I'll send over some alms tomorrow."

The Living Buddha retreated with his hands clasped in front of him.

Inside the tent, Special Emissary Huang's soldiers had been replaced by our young girls, and his eyes glistened like a night prowler.

The final activity of the day was the taking of photographs.

I didn't discover that my older brother was missing until our family was seated around Special Emissary Huang. It turned out that he was traveling with the weapons – rifles, machine guns, and plenty of ammunition.

Our photographer was the *thongsi*, or what people now call an interpreter. Back then, anyone who could turn one language into another was called a *thongsi*. The special emissary sat between Father, who held me in his lap, and Mother. That was the first photograph in the history of the Maichi family. Thinking back now, I realize how timely the introduction of photography was, for it preserved a picture of what turned out to be our waning days. But at the time, we treated everything as the beginning of an even more prosperous era for our family. My father and mother were energetic in real life, but the photograph turned us all into dull figures, as if we were doomed to disappear soon. See there, Father looks half-dead in the picture. Looking at it now, who'd have thought that he was filled with ambition and ready to deal a deathblow to a neighbor who had insulted us? To a certain degree, he was a man whose fists landed wherever his mind settled.

A few days later, my brother returned with the newly purchased munitions.

A stretch of land close to the estate house, so vast that a galloping horse couldn't reach the end before tiring out, was now our drill ground, and it was constantly shrouded in rolling dust. The soldiers who accompanied Special Emissary Huang were our drill instructors. Whenever one of them barked a command, our men would shout cadence and goose-step in tight formation. Of course, they had no clear goal yet, so they just shouted and sent yellow dust flying. When they reached the far end, they executed an about-face and shouted their way back, followed by more rising dust. This was a far cry from what we knew about combat training.

Father wanted to ask what this drill accomplished, and whether the training could actually help him defeat Chieftain Wangpo. But before he could open his mouth, the special emissary said, "Congratulations, Chieftain Maichi. You are now the only chieftain who commands a modern army. You will be invincible."

Puzzled by this comment, Father asked Mother, "Have you ever seen an army train like this?"

"I haven't seen any other way to do it," she replied.

Special Emissary Huang laughed, and Father had no choice but to take the man's word for it. What else could we do, since we had no other means of dealing with a traitorous headman? For the longest time, none of the soldiers Father had brought to help us out ever taught our men how to fire a rifle.

Even as the weather warmed up, all that our men did was march and shout to high heaven. No one could figure out why they had to learn how to march before they learned to fight. Dust flew all over the place, even in the third month, when the air should have been turning moist. My half brother marched with the other men, a rifle over his shoulder, his sweaty face streaked with dust. Eventually, even he could take it no longer, and came to ask Father, "Shouldn't they be giving us bullets by now?"

So Father brought up the matter with Special Emissary Huang, who dispensed bullets, three per man, to the soldiers, but they weren't allowed to fire them. The only difference was that now bayonet training was added to the marching drills. A few days later my brother went again to Father, who said to the special emissary, "The planting season will soon be here and the fortress is still under Chieftain Wangpo's control."

But the special emissary said, "What's the hurry?"

Chieftain Maichi now knew that he'd invited in a deity that was hard to send away. Bothered by a disturbing premonition, he had a lama cast divining blocks. The lost fortress would be retaken, the lama told him, and perhaps a new one or two as well. But there would be a price.

Father asked if any lives would be lost. The answer was no.

He asked if any money had to be spent. Again, the answer was no.

Finally he asked what exactly would be involved. The lama said he couldn't see clearly.

The resident lama being found useless, the Living Buddha was sent for. But his divination turned out the same. He saw flaming flowers, but was unable to foretell what sort of price the flowers portended.

Chieftain Maichi ordered that two new girls and a casket of silver dollars be sent to the special emissary. Putting Mother in charge of the matter, the chieftain said to her, "I think you should go, since I don't understand the Han people." Mother was happy that the chieftain felt that way; from now on, she would enjoy the authority of the chieftain's wife in dealing with such matters. Before becoming the chieftain's wife, it was unthinkable that one day she might ever be the equal of anyone as important as the special emissary.

The next day the special emissary said, "The girls are fine, but I must return the silver. Our government has come to help you barbarians, not because we desire your silver, but because we want all five ethnic groups to live harmoniously for the stability of the Republic of China. I will accept the girls so as not to make you lose face. I understand that this practice is not considered immoral in places outside the influence of Chinese civilization." Then he added, "Mistress, I hear you are a Han Chinese. In the future, we will rely on you for many things. Though I cannot say for sure, one day this place will no longer be alien territory, but your fiefdom."

"Please, no talk of fiefdoms. I wouldn't have fallen so low if your army hadn't looted my father's shop."

"For that we can easily compensate you."

"Can you compensate for the loss of human life? Both my parents. That's two lives."

Not having expected to fail in his attempt to find a collaborator, the special emissary said, "The mistress is the equal of a great man. I truly admire you."

Mother handled this delicate situation in an open, forthright manner; but she told Father only that the special emissary had returned the silver. The chieftain could do nothing but gnash his teeth, and say, "One day I'll kill that man."

Then the special emissary came to see him. "I think I should meet with Chieftain Wangpo."

Father looked at the special emissary, whose yellow face showed that he was serious, so he said to the steward, "Send a courier."

The courier soon returned. Who could have guessed that heaven would send such good fortune Chieftain Maichi's way? For what Chieftain Wangpo sent to "the son of a bitch Han official" was not a response, but a pair of handsome boots, which clearly meant for him to get the hell back to where he came from. Since the significance of the gift was lost on the special emissary, Mother gave him a vivid and thorough explanation.

Our honored guest was outraged.

Volleys of gunfire now sounded on the drill ground, and everyone knew we were preparing for war.

Three days later, armed government troops and several hundred of our soldiers arrived at the border. From the outset, the weapons we received from the military government overwhelmed the enemy. They could only yelp as their local weapons jammed. In the time it takes to eat a meal, we reclaimed the defector's fortress. The headman acknowledged his guilt by fleeing, leaving his kinfolk to die in his stead. All the members of his family, strung together, knelt beneath a walnut tree in front of their gate as the rising sun dried the dew on the grass under their feet. When they realized that the swords and guns held by the guards were not being used on them, they assumed that Chieftain Maichi had spared them, and the color returned to their ashen faces. What they could not have known was that Chieftain Maichi, unlike other chieftains, had never allowed soldiers to kill his prisoners. Ever since the Maichi family came into existence, hundreds of years ago, we have always had a designated executioner.

On the land governed by the Maichi family, there were three hereditary lines: the chieftain; Aryi, the executioner's family; and the historian. Unfortunately, the historian's line had been eliminated by the fourth chieftain after the third historian had advocated "factual recording." By now we had no idea how many generations had passed in the chieftain's family, let alone that of the executioner.

The executioner arrived. With his long arms, long legs, and a long neck, he looked exactly like someone whose specialty was taking people's lives. Prior to the execution, Father said to those who were about to die, "One of your own left you behind to be punished, so I will show no mercy. If that traitor hadn't fled, you would not have to lose your insignificant lives."

Up till then, they had been hoping that the chieftain would spare them; now the resolute looks on their faces disintegrated, as if they had suddenly realized that they were traitors to their master, not enemy prisoners. Their knees buckled and they knelt on the ground to beg for their lives, which was precisely the effect Father sought. Once they were on their knees, the chieftain waved his hand, and the executioner's sword flashed. Heads rolled. Each of the faces was still expressive, whereas the headless bodies remained erect for a brief moment before twirling and crumpling to the ground, as if caught by surprise.

I looked into the sky but failed to see any souls rising up to heaven. They say we have souls, so why wasn't I seeing any?

I asked Mother, but she just gave me a mean look and walked over to join her husband.

That was the first day of battle.

On the second day, the flames of war spread to Chieftain Wangpo's territory.

The special emissary, the chieftain, and his wife, along with some servants, observed the battle from a safe distance. I was among them. The officers in charge were my brother and the platoon leader of the special emissary's army. Our men quickly bored their way into the scrub brush after crossing a stream in the valley separating the two chieftains' territories. We were now watching an invisible battle, the only sign of which was crisp gunfire echoing in the radiant sky. Chieftain Wangpo's men put up a better fight this time, because they were now fighting for their homeland. But our men, with their overpowering weapons, continued to advance. It did not take long for them to reach a fortress, where a raging fire erupted from one of the buildings. A man flew out of the flames like a bird, was shot in the air, and thudded to the ground facedown.

A moment later, another fortress was reduced to a giant pyre.

The special emissary was watching through a pair of binoculars. When a third building caught fire, he opened his mouth wide, showing his yellowed teeth, and yawned. He was then helped by a fair, young soldier over to a shade tree, where he began to smoke. Father held the binoculars up to his eyes but couldn't see a thing, since he didn't know how to adjust the lenses. I took them from him and played with them for a while before I located some sort of dial. After I twisted it back and forth, suddenly the scenery on the opposite hills jumped up under my nose. I saw our men, crouching as they darted between hills, rocks, and the scrub brush. Green smoke issued from the muzzles of their guns.

Someone crumpled in a clearing.

That was one, then another. When they fell, they flailed their arms before opening their mouths to chew the ground. The two men turned to crawl down the hill. Then another man fell, his gun flying off into the distance. I couldn't help but yell, "Go get your gun, you idiot! Go get it!"

But he lay there, motionless, ignoring my command. It occurred to me that he'd probably obey only my brother's commands. For it was my brother, not I, who was the future Chieftain Maichi. These soldiers weren't mine; they belonged to him. That thought filled me with sadness. My brother, always brave, always at the head of his soldiers. Now he was walking crablike, his gun at the ready, his silver amulet shimmering in the sun. Each time he raised his gun, a man flew off a tree, flapping his arms like a bird before dropping into the bosom of the earth. I shouted excitedly, "You killed one, he's dead!" but I felt in my heart that my brother had actually finished me off. Yet at that moment, Chieftain Maichi was more worried about his older son, and when he saw me grasping the binoculars and yelling, he waved impatiently. "Someone take him inside. How can an idiot see anything with those if I can't?"

I wanted to tell him I could see everything, and not just of today, but everything of tomorrow as well. The words were on the tip of my tongue, but I didn't dare say them, since I wasn't altogether sure what it was that I could see of tomorrow. By now, our men had taken their objective and were crossing the ridge to attack the next valley.

Nighttime brought a cease-fire. As a peace offering, Chieftain Wangpo sent a messenger over with the traitorous headman's ear, a silver earring dangling from the lobe. When the covering cloth was removed, the ear twitched on the platter, sending the earring clanging loudly against the brass.

Father said, "The traitor isn't dead yet."

The messenger shouted, "Kill me, then."

"Do you expect me to taint my reputation?" Father replied.

"You've already tainted your reputation by seeking help from the Han Chinese. You have violated the rules, so how can you expect to preserve your name? Compared to asking an outsider's help in a family feud, killing a messenger means nothing."

It's true, here we check each other's "bone" when marriage is contemplated, so all chieftains are related. With so much intermarriage, we have multiple kinship relations. Chieftains Maichi and Wangpo were both maternal and paternal cousins. After the battle, the two families might intermarry once again, making it nearly impossible to tell which relationship was more dependable.

"I don't want your life," Father said. "But since you tried to deceive me with an ear, I'm going to take one from you, so you'll remember how to talk to a chieftain."

In the firelight, with a cold, narrow glint from his dagger, an ear fell to the ground and was covered with dirt.

Special Emissary Huang walked out from the shadows, and said to the now one-eared messenger, "I am the recipient of your chieftain's boots. Go back and tell him that boots from a chieftain will never befit me, a proud special emissary of the provincial government. Chieftain Maichi is a model supporter of the government. Go back and tell your chieftain to follow his example. Then send that traitor's head over before midnight, or I'll send him something faster than those boots and more lethal than that dagger."

The man nonchalantly picked up his ear and blew off the dust before bowing and retreating.

Sure enough, the traitorous headman was decapitated. Chieftain Wangpo also sent word that, as the defeated party, he would hand over a piece of land double the size of the defecting fortress as reparation.

Victorious shouts erupted in the night sky; a bonfire was lit and liquor vats were opened. People danced around the fire and the vats. But, gazing up at the crescent moon, I thought only of the girl Dolma, who was back at the estate – her smell, her hands, her breasts.

My brother, the conquering hero, opened his arms and joined the circle dance, which headed toward its climactic moment as the pace quickened and the circle grew smaller. The girls whose hands he held yelled shrilly, exaggerating a bit so everyone would know how honored and happy they were to be dancing with the noble hero. As people cheered for my brother, his face, glowing from the fire, became more animated, more radiant than usual.

But in the house behind the dance ground, the relatives of two fallen soldiers wept beside the corpses.

Far greater numbers of enemy bodies lay exposed to the wild. Packs of wolves made their move, their long howls echoing in the valley.

And Father wasn't happy on that victorious evening, for the birth of a new hero could mean only that the former hero was past his prime. Even though the new hero was his own son, he could not help but feel sad. Fortunately, the new hero wasn't arrogant, as most heroes would be; he was simply wrapped up in merriment, and that made his father envious. My brother's joy came from the fact that, like me, he never tried to separate himself from the serfs. See there, he's drinking with a man and flirting with the man's sister at the same time. In the end, he takes the girl into the woods and, when he reemerges, glumly joins the vigil for the fallen soldiers.

I, on the other hand, was getting sleepy.

Father didn't awaken from his drunken stupor in time for the cremation rites for our fallen soldiers.

Sprawled across my horse, I watched the people rock back and forth and sing funeral dirges as the long procession moved down the dusty spring road.

My brother gave me a knife, his trophy, which he had snatched from an enemy's hand. "May it make you brave," he said. I touched the hands he'd used to kill people; they seemed too warm to have taken lives. So I asked him, "Did you really kill them?" He tightened his grip on my hand, the pain creasing my brow. At that moment, he didn't have to speak for me to believe that he had.

Two ⁓

5 Flowers in the Heart

A three-day feast was held on the Maichi estate after our army returned. At the end of those three days, the square in front of the house was littered with fresh cattle and sheep bones, which the family slaves piled into a small hill. The chieftain said to burn them, but the steward argued that the smell would attract packs of hungry wolves. Chieftain Maichi laughed heartily. "The Maichi family is no longer what it once was. We can put all those new rifles to good use when the wolves come." And to Special Emissary Huang he said, "Why not stay a few more days? Don't go home until you've shot a few wolves."

The special emissary, crinkling his nose, didn't reply. At that point, no one had yet heard him so much as mention going home.

The stench of burning bones permeated the spring air. At dusk, hungry wolf packs came down from the mountain, expecting a meal, not a bonfire. They were denied the taste of grease from the bones, which were now sizzling and turning into blazing light. What little meat remained after the humans had finished with them turned to ashes, and the enraged wolves sent piercing howls into the evening sky. The bones were burned on the right edge of the square; on the opposite edge, a pair of sheep was tied to a stake, wailing pitifully in response to the howls of wolves. One after another, amid the crack of rifle fire, the wolves fell at the feet of the sheep. This went on for three days. Then no more wolves came down the mountain, and the smell of burning bones faded away. It was time for Special Emissary Huang to take his leave, but still not a word about going home. Father said, "We're going to start planting soon, and I won't be able to keep you company."

"This is a good place," the special emissary replied. Then he

33

closed himself up in his quarters under the pretext that he was avoiding gift-seeking lamas. Government soldiers stood guard outside his door. Father didn't know what to do with him. He wanted to consult my brother, but no one knew where his elder son was. Father would never ask my opinion on such matters, even though I might have been able to give him some useful advice. So he said to my mother resentfully, "You know how Han people think. What's going on in that Han head of his?"

"Don't blame me," Mother replied indifferently. "I didn't do anything."

Realizing how inappropriate his comments had been, Father scratched his head, and said, "He's sticking around. What does he want from us anyway?"

"Did you actually think he came here for our good? It's easy to send for a deity, but hard to get rid of one."

After discussing with his wife how to get rid of this particular deity, Father devised a plan. The same day, followed by servants bearing caskets containing eight thousand silver dollars, he went to the stairs leading to the special emissary's quarters. The guard saluted but blocked the way with his rifle. Father was about to slap the man when the *thongsi* came down, smiling broadly. He told the soldier to put away the caskets, but would not permit the chieftain entry upstairs.

"Please wait awhile," the *thongsi* said. "The special emissary is composing poetry."

"Wait? Why should I wait to see someone in my own house?"

"Then please return to your quarters, and I'll come get you as soon as the special emissary is free."

So the chieftain returned to his quarters, where he smashed three wineglasses and flung a cup of tea at a maidservant. Stomping his feet, he fumed, "Wait and see if I don't kill him one day!"

Historically, in the Maichi estate, people requested audiences with the chieftain. But here was this man, a houseguest staying in lavish quarters and acting as if he owned the place. Father's anger was understandable. Even I was so upset that my head swelled. Boldly I went to Father, but he shouted for someone to find his son. As if *I* weren't his son.

The servant returned to report that First Young Master was performing in a long, sacred play in the square. Father ordered him to come back and learn how to be a chieftain and to leave the acting to monks. The command was sent down from one floor to the next, from inside the estate house to out in the square. The response came back in reverse order: the fight between a demon and a spiritual deity had reached its climax, and my extraordinary brother could not be identified among all the actors in their costumes and masks.

Chieftain Maichi shouted, "Tell them to stop the play."

The lama, who had always obeyed the chieftain, replied, "You mustn't stop it. That would go against the will of the gods."

"The gods?"

"Yes, the play is a creation of the gods. It is our history and our poetry, and cannot be stopped midway."

True enough. We were often told that drama, history, poetry, and the like fell within the monks' special domain. This authority instilled in them a sense of transmitting the will of heaven. Chieftain Maichi could do nothing but vent his anger on his son. "Does he think he can rule a country just by knowing how to fight?" By then my father was screaming.

Please note that Father used the word *country*. That doesn't mean that he really believed he ruled an independent nation. It's all a matter of language. The word *thusi*, or *chieftain*, is a foreign import. In our language, the closest equivalent to *chieftain* is *gyalpo*, the term for "king" in ancient times. Chieftain Maichi had used the word *country* instead of other terms, such as *territory*.

I felt so sorry for him at the moment that I tugged at his sleeve and urged him not to be so angry. But he brushed me off, and cursed, "Why don't you perform in that play? Do you honestly think you could learn how to rule a country?"

Mother snickered. "How do you know my son could not?"

Then she took me to the special emissary, with Father staying behind and grumbling that we couldn't possibly carry more weight than he. But we soon returned to tell him that the special emissary was ready to see him now. Caught by surprise, Father could only look at Mother with a vicious glint in his eyes. Then, with an exaggerated flick of his sleeve, he went off to see the special emissary. The guards' salutes elicited only a grunt in response. Inside the room, Huang Chumin was sitting bolt upright, his eyes half-closed, as if indulging himself in something others could not see.

Before the chieftain could speak, a servant placed his finger to his lips. "Ssh." So the chieftain stood there with his hands at his sides for a while, until he realized that might appear overly respectful. Furious, he sat down heavily on the carpet.

The special emissary was facing a sheet of blank paper, which seemed to Chieftain Maichi to flutter as the man breathed on it. Finally the special emissary opened his eyes and took up a brush to write frenetically, as if possessed. Sweat dampened his hairline. Then he tossed down the brush and let out a long sigh, his body falling limply against a leopard-skin cushion. After a long moment, he smiled at the chieftain weakly. "Since I have no silver for you, why don't I give you a poem in my own calligraphy?"

He laid the paper on the carpet, the ink still wet, and recited loudly:

Tall flags flap in a spring breeze,
Arrows from jade tents rain down on the enemy camp.
The Maichi territory in the clouds has been recovered,
Wangpo's fortress beyond the snow will also be conquered.

Now, Chieftain Maichi knew nothing about poems, let alone one written in a tongue he didn't understand. Still, he bowed slightly as a sign of gratitude, planning to hang the gift in the guest room to show others that the Nationalist Government, like the emperors before them, were supporters of the Maichi family. Already proudly displayed in the room was an imperial plaque bestowed by a Qing emperor, with a four-word inscription, INSTRUCT AND ASSIMILATE BARBARIANS.

The special emissary was now seated beneath those gilded characters, in a stuffy guest room reeking of Indian incense.

"How can I thank the government and its special emissary?"

"I want nothing from you," the man said, "and the government has only a modest request." He told one of his men to bring in a cloth bag. The special emissary, a scrawny man with small hands and long fingers, reached into the bag and took out a handful of tiny gray seeds. Father had never seen such seeds. The special emissary let the seeds slip back into the bag through his fingers, and when the chieftain asked what they were, he was asked in return if all the grain harvested from his vast holdings was consumed each year. The atmosphere turned warm and cordial at the mention of food. Father said that some of the grain inevitably rotted in warehouses every year.

"You don't have to tell me. The smell hangs over the estate."

Not until that moment did I realize that the sweet odor permeating the estate each spring was actually the stench of rotting food.

The special emissary continued, "Do you have as much silver as grain, so much that no one cares when it slowly rots in a warehouse?"

"No one could ever have too much silver. Besides, silver doesn't rot."

"Good. Now we can talk. We don't want your silver. In fact, we'll give you more of it just to grow this. You can plant it in a space the size of the fortresses you've just taken."

"Exactly what is it?" it finally occurred to the chieftain to ask.

"The opium I enjoy so often. It is highly valued."

With a long sigh of relief, Chieftain Maichi gave his whole-hearted consent.

And with that, the special emissary took his leave, saying to Father, "I shall see you in the fall." But before leaving, he gave the chieftain's wife a set of intricately carved opium paraphernalia.

Uneasy about the gift, she asked Dolma, "Why didn't he give this to the chieftain?"

"Maybe he's in love with you," Dolma said. "After all, Mistress is also a Han."

Rather than react angrily to the insolent servant, the worried chieftain's wife said, "I'm afraid that's exactly what the chieftain is thinking."

Dolma simply snickered.

The chieftain's wife was no longer a young woman. Except for her fancy clothes, there wasn't much about her that was still appealing. People were always saying she'd once been a beauty but that she'd left her youth behind. I heard that my sister was also a beauty, but had no idea what she looked like. She had left with my uncle for Lhasa long ago, then gone on to Calcutta, from where they had sailed across the ocean to England on a beautiful floating house. Each year, we received a letter or two, months after she'd sent them. But since no one could read the English script, we just looked at the enclosed photographs. My sister was dressed in strange clothes, and, to be honest, seeing someone whose taste in clothes was so different from ours, I had trouble deciding if she was pretty or not.

So I asked my brother, "Is Sister pretty?"

"Of course she is. How could she not be?" Seeing the look of doubt on my face, he smiled. "God, I don't know either. Everyone says she is, so that's what I say." We had a good laugh over a family member who was off in some distant foreign land.

Since we couldn't read her long letters, we had no way of knowing that she was asking permission to remain in England. She was expecting to be summoned back to marry the son of another chieftain, someone who might someday become a chieftain himself, or who might turn out to be nothing. So she argued her case passionately, we were told, in a language we could not understand. Each letter extended the argument of earlier letters.

Everyone in the chieftain's family had a high opinion of himself; my sister in far-off England was no different, behaving as if the Maichi family would collapse without her. I was the only member of the family who didn't think he was that important to the world. My sister could not know that no one had read her letters, and that we merely hung the pictures on the walls of her room. Every once in a while a servant would clean the room; it no longer looked like a room for a living person, but one that had been lived in long before, and was now a space for that person's soul.

The battle with Wangpo had delayed planting a few days, but had helped the crops escape a frost when they sprouted. An unfortunate event had produced fortunate results, showing that, since my earliest memories, events had already begun to take an extraordinary course.

The center of the Maichi territory, that is, the land surrounding the estate, was planted with opium under the supervision of my father, my brother, and me.

Now let's take a look at the farming picture. Led by a child, two yoked oxen pulled a heavy wooden plow. A sliver of precious, shiny iron fixed to its tip guided the plow deep into the black soil, turning it over like ocean waves. The fellow at the plow regularly shouted out the names of the oxen or of the women following him. The seeds cascading into the soil from the women's raised hands produced the pleasant, rustling sound of spring rain, as the heavy fragrance of moist, newly planted soil filled the air.

Rest periods in the field quickly gave way to frenzied games. The women would throw the men to the ground, lift up their long robes, and remove their baggy underpants so they could paste manure on their devilish little things. The men's targets, on the other hand, were the girls' blouses, as they hoped to see the girls' lovely breasts exposed under the clear blue sky. These sorts of games during spring planting not only cheered the people, but, so I was told, also increased the yield. Chieftain Maichi told his sons that in olden times men and women actually did it in the fields.

Father had a cauldron set up in the field to make tea with a generous addition of butter and salt, which was a rarity back then. "This will enhance their strength," he said.

Two shrieking girls ran in front of our horses, their breasts jiggling like perky doves. The men chasing them were about to kneel down to us when my brother waved his whip. "Don't bother. Go after them!"

After the planting season, everything – the people, the sun, and the land – turned languid. Even the water in the river and the grass on the mountains took their own sweet time turning green. Everyone was anxious to know what would emerge from the seeds left by Special Emissary Huang.

The pampered family of the chieftain began to concern itself with farm work. Each day the family, followed by a long procession of maidservants, grooms, various attendants, the steward, and duty headmen from other fortresses, set out to inspect the distant land. Even before the poppies appeared, their boundless magic enthralled us. I kept bending down to part the loose soil and see how the seeds were coming along. This was the only time no one called me an idiot. The others, with their normal intelligence, were as curious as I but didn't want to show it, so the job was left to me. When I scooped a seed out of the ground, they couldn't wait to take it from me and wonder out loud how such tiny seeds could sprout such strong, thick tendrils. Then one day the sprouts ripped through the ground and tender buds spread out to form thick leaves shaped like a baby's delicate hands.

The next two or three months passed quickly.

When the poppies bloomed, the giant red flowers formed a spectacular carpet across much of Chieftain Maichi's territory. This plant captivated us. How lovely those poppies were!

Complaining of headaches, Mother regularly pasted slices of garlic onto her temples. Garlic, an effective medicine around here, could be cooked and ingested to stop diarrhea or sliced raw to put on the temples for migraines. The chieftain's wife often used her homesickness and her migraines to remind people that she lived in agony. And so a disagreeable, spicy odor followed her wherever she went.

On one of those days, the family was happily preparing an outing to celebrate the balmy summer weather. All except for Mother, who stood alone upstairs, behind the curved railings, slices of milky white garlic stuck to the sides of her head. The grooms, the maidservants, even the executioner, strolled outside in high spirits, their happy chatter and laughter drifting over the high walls. Seeing that no one was paying her any attention, she moaned. "Tell Dolma to stay with me."

But I said, "Dolma, I need you up here on my horse to hold me."

Sangye Dolma looked over at the chieftain.

"Do what Young Master says."

And so the always redolent Dolma climbed up and held me tightly. Amid the raging sea of red poppies, I pressed my head back against her full breasts. The field was saturated with burning red flowers and the pungent smell of horses. I ached from wanting a woman, inflamed by the soft curves of the beautiful maid and her moist, warm breath. It felt to me as if the poppies, raging like a wildfire across the hills, were flowering in my heart.

Some girls were playing seductively in a patch of flowery bushes ahead. My brother reined in his horse, about to go after them, when Father stopped him.

"We're nearing the Tratra fortress. Its headman will come out to greet us."

So my brother picked up his rifle and began shooting birds in the sky. The cracks of gunfire were swallowed up by the vast river valley, above which the deep blue of the sky was broken only by puffy white clouds hanging lazily atop mountain trees. My brother even held his rifle elegantly, and once he started firing he couldn't stop. Before the echo of one shot died out, the next one followed. Bullet casings skittered on the ground, reflecting the bright sunlight.

Off in the distance, the headman of the Tratra fortress emerged ahead of a contingent of people. Just before we reached the hitching posts, as his servants were bowing low and reaching out for our reins, my brother abruptly turned and fired a shot at the headman's feet. The screeching bullet hit the ground just beneath the man's handsome boots, its force seeming to lift him into the air. I'm sure he'd never jumped so high before, or so nimbly. His landing was just as nimble.

My brother dismounted and stroked his horse's neck. "It went off accidentally," he said. "The headman must have been startled."

Headman Tratra looked down at his feet, which, unharmed, still supported his hulking body. But his handsome boots were covered with dirt. Wiping the sweat from his forehead, he tried to smile, but instead of masking the anger, the smile distorted his expression horribly. Knowing how transparent his feelings must be, he gave up all pretenses and dropped to his knees before Father. "What law has Tratra broken? Why does the young chieftain treat me this way? Why doesn't Master just tell him to shoot me dead?"

Not realizing that this exchange was all for show, Yangzom, the headman's lovely wife, squealed and fell to the ground. The look of fright on her face only enhanced her beauty, which immediately attracted the chieftain's attention. He walked up to her. "Don't be afraid," he said. "It's just a game."

As if to prove the truth of his words, he burst out laughing, which lightened the atmosphere somewhat. Headman Tratra, helped up by the young future chieftain, wiped the cold sweat from his face, and said, "I had food and drink prepared as soon as I saw you, Chieftain. Please instruct us where to set up the tables, inside or outside?"

"Outside," Father said, "closer to the flowers."

So we ate and drank in sight of the incredibly beautiful poppies. Father kept turning to look at the headman's wife, which did not escape her husband, who was powerless before the mighty chieftain. He could only say to his woman, "Don't you have a headache? Go inside and lie down."

"Does your woman have headaches too? She doesn't appear to.

41

My woman is forever troubled by them." He turned to the headman's wife. "Do you have a headache?"

Yangzom smiled but said nothing.

The chieftain returned Yangzom's smile and gazed into her eyes. Finally she said, "Not anymore. The young chieftain's gunshot drove it away." Her response enraged the headman, but he kept his anger in check and merely showed the whites of his eyes to the cloudless sky.

"Don't be upset, Tratra. Look how beautiful your woman is!"

"Does the chieftain wish to take a rest? I'm not sure you are quite clearheaded."

The chieftain burst out laughing. "*Someone* here isn't clearheaded." It was the sort of laughter that made a man shudder. The headman looked down at his feet.

During that first summer, when the poppies took root in our land and produced beautiful flowers, a strange phenomenon occurred – both my father's and my brother's sexual appetites grew stronger than ever. My own desire, which had been awakened in the early spring, now exploded, fed by the vibrant red blossoms of summer. During the banquet that day, Chieftain Maichi was bewitched by Tratra's wife, while my head was sent spinning by the redness all around and the fullness of Dolma's breasts.

Tratra gulped down huge mouthfuls of liquor. My head was buzzing, but I could still hear his mumbled comment to the chieftain: "These flowers offend the eye. What's the point of planting so many of them?"

"You don't understand," the chieftain replied. "If you did, then you would be chieftain, not me. These aren't flowers, they're silver. Do you believe me? Of course you don't. Now have one of your women refill my cup."

My brother had already left the banquet, for a spot where there were girls, so I tugged at Dolma's arm. We walked slowly away from the table, then began to run hand in hand after we'd gone around a low wall. We ran straight into the dazzling sea of flowers, whose fragrance made my head throb again. I tumbled to the ground and lay in the shadows of their petals. As if reciting an incantation, I called out, "Dolma, oh, Dolma, Dolma."

There must have been magic in my moans, because Dolma fell down beside me.

With a giggle, she hiked her long skirt to cover her face, exposing the beast's mouth between her legs. I called out again, "Dolma, Dolma."

The mouth swallowed me up as she wrapped her legs around me, and I entered a patch of darkness surrounded by brightness, searching for something as if I'd gone mad. She was too big for my still growing body. Poppies were broken, the milky substance oozing from the injured stalks covering our faces. It was as if they were ejaculating, just like me. With a giggle, Dolma pushed me off and told me to arrange flowers around her navel. Sangye Dolma was my teacher, not my lover. I called her sister and she held my face and cried. "Good brother," she said. "Good little brother."

For Headman Tratra, it was a calamitous day.

As I've said, Chieftain Maichi had his eye on the headman's wife. We couldn't know exactly how the headman felt about this, but in any case, this stubborn man, a die-hard loyal servant to the Maichi family, would surely draw the line at putting his woman on a horse and sending her over to the estate house.

A couple of weeks later, the headman was walking through the vast poppy field with his steward. By then, the unsettlingly bright and beautiful flowers were undergoing a change, with tiny green berries forming in the middle of each one. Pistol in hand, his steward asked, "What does the headman plan to do?"

The headman knew what the steward was talking about but had no answer, so he pointed at the green berries, and asked, "Can these things really be converted into silver?"

"If the chieftain says so."

"I think the chieftain is losing his mind. No one with his head on straight would grow so many inedible things. He's mad."

"Don't you want to do something about this madman? Such as get rid of him." Tratra's steward held up his pistol. "It's clear he wants your wife, and clear that you don't want to give her away. So what are you going to do?"

"Are you telling me to rebel? No, no, I cannot."

"Then you must die. If you had chosen to rebel, I'd have followed you. But since you didn't, you'll have to forgive me. The chieftain has ordered me to kill you."

Before Tratra could say another word, Dorjee Tsering, his steward, shot him in the chest. The headman opened his mouth to speak, and out came a mouthful of bright red blood. In the end, he was unable to say a word. Trying not to fall, he opened his arms to embrace a cluster of poppies, as if for support. But the poppies, unable to sustain his weight, fell with him.

Dorjee Tsering then raced toward the chieftain's compound from the main road, yelling, "Tratra is rebelling! Tratra is rebelling!" Meanwhile, the headman lay on the damp ground amid the poppies, his mouth filled with dirt. His legs stretched out one final time, and he breathed just once more as gunfire erupted behind the killer. At last, the man who had murdered his own master ran into the house. The people chasing him stopped some distance away, not daring to get closer, as rifles quickly filled the slots in the blockhouse. The chieftain stood on top, and shouted, "Your headman was plotting against me, and now he's been taken care of by someone loyal to me. Do you plan to rebel against me too?"

The mob quickly dispersed.

The raging red poppy flowers were beaten down by the onslaught of rain.

When the autumn sun shone on them again, the flowers had given way to green berries. My father, meanwhile, took up with the dead headman's wife, Yangzom, in the field as soon as the rains stopped. Dorjee Tsering, who had killed her husband, Headman Tratra, repeatedly told the chieftain that he should be returning to his fortress. But this was actually a reminder to the chieftain to fulfill a promise made to him. After the man had spoken once too often, the chieftain replied with a smile, "You must be foolhardy. Do you honestly think that people back at the fortress believe that Tratra was a rebel? No one believes that. People have not forgotten that his family has been around for many generations. Are you so anxious to return because you want to be killed?"

After uttering this comment for Dorjee Tsering to mull over, the chieftain went into the poppy field for another tryst with Yangzom.

But while he was with his other woman, Mother grew increasingly arrogant.

The poppies flourished beyond imagining, as we could see from the windows of the house. These plants, which were appearing on our land for the very first time, were so thrilling that they drew out the madness hidden in the people's marrow. Maybe it was their mysterious power that had caused the chieftain to fall so much in love with Yangzom, a lovely but rather stupid woman. And Yangzom, who had just buried her husband, was equally mad. As soon as the sun rose each morning, they set out from their respective stone buildings to meet and fall into each other's arms before dashing into the crazed poppy field. With the wind blowing on the new plants, the berries surged in waves like raging sexual desire. Everyone knew that Father and Yangzom were making passionate love out there deep in the field, while Mother, who stood by the window watching the undulating green waves, clutched her chest as if in excruciating pain.

Father's newfound love played a mouth lyre, the vibrating sounds from its bamboo fingers floating over on the wind from far away. The chieftain's wife told people to shoot at the place the sounds were coming from, but who would dare to fire at the chieftain, their ruler? So she did it herself, but the bullet could not possibly have reached its distant target. Instead, it fell to the ground midway, like the droppings of a passing bird. Her anger dried up the garlic slices on her temples, some of which fell to the floor, one by one.

Indian snuff was another of Mother's headache remedies. But her method of using the yellow powder was unique. Others snorted it directly from their thumbnail. She, on the other hand, slipped a gold thimble on her pinkie, poured a bit of the powder on top, and raised it to her nose. She'd scrunch up her face for a long time before snorting deeply, then raise her suddenly reddened face skyward and open her mouth, wider and wider. Finally, she'd stomp her foot and jerk her head to release a ringing sneeze or two. Dolma, who had to clean the snot and spit from her mistress's clothes, would say, "Does the mistress feel better now?"

Normally, she would answer softly, "Much better." But this time, she screamed, "How is that supposed to make me feel better? Nothing can do that. This rage will kill me!"

The servants could say nothing. But I said, "Father's the one who ordered Tratra's death. It's not the woman's fault."

Mother immediately burst out crying. "Idiot! Idiot! You're a good-for-nothing idiot!" Snot flew onto the crippled steward's boots. After a while, her cries turned to muted sobs, which rose to the ceiling and buzzed around like a housefly. At times like this, we all turned our attention to the poppies blanketing the fields outside. Out there, Chieftain Maichi embraced his beloved woman as he entered her, crushing the fallen flowers around them. Having rediscovered love, Father felt the earth move under the woman as she cried out in ecstasy. Her cry traveled all the way to the estate house, where it echoed around the walls of our stronghold. We all covered our ears, except for my poor mother, who grabbed her head, as if the happy, lascivious cry would split it like an ax. Fortunately, there was a limit to Chieftain Maichi's vitality, no matter how crazed he was, and calmness soon returned to the surging center of the poppy field. The vast patch of green rose and fell in the breezes, along with the rhythmic breathing of the now sated Chieftain Maichi and his new love.

Mother also returned to normal. Dolma peeled the remaining garlic slices off Mother's temples. Now she could calmly wash her face in the brass basin. She spent more time at it than usual, and as she was applying lotion she ordered a servant to summon the head of the family guard.

The man came, but as he was stepping across the threshold, Mother said, "No need to come in. Just stand there."

So he was forced to stand with one foot inside and one foot out. "Mistress," he said, "what would you have me do?"

The chieftain's wife told him to give a gun to Dorjee Tsering, the man who had killed his own master. "Since he can kill his own master, he can get rid of that slut too."

"Yes," the head of the family guard replied, clicking his heels, something our men had learned from the special emissary's troops.

"Wait," the chieftain's wife said. "I want you to get rid of him too after he's killed that woman."

6 Killing ⟅

I said to the chieftain's wife, "Ah-ma, let me do it. They won't kill Yangzom. They're afraid of Ah-pa."

A contented smile spread across her face as she said, "You're such a little fool."

46

My brother walked into the room at that moment. "What's he done this time?" he asked.

My brother got along well with both my mother and me. "He's had one of his foolish ideas again," she said, "so I scolded him a bit."

He looked at me with pity in his eyes, the eyes of a smart person. For me, that sort of look was poison. Luckily, because of my low intelligence, I suffered little, if any, hurt at all. An idiot has no strong loves or hates, and can see nothing but basic truths. That, in turn, keeps his fragile heart relatively safe from harm.

The future Chieftain Maichi rubbed my head, but I ducked away, and while he was talking to Mother, I stood behind Dolma, playing with the tassels on the silk ribbon around her waist. After a while, a warm current swelled the thing that had so recently enjoyed the taste of carnal pleasure, prompting me to pinch her leg viciously. The sweet-smelling Sangye Dolma reacted with a soft cry.

Ignoring us, Mother said to First Young Master sternly, "Just look at him. After we're gone, you'll have to take good care of him."

My brother nodded and waved me over to whisper, "Do you like girls too?"

I didn't answer, not knowing if he expected me to say yes or no.

"I think you do."

So I stepped into the middle of the room, and declared loudly, "I–like–Dol–ma."

He laughed, the sort of laugh that showed he was made of the right stuff to be a leader. It was so contagious that Dolma and Mother started to laugh too. So did I. That laughter was a happy, flickering flame that shattered the noon tranquillity and made it quiver. But no sooner had we stopped laughing and were about to speak than we heard a gunshot.

It was a strange sound, like someone striking a brass gong.

Crack! It was so loud.

Mother shivered.

Crack! Another loud shot.

Sounds of hurried footsteps and shouts erupted on the estate, followed by the crisp, ominous sound of rifle bolts being pulled. Then came the creaks of gigantic wooden wheels as our family guards positioned cannons in the tower. Silence returned to the compound in the bright autumn sun once the cannons were in

47

position. The silence made the tower seem more imposing and magnificent than ever.

After making sure that all was ready, my brother stood with me between two bronze cannons to survey the spot from which the gunfire had come. I knew what the shots were all about, but still I yelled along with my brother, "Kill whoever fired his gun!"

Outside, the field, with its boundless, thriving poppies, was calm. Women were rinsing white linen in the river. At the Kaba fortresses below, people were weaving wool blankets or tanning leather on their rooftops, as the river flowed east to some faraway place. While I was caught up in the scenic panorama, my brother blurted out, "Do you really think you could kill?" I turned to look at him and nodded. He was a good brother, someone who wished that I could be as brave as he, and was trying to cultivate courage in me. He thrust a gun into my hand, and said, "Go ahead, kill anyone you wish. Don't be afraid."

With the gun in my hand, I saw everything that was happening out in front of me, especially the activity amid the poppies. Now if you'd asked me just what it was I saw, I'm sure I couldn't tell you. But I *did* see everything. See there, I fire a shot, and the head of the family guard drags Dorjee Tsering's body by the legs out from amid the poppies. I fire again, in another direction, sensing that my aim is better than any marksman. See there, with this shot Father leaps out of the place where he had been indulging in carnal pleasures, roaring like a bear. Holding the hand of his new woman and waving his yellow sash in the other hand, he runs through the ocean of green.

My brother grabbed my wrist with a force that sent the next few bullets up into the sky. Then we went down to the poppy field, where we found Father completely dressed. Without a word he slapped my brother, thinking that his heir had fired the shots. My brother smiled at me, the look devoid of any resentment over having assumed the blame. On the contrary, it was more the look of embarrassment for a smart person who had done something stupid.

"It wasn't him," I said. "I fired the shots."

Father turned to look at me grimly, then looked over at my brother, who nodded. Ignoring the woman, Father snatched the pistol from my brother's belt, released the safety, and handed it to me. I swung my arm, and the dead Dorjee Tsering, who was lying in the road, waved his lifeless right hand at us.

Yangzom looked at her former steward, a scream escaping from her lovely mouth.

I fired again, and the dead man who had betrayed his master waved his left hand at his former mistress. Unfortunately, she didn't see it because she had her own hands over her face.

Father laughed hollowly as he patted me on the head, and said to the woman, "Ha-ha. Even my idiot son is a crack shot." With that we were introduced to his new love. Then he added, "Just wait. When Yangzom gives me another son, you three will have no peers." And that was how we learned that Yangzom was to become a new family member. At the same time, he snatched the gun out of my hand and tucked it back into my brother's belt.

The corpse was now covered with flies. Chieftain Maichi said, "I was thinking of making him the headman of the Tratra fortress. Who shot him?"

The head of the family guard knelt. "He planned to shoot the master, so I took care of him."

Scratching his head, Father asked, "Where did he get the gun?"

I smiled foolishly, but my brother and the head of the guard kept quiet.

"What are you smiling at?" Father asked. "Do you know something?"

I was receiving a great deal of attention that day.

Seeing that they were all looking at me quizzically, how could I disappoint them? So I told them about the chieftain's wife, who was behind it all. As I spoke, sweat trickled down my face, not because I was afraid, but because it was all so involved. It was much too hard on my idiot's brain to recall things arranged by a smart person. As far as I was concerned, smart people were like marmots up on the mountain, always watchful, always jittery. They can't take a nap in the sun after a meal, but they must dig a hole here and pee there to create countless false trails for the hunters. Yet their tricks always fail them. Maybe the sun was too hot for Father, Yangzom, and the head of the guard, because as I spoke, I noticed that sweat was oozing from the tightly knit brows of Father and Yangzom, the shiny beads slithering down the tips of their noses and falling to the dusty ground, while it seeped murkily from the guard's hairline and spread out unevenly from his eyebrows.

In my tale, two people deserved to die, a man and a woman. But only the man had died. His mouth was open, as if he were confused about all that had happened. My brother stuffed a green berry into the dead man's mouth to improve its appearance.

"Very well, then," Father blurted out. Then he turned to his mistress. "Now that it's come to this, I'll have to keep you here with me for your safety."

And so Yangzom, whom Mother hated with all her being, entered the Maichi household as a matter of course. Now the couple could make a big show of sleeping in the same bed. Some people said it was I, the idiot, who had given Father the excuse to house his mistress. But I've forgotten all the details. Besides, a chieftain needs no excuse to bed a woman. Anyone who says otherwise is more stupid than I.

As we walked back to the estate, the head of the corpse being dragged along by the feet banged against the roadway with a muffled, unsettling sound.

The chieftain's wife appeared on the platform balcony, flanked by lamas, the steward, and her maidservant. Dressed in a dazzling pink dress with billowing white sleeves, she looked down at Father approaching the gate with his new love. Mother had been born into a poor Han family and bought by a rich man as a present for Father. Normally, it would have been unusual for Chieftain Maichi to stay in love with her for such a long time, given the difference in status. But where feelings were concerned, Chieftain Maichi always surprised people. Soon after his first wife died, a constant stream of people from far and near had come to propose marriage; but he had turned them all away. Then, just as people were praising his deep devotion to his late wife, a wedding announcement arrived. He and my mother, a woman without status and from a different race, became husband and wife. People said, "A Han woman! Just wait and see. He'll soon propose marriage to a chieftain's daughter."

In fact, among the chieftains in our area – such as Wangpo, Lha Shopa, Rongong, and one called Gyalwa, and even the late Maichi – it was usually a matter of: you marry my daughter, then someday I'll come and marry another chieftain's younger sister. Intermarriage occurred even more frequently with chieftains farther away. Take our family, for example. Over the years, Maichi chieftains have been involved in marriages with three chieftains on the Tadu River, two from the mesas west and north of Mount Tsechong, even some who, no longer titled, served as border guards for the Nationalist Government. This group, although no longer as powerful as before, still owned land and people. They were our relatives, either distant or close. Even though we might turn on one another sometimes, where marriage was concerned, we'd rather join the enemy than find someone whose "bone" was inferior to ours. That's how it had always been. But Father broke that tradition, which was why, from the beginning, people predicted that Chieftain Maichi would not be happy with the Han woman for long. Many chieftains and the people on the vast lands they governed said that the marriage was nothing but a novelty for Chieftain Maichi. But messengers bearing his marriage proposal never appeared at the borders of a single chieftain's territory.

I was the product of the union of the chieftain and the Han woman. During my first two years, they wondered if something was wrong with me, but it took them another two years to confirm the fact that I was an idiot.

My status rekindled hope in people. But again they were disappointed. All they heard was that the chieftain's wife was getting increasingly temperamental, and that the chieftain would occasionally take his pleasure with one of the serving girls. News like that certainly didn't bring them any hope. As a matter of fact, all the women who had once waited for Chieftain Maichi's marriage proposal were by then married themselves. Yet people never stopped paying attention to Chieftain Maichi's love life simply because they'd gotten used to observing the foolishness of someone so smart.

But Mother knew that the day had finally come. For a woman, there's no escaping this day, so she greeted it in her finest clothes. The daughter of a humble family had become a graceful noblewoman. Watching the chieftain draw up to the estate house with his new love was like witnessing the arrival of the lonely, second half of her life. Dolma told me that she heard the mistress say over and over, "I see it, I see it now."

The procession arrived at the gate amid Mother's muttering.

People looked up to admire the gracious figure of the chieftain's wife. Unlike Father's new love, whose beauty made a man want to possess her, Mother's charm was overpowering. Even Yangzom was overpowered by it. "Please," she begged Father, "let me go. I want to go home."

My brother said, "Go home, then. Plenty of people are lying in wait to kill you on the road."

"Why would they want to kill me?"

He smiled and said to this beautiful woman, who was his own age but was about to be elevated to the status of his mother's generation, "Because they think you had Headman Tratra killed so you could become the wife of the chieftain."

Father looked up to the balcony. "Are you afraid of her? Don't be. I won't let her harm you."

By then, the dead man had been tied upside down to a stake by the executioners, a father-and-son team. After an ox horn was sounded, people from far and near gathered at the estate, quickly filling the square, where the chieftain explained how this man had killed the loyal Headman Tratra, and how he himself had detected the plot and punished the man as he was about to take over Tratra's position. That's how the people learned that another headman's territory had fallen under the direct control of the chieftain. But since that had no real effect on them, as serfs, they formed a line and walked past the corpse with its expressionless face. Custom required that they spit in the dead man's face so he'd sink to the bottom of hell, never to be reborn. They spat so much that flies drowned on a face that was becoming more and more swollen.

Mother stood up there the whole time, taking in everything.

Father was mightily pleased with himself. He had deftly turned Mother's careful scheme to his own advantage. And he didn't stop there. He told the family slave, Sonam Tserang, "Go ask the mistress how she'd like to curse this criminal who turned a gun on his own master."

Without a word, the mistress loosened a piece of jade from a sash around her waist and spat on it. The slave carried it downstairs and threw it on the corpse. The crowd was astounded by her disdain of a valuable piece of jade.

She turned and went back to her own room. The people below watched her disappear from the third-floor balcony, then heard her shrill voice echo down the shadowy veranda. She was calling for her personal maid, my teacher. "Dolma! Sangye Dolma!"

Dolma's figure, in a long, pale green robe, also disappeared.

Father installed Yangzom in a third-story room on the east side, with a southern exposure, where they could sleep in the same bed for as long as they wanted. Prior to then, no Maichi chieftain would have remained long in the same room with the same woman, let alone sleep in the same bed with her for years.

But let's leave that and take a look at the chieftain's bed, which was actually a giant closet built into the wall. Dim lights made it dark and deep. Once I asked Father, "Are there monsters in there?"

Instead of giving a direct answer, he smiled like an ordinary, guileless father, and said, "You're such a little fool."

But I believed there was something scary inside.

Late that night, grief-stricken sobs sounded outside the estate house. Draping his clothes over his shoulders, Chieftain Maichi got out of bed, while Yangzom rolled to the edge, terrified of the deep, dark shadows inside. The chieftain had only to clear his throat for lanterns to be lit inside the house, followed by torches outside. As soon as he appeared on the balcony, someone shone a lantern on his face. He shouted down at the darkness, "This is Chieftain Maichi. Take a good look."

Down below, three shadowy figures knelt in the misty night. They were the wife and two sons of the slain Dorjee Tsering, whose body hung upside down and swayed gently on the stake.

Father shouted, "Though I should have you all killed, I'll let you off this time. But don't blame me for what happens if you're found on my territory three days from now." His voice boomed throughout the estate.

A boyish voice emerged from the dark: "Chieftain, have them shine a light on you again, so I can remember your face."

"Are you afraid you might kill the wrong person someday? All right, take a good look."

"Thank you. I've seen it now."

Father laughed out loud. "Good boy. Must I wait for you if I feel like dying before you come?"

No answer, as the three of them, mother and sons, had already vanished in the dark.

When Father turned around, he saw Mother looking down at him from her quarters. She liked the effect of Father looking up at her. Gripping the smooth, chilled wooden banister, she asked, "Why didn't you kill them?"

Father could have asked if she thought he was that small-minded, but instead he said softly, "I'm sleepy."

Mother added, "I heard them cursing you."

Father quickly composed himself. "What do you think an enemy does, sing to you?"

"Why are you so edgy? You may be the chieftain, but a woman has caused you to lose your head. What would you do if there were ten of them?"

She spoke so convincingly that Father didn't know what to say. As the torches died out, turning the estate back into a gigantic black hole, Mother's clear, crisp laughter echoing in the dark sounded wonderful. "Shouldn't the master return to his room?" she asked. "His concubine must be frightened in that big bed."

"You should go inside as well. It's too windy up there for someone as frail as you."

Naturally, Mother detected the hidden meaning in his words. Father wouldn't have said something like that if she hadn't complained about her health so often. I think she mistakenly applied the Han definition of wistful beauty to everyone. But she was not prepared to give up so easily. "Would it matter if I died? The Maichi family may need lots of things, but it certainly isn't short of wives. You can buy one with money or take one with a gun. What could be easier?"

"I don't feel like talking with you anymore," Father replied.

"Then go back to your room. I'm waiting to see what sort of drama unfolds tonight."

Back in bed, the image of that cold face, like a silver platter, swam before his eyes. He ground his teeth, and said, "She's turning into a witch."

Yangzom rolled into the chieftain's arms. "I'm scared. Hold me."

"You needn't be afraid. You're Chieftain Maichi's third wife."

The woman's warm body calmed him. All the while he was telling her how he would arrange a grand wedding ceremony, he was thinking about how Headman Tratra's property now belonged to him. For generations, Tratra had been his most loyal headman, but he should not have had such a beautiful wife, or so much silver, keeping the chieftain awake at night. Things would not have turned out so badly had Tratra offered to share his wealth with the chieftain. Father sighed over man's insatiable greed.

The woman fell asleep in his arms, her tender round breasts shining in the dark. She really was a stupid woman. After all that had happened over the past few days, no one with any sense could possibly sleep; but she rolled over and fell into a deep slumber. Along with her deep, even breathing, a seductive, animal-like smell from her body filled the room, arousing his desire. As a man, the chieftain knew that after this bout of madness, there would be little left, and that time was running out for him. He wanted to wake the woman and travel with her into the valley of ecstasy.

Upstairs, his second wife was clapping her hands and shouting gleefully, "It's burning! It's burning."

Chieftain Maichi sighed over this petty woman. He would have to send for the lamas to recite exorcist sutras, or she might go crazy. But now more people were shouting and running around in the dark, making the stone stronghold quake. This quaking had the power to make people uneasy about a lot of things.

Chieftain Maichi opened his eyes and saw a red light outside his window. At first he thought that someone had set the estate on fire. That proved not to be the case, but still, he sensed an aura of hate.

The population of the estate had all been in bed, except for Mother, who had been standing upstairs the whole time, beneath dim, flickering starlight. But now everyone was awake. The chieftain's family and their lamas and steward were upstairs, the family guard and slaves down below. The new third wife buried her head under the covers and rolled toward the inside of the closet-bed. It turned out that the three people who had left that night vowing vengeance had set fire to Headman Tratra's fortress. Flames raged under the cold, starlit autumn night; it shone over the vast, pitch-black poppy field and on the grand estate of Chieftain Maichi. We stood there watching gravely as our newly acquired property turned to ashes.

Behind us, winds off the river got colder and colder. The flames in front and the chill behind put all sorts of thoughts in our heads.

The servants clapped and hooted each time a fire dragon leaped from a window in the distant fortress, and I could hear the voices of my wet nurse, the maidservants, the silversmith, and the young family slave, Sonam Tserang. Dolma was with them; even though she had been granted the rare privilege of living with the family, she joined the other servants whenever she had the chance.

It was daylight by the time the fire died out.

Instead of fleeing with her two young sons, Dorjee Tsering's woman had thrown herself into the fire she'd set and had died a horrible death. She exploded along with her curses, her belly opening up like a beautiful flower. She had placed a murderous curse on what appeared to be a rock-solid family. Father knew that the childish promise of vengeance would someday be carried out, and he wanted to send people after the two sons. But my brother said, "You let them go in front of all those people. So instead of chasing after them now, I say we just be more careful."

The chieftain sent pursuers anyway. But our two future enemies were not caught in three days, and by the fourth, they'd have fled the territory ruled by the Maichi family. No one could pass beyond our territory in less than three days.

From then on, the incinerated woman and her sons entered my father's nightmares, and his only path to tranquillity was to hold a large-scale Buddhist ceremony.

Lamas from our sutra hall and from the Mondron Ling Monastery were brought together to craft animal and human figurines from dough. In the solemn rite that followed, all the curses and latent hatred were transferred to these figurines, which were taken to the foothills for cremation on a pyre made of desert thorn, which everyone said could reduce anything in the world to ashes. The ashes were then scattered so widely that nothing could bring them together again.

Meanwhile, poppies ripening in the field filled the air with an intoxicating fragrance.

Those few days of favor caused Jeeka, Mondron Ling Monastery's Living Buddha, to forget the cold shoulder he'd endured for years. In a somber, earnest tone, he said to the chieftain, "In my view, none of this would have happened if you hadn't planted those flowers. They have a corrupting influence."

The Living Buddha actually grasped the hands of the chieftain, who pulled them back and hid them in his robe. "What's wrong with these flowers?" he asked coldly. "Aren't they pretty enough for you?"

Realizing that he had made one of those mistakes so common to the learned – the inability to hold one's tongue – the Living Buddha brought his palms together as a sign to leave. But the chieftain took his hands. "Come, let's take a look at those flowers."

The Living Buddha was obliged to follow the chieftain out into the corrupting field, which had undergone a transformation. The bright flowers had withered, and the leaves now held green balls like monks' heads. The chieftain laughed. "Why, they look like the heads of your little monks." A sweep of his dagger sent berries rolling onto the ground.

The Living Buddha sucked in his breath as he watched milky sap ooze from the decapitated stalks.

The chieftain said, "I've heard that the blood of an accomplished lama is different from that of ordinary people. Could it be this same milky color?"

Holding his tongue, the nervous Living Buddha stepped on the round poppy berries, which exploded like human skulls. He looked up into the cloudless sky, where a white-shouldered hawk was surveying the surroundings below, rising and falling with the air currents over the valley. The sun cast its enormous, powerful shadow on the ground as the hawk soared and cried out shrilly.

The Living Buddha said, "It's summoning the wind and the rain."

Here we have yet another problem of the learned – they think they must explain everything. Chieftain Maichi smiled, but didn't feel the need to remind the Living Buddha of his current situation. He simply said, "Yes, the hawk is the king of the sky. And when the king appears, snakes and rats must run and hide in their holes."

The king of the sky swept past the chieftain and the Living Buddha with a gust of wind and soared upward after snatching a shrieking bird out of the shrubbery, then landed on the highest branch of a cliff-top tree.

Chieftain Maichi later told people that he'd taught the Living Buddha a lesson that day, just to make sure he wouldn't consider himself infallible. When a curious person asked the Living Buddha if that was true, he said, "Amita Buddha. We monks have the right to interpret what we see."

7 The Earth Trembles ⌒

I was taught that land is the most stable thing in the world, followed by the kingly power of the chieftain who governs it. But during the first year poppies grew on our land, the earth trembled. At the time, Living Buddha Jeeka was in his prime and the chieftain's threat had failed to seal his mouth. It's not that he didn't fear the chieftain; rather, he was driven by that habit common to the learned of voicing an opinion on everything.

As he sat in his monastery, he grew restless over the fact that he could not divulge the omens he saw. He sat rigid on a Buddhist throne gilded with five catties of gold, calming himself and regulating his breath. Once he focused his mind, the glittering iconic Buddha would show himself. But one of his fleshy eyelids began to twitch, so he interrupted his meditation to wet his eyelids with bits of saliva. When that didn't work, he summoned a young monk to place a piece of gold foil on the eyelid. The next twitch sent the gold foil gliding to the floor.

The Living Buddha asked what was happening outside.

Someone answered that snakes were coming out of their holes.

"What else? There should be more than snakes."

Someone complimented the Living Buddha on being so wise. Dogs were climbing trees like cats, and many sightless things that should have remained underground were emerging.

Flanked by retainers, the Living Buddha went to the monastery gate to see with his own eyes if things were truly happening as described to him.

The monastery had been built on a cliff shaped like a dragon's head.

The Living Buddha's magic eyes took in everything as he stood at the gate. Not only did he see what his disciples had told him, but he also saw Chieftain Maichi's estate shrouded in a haze of indescribable color. Children were beating the roaming snakes. Led by the slave Sonam Tserang, and holding sticks encircled with dead snakes of all colors and patterns, they walked through the field beneath a clear autumn sky. They were singing:

The yak's meat has been offered to the spirits,
The yak's skin has been made into ropes,

The yak's tassel-like tail
Has been hung on the mane of Kurongmenda,
Friendship will be rewarded, evil intentions will be punished.
The demons are rising from the ground,
King Bende is dead,
The flawless jade is shattered,
It is completely shattered.

The Living Buddha was astounded. This ballad had been part of an old tale called "The Story of the Horse and the Yak," which was widely circulated even before the first Maichi chieftain had come into existence. After there was a chieftain, people began to sing more of praise and forgot all about historical ballads.

Only widely read lamas could find such stories in ancient texts. Living Buddha Jeeka, who had once devoted himself to the study of local history, knew of their existence. But, now, without being taught, young slaves ignorant of worldly affairs had suddenly revived this long-lost ballad. Sweat dripped from the Living Buddha's shaved head. He told his disciples to set up a ladder by the sutra tower, where he found a volume containing the story. A young monk blew away the dust to reveal the yellow silk wrapping.

After changing into a fresh cassock, the Living Buddha left the monastery with the yellow bundle tucked under his arm. He intended to relate the story to Chieftain Maichi and convince him that the revival of a ballad like that by youngsters was no mere coincidence.

But he went in vain, for the chieftain was not in the house. The servants said they did not know when he was expected back, and the worried looks on their faces told him they weren't lying. The Living Buddha said he'd like to see Monpa Lama, who was in charge of the family sutra hall.

Monpa Lama told the messenger, "Let him come up if he wants to."

The Living Buddha was waiting in the steward's second-floor office; the sutra hall was on the fifth floor. The resident lama's haughtiness caused even the steward to steal a glance at their guest. But the Living Buddha said calmly, "See how he treats me, steward? But I can't be bothered by that, since a calamity is about to occur." He went upstairs, enduring the humiliation and weighed down with his sense of duty.

And where was Chieftain Maichi?

Shh! It's a secret. I hold up my finger, yet cannot stop myself from telling you that Chieftain Maichi had led his new love into the field to take his pleasure.

The binoculars left behind by Special Emissary Huang had a new use, for I fixed my gaze on Father and his new love as they tore through the sea of poppies. Now let me tell you why they had to go outdoors. Chieftain Maichi's third wife was in constant fear in the bed she shared with the chieftain, always filled with apprehension whenever he wanted her. If he forced himself on her, she resisted as if her life were at stake, digging her long nails deeply into him as she begged, "Daytime, let's do it in the daytime. Please, I beg you. Let's do it outside during the day."

"Have you seen something?" he asked her.

With tears streaming down her face, Yangzom said, "No, I haven't. I'm just afraid."

Holding her in his arms, the chieftain was surprised at his own patience and tenderness toward a woman, just as he was surprised by the powerful sexual desires raging inside. "All right," he said. "We'll wait until tomorrow."

But daylight did not bring them any better prospects. I watched them hurry through the field trying to find a spot to lie down in. Let me remind you that this impatient man was the master of boundless lands, yet he could not find a place to lie with his beloved woman. The empty spaces were all taken up by animals of unknown origin.

There was a giant flat rock by the creek, but they discovered that it was occupied by toads. He tried to chase them away, but instead of fleeing, they croaked loudly.

Then when Yangzom lay down on a grassy spot, she leaped up, screaming as she brushed voles from under her skirt.

The chieftain was forced to prop her up against a tall Chinese larch tree. But as soon as she hiked up her skirt and he dropped his pants, their lower bodies were assaulted by ants and angry cuckoos. In the end, they had to give up their attempt to have sex in the wild.

I witnessed every failure. Their only chance, it seemed, was to levitate. But of course they didn't know such magic. I've heard of a magic that lets people fly, but nothing about mounting a woman in the air.

By the time I put away my precious binoculars, Father and his third wife had returned from the field, frustrated and angry.

The slave children, still holding sticks wrapped with colorful snakes, were singing their ballad in the square:

King Bende is dead,
The flawless jade is shattered,
It is completely shattered.

As the chieftain's sexual desire turned to flames of rage, the executioner's whip drove off the screaming slaves. The chieftain's face was twisted by anger, but Yangzom, her face tilted to look at him, was laughing heartily. I'd always thought that women were just women, that there wasn't much difference between her, a woman taken by force by the chieftain, and my mother, who had been bought. Now Yangzom's laugh proved that she was truly a demon. Later, Living Buddha Jeeka told us that some demons are self-aware when they cause trouble, but that some aren't. "Third Mistress clearly belongs to the latter category," he'd said, "so don't harm her after your father passes on."

At some point, my brother, Tamding Gonpo, had come out to stand beside me. "I like pretty women," he said, "but this one scares me."

Out in the square, Yangzom said to the chieftain, "Master, since they like to make up songs, why not tell them to make one up about me?"

My brother and I walked up to them. "According to the Living Buddha," he said, "this is an ancient song. The mistress should not have lowly people make up songs about her. They know only the patterns on poisonous snakes, not the beauty of a peacock."

The third mistress smiled at him magnanimously.

My brother then waved the children away.

The chieftain and his third wife passed through the massive gateway and went upstairs. Singing suddenly erupted among the servants who were pounding glutinous rice into paste, washing grain, milking the cows for the second time, and polishing silverware. Father rushed out of his room like an enraged lion. But the servants' songs were different from the one sung by their children, and he could find no fault with them. So he shook his head and returned angrily to his room.

The chieftain told the steward to get some silver to make a set of ornaments for Third Mistress. The silversmith who had given me something to drink on my horse that day was summoned. He was a man whose skillful hands were always tucked beneath his leather apron. I could sense the world fill up with the sound of him banging on silver each time the estate, like a gigantic beehive, quieted down. People listened to that sound as it echoed throughout the world.

Ding clang!

Ding clang!

Ding – clang – !

He smiled at the singing women as he sat in the shadow of the giant pillars that supported our grand estate house, his face expressive, as always. Thin sheets of silver foil shone before him like the lucid surface of a pond. He'd told me his name once, but I couldn't recall it, no matter how hard I tried. Dolma must know. Why I assumed that, I couldn't say, but I was sure she did. She pinched me. "Idiot."

"Tell me."

"He served you once, how could you forget his name? Will you forget mine someday too?"

She told me his name only after I promised I wouldn't forget. It was Choedak. Dolma had met him only once – at least that's what I assumed – but she had his name down pat, and my sensitive heart ached. I looked away. Dolma walked over, brushing my head with her full breasts, which quickly softened me. Knowing I was giving in, she said gently, "I'm surprised that a nursing baby like you understands jealousy. Don't be like that."

"I'm going to kill that man."

She buried my head between her breasts, nearly suffocating me. "Young Master looks angry," she said. "Young Master looks upset. You're not serious, are you?"

I didn't like the idea that just because she'd given me her body she felt she could talk to me that way. So, pulling away from her breasts, which were as soft as ripe cheese, I said breathlessly, my face red, "I'm going to stick his silver-making hands into boiling oil."

Dolma turned around and covered her face with her hands.

My idiot brain was thinking that although I'd never be the chieftain, at least I was the chieftain's son and the future chieftain's brother. Women were there for the taking for someone like me. So I left her and went for a stroll. Everyone was busy. The chieftain was with his third wife, whom he finally owned but was unable to enjoy. His second wife was sitting on a flower design woven into a Persian rug, meditating. I called out to her, but only whiteness showed in her eyes, which were as empty as the essence of things, as described in the Scriptures. Living Buddha Jeeka was opening his yellow bundle to show Monpa Lama. The children of the family slaves were roaming the fields with sticks spiked with snakes and singing a long-lost ballad that had suddenly been revived. After the incident with the thrushes, they'd been displaying aloof respect toward me, a lonely noble.

I really was lonely. So too were the chieftain, the future chieftain, and the chieftain's wives, now that there were no wars, no holidays, and no reason to punish the servants. Suddenly I understood why Father kept creating incidents: over the defection of a minor fortress, he'd gone inland to petition the provincial government, planted opium, and ordered his soldiers to undergo a new style of training; over a woman, he'd killed a loyal headman; and he'd let monks fight over favors, like women do. But understanding this didn't lessen my loneliness. My brother wasn't in the estate house, and no one knew where he'd gone. None of the other people were lonely. They had work to do: turning the millstone, milking the cows, tanning leather, spinning wool. And they gossiped among themselves while they worked. The silversmith was pounding silver: *Ding clang! Ding clang! Ding clang!* He smiled at me, then went back to work. He seemed okay, so why shouldn't Dolma remember his name?

"Choedak," I called out.

He responded by making music with his little hammer, and I quickly forgot my glum mood. I returned to my room, banging the railing with a rock along the way. Dolma turned her face to the wall as soon as she saw me. She needed an idiot, a little boy, to butter her up. So that's what I decided to do. "The silversmith isn't a bad guy," I said.

"That's what I told you." I was right, she was treating me like an idiot. "I like him because he's an adult, and I like you because you're a child."

"You don't like me because of my aristocratic background, and like him because he's a silversmith?"

She gave me a guarded look. "Yes," she said as she lowered her head bashfully.

So we showed our love for each other atop the bright woven flowers on the rug. Afterward, she smoothed her clothes and sighed. "Someday, the master will give me to a servant. Please, Young Master, when that time comes, give me to the silversmith."

My heart ached again, but I consented with a nod.

Then this girl, who was so much taller, so much more grown-up than I, said, "Actually, it's not up to you. But I won't consider my service to you in vain, so long as you feel that way."

I said, "It will be done if I say so."

Dolma rubbed my head. "You can't succeed the chieftain."

My God! At that moment, I actually felt like wresting the position for myself. But as soon as I reminded myself that I was an idiot, the idea vanished like bubbles in a spring. Just think, how could an idiot be a chieftain who ruled over thousands of people, be the king of the world? How could an idiot have such thoughts? My only excuse was that a woman had put the idea in my head.

Now let me think. What else happened that day?

Ah, now I remember. That day, Living Buddha Jeeka, who had hoped to predict what was about to happen, got the cold shoulder when he opened the ancient text for Monpa Lama, and the ballad sung by the children appeared before the two scholars. In the Living Buddha's treasured text, every word had been commented upon by many people over the years. So these stories could now foretell the future. Beneath this particular ballad was the following commentary: "One day, someone sang this ballad, and a plague rampaged for years. Then the ballad was popular during another year, after which a Central Plain dynasty fell, the lack of support causing the demise of a sect in the Land of the Snows." Shaking his head, Monpa Lama wiped his sweaty brow. "I cannot report this to the chieftain. Since we cannot escape disaster, it is useless to talk of fate. Besides, do you think the chieftain is a man who takes advice from others?"

The Living Buddha said, "The chieftain has wasted his favors on you."

"Then why don't you move in here, and I'll take over your monastery?" Monpa replied.

The Living Buddha had been planning a pilgrimage to the

Buddhist realm of Tibet, or perhaps to a quiet cave somewhere to meditate in isolation. But he knew he couldn't make the trip, for if he left, the monastery residents would lose their support. Only a Living Buddha who pondered deeply such matters truly understood that no one survives by his wits alone. He had come calling this time out of concern for the residents of his monastery, since only he could feed them. To him, sitting in a glittery sutra hall with the lama, casually discussing matters that were anything but casual, was much better than being cooped up in his monastery, and he was actually worried that Monpa Lama might end the conversation too early. Personal conduct aside, at least the man was his intellectual peer, he thought. In pursuit of this little pleasure, he might even be treating Monpa Lama with more deference than he deserved. The Living Buddha heard himself ask cautiously, "How do you think I should broach this matter with the chieftain?"

Monpa Lama shook his head. "I have no idea. It's getting harder and harder to figure out his moods. Would you like another bowl of tea, Living Buddha?" This was an obvious invitation for him to leave.

"Very well, then," the Living Buddha said with a sigh. "We've been vying to see who has more say with the chieftain. But where this matter is concerned, I'm more worried about the black-haired Tibetans, the sons and grandsons of Gesar. So I'll do it. I'll tell him not to incur the anger of Heaven and the people. I don't imagine he'll lop off my head for that. At least, I hope not."

Without drinking the tea, he walked downstairs, the bundle tucked under his arm.

Monpa Lama turned to look at the murals on the walls. The largest one, out on the veranda, portrayed the three realms: heaven, earth, and hell. Within each realm, many levels of worlds were piled upon a pagoda-like water monster. With a blink of the monster's eye, the earth would tremble, and once it began to tumble, this world and its past, its present, and its future would be gone. Monpa Lama believed that such a picture should never exist in a religion. With a world depicted as always on the verge of toppling, how could you make people believe there was an eternal place in the clouds at the topmost level?

The Living Buddha located the steward. "I'd like to see the chieftain," he said. "Please announce me."

Our steward had once commanded the family guard, and only became steward after being crippled in battle. He'd been such a good commander that he'd received the highest award: a tiger-skin cape from India. In contrast with the average cape, it was a whole skin that was worn over a down coat. The tiger's head hung over the chest; its tail fell over the back. Anyone wearing it, even the most benign of men, became a tiger. Its recipient had since become an excellent steward, and it was precisely his outstanding skills that made it possible for my father and brother to go on their pleasure excursions.

The steward said, "Oh my, we're ignoring our honored guest." He brought tea for the Living Buddha, touching his forehead to the man's hand as an act of spiritual deference. How soft the hand was, like the gentlest cloud in the sky. This ritual restored self-respect to the Living Buddha, who took a sip of the tea, letting its fragrance linger on his tongue briefly before it flowed warmly into his stomach.

"Something bad is about to happen, I take it," the steward said.

"Yes, very soon."

"The chieftain won't be happy to hear that."

"It doesn't matter if he listens or not. But if I don't tell him, later generations will laugh at me for not predicting such an important event. Besides, people like us always have something to say on occasions such as this."

So the one-time commander, looking like a typical steward with no military background, hobbled into the chieftain's room to announce the Living Buddha. Only if the steward himself interceded would the chieftain, who happened to be in bed with his third wife, deign to receive the Living Buddha.

"Living Buddha Jeeka is here to see you."

"Has he come to lecture me again?"

"He came to tell you why so many strange things have been happening lately."

The chieftain thought about the lamas he had installed in the estate sutra hall. "What about our own lamas? Why didn't Monpa come with this news?"

The steward smiled meaningfully, a look that lent itself to a range of speculation and interpretation. What else can you do with a stubborn chieftain, the ruler of a vast land, but smile? The chieftain saw something in that smile. "Send him in." Agitated by his own sexual desire and all the strange phenomena around him, he asked with an affected ease, "Should I put on my boots?"

"Yes, and you should go out to meet him."

Following the steward's advice, the chieftain put on his boots and greeted the Living Buddha at the top of the stairs. The Living Buddha looked up and smiled.

"Ah, Living Buddha. What do you plan to lecture me about this time?"

Halting on the stairs, the Living Buddha took a deep breath. "For the eternal stability of your territory and the happiness of the black-haired Tibetans, please forgive me if I speak out of turn."

"I'll hear you out. Come on up." He reached out to help the Living Buddha. But just as the two hands were about to clasp, a roar like spring thunder rumbled in from the east. Then the earth shook like a huge drum being beaten by a gigantic, invisible hand. Amid the booming roar, the earth throbbed like a leather membrane. The Living Buddha tumbled down the stairs at the first tremor. The chieftain saw him open his mouth, but he bumped and rolled all the way down to the first landing before he could make a sound. The earth stopped moving for a moment, then began to shake from side to side like a sifter. Unable to keep his footing, the chieftain crashed to the floor. Worst of all, he tried to shout to the Living Buddha but was on the floor before the words came out, and he bit his tongue. As he lay on the floor, he felt as if his stronghold were about to disintegrate. In the grip of such violent shaking, it was no longer indestructible and was now little more than a pile of wood, stone, and clay.

Fortunately, the shaking soon stopped. Spitting out the fresh blood in his mouth, the chieftain got to his feet in time to see the Living Buddha start climbing back up the stairs, and he suddenly realized that this slighted lama was actually very loyal to him. He reached down to help him up. Then, sitting side by side on the veranda floor, the two men looked in the direction of the source of this mysterious power, hearing the shouts of startled people who had barely recovered from the shock. These shouts told them that buildings had collapsed and that people had died, while powerful waves of river water had washed away the wooden bridge. Seeing that his house was still standing, the chieftain smiled, and said,

"Living Buddha, you'll have to stay here now, since the bridge is gone and you can't go home."

The Living Buddha wiped the sweat from his forehead. "I've come too late. It's already happened."

His face covered in dust, the chieftain grabbed the Living Buddha's hands and laughed hoarsely, interrupting his laughter to spit out some phlegm before starting in again. He did so over and over, until he was finally able to catch his breath. He sighed, his hands pressed against his chest. "How many stupid things have I done?"

"Not too many, but enough."

"I know what I've done, but it all seems like a dream."

"You're fine now."

"Am I really? Then what do you think I should do?"

"Aid the survivors and recite prayers for the dead."

"Let's go in and rest. My wife must be scared witless."

He led the Living Buddha into the second wife's room. As soon as they entered, my mother knelt at the Living Buddha's feet and banged her head against his handsome boots. The chieftain reached down for this woman he'd ignored for so long. "Get up," he said, "and have someone bring us some good food." He sounded as if he'd been in this room all along, as if he'd never gone astray.

He added, "I'm hungry. How long has it been since I last ate?"

Mother gave the order, which was relayed all the way down. Then she looked at the Living Buddha with tears glistening in her eyes, wanting to express her gratitude. The man she'd thought she'd lost forever had returned to her.

The strange phenomena out in the fields disappeared after the earth trembled. The chieftain came to the aid of those suffering the loss of family members and of their houses.

Soon afterward, the poppies were ready for harvest.

Three ⁓

8 White Dreams ⁓

White permeated our lives.

If you had looked at the stone and rammed-earth houses and temples in the chieftain's territory, you'd have seen how much we liked this simple color. Sparkling white quartz was piled above the doorframes and on the windowsills, while the doors and windows were accented in clean, pure white. Yak heads and Buddhist warrior gods powerful enough to exorcise spirits were painted in white on towering walls; inside the houses, walls and cupboards were decorated with eye-catching sun and moon symbols and designs of longevity and endless good fortune, all created with snowy white barley flour.

But now I saw a different kind of white.

Sticky whiteness oozed from poppy berries and gathered in a jiggly mass before falling to the ground. The poppies squeezed out their white sap as if the earth were crying. On the verge of falling, the teardrops hung on small, shiny green berries that seemed to be choking on sobs, unable to speak. What a touching scene! Farmhands who had wielded sickles when harvesting the barley now made tiny slits in the berries with sleek bone knives to let the white sap seep out. One drop after another gathered silently between heaven and earth, crying wordlessly in the wind. When the farmhands went back out to the field they took along ox-horn cups to catch the giant drops of sap hanging from the slit berries, which they scraped off with their bone knives.

Then a new slit was made on each green berry so there would be another swollen drop of white sap to harvest the following day.

Special Emissary Huang sent people from the land of the Han to process the white sap. They erected a wooden shed on the estate, then set up a stove and closed the door to process the opium, as if preparing herbal medicine. We needed only to breathe in a whisper of the aroma floating out of the shed to fly up into the heavens. Chieftain Maichi, our great chieftain, liberated his people with this unprecedented, wondrous thing, an elixir that could make you forget all the troubles and suffering of the human world.

Monpa Lama, who had been ignored for some time, came with a new interpretation for the earthquake, one completely different from that of Living Buddha Jeeka. He said that such a wondrous thing came from the gods, and that only the chieftain, with his boundless good fortune, could bring it to black-haired Tibetans in the human realm. The earthquake was simply the result of gods who were upset over losing something so precious. Monpa Lama even declared that he had appeased the gods through prayers and Buddhist rites. Taking a deep breath of the intoxicating fragrance in the air, the chieftain glanced over at the Living Buddha and smiled. The Living Buddha said, "If the chieftain believes Monpa Lama, then I'd better leave and return to my monastery."

"Oh my, our Living Buddha is upset again. But I know he doesn't mean what he says. Even if he does, I'll keep him around," said the chieftain, as if the Living Buddha weren't there.

"What does it matter to me whose words the chieftain cares to believe?" the Living Buddha said, also as if the chieftain were elsewhere. "My master once told me that no one can stop something preordained in heaven."

The chieftain laughed. "See how clever our Living Buddha is."

"Let Monpa Lama accompany you, since it is he to whom you listen."

Not wanting to say more, the chieftain picked up a nearby bell and rang it to summon the steward, who hobbled down the stairs and saw the Living Buddha to the door. "Living Buddha," he said abruptly, "do you think the berries will really bring bad luck?"

Opening his eyes wide, the Living Buddha saw the worried look on the man's face, and said, "Of course. Do I make a living by lying to people? Just you wait and see."

"Then the Living Buddha must recite sutras for the protection of our master's estate."

The Living Buddha waved and walked off.

People continued to harvest opium on the vast land as the white sap was turned into a black paste that sent a fragrance unknown in this land wafting through the air. Lines of mice emerged from their hiding places to sit on the roof beams of the opium-processing shed and savor the intoxicating aroma. Mother, who was in high spirits, hadn't complained about headaches in a long time. She took me to the shed, which was off-limits to most people, and where armed guards stood at the door while Special Emissary Huang's people were working.

"You won't let me in?" Mother complained. "Then why did the special emissary give me an opium pipe?"

After considering her words, the guards lowered their rifles to let us pass.

I didn't pay much attention to how they made opium in the big cauldrons; instead, I was gazing at strings of meat hanging in front of the stove, looking like the thrushes I'd hunted with the slave children. Just as I was about to ask for one, I heard a squeal and saw a mouse fall from a roof beam. One of the men cooking opium laid down the tool in his hand and picked up a knife to lightly pry open one of its hind legs. The mouse squealed again as its skin was peeled away like a layer of clothing. The worker then sliced open the mouse and removed its throbbing lungs and beating heart. After being dipped in a bowlful of sauce, the mouse was quickly added to the hanging strings of meat.

"You're frightening my son," the chieftain's wife said with a smile.

The workers laughed. "Would the mistress like to try some?"

The chieftain's wife nodded. Grease from the smoked mice sizzled on the stove, giving off a smell as mouthwatering as that of the thrushes. If I hadn't happened to look up and see all those beady-eyed mice on the roof beams, I might have tried this Han delicacy. But their pointy mouths seemed to be gnawing at my guts as my mother bared her white teeth and bit into her mouse, completely oblivious to me as I stared wide-eyed at her. She purred like a cat as she tore at the mouse. "It's delicious, just delicious. Come, my son, try some."

I felt like throwing up.

I ran out the door. I'd never believed all that nonsense about how scary the Han people were. Father had told me not to. "Is your mother scary?" he'd asked. Then he'd answered his own question.

"No, she's not. It's just that strange Han temperament." My brother, on the other hand, believed that everyone had peculiarities. Later, after my sister returned from England, she answered the question. She didn't know if the Han were scary or not, but she didn't like them. I told her they eat mice, and she said they also eat snakes and lots of other bizarre things.

After she finished eating, Mother looked very contented, licking her lips like a cat. It was unsavory for a woman to unconsciously act like a cat. Now she really scared me.

But she just giggled. "They gave me some opium. I never tried it before, and now I've had my chance."

When I didn't say anything, she added, "Don't be upset. Opium is bad, but not *that* bad."

"I wouldn't have known opium was bad if you hadn't said so."

"It's bad for poor people, but not so bad for those who can afford it." She went on to remind me that the Maichis were the wealthiest family in a radius of hundreds of li. Then she reached out and grabbed my arm, her long nails digging into me. I squealed as if they were the sharp teeth of a mouse. When she noticed the look of terror on my face, she knelt and shook me. "My son, what have you seen? Why are you so scared?"

I started to cry. You ate a mouse, I wanted to say. You ate a mouse. But instead I pointed to the sky, empty but for several puffy clouds floating above us. They had shiny white edges but were dark in the center. They seemed to be lost in the vastness of the sky and weren't moving because they didn't know where to go. Mother looked to where I was pointing but couldn't see anything. She was incapable of finding meaning in the clouds, since she cared only about things on the ground. At that moment, mice on the ground were moving toward the place with that special aroma. I wasn't about to say anything. So long as a drop of a ruler's blood flows in one's veins, even an idiot realizes the advantages of knowing other people's secrets. So I kept pointing at the sky, and that made Mother afraid. Holding me tightly, she walked off quickly, and before long we had arrived at our house, where the executioner Aryi was tying someone to the stake in the square. When he spotted us, I saw that tall, skinny body, so typical of his family, bend at the waist. "Young Master, Mistress," he said.

I stopped trembling immediately.

Mother spoke to the executioner. "The smell of death on you has frightened off the unclean entities on Young Master. Have your son spend more time with Young Master from now on."

No one knew how far back it went, but every generation of the Maichi executioners was called by the name Aryi. If they'd all been alive, it would have been difficult to tell them apart. Fortunately, no more than two generations ever lived at the same time. The sons grew up and learned the skills while the fathers served as executioners. Aryi Senior carried out the executions; Aryi Junior waited to take over. You can say that the Aryis were the scariest, loneliest people anywhere in the world. We often wondered if Aryi Junior was a mute. So I stopped, turned, and said to the executioner, "Can your son talk? If not, you should teach him how to say something."

He bowed deeply.

Mother lay down as soon as we reached her upstairs room. She had Dolma open a chest and take out the pipe from the special emissary. Then, after telling Dolma to light a small lamp, she removed a mud-colored lump of opium from an inside pocket and rolled it into a pellet, which she stuffed into the pipe to heat over the lamp. She went limp immediately, and a long time passed before she was awake again. "From now on," she said, "I will fear nothing." Then she added, "The silver utensils sent over by the special emissary aren't nearly as nice as ours."

She was talking about the silver tray containing opium paraphernalia, a small teapot, and a few opium pokers.

Dolma spoke up. "I have a friend who is a skilled silversmith. Why don't we have him make a set for you?"

"Your friend?" Mother asked. "You mean that fellow out in the yard?"

Blushing, Dolma nodded.

The late autumn sun set behind the mountain. Waning sunlight gilded the outdoors. It was much darker inside the room, but the eyes of the chieftain's wife actually brightened, reminding me of the mice in the opium shed. I grabbed Dolma's hand, but she flung it back onto my chest; she made me hurt myself. I cried out because it hurt, but also because I was terrified of my mother's shifting, shiny eyes. "What's wrong?" the two women asked in unison.

Then Dolma took my head in her soft, warm hands.

I got up and walked over to the window, hands behind my back, where I watched stars leap into the blue night sky, one after the other. "It's getting dark," I cried out in a voice that was already changing. "Light the lamp."

The chieftain's wife demanded of Dolma, "It's getting dark. Why haven't you lit the lamp?"

Not even turning to look at them, I continued staring at the night sky as the pleasant aroma of sulfur spread throughout the room. The maid had struck a match. Then she lit the lamp. I turned around, holding my wrist, and said, "You little tramp, you hurt me."

As her eyes filled with emotion, Dolma knelt down to hold my hand and blew perfumed air on it, turning the pain into a tickle. I started to laugh. She turned to Mother. "Mistress, the young master looks like a true young master today. Maybe one day he'll be the Maichi chieftain."

Her words were heartening, although I could never be the chieftain of our land. Even if I weren't an idiot, the future chieftain would not be me. But the expression on Mother's face showed how pleased she was. Nonetheless, she scolded Dolma, "Talk like that is out of line."

Just then, the chieftain walked in. "What's out of line?"

"These two children were talking nonsense," Mother said.

The chieftain demanded to hear what that childish nonsense was, so Mother put on the same ingratiating look Dolma gave me. "I won't tell you unless you promise not to get mad."

Father sat on Mother's opium bed, his hands on his knees. "Tell me."

So Mother told him what Dolma had said about me.

With a burst of laughter, the chieftain waved me over. "Do you want to be chieftain, son?"

Dolma walked up behind Father and waved her hands. But I roared, "Yes!" like a soldier answering his commanding officer.

"Good." Then he asked, "Your mother didn't put that idea in your head, did she?"

Clicking my heels like a soldier, I roared back, "No! She refuses to let me entertain that kind of idea."

The chieftain looked sharply at his wife. "I prefer to believe the words of an idiot. People who think they're clever worry me sometimes." Then he said to me, "It's all right for you to want to be chieftain, and it's right for your mother to forbid you from wanting it."

Then Mother told Dolma to take me back to my room. "It's bedtime for Young Master."

While she was helping me undress, Dolma put my hand on her breast, where her heart was beating wildly. She said I'd scared her half to death, and that I was a lucky idiot. I said I wasn't an idiot – an idiot wouldn't want to be chieftain. She pinched me savagely.

Then I fell asleep between her breasts.

For some time, I'd been dreaming in white, and that night was no exception. I saw whiteness rage toward me but couldn't tell whether the source was a woman's breasts or the sap of poppies. White crests picked up my body and sent it drifting along. I screamed and woke up. Dolma held my head, and asked, "What's wrong?"

"Mice!" I said. "Mice!"

I had seen mice streaming in the window with the pale moonlight.

I was afraid of mice.

From then on, I didn't dare walk alone on the estate.

9 Sick ⌒

I was afraid of mice.

But they all said the young master was sick.

I wasn't sick; I was just afraid of those squealing critters with their beady eyes and sharp teeth.

But they continued to insist that I was sick, and there was nothing I could do to change their minds. So all I did was hold Dolma's hands tightly whenever Mother came to see me. Each and every day, the steward had the family slave Sonam Tserang and Aryi Junior wait by my door. As soon as I stepped outside, they followed me everywhere I went.

Dolma said, "The young master isn't chieftain yet, but he looks more impressive than one."

I said, "I'm scared."

"Look at you," she said impatiently. "You silly little thing." But her gaze kept shifting toward the silversmith, who was looking up at us from the yard below. I laughed when I saw him hit his own hand with his hammer. I hadn't laughed like that for a long time; only people who haven't laughed for a long time know how good it feels. It was better than sleeping with a woman. I was laughing so hard that I fell to the floor. Everyone who saw me said that the young master was really sick.

So Monpa Lama and the Living Buddha engaged in another contest, both claiming they could cure me. Monpa Lama, who lived with us, could recite sutras and write prescriptions. He used sutras as the primary treatment, supplementing them with elixirs. That didn't work. Then it was the Living Buddha's turn; his method was not all that different, except that he used elixirs as the primary treatment. I didn't want these two to cure me – if I was really sick, that is. When I took the elixers, by closing my eyes I could see them flow from my mouth down to my stomach and then quickly slither into my intestines. What I'm saying is, the elixirs couldn't reach the center of my fear of mice; instead, they slid right past that spot, separated from it by the lining of my stomach.

It was funny to see how much those two treasured their medicine and how seriously they took everything. Monpa Lama's medicine always came in the form of black pills packed in a lovely box, as if they were precious stones and not medicine. The Living Buddha's medicine, on the other hand, was powder wrapped in individual paper packets inside layers of yellow silk. As his pudgy hands unfolded the silk, I felt that a whole world was about to spring forth from the seemingly endless layers. But it was only gray powder over which the Living Buddha recited a sutra, as if it were virtually priceless. The spot of fear inside me was about to burst out laughing. When the powder was poured into my mouth, it felt like a herd of wild horses running across arid land; my stomach was muddy, and dust flew before my eyes.

I asked the two doctors with their magic powers what kind of illness I had.

Monpa Lama said, "The young master has run into something foul."

Living Buddha Jeeka said the same thing.

The word *foul* held two separate meanings, one dirty, the other evil. I didn't know which one they meant this time, but I didn't feel like asking.

Sonam Tserang imitated the voices of the two doctors perfectly as he said, "Young master, I think you have run into something foul." We laughed out loud; the future executioner laughed too, but soundlessly. He just smiled shyly, whereas Sonam Tserang's laughter boomed like water gushing out of a bucket. You see, I favored my young servants, so I said: "I like you both, and I want you to follow me for the rest of your lives."

Then I told them I hadn't run into anything foul.

I was the only one who talked when the three of us were together. Sonam Tserang was quiet because he had little to say. Aryi Junior, on the other hand, had a lot to say, but didn't know where to begin. Someone like him should have been sent to a monastery to study the sutras, but he had been born into an executioner's family for the chieftain.

On this particular day, the two young servants followed me out into the vast field under an autumn sky that was getting higher and bluer by the day. The smell of poppies all around made us feel as if the whole world were drunk. I turned to Aryi, and said, "Take me to your house."

His face paled as he fell to his knees. "Young master, in my house there are things much scarier than mice."

Now I *really* wanted to go. I'd never been a coward and hadn't been afraid of mice before this. Only Mother knew why I was afraid. So I insisted on seeing the executioner's house.

Sonam Tserang asked Aryi what was so scary in his house.

"The instruments," he said. "They're all bloodstained."

"What else?"

Aryi's eyes darted this way and that. "Clothes stained with dead people's blood."

"Lead the way," I said.

To my surprise, the executioner's house was more peaceful than any other household.

Herbal medicine was drying in the yard. The executioners, with their special knowledge of the human body, were the real surgeons around here. Unable to accept the fact that she was married to an executioner, Aryi Junior's mother had died soon after giving birth to him. The woman of the house now was Aryi Junior's eighty-year-old grandmother. After she learned who I was, she said, "Young Master, I shouldn't be alive at my age, but there's no one to care for the two executioners in your family. Men need women to take care of them, so I can't die yet."

Aryi told her that the young master hadn't come for her life.

She said, "The masters never come to a slave's house for no reason at all." Her eyesight was failing, but she could still polish the copper teapots and make them shine.

The first room we visited contained instruments of torture. First there were whips: whips made of raw or tanned leather, whips made of rattan, whips woven with gold threads, and so on. Lots of them, all bestowed upon the executioners by generations of chieftains. Then we saw knives, of different sizes and shapes, but not for aesthetic reasons. They were designed for different parts of the human body. The thin, wide ones were good for the neck, while the long, narrow ones could easily pass through the ribs and reach the steaming organs underneath. Those more curved than a crescent moon were used on the knee. There were many other instruments, such as scoops for eyeballs and a straightener that could be used to cure toothaches but could also quickly unburden a person of every tooth in his mouth. Things like that filled the room.

Sonam Tserang greatly appreciated them all. He said to Aryi, "It's great the way you can kill anyone you want."

"It's painful to kill them," Aryi said. "They may have violated the laws, but they aren't enemies of the executioners." Then he looked at me, and said softly, "Besides, some of the executed didn't really commit the crimes they were accused of."

I asked, "How do you know?"

The future executioner of the Maichi family replied, "I don't know. I haven't killed anyone yet, but those who have say so." He pointed upstairs. "I hear you can tell by the clothes."

The clothes of the condemned were stored in an attic specifically added to the house for that purpose. Aryi's face grew paler than ever when we reached the bottom of the wooden stairs leading to the room. "Young Master, let's not go up there, all right?"

I was afraid too, so I nodded. But Sonam Tserang demanded, "Young Master, are you scared or are you an idiot? We're almost there and now you've decided you don't want to take a look. Then I won't play with you anymore."

He called me an idiot, but I thought he was the true idiot. Did he really think it was up to him whether he played with me or not? So I told him, "I'm going to remember what you just said. Don't you ever forget that you're not playing with me, you're waiting on me."

I was happy to see him stunned by my words. That foolish mouth of his hung slack; Aryi stood beside me, also stunned.

I gestured with my mouth, and Aryi, his face ashen, climbed a ladder that ended at the attic door, which was protected by an amulet inscribed by a lama; the gold sprinkles on the writing glittered under the sun. I climbed up behind Aryi; my head was right beneath his feet when he turned, and said, "Here we are." Then he asked me if we were really going to open the door. He said there might be ghosts of wrongfully condemned men that could escape if we did. From down below, Sonam Tserang cursed Aryi, saying he looked like the real wronged ghost. I looked up at Aryi, and had to agree – he did look a little like a ghost.

"I'm not afraid," he said to me. "I'm worried that something might emerge to harm the young master."

One of my two young slaves was bold; the other had a clever mouth. The bold one was often insolent, while the one who knew how to make me feel good was a bit timid. How could I help but like them both?

The executioner's house was located on a hill, lower than the estate but higher than other houses. Standing at the top of the wooden ladder, I looked out over a vast field where a flock of pigeons wheeled in the autumn sky. We were above the pigeons and could see the river flowing off to the edge of the sky.

I said, "Open the door."

When Aryi removed the lock, I heard Sonam Tserang gasp, just like me. But Aryi remained calm as he whispered, "It's open."

The door creaked at the touch of his hand and released a gust of chill wind, causing all three of us to shudder. We climbed in and stood in a pool of sunlight that had crept through the partly opened door. Items of clothing were arrayed on horizontal pine poles around the room. Hanging undisturbed, they looked like people asleep on their feet. There were faint traces of blackened blood around the necks. It was all fine, holiday clothing. Before being put to death, the condemned put on their best clothes, which were then left behind in the mortal world, stained with their blood.

Holding up a robe edged with sealskin, I expected to see a gaunt face, but I found nothing but a satin lining that gave off a dark glint. Sonam Tserang boldly draped a garment over his shoulders – nothing happened.

In fact, nothing out of the ordinary happened at all, and that was disappointing.

On our way home, we saw a figure appear at the mountain pass to the east, followed by another to the west. My young slaves wanted to wait to see who they were. They knew that everyone who passed through here was obliged to travel to the estate. Some brought money, others brought gifts, while those with nothing to give were prepared to say something pleasing to the chieftain's ears.

Dolma brought me tea after we returned upstairs. When I told her to pour some for Sonam Tserang and Aryi, she gave me an angry look. "Am I here to pour tea for slaves?" But I ignored her, and she had no choice but to pour two more bowls of hot tea. I heard her scold them, "Don't you know anything? How dare you sit in front of the young master and drink tea! Stand over there by the door and drink your tea!"

Just then the guard dogs started barking.

"There's a stranger at the gate," Dolma said.

I said, "He's here to marry you."

She looked down in silence.

"Pity it isn't the silversmith."

I wanted to study her face, but from downstairs came the announcement that a guest was asking to be received. With a slave on either side, I leaned over the railing to look down. I was wearing a floral silk robe that day, with a light red belt and a scabbard decorated with three large pieces of green coral. When the visitor looked up and saw me, he waved. Then Father, my brother, and my mother all came out of their rooms. We normally didn't greet one another like that around here, but I knew he was greeting me, so I waved back.

By the time the visitor was upstairs, the entire Maichi family was seated to receive him.

He entered the room.

I thought I was seeing a monster. Even though he was dressed in a loose Tibetan robe, the visitor had blue eyes. Then he took off his hat to reveal a full head of golden hair. His sweaty body gave off a repugnant odor. I asked my brother if he was a monster. "A Westerner," he whispered.

"Our sister is living in a country full of people like him?"

"I guess so."

The visitor was speaking our language, but it sounded strange, more like the Westerner's tongue than ours. He yakked away until finally the Maichi family understood that he'd traveled from England in a seafaring house. He reached into his saddlebags and took out a clock; it was a present for the chieftain. Both Mother's and Father's rooms had clocks, but this one, with its enamel face, was much prettier.

He had a nice-sounding name – Charles.

With a nod, the chieftain said, "It sounds more like our names than Han names do."

First Young Master asked Charles, "Where are you headed from here?"

Blue-eyed Charles blinked, and said, "The chieftain's territory is my destination."

The chieftain said, "Tell us what good you can bring us."

Charles said, "I have followed God's command to come here and spread the Gospel."

Father and Charles began discussing whether God could or could not exist in our land. The missionary was optimistic about the future, while the chieftain was dubious about everything. He asked Charles if his God was Buddha.

Charles said no, but that God and Buddha both bring relief to the suffering masses.

The difference was too subtle for the chieftain, not unlike the issues raised when Monpa Lama and Living Buddha Jeeka competed to show who was more knowledgeable, raising issues such as: How large, in leagues, is a bodhi leaf in the pure land of Amita Buddha? How many enlightened Buddhas can the leaf accommodate? And so on. The chieftain had never been happy with the things the lamas fought over, not because he thought their tedious philosophy was boring, but because the arguments made him appear uncultured. So he said to blue-eyed, golden-haired Charles, "Since you're here, you'll be our guest. Please stay awhile."

The smell of Indian incense, lit to drive the mildew smell out of the guest room, drifted in on the air.

Mother clapped her hands to summon the steward, who turned to show Charles to the guest room. As people were leaving, I said, "We have another guest, but he came leading a donkey, not a mule."

Sure enough, the dogs started their frenzied barking again.

Father, Mother, and Brother looked at me in a very peculiar way, but I ignored their needlelike stares, and said, "See, our guest is here."

10 The New Sect Gelukpa ~

The second uninvited guest was a cassock-clad lama.

He deftly tethered his donkey at the door. His purple cassock flapped like billowing flags as he climbed the stairs spryly, but there wasn't a breath of wind anywhere. He reached the fifth floor, where every door looked exactly the same, yet he pushed open the correct door; we were all waiting for him.

A young, enthusiastic face appeared before us.

Tiny beads of sweat dotted the tip of his nose, and he was breathing hard, like a horse at the end of a long journey. I could tell that everyone in the room instantly liked the face they saw. But instead of pleasantries, he blurted out, "I've been looking for this place. This place of yours is it."

The chieftain stood up. "You come from far away. I can tell by your boots."

The guest finally bowed to the chieftain, and said, "I come from the Holy City of Lhasa."

He was a warm, outgoing fellow. "Give me a bowl of tea," he said, "a bowl of hot tea. I've drunk nothing but mountain spring water on my way here. I've spent more than a year looking for this place. I've tasted many different kinds of spring water – sweet, bitter, salty. No one has ever tasted so many kinds of water before."

Father interrupted him. "You have yet to let us learn your honorable name."

The guest slapped his own head, saying, "Look at me, I'm so happy to have found your place that I've forgotten everything." He told us he was called Wangpo Yeshi, a name given to him by his master when he received his *geshe* degree.

Brother said, "You're a *geshe*? We've never had one of those around here." *Geshe* is the highest degree for a monk; someone said it was like a *boshi* degree, what we now call a doctorate.

Father said, "See, we now have another learned guest. You may stay here, either in my house or at the monastery. It's up to you."

"I wish to establish a new sect here," Wangpo Yeshi said. "It is the Gelukpa Sect, founded by the most venerable Master Jetsongpa. It can replace evil sects, which reek of secular heresy and lack discipline."

"What evil sects are you talking about?" Father asked.

"Those Nyingmapas under the chieftain's protection, sects that believe in sorcery."

Once again Father interrupted Wangpo Yeshi, and ordered the steward, "Smoke a room with the best incense for our guest from afar."

To our surprise, the guest ordered the steward, in front of everyone, "Have someone feed my donkey. You never know when your master will need my donkey to carry precious good tidings out of his territory."

Mother said, "I've never seen such an arrogant lama."

The lama said, "Your Maichi family hasn't become an alms giver to our omnipotent sect yet, has it?" Then he retreated from the room in a leisurely way.

By then, I already liked him more than I could say.

The chieftain, on the other hand, didn't know what to do with Wangpo Yeshi, who had come to us from the Holy City.

Soon after Wangpo Yeshi's arrival, Monpa Lama went to the monastery to pay Living Buddha Jeeka a visit. Father said that Wangpo Yeshi was a man to reckon with, since his appearance had turned mortal enemies into friends. So Father sent for him. When Wangpo Yeshi arrived, the chieftain placed an elegant cushion before him, and said, "Your boots are so tattered I should have given you a new pair, but I'm giving you a cushion instead."

"I congratulate the chieftain," Wangpo Yeshi said. "One day, when you establish connections with the Holy City, your family enterprises will truly become your eternal heritage."

"You won't decline a bowl of light wine, will you?"

"Yes, I will."

"None of the lamas here would."

Wangpo Yeshi, his forehead shining, said, "That is why the world needs this new sect of ours."

And so, just like that, Wangpo Yeshi moved in with us. But the chieftain gave him no special authority, granting only that he could freely preach to the people. Wangpo Yeshi had hoped that the chieftain would drive out the old sects and present him with believers and territory. The zealous lama thought of nothing but his master's teachings and his dream to proselytize in a new place.

Generally speaking, before a lama, from either an old or a new sect, traveled to a new place to spread his teaching, he would have a prophetic dream. Shortly after receiving his advanced *geshe* degree, Wangpo Yeshi had in fact had such a dream. In a small Lhasa cell of yellow clay, he had dreamed of a valley that opened to the southeast. Shaped like a seashell, it was fed by a river whose flowing water sounded like worshipers chanting sutras. After awakening, he sought an interpretation of the dream from his master, who, as someone passionately interested in politics, was entertaining some sort of English colonel. Upon being told of the dream, the master said he was destined to travel to farmlands near the Han border, since both the valleys and the people in such places faced southeast. He knelt down and vowed that he would build many temples and monasteries for the sect in such a valley. His master then gave him nine volumes of the classics of their sect. And when the Englishman heard that Wangpo Yeshi was going to proselytize near the Han border, he presented him with a donkey, an English donkey. Wangpo Yeshi wondered at first if donkeys came only from England, but on the trip, he would discover that it was indeed a fine animal.

The chieftain told him to seek out his own believers.

But who would become his first convert? He thought about the four people in the Maichi family: the chieftain certainly didn't fit the bill, whereas the chieftain's wife seemed absent-minded. There was no way to tell if the chieftain's younger son, with his mouth hanging slack, was highly focused or an idiot. The chieftain's older son was the only one who smiled at him. So one day, when my brother was going out for a ride, Wangpo Yeshi grabbed hold of his reins, and said to the future chieftain, "I have great hopes for you. You and I belong to the future."

But my brother said, "Stop it. I don't believe a word you say. I don't trust you or any other lama."

The lama was shocked. Never in his life had he heard anyone openly declare that he did not believe in the teachings of the most venerable, the most powerful Buddha.

First Young Master spurred his horse and rode off.

At that moment Wangpo Yeshi realized that even the air here was not quite right. He detected the aroma of opium, which made him feel good and yet dizzy at the same time. The smell was more powerful than a demonic temptation. He began to see just what sort of place his dream had sent him to. But he couldn't return to the Holy City without accomplishing anything.

He sighed, the long, deep sigh of someone skilled in yoga.

If Wangpo Yeshi had known that Monpa Lama was right behind him, he wouldn't have let out such a heavy sigh. Monpa Lama laughed; without turning to look, Wangpo Yeshi knew that the laughter had come from a monk. Wangpo Yeshi could tell that his rival wanted to display his inner power, but his second breath revealed his weakness.

"I heard that a member of a new sect had come," Monpa Lama said. "I was planning to go see you, but chance would have us meet here."

Wangpo Yeshi cited an allusion.

Monpa Lama did the same.

The first allusion indicated that the act of going to see someone was actually a contest.

The second implied that they would coexist in peace if both sides were willing to compromise.

But since they could not reach agreement, they turned their backs on each other and walked off.

The following day, Wangpo Yeshi went into the countryside to spread the word after tying the guest room key to his waist.

Meanwhile, Charles was telling the chieftain's wife a story about someone who had been born in a manger. I stopped by from time to time to listen to him and learned of someone who had no father. When I said he was just like Sonam Tserang, Mother spat at me.

Then one day, Sangye Dolma emerged in tears. When I asked who had made her cry, she sobbed, "He's dead. The Romans crucified him."

So I walked into the room, where my mother was drying her

eyes with a silk handkerchief. Charles looked triumphant. He had placed a nearly naked human figure on the windowsill, so skinny that his ribs showed. I figured he must be the person who had made the two women cry. He was strung up like a criminal, his bloody hands nailed to a piece of wood. Blood dripped from his wounds. The thought that he was about to bleed to death made me laugh. Why else would his head be slumped onto his chest, as if his neck were broken?

Charles said, "My Lord, the ignorant must not be considered irreverent. Please forgive this ignorant young man. I'll convert him into one of your lambs."

I asked, "Who's the guy bleeding there?"

"Lord Jesus."

"What can he do?"

"He suffers for you and gives you salvation."

"But he looks so pitiful. How can he help anyone?"

Charles merely shrugged his shoulders.

With the chieftain's permission, Charles roamed the mountains and fields to search for rocks. One day he returned with news of Wangpo Yeshi, who was living in a cave and preaching a Gospel of benevolent ideas and strict self-control. Charles said, "I must say, he seems to be a good monk. But you are incapable of accepting good things, so I'm not surprised that he has been slighted by you and ridiculed by your people. That is why I am content to be permitted to collect mineral rocks."

His pile of rocks was getting higher and higher.

Monpa Lama said to the chieftain, "This man will one day take away our greatest treasures."

"If you know where those treasures are," the chieftain said, "go guard them. If not, then don't worry me by talking about them."

Monpa Lama had no response.

The chieftain then asked Living Buddha Jeeka about the treasures. "Those are the words of a sorcerer. He has no knowledge of such things."

"You know," the chieftain said, "when the time comes, I will rely upon a new sect like yours, neither too old nor too strange."

Not quite ready to accept the chieftain's compliment, Living Buddha Jeeka replied coolly, "I hope you are as good as your word."

Charles was getting ready to leave when the first snow fell. By then, he and Wangpo Yeshi had become friends, so he swapped his mule for his friend's strong donkey. He'd sifted through the rocks he'd collected several times and now put the finest into a leather sack, which he then placed on the donkey's back. The snow was as dry as powder, as dry as sand. Charles looked toward the distant mountain, where Wangpo Yeshi's cave was located, and said, "My friend couldn't feed his own big animal, but I hope he'll be able to feed himself and that docile mule he now owns."

I said, "You swapped with him because your mule couldn't carry your rocks."

Charles laughed. "Young Master is a fascinating person. I like you."

As he hugged me, I detected a strong animal odor on his body. He then whispered in my ear, "If you become chieftain one day, we could become very good friends." His blue eyes were smiling. I was thinking, He doesn't know I'm an idiot. No one's told him yet.

Charles's parting words to the chieftain were: "I don't think you should make someone so devout suffer like that. Fate will reward you." He then put on his gloves, slapped the donkey on the rump, and disappeared into the silent, falling snow. The sounds of his donkey's hooves did not die out until long after his tall figure had disappeared from sight. Everyone let out a long sigh, as if shedding a heavy load.

They said, "The special emissary should be here soon. He'll show up before the mountains are sealed off by snow."

But I was thinking about Wangpo Yeshi. How intriguing to be a monk who spreads a Gospel that no one accepts. Except for his mule, grazing nearby, he was all alone as snow fell in front of his cave, like a beautiful curtain. At that moment, I too experienced the elation of being abandoned by the world.

11 Silver ∼

Where silver is concerned, don't think that our perception of it is limited to its monetary value.

You will never understand us if you equate our worship of

silver with a love of wealth. That would be much the same as the bewilderment felt by Charles when he saw us reject Wangpo Yeshi's beliefs after we had turned down his. "Why would you prefer a bad religion to a good one?" he asked, then added, "If, like the Chinese, you are worried about the intentions of Westerners, then wouldn't Wangpo Yeshi's religion be a good one for you? Isn't his derived from the teachings of your religious leader, the Dalai Lama?"

But enough about religion. Let's return to silver.

Our ancestors mastered the skill of mining precious metals, such as gold and silver, a very long time ago. The yellow of gold is associated with religion, like the glittery powder on the Buddha's face, or the silk chemises the lamas wear under their purple cassocks. We know that gold is more valuable than silver, but we like silver, white silver. So never ask a chieftain, or a member of a chieftain's family, if he likes silver, because not only will you get no answer, but he will be wary of you. The answer you'll get is: We like our people and our territory.

One of my ancestors was a dedicated writer. He once said that you had to be either the smartest fellow in the world or an idiot if you wanted to be a ruler, a king. To me that was a very intriguing idea, because I, well, I was a certified idiot. My brother began his studies as a child, in order to become a smart person, since he would be Father's successor as Maichi chieftain. And I was content to enjoy the benefits of being considered an idiot. My brother treated me well, since he wouldn't have to guard against me, unlike brothers of earlier generations.

My brother liked me because I'm an idiot.

And I liked him because I'm an idiot.

Father had said many times that he was spared much of the trouble encountered by earlier chieftains in this regard. He had had to part with a large sum of silver to pacify his own brother, the uncle I'd yet to meet. Father said repeatedly, "My sons won't be a worry to me."

A pained expression appeared on Mother's face whenever he said that. She knew I was an idiot, but deep down she retained a sliver of hope, and it was precisely this tiny bit of hope that caused her so much pain, desperation even. I think I mentioned earlier that I was conceived when Father was drunk. Too bad the ancestor who wrote about how chieftains govern hadn't considered this method of preventing power struggles between sons of later generations.

That day, Father mentioned the same thing.

A pained expression appeared on Mother's face again. But this time she rubbed my head as she said to the chieftain, "I didn't bear you a son who causes you to lose sleep. But what about that woman?"

Yes, there was the woman called Yangzom on our estate who was now carrying the chieftain's child. No one doubted that Yangzom would be a source of trouble. She had already caused the death of one man, and we wondered who would be her next victim. But no one died, and people began to feel sorry for her once she fell out of favor with the chieftain. They said she was guilty of nothing, and that the downturn in her life was a result of bad karma and retribution.

After several bouts of nausea, Yangzom told the steward that she was carrying the old master's baby and that she'd present him with a future chieftain. The chieftain had not visited her room for a long time, and that is where she waited for her pregnancy to reach full term. People said she would give birth to a crazy baby, since the mad, raging love between her and the chieftain had nearly turned them both to ashes. So many people were talking about them that she refused to leave her room, saying that someone wanted the son in her belly dead.

Now I really ought to talk about silver.

But first, the whiteness dream.

Many years ago – we don't know exactly how many years ago, but it was at least more than a thousand – when our ancestors came here from far-off Tibet proper, they met with strong resistance from the natives, whom our legends described as sprightly as monkeys and ferocious as leopards. There were many of them, and few of us, but we were there to be their rulers, so we had to conquer them first. One of the ancestors had a dream in which a silver-bearded old man told him that they had to use white quartz as a weapon in the next day's fight. The old man also gave the natives a dream in which he told them to fight us with snowballs. And that was how our ancestors became the rulers of this land. The person who dreamed about the silver-bearded old man became our very first *gyalpo*, the first king of the Maichi family.

Later, when the Tibetan kingdom fell, nearly all the aristocrats who had come here had forgotten that Tibet was our homeland. And we gradually forgot our mother tongue. We spoke the language of the conquered natives. Of course, there were still signs of our own language, but they were barely perceptible. We were the rulers of our territory with the title of chieftain, bestowed upon us by the Imperial Court in the Central Plains.

Quartz has another important use. Carried in a pouch around a man's waist, along with sharp pieces of crescent-shaped metal and wicks, it can be struck to start a fire. It always gave me a wonderful feeling to see white quartz strike a shred of gray metal. As sparks flew, I felt myself burning happily like the soft, dry wicks. Sometimes I thought I'd have been a great figure if only I'd been the first Maichi to see the birth of fire. Of course, I'm not that Maichi, so I'm not a great figure, and all this was just the idle ruminations of an idiot.

What I wanted to know was, was I the stupidest person ever since the appearance of the Maichi family? I knew the answer, and had nothing more to say on the matter, except that I believed I was the descendant of fire. Otherwise, how could I explain why I felt such an affinity with fire, as if it were my own grandfather or great-grandfather? But when I said that, everyone – Father, my brother, the steward, even the maid, Sangye Dolma – laughed. Mother was upset, but she laughed too.

Dolma said, "Young Master should go see the murals in the sutra hall."

Of course I knew there were murals in the sutra hall. The paintings told everyone in the Maichi family that we were hatched from the giant eggs of wind and fantastic birds called rocs. According to the paintings, when heaven and earth were a void, there was only the howling wind. Then a god appeared in the wind, and said, "Ha!" A world was created out of the blowing wind, which swirled in the void around it. The god said, "Ha!" and new things appeared. I had no idea why the god had to say "Ha" all the time, but when he uttered his last "Ha," nine chieftains were hatched from a gigantic egg laid by a roc at the edge of the sky. The nine chieftains, staying close to one another, intermarried, and were all related. At the same time, the land and the people turned them into mutual enemies. Moreover, even though they considered themselves kings, they still had to kneel before those in power in Beijing and Lhasa.

Yes, I know, I haven't yet spoken about silver.

But didn't I start already? Anyway, silver, whose function is similar to gold, was our favorite. We especially liked it because its whiteness had brought us good luck. That makes two excellent reasons to like silver, and I can add another. Silver can be made into all sorts of ornaments, small ones like rings, bracelets, earrings, scabbards, milking hooks, fingernail caps, and tooth straighteners, and big ones like belts, sutra cases, saddle fittings, dinner services, and ritual accessories.

Silver mines were scanty in chieftains' territory, and completely absent on Maichi land, though there was gold in the sand by the river. The chieftain had people pan the gold, some of which we kept for our own use, but most of which was exchanged for cases of silver, which we stored in a cellar near the dungeon. The key to the silver storage was placed in a multileveled chest, whose key in turn hung at Father's waist. This key, over which a lama had read a sutra, was connected to a part of his body, and when it was missing, it felt to him as if an insect were gnawing at his flesh.

One of the reasons Living Buddha Jeeka had fallen out of favor with the chieftain in recent years was that he'd once said that since we now owned so much silver, we should stop panning gold by the river in order to preserve our *feng shui*. He said that having a treasure in the house doesn't mean anything; our land is the true treasure. With treasure in the land and good *feng shui*, the chieftain would enjoy a promising and solid future, because only the land can sustain generations to come. But of course, it was not easy for the chieftain to heed his words. As the silver piled up, our estate emitted a sweet, silvery fragrance. But for years we weren't considered particularly wealthy, especially when compared to other chieftains.

Now all that was changing. As the harvesting of poppies came to an end, our wealth was about to eclipse that of all the other chieftains. The opium processors sent by Special Emissary Huang did a rough calculation; the figure absolutely shocked us. Who'd have thought that such a skinny old Han could bring such incredible wealth to the Maichi family? "How could the god of wealth turn out to be a spindly old man?" the chieftain wondered aloud.

Special Emissary Huang arrived amid our anticipation.

Rain was falling from deep in the sky the day he came. Winter was almost upon us. All that morning a freezing rain poured out of the gray clouds high above; in the afternoon it turned to snow that melted as soon as it hit the ground. The horses carrying Special Emissary Huang and his attendants rode up through the slush; the only snow that hadn't melted was the little bit piled on top of the special emissary's felt hat. The steward rushed out to begin the welcoming ceremony, but Special Emissary Huang waved him off. "We'll skip all that," he said. "I'm freezing."

He was escorted to the fireside, where he sneezed twice. He shook his head at the various cold therapies proffered to him, saying, "The mistress is a Han, so she'll know what I need."

The chieftain's wife handed him her opium paraphernalia. "Please try the opium that came from the seeds you gave us and was processed by the men you sent."

Special Emissary Huang's eyelids drooped after he sucked in the smoke and swallowed it. When he finally opened his eyes, he said, "Terrific stuff! This is truly terrific stuff."

The chieftain asked anxiously, "How much silver do you think we can get?"

Mother signaled Father to be patient, but Special Emissary Huang just smiled. "Don't worry, Mistress. I prefer the chieftain's straightforward style. He'll receive an undreamed of quantity of silver."

The chieftain pressed him to say just how much.

"Tell me how much is in the chieftain's estate at this moment. Please be precise. Don't exaggerate and definitely don't give me too low a figure."

After sending the servants away, the chieftain divulged how much silver we had.

Stroking his yellow beard, Special Emissary Huang mulled this over for a moment. "That is not a small amount, nor is it too great. I will double the quantity for your opium, provided that you use half of one half of the amount to buy new weapons from me to arm your people."

The chieftain gladly agreed.

After Special Emissary Huang had enjoyed a meal and a round of musical entertainment, the chieftain's wife sent a maidservant up to him to share some opium and his bed for the night. Then the family was called together. For what reason? To hold a meeting. Yes, we held meetings too, except that we didn't say, Well, there'll be a meeting tonight, or, The agenda for tonight's meeting will be such and such. In any case, we decided to expand our silver storage. Messengers were sent that night to summon stonemasons and workers from all the headmen's fortresses. The family servants were also summoned from their quarters, while the chieftain ordered that the prisoners in the dungeon be consolidated to make room for the large quantity of silver that would soon arrive. Squeezing prisoners from three of the cells into others that were already occupied led to considerable grumbling. One fellow, who had been locked up for over two decades, was especially unhappy. He said that the current chieftain must be worse than his predecessor. Otherwise, why would he have to give up the spacious cell he'd occupied for so many years?

His complaint was quickly reported upstairs.

The chieftain took a sip of wine, and said, "Go tell him not to be so insolent just because he's been there longer than anyone else. One of these days I'll send him to a place with nothing but space."

The Maichi family was about to possess more silver than the other chieftains could ever imagine. We would soon be richer than the wealthiest chieftain in history. But of course the prisoner knew none of this. "Don't tell me what tomorrow will be like," he said. "It's not even daybreak, and I'm already doing worse than I was at early nightfall."

The chieftain smiled at his words. "He can't see daylight? All right, get the executioner over to send the prisoner to that ultimate spacious place."

By then my eyelids were getting so heavy that I couldn't have propped them open with house beams. The night may have been filled with excitement, but I couldn't stop yawning. Mother looked at me with disappointment in her eyes. I didn't feel like apologizing. Even Dolma didn't want to get up and help me to bed, but she had no choice but to walk me back to my room. I told her not to leave me because I knew I'd be frightened when I thought about mice. She pinched me. "Why didn't you think about mice earlier?"

"I wasn't alone then. I only think about mice when I'm by myself."

She laughed despite herself. I really liked Dolma, especially the bovine smell that came from between her legs and from her bosom. Of course, I didn't tell her that, since that would only have gone to her head. Instead, I pointed out that she needn't get excited like

Father and the others over the silver that would soon be added to our coffers, because not a single piece of it would be hers. That did the trick. She stood in the dark by my bed for a long time before sighing and lying down beside me fully clothed.

When I got up the next morning, the prisoner who had complained about his crowded cell had already been executed.

Every time someone was executed, our household was shrouded in a strange atmosphere, even though everyone looked as normal as any other day. For instance, the chieftain would cough loudly before breakfast, while his wife would place her hand over her chest, as if unable to withstand the beating of her heart, which might fall to the floor if she let her arm drop to her side. My brother always whistled before breakfast, and that morning was no different. But I could tell they were disturbed. Killing people was nothing we shied away from, but afterward, our hearts would still be uneasy. It would be wrong to say that the chieftain enjoyed killing people, but sometimes he simply had to. The commoners lived with things beyond their control, and so did the chieftain. If you don't believe me, then tell me why we retained an executioner if the chieftain himself enjoyed killing so much. And if you still don't believe me, then you should share a meal with us after the execution order is given. You'd see that we drank more water than usual and ate less food. The meat was hardly touched, maybe a symbolic bite or two at most.

I was the only one whose appetite was never affected. This morning was no exception.

I was a very noisy eater. Dolma said I sounded like someone sloshing through mud. Mother said I sounded like a squealing pig. That just made me eat more loudly. Seeing a frown on Father's face, Mother said, "What do you expect from an idiot?" That shut him up. But how could a chieftain simply keep quiet? So after a while he said crossly, "Why isn't that Han fellow up yet? Do all you Han people laze around in bed in the morning?"

My mother was, as we know, a Han and, on mornings when she didn't have anything to do, she slept in, skipping breakfast with the family. But she just laughed, and said, "Don't get so worked up. That silver hasn't fallen into your hands yet. Instead of getting up early and coughing your heart and lungs out, why not spend some quiet time in bed?"

At moments like that, it would be wrong to assume that the

94

chieftain and his wife were on bad terms. It was when their conversation dripped with politeness that they were unhappy with each other. They carped only when they were getting along.

The chieftain said, "You see, it's our language that has taught you how to talk." What he meant was, a good language makes a person articulate, and ours is a good language.

"I'd show you what a sharp tongue can do if you knew Chinese," Mother said, "and if your language weren't so simple."

Dolma whispered to me, "You know, Young Master, the master and the mistress did you-know-what last night."

After swallowing a big slice of meat, I opened my mouth wide and burst out laughing.

My brother asked what I was laughing at. I said, "Dolma said she wanted to go wee-wee."

Mother fumed. "What kind of talk is that?"

I said to Dolma, "Go wee-wee. Don't be afraid."

My hoodwinked maid, Dolma, left the table blushing. The chieftain laughed. "Well, my idiot son has grown up." Then he turned to my brother. "Go see if the workers are here. Blood has been shed, and it would be inauspicious if the work didn't start today."

Four ~

12 Visitors ~

The three spare cells in the dungeon were converted into two large storage rooms, one for silver and the other for the new-style weapons that Special Emissary Huang had bought for us from the provincial military government.

The special emissary departed with a large shipment of opium while leaving behind some men to train our soldiers on a piece of land big enough to sow eight hundred bushels of barley. The soldiers' shouts on the drill ground shook the earth and dust whirled all through the winter. Before our previous battle, our troops had learned formations and how to fire their weapons; now they were looking more and more like real soldiers. The chieftain summoned tailors to make uniforms for them: black Venetian robes decorated with red, yellow, and blue cross-stitched edges, and red silk belts on which bayonets could be sheathed. Lower-ranking officers had seal-skin trim, while those of higher ranks sported leopard skin. The highest-ranking officer was my brother, Tamding Gonpo; as officer in charge, he wore a uniform edged with the skin of a whole Bengali tiger. Never, since the beginning of history, had any chieftains commanded such a well-equipped, well-turned-out army.

The dust on the makeshift drilling ground didn't settle until the eve of the new year.

When the snow began to melt, a new line of traffic appeared on the main road.

It was our neighboring chieftains, leading long processions of servants and guards.

Dolma asked me to guess why they were coming. I said they had come to visit relatives. Then why, she asked, hadn't they come in years past?

The Maichi family had to send its servants far out of the estate to

96

prepare proper welcomes, to lay our best carpets, upstairs and down, and to lay less fine carpets from the foot of the stairs all the way out to the square beyond the gate, where horses were tethered. The young family slaves were all there with their backs bent, waiting to serve as footstools for the visitors when they dismounted.

Chieftains always traveled with a team of horses, whose bells rang out in the cold, clear air before they were in sight in the valleys. Members of Chieftain Maichi's family sipped cup after cup of buttery tea, so that when they appeared before their guests, their faces would be red and shiny, in striking contrast to the visitors, whose faces would be dusty and weary from the rigors of travel and the cold. That way, chieftains who had traveled a great distance would immediately lose the psychological edge.

At first, we were very courteous to our guests, for Father wanted to make sure we didn't look like upstarts. But the guests were intent upon making us feel superior through their requests, which could be roughly divided into two types.

One was quite straightforward: they wanted the magical seeds that had made the Maichi family rich overnight.

The other was more indirect: they wanted to marry their sisters or daughters to Chieftain Maichi's sons. Obviously, they too sought our magical seeds.

But all they managed to achieve was to turn a family that had tried to appear humble into one that was lofty and arrogant. We agreed to all the marriage proposals.

My brother said cheerfully, "My brother and I can each get three or four."

"Hush!" Father said.

My brother smiled as he left to look for a place where he could play with his two favorite objects, guns and women, both of which liked him in return. All the girls considered it a great honor to be close to him. So did the guns. Locals had a saying that guns were the extended arms of the first young master of the Maichi family. The rifles were his long arms, the pistols his shorter arms. By contrast, they assumed that I neither knew how to play with guns nor appreciated the wonder of women.

On that happy winter day, the Maichi family made enemies of every neighboring chieftain, since none of them received any of the magical poppy seeds.

Talk spread like lightning, from east to west and north to south. Even though every chieftain had been granted his fiefdom by the Chinese emperors, they now said that the Maichi family had thrown its lot in with the Chinese. Overnight, the Maichi became traitors to the Tibetan people.

Actually, the three smart people in my family – Father, Mother, and my brother – plus me, the idiot, had discussed whether to give the seeds to our neighbors. As normal people with normal brains, the others were against giving anyone a single seed. But I said, Why not? It isn't silver. They said, Hush, what do you mean "It isn't silver"? That wasn't what I meant, but they wouldn't let me finish. What I wanted to say was, The things growing out in the field could not be stored like silver in the cellars under the Maichi estate.

I managed to finish my thought: "The wind will scatter them anyway."

But no one listened to me, or else they pretended not to hear the truth in my words. Dolma tugged at my arm to shush me. When she tugged it the second time, I left with her.

"You idiot," she said, "no one will listen to you."

"Tiny seeds like that can hitch a ride to a neighbor's land on the wings of a passing bird," I said as I hiked up her skirt.

The bed began to shake and squeak, the rhythm matched by Dolma's shouts: "Idiot, idiot, i-di-ot."

I wasn't sure if I was an idiot or not, but I sure felt good doing it with Dolma. Afterward, I felt much better, and said to Dolma, "You hurt me."

She suddenly knelt down before me, "Young Master, the silversmith has proposed to me."

Tears gushed from my eyes, and I heard myself say in a funny voice, "I don't want you to go."

While the normal people out in the meeting room were worrying about seeds, I was cushioning my head between Dolma's breasts. She said it was enough for her to see me cry after serving me all these years, even if I was an idiot. She added that I wouldn't let her go because I'd never had another woman, and told me I'd get a new personal maid. At that moment, I sobbed like a little boy, her son, and said, "But I don't want you to go."

Rubbing my head, she said she couldn't spend the rest of her life with me, that I would no longer want her after I knew more about women. "I've picked out the perfect girl for you."

The next day I told Mother it was time for Dolma to get married.

She asked if that rotten girl had said something to me. Even though I felt empty inside, I replied indifferently, like my brother when he talked about women, "I just want a girl my own age."

Mother began to cry. "My foolish child. You finally know something about women."

13 Women ∼

Sangye Dolma was right. They quickly found me a new personal maid, a girl with a small body, a tiny face, small eyes, and dainty hands and feet. Standing before me with her arms at her sides, she neither wept nor smiled. I discovered that she lacked the smell of her predecessor, and I told Dolma so.

The maid who was soon to be relieved of her duties said, "Give it some time. She'll have it once she's been with you awhile. That smell is given by men."

"I don't like her," I said.

Mother told me that the new girl's name was Tharna. After mulling that over, I decided that even if it was a girl's name, it was the wrong one for this girl. Fortunately, she was to be my maid, not my wife, and there was no need to be so picky. When I asked the girl with dainty hands and tiny feet if her name was really Tharna, she finally spoke. Her voice trembled out of nervousness, but at least she spoke. "Everyone says my name is kind of strange. What do you think?"

Her voice was soft, but I was sure it could be heard no matter how far away she was. Only a well-trained maid had a voice like that. She was the daughter of a groom, who, before entering the estate, had lived in a squat hut. Her mother's eyesight had been ruined by smoke, so from the age of seven or eight, she'd been getting up in the middle of the night to feed the animals, every night, until the day our crippled steward walked into their house. As if in a dream, she took a bath in a warm spring and put on new clothes to come live with me.

Before I had a chance to ask her any more questions, she was taken away by another servant to bathe and change clothes.

Which gave me time to see Dolma.

But Dolma's heart was elsewhere. I could see it fluttering away from me.

She was sitting behind the upstairs railings doing embroidery and singing softly to herself. It was part of a long narrative poem, a tune unrelated to love, but romance clearly filled her heart.

Her flesh, eaten by the birds, *gezhi*, *gezhi*,
Her blood, drunk by the rain, *gudong*, *gudong*,
Her bones, gnawed by bears, *gazhi*, *gazhi*,
Her hair, loosened by the wind, one lock after another.

By mimicking the sounds of the birds eating, the rain drinking, bears gnawing, and the wind blowing, her song was exceedingly meaningful and full of emotion. As she sang, the silversmith's little hammer pounded out a pleasant rhythm. The Maichi family had so much silver that he would never lack for work. And everyone said that his work was getting better day by day. Chieftain Maichi liked this clever, skillful fellow, so when he heard that the maid Dolma was to marry him, he said, "She did not live with us in vain. She has good taste, she's made an excellent choice."

He sent word to the silversmith that, even though the master liked him, he would become a slave if he married Dolma. To which the silversmith replied, "What's the difference between a freeman and a slave? I'll have to work in this compound for the rest of my life anyway."

As soon as they were married, Dolma would change from a fragrant-smelling personal maid into a cook whose face was constantly smeared with soot. But she said, "Such is my destiny."

So, these few days would be the best in the life of Dolma, my private tutor in the ways of men and women. In this regard, the chieftain's wife displayed the ultimate kindness one woman could bestow upon another. As Dolma was hurrying downstairs, the mistress said she would have plenty of time to be with her man, but the time before marriage, once gone, would never return. She took out some things. "These are for you. Use them to embroider something you like for yourself."

Each day, when the silversmith's hammer sounded in the courtyard, turning silver into ornaments, Dolma went out and sat on the veranda to sing and do embroidery. The little hammer drew her attention away, and she didn't even turn to look at me. So my idiot brain began to think that women were so fickle that they would forget you in a moment. My new maid, Tharna, was playing something with her slender fingers behind me while I stood behind Dolma as she sang, clearing my throat the whole time. But she carried on with her singing, not sparing a moment to look at me. *Gazhi, gazhi, gudong, gudong*, there was no end to it. Not until the silversmith was away one day did she look around, blushing and smiling. "I'll bet the new maid gives you more pleasure than I did."

I told her I hadn't so much as touched Tharna.

She gave Tharna a searching look, and was assured that I was telling the truth. Though I often lied, this time I did not, and Dolma's tears began to flow. "Young Master," she said. "I'm leaving tomorrow. The silversmith went to borrow a horse." She added, "Make sure you think about me every once in a while."

I nodded.

The next morning I was still in dreamland when I heard Dolma's singsong, tearful voice. I stepped out to take a look, only to discover the silversmith standing upstairs in brand-new clothes while Dolma was weeping at the mistress's feet, telling her what she'd said to me the day before. As her eyes turned red, the mistress said to her, "Come tell me if anyone dares to make trouble for you." Then she turned to say to the servants, "No one is to stop Dolma if she comes upstairs to see me or Young Master."

The servants answered in unison, "Yes, Mistress."

Then the silversmith bent down to lift Dolma up on his back, and I watched as they descended, one step at a time. Two male servants carried the chieftain's dowry, followed by two maidservants holding gifts from the chieftain's wife. In the servants' eyes, Sangye Dolma was bathed in utmost favor.

After setting his woman on the back of the horse, the silversmith leaped into the saddle. They rode out through the gate and began galloping on the dirt road, trailed by puffs of yellow dust that thinned out the higher it rose in the clear winter sky. Then they disappeared around a bend in the road, to the accompaniment of servants' shouts in the yard. I knew what those peculiar shouts meant: the new couple was off to find a discreet place somewhere under the sun to do their business. I'd heard that especially adroit couples actually did it on horseback. Then I spotted my two little slaves among the spirited servants. Sonam Tserang, his mouth opened wide, was making a lot of noise, while Aryi stood off to the side, near the stake where his executioner father carried out his duties. He looked lonely, but no one knew that I was just as lonely, and sad, now that my Dolma was being carried away on horseback. I waved at Aryi, but he was so focused on the disappearing horse that he didn't realize that the person in the fox-skin robe upstairs was more pitiable than he. The spot where the horse had disappeared, a sun-drenched patch of dead grass between a pair of juniper trees, looked empty. I felt the same kind of emptiness inside.

Finally the horse reappeared at the same spot, galloping back.

Another round of cheers erupted from the crowd.

The silversmith helped his charming bride off the horse and carried her into a dank, smelly little room in the lowest level of the estate house. Out in the yard the servants sang as they worked. Then the silversmith emerged from the room to resume his work, his hammer emitting a series of crisp and very loud *ding-dang! ding-dang! ding-ding-dang-dang!* noises.

Behind me, the dainty-limbed, tiny-voiced Tharna said, "I want to come down the stairs like that someday. Will I look as dignified and lovely?"

Without waiting for an answer, she added, "And will Young Master be as sad?"

Surprised by her astuteness, I said, "I'm not happy that you know about such things."

She giggled. "But I do."

I asked her if it was her mother who had taught her.

"Can a blind woman teach me that?" She sounded more like a master talking about a servant than a daughter discussing her own mother.

That evening, the servants received permission to build a bonfire in the yard, around which they drank and danced. Leaning up against the high railing, I looked down to see Dolma mingling happily with them. As the night deepened, stars twinkled above. Under a sparkling sky, people mired in the bitterness of the human world enjoyed a rare joyful moment. They must have been warm and toasty, unlike me, who shivered with the chill air assaulting my back.

When I went back into my room, the only light came from coals smoldering in the brazier, where I went to warm myself. Tharna was already in bed, her bare arms lying atop the blanket. I gazed at her smooth, slender neck and white teeth, and when she opened her eyes, they glimmered like fine gems. Finally, like flames igniting, desire surged up in my body. When I called her name, I felt a strange quiver between my lips and teeth.

The girl said, "I'm cold."

The body that rolled into my arms was smooth and cool, with a thin waist, tiny buttocks, and small breasts. With Dolma, I had always sunk into her body, but now Tharna's body was buried under mine. I was not yet fifteen but had already grown into a real man. I asked her if she was still cold; she giggled and said she was hot. It was true; her body had suddenly turned boiling hot. When I was with Dolma, I often felt that I was still outside even when I wasn't, but with Tharna I couldn't get inside. Each time I tried, the little tramp let out a horrifying scream. But when I moved away, she held onto me tightly. We went on like that, back and forth, until the birds on the mountains, by the rivers, and in the trees, all started to chirp. Day was breaking. Tharna told me not to worry about her, so I thrust in with all my might. Finally, I knew she was a woman. I felt myself fill up the inside of a woman! It was wonderful to be with a small woman! Just wonderful! I quickly grew larger inside her, and the world swelled. The earth expanded, sending water to the lower end; the sky inflated, pushing the stars off to the sides. Then, *boom*, the world collapsed. Daylight had arrived. Tharna pulled out a piece of white silk that was speckled with bright red drops of blood. She waved it in front of me. I smiled, knowing that was my doing, before falling into a contented sleep. I slept through the day. When I woke up, Mother was sitting on the edge of my bed. Her smile told me that she now considered me a full-grown adult, someone who knew everything about what went on between a man and a woman. I'd been there before, but to tell the truth, this time it felt like the real thing.

Reaching out from under the blanket, I said, "Give me some water."

I could tell that my voice had changed overnight; now husky and low, it seemed to resonate from deep in my chest.

Instead of putting her hand on my head, as she had done before,

103

Mother turned to Tharna. "He's awake and wants water. Maybe it would be better to give him some light liquor."

So Tharna brought the liquor, which produced a wonderful sensation I hadn't experienced before as it slid down my throat. Mother said to Tharna, "Now Young Master is your responsibility, and you must do your best in waiting on him. Everyone says he's an idiot, but he isn't stupid in some ways."

Smiling shyly, Tharna answered in a low but audible voice, "Yes."

The chieftain's wife took a necklace from her pocket and put it around Tharna's neck. After Mother left, I thought Tharna would promise to follow the order of the chieftain's wife and take good care of me. But instead, she buried her head in my chest, and said, "From now on, you must be good to me."

I had no choice but to say, "I will."

She looked up at me, her eyes brimming with things she wanted to say.

"I've already promised you," I said. "What else do you want?"

She asked, "Am I pretty?"

I didn't know what to say. Truth is, I couldn't really tell if a woman was pretty or ugly. If that's what makes someone an idiot, then I surely was one. I knew only whether or not I felt a desire for someone; I was familiar with the curves of a woman's body, but not what makes her pretty. Yet I knew that I was the young master, who could talk to her when he felt like it, and who didn't need to say a word if it didn't suit him. So I didn't say anything.

I decided to get up and have dinner with my family.

While waiting for dinner to be served, my brother patted me on the head and Father gave me a large gemstone. Following me like a shadow, Tharna knelt behind me when I sat down.

Our dining room was a rectangle. The chieftain and his wife sat at either end of the room, my brother and I sat on opposite sides, all of us on soft cushions: Persian rugs with lovely designs in the summer and bearskins in the winter. In front of everyone was a low, gilded red table. Shortly after the Maichi family made its fortune from opium, the quality of our dinnerware improved; much of it was now made of silver, and we drank from coral wineglasses. In addition, we imported a large amount of wax, which was then made into candles by Han wax workers. Before everyone stood a candelabra, in which several tapers lit up the room. When it wasn't particularly cold, the candles alone warmed the room. On the walls behind us stood cabinets for our dinnerware and curios: two gold-plated telephones from England, a German camera, and three radios made in America. There was even a microscope and some square flashlights with handles. We had many such things, and though we could not find uses for them, we displayed them because other chieftains didn't own any. If an object disappeared from the shelf, it was because a particular chieftain also owned one, not because ours had been stolen. Several alarm clocks that had once been displayed had suffered that fate, for we had heard that after leaving our place, the missionary Charles had gone to visit other chieftains and had given them similar gifts. My brother told the servants to empty out two .60-caliber cannon shells and put them in the spots where the clocks had once stood. The bases of the shiny, painted shells were exquisite enough for our tastes.

It was dinnertime for the family.

Though there weren't many dishes, there was plenty of food, steaming hot and nutritious. Kitchen servants brought the dishes out and handed them to the personal servants kneeling behind us to place on our tables. Dolma came in that day at the end of the meal with a large bowl. Kneeling on the floor, she walked on her knees as she served each of us in turn. Since it was her first day in the kitchen, she'd made a special cheese dish for the masters. But this was not the Dolma I'd known; the fragrance was gone and her silk clothes had been replaced by coarse linen.

When she came to me, she said, "For your enjoyment, Young Master." Even her voice sounded old, no longer able to evoke the pleasant feelings of before. Yesterday Dolma had been a nicely dressed young woman oozing a delightful fragrance; today she was a lowly kitchen maid. Kneeling as she presented us with the cheese dish, she was encased in kitchen smells of smoke and soot. When she said in her humble voice, "For your enjoyment, Young Master," I didn't answer. I was too sad. Watching her retreat from the light into the dark, for the very first time I experienced the feeling of having something vanish from my life and knowing it will never return. Before then, I'd always thought that everything would remain forever, that once something appeared before me, it would never disappear.

While the Maichi family members were yawning or picking their teeth after dinner, it was mealtime for the personal servants, Tharna among them. She chewed her food so fast that she sounded like a little mouse – *ji-ji, ji-ji-ji-ji*. The thought of a mouse sent shivers down my spine, and I nearly jumped up from my cushion. I turned to look at her; she was so unnerved at being observed that she nearly dropped her spoon.

I said, "Don't be afraid." She nodded, but I could tell she didn't want me to watch her eat. I pointed to the meat. "Have some." She picked up a piece and ate it, this time without sounding like a mouse. Then I pointed to the boiled broad beans. "Try some of those too." After shoveling in several beans, she couldn't keep from making the mousy noise – *ji-ji, ji-ji-ji-ji* – no matter how tightly she closed her tiny mouth. I started to laugh. This time she was so unnerved that she actually did drop her spoon.

I announced loudly, "I'm not afraid of mice anymore."

Everyone looked at me strangely, as if I'd said that the sky overhead had vanished. So I repeated loudly, "I'm – not – afraid – of – mice – anymore."

They remained quiet.

I pointed at Tharna. "She eats like a mouse, *ji-ji-ji, zha-zha-zha-zha* …"

They were still silent, as if trying to embarrass me, and I began to wonder if I was truly no longer afraid of mice. Suddenly, Father burst out laughing. "Son, I know you're telling the truth." Then he turned to his wife and said in a low voice that was still audible to all, "Do you know why men want women? Women can make a man out of you! See, now he's cured himself."

After we returned to my room, Tharna asked, "What made Young Master think of that?"

I said, "It just came to me. You're not upset, are you?"

She said she wasn't. Her horse-groom father had also said she was like a mouse. Whenever a fine new horse given to the chieftain wouldn't eat, her father would send her to feed it in the middle of the night, saying the animal would not be afraid of anyone who resembled a mouse.

We climbed into bed and did it again. Afterward, she giggled while she put on her underwear. She said it felt so good, why didn't others want to do it. I asked her what others she was talking about.

She said, the mares never wanted to do it, her mother either. I felt like asking more questions, but she'd already fallen asleep, a contented look on her face. So I blew out the lamp. Normally I fell asleep easily when I was in the dark, no matter what time of day. But this night was different. The light was out, yet I kept hearing the wind howling over the roof, like flocks of birds flying overhead.

The following morning, Mother noticed the dark shadows under my eyes. "Didn't you sleep well again last night?"

I knew what she meant, but I didn't want her to blame Tharna, so I told her I had trouble falling asleep. She asked me why. I said it was nothing, just that I was annoyed by the wind blowing across the roof.

"I thought it was something else," she said, then added, "My dear child, we may be the chieftain's family, but we can't stop the wind from blowing over the roof."

"Didn't Dolma know?" I asked her.

She laughed. "I knew it wasn't anything as simple as the wind. Didn't Dolma know what?"

"Didn't she know she'd have to wear tattered clothes, be covered in soot and dust, and smell bad?"

"She knew."

"Then why did she want to go down there?"

Her voice turned cold. "Because she had to eventually. If she went early, she could find a man. But if she waited till later, there wouldn't be a man for her."

As we talked, the steward came in to report that my wet nurse had returned. Dechen Motso had traveled to inner Tibet with a group of pilgrims a year before. To be honest, we'd all but forgotten her. It is unwise for someone to return after people have forgotten about her, because everything from the past is erased from their memories. We'd talked about her shortly after she left, saying that the old woman would die on her Buddhist pilgrimage. And just before she set out, we offered her fifteen silver dollars for traveling expenses. But she wanted only five. A stubborn woman, she wouldn't accept more. She said she was going to visit five temples, and would need only five, one for each temple. She also said that the Buddha cared about a poor old woman's heart, not her money. We asked her why she was going to only five temples. She said she had dreamed about only five temples at any time in her life. As for traveling expenses, she said no one who truly wanted to worship the Buddha would spend money on the road, not even the wealthy. She spoke the truth, for it was our belief that the trip would be made in vain if a pilgrim didn't beg or seek alms on the road. And that was one of the reasons the chieftains could never make up their minds about pilgrimages. One of our Maichi chieftains had made one. All his entourage made it back; he didn't. Chieftains were the people least able to endure hardships.

We gradually forgot about Dechen Motso after she left, which proved that we hadn't liked her much. So imagine our shock when she walked in. Not only had the old woman weathered the trek over high mountains and across icy waters, but her bent back had straightened. Even the many wrinkles on her face had smoothed out. Standing before us was not a sickly old woman, but a tall, younger one with a ruddy face. She pecked at my cheek, bestowing upon me the smell of distant places and times.

She'd always had a booming voice, and now it was louder than ever. "Mistress, I nearly died from missing the young master."

The mistress said nothing.

Dechen Motso continued, "Mistress, I'm back. I did a calculation yesterday, when we were nearing home. I've been gone for exactly one year and fourteen days."

The chieftain's wife said, "Go get some rest."

But she wouldn't listen. Shedding a few tears, Dechen Motso said, "I can't believe the young master has a personal maid. He's truly a grown man now."

"Yes, he's a grown man," the mistress said, "and we needn't worry about him anymore."

But the wet nurse said, "No, we still need to worry. No matter how old he gets, he is still a child." She asked the mistress to send for Tharna, so she could look at her.

The old woman touched Tharna's face and felt her bones before saying bluntly, "She's no match for the young master."

The mistress's face darkened. "You've said enough. You can go now."

Her mouth agape, the wet nurse was unable to comprehend what was happening. She didn't know we all thought she'd died on the road and had already forgotten her. Now that we had, she shouldn't have come back. But, ignorant of that fact, she said, "I

108

want to see the master and the first young master. I haven't seen them in a year and fourteen days."

The mistress said, "I don't think that will be necessary."

"I'll go see the little tramp, Sangye Dolma, then," the old woman said.

So I told her that Sangye Dolma had been married to the silversmith, Choedak. Apparently, the pilgrimage had changed her looks, but not her personality. "The little tramp was always trying to seduce the young master," she said. "Now I see she's gotten what she deserves."

Now even I could contain myself no longer. "Get out of here, you old hag," I screamed.

The story of such an insignificant person should have ended much earlier.

Still seething with anger, I issued a relatively important order for the first time in my life. I told the servants to move the wet nurse's things downstairs and tell her she must not step foot on the third floor or higher anywhere in the house. When I heard her crying in the yard, I augmented my order: "Give her a room to herself, complete with kitchen utensils, so the only thing she'll ever have to do is cook for herself."

It appeared that my order pleased everyone; otherwise, Father, Mother, or my brother could easily have overruled me. With nothing to do, the old woman spent her days with the servants, telling them stories of my childhood and of her pilgrimage. That news led me to issue a supplemental order, permitting her to talk about her pilgrimage, but prohibiting her from relating anything about my childhood. She had no choice but to obey my orders. I thought about revoking them when I noticed her hair getting grayer by the day. But I changed my mind when I saw how she regularly spit on the shadow I cast from above.

Later, by the time she was so old that she'd even forgotten to spit on my shadow, I'd given up concerning myself with her. I didn't learn about her death until a year after it had happened. Even at that, people said that the Maichi family had not done wrong by the idiot son's wet nurse.

That's what I figured, too.

I thought about that when I looked up at the stars on clear nights. I thought about it in bed as I listened to the river raging to a faraway place on nights of bad weather. But gradually I stopped thinking about her altogether. Instead, I began to think about Wangpo Yeshi, the monk of the new sect that the chieftain had found unacceptable. He had a mule he'd swapped his donkey for, he had some sutras he considered to be rare treasures, and he lived in a cave.

When the wind changed its direction, willow branches on the riverbanks would turn green and bloom, sending puffs of white catkins flying everywhere. Spring would arrive before we knew it, faster than the arrival of winter.

14 Heads ∼

Because of the gray poppy seeds, Maichi became the hated target of other chieftains.

They came, one after another, and left empty-handed, but that didn't stop the next chieftain from coming to try his luck. Those whose territory was close to ours said we could unite and become stronger, the overlords to whom the other chieftains bowed low. Chieftain Maichi replied that he wanted only to enrich himself and his people, and had no intention of becoming an overlord. Distant chieftains said that since great spaces separated us, we had nothing to fear, even if they grew stronger. To which Chieftain Maichi said, "For a giant, no river is impassable."

When spring arrived, Father said, "No one will come now."

My brother reminded him, "There is still one chieftain who hasn't yet shown his face."

Father counted slowly on his fingers. There had been eighteen chieftains, including Maichi, before the Han emperor eliminated three of them. Then a feud between brothers had divided one chieftain into three. There was also one childless chieftain whose territory had been split between his wife and his steward. So in the end there were still eighteen. Now sixteen had come. The only holdout was Wangpo, who had recently waged war against us. Father said, "He won't have the face to come."

"Yes, he will," my brother said.

"He wouldn't be a Tibetan if he visited his enemy over something so insignificant. Even chieftains who hate us would look down on him."

"My God, Father, you're so old-fashioned."

"Old-fashioned? What does that mean?"

"Nothing, really. He doesn't have to come to us humbly with bent back. He can try other means to get the seeds."

"I defeated him!" Father screamed. "Do you think he'll try to take them by force? Didn't I frighten him off already?"

In fact, Chieftain Maichi knew what his son was trying to tell him, and he felt the pain of desperation, as if he could already see his precious seeds spreading into other people's fields, where vast expanses of flowers were bursting into bloom.

Even I felt the pain in Father's heart, tasted the bitterness that rose in his mouth, and understood his reluctance to mention the word *steal*. We all knew that other chieftains would do that, and we had no way of preventing it. So what was the point of mentioning something beyond our control, except to make ourselves feel even worse?

In this matter, my brother exposed the folly of a smart person. He often saw in simple matters a complexity others failed to perceive. On this particular day, that is exactly how the future Maichi chieftain acted. He said confidently, "They'll send someone to steal our seeds."

The word *steal* was so powerful that it hit Father like a bullet, but he kept his anger in check. Instead he asked my brother, "Do you have a plan?"

He did. He wanted Father to retrieve all the seeds and hand them back to his people at planting time. The chieftain said sarcastically, "Planting time is fast approaching. Wouldn't the people think I didn't trust them if I took back the seeds now? Besides, if stealing was what they had in mind, they'd have done so long before now. I tell you, there are other ways for the chieftains to get their hands on the seeds. Payoffs, for instance."

The future chieftain looked at the current chieftain, speechless.

In the face of this awkward situation, the chieftain's wife wore a look of gleeful satisfaction.

The chieftain added, "Now that we've considered that possibility, we must be prepared, so as to have no regrets later on."

Mother smiled at my brother. "So go take care of it. There's no need for your father to worry himself over such matters."

111

The future chieftain carried out his duties, sparing no effort.

Orders were sent down and seeds were sent back up on fast steeds. Since it was impossible to tell how much had been hidden away or fallen into the hands of other chieftains, no time was wasted trying to figure that out. As it happened, when Headman Yingolok was out collecting the precious poppy seeds, he caught a thief stealing some. It was a man sent by Chieftain Wangpo. Yingolok sent a messenger to ask if the thief should be delivered to the estate. "Of course!" my brother demanded. "Why even ask? I knew it. I knew they'd try stealing. But they failed. Send him over and tell the executioner to get ready. We'll see what the impudent thief looks like."

Aryi Senior was summoned to the execution ground in the estate courtyard.

On the right edge of the yard were several hitching posts for horses; on the left stood an execution stake, a solid log that, in addition to its practical function, was a symbol of the chieftain's power. For some crimes the offenders were tied to the stake and bitten to death by poisonous insects released into a funnel attached to the top. Iron clamps beneath the funnel could be locked from behind and fastened around the prisoners' necks. Two arms stretched horizontally under the clamps, which, together with the funnel, made the stake appear from a distance like a scarecrow, creating a bucolic aura around the estate grounds. These arms were in fact iron bars stuck through the stake to hold the prisoners' arms out straight. Someone had wisecracked that the bar created the image of a prisoner flying up to heaven. Closer to the ground were two iron rings for fastening the ankles. And there were other objects near the stake: large round stones with a metallic sheen, a trough made of hollowed-out pine, and a number of smaller odds and ends. All in all they formed an extraordinary sight, with the stake as the center. And of course, there was Aryi the executioner, whose absence would have greatly diminished the atmosphere.

Now they had both come – Aryi Senior in the lead, followed by Aryi Junior.

Both had long arms and legs; they walked like stumbling goats, while their thrust-out necks swiveled like startled deer. The executioner's family had come into existence at the beginning of the Maichi hereditary line. Over the centuries, no two people in the Maichi family had looked alike, but each Aryi resembled all the others. They made their living dealing out punishments: lashings, mutilations, and all manner of death. Many people liked to pretend that the Aryis did not exist in this world, but they did, in the form of a powerful silence.

They walked into the yard, Aryi Senior carrying a leather satchel over his shoulder, and Aryi Junior a smaller one on his back. Having been to their house, I knew what those satchels contained.

When he saw me, Aryi Junior smiled childishly before bending down to go to work. All sorts of execution equipment glistened in the sunlight when the satchels were opened. The thief was pushed forward; he was a brawny, towering man, nearly taller than the stake. Apparently, Chieftain Wangpo had sent his best man.

The leather whip danced in the hand of Aryi Senior. It curled like a snake whenever it landed on a victim, each lash unerringly peeling away a layer of clothes or a patch of skin. This particular thief received twenty lashes, each aimed at his legs. When Aryi Senior halted his whip, there was nothing left covering the man's legs, and the people could tell by what they were seeing that it was a thief who was tied to the stake. The man nearly fell apart when he looked at his legs, virtually unscathed, but without a shred of clothing. He shouted, "I work for Chieftain Wangpo. I am not a thief. I was sent by my master to look for something."

The first young master of the Maichi family appeared in the courtyard. "And how did you go about looking for it? Yelling and screaming like this, or sneaking around?"

The people's hatred toward the enemy was already in place, like the silver in storage, and could be put to use whenever needed. The words were barely out of the future chieftain's mouth when the crowd began to yell, "Kill, kill, kill him!"

The man sighed. "Pity, such a pity."

"Feeling sorry for your head?" the future chieftain asked.

"No, I only regret I wasn't fast enough."

"That wouldn't have saved you."

The man laughed. "Did I really think I'd return alive when I came to do something like this?"

"You are a man worthy of the name. Tell me your wish and I'll grant it."

"Send my head back to my master so he'll know that I was loyal to the end. I won't close my eyes until I'm with him."

"A true man. I'd value you if only you'd worked for me."

The man's final request was that his head be rushed back because he didn't want to meet his master after the last glint was gone from his eyes. "That would be humiliating for a warrior."

The first young master ordered a fast steed brought over; and what remained was simple, very simple. The executioner unbound the man's upper body, leaving his feet tied to the stake, which would force even the strongest man to kneel. The executioner knew that the future chieftain, who had kindred feelings toward all brave warriors, would not want the man to suffer. So he raised his sword and swiftly sent the head rolling to the ground. Normally a severed head fell facedown and got a mouthful of dirt, but not this one; it faced the sky with a glint in its eyes and the trace of a mocking smile at the corners of its mouth. It looked like a victor's smile to me, but before I could get a closer look, it was wrapped in a piece of red cloth and carried off on horseback like a whirlwind. Still I sensed something unusual in that smile and wondered about it aloud. My brother laughed at me. "What can we expect that brain of yours to tell us?"

Before I had a chance to argue, Mother said, "His idiot mind is right once in a while. How can you be sure he's wrong this time?"

Generally good-natured, the first young master said, "It was nothing more than the smile of a slave after displaying his loyalty to a master."

Smart people are like that, good-natured, but unwilling to yield to others. Easy to get along with, they can also be very stubborn.

Surprisingly, Chieftain Wangpo sent more people over, two this time. We dealt with them in exactly the same fashion. As the still warm heads sped away on horseback, the future chieftain said softly, "This is becoming a problem."

Then Chieftain Wangpo's men came again, three of them this time. My brother burst out laughing. "Wangpo is using his slaves' heads to taunt us. All right, we'll lop off as many heads as he sends."

But we didn't return the last three heads. Instead we sent a fast steed with a messenger. The message was simple: after the required cordialities, Chieftain Maichi congratulated Chieftain Wangpo for all the loyal and brave slaves under his command. Chieftain Wangpo didn't respond, except to send people over to collect the heads. As

114

for the bodies, he asked that they be cremated on the riverbank after being blessed by lamas.

With all these spectacular events occurring, we hardly noticed that spring had arrived.

The seeds that had been collected were redistributed, to be sown in even vaster expanses.

15 Missed Cure ~

My family decided that I should go on an inspection tour of the Maichi territory.

It was a required lesson for every son of a chieftain, once he came of age.

Father told me that I could take anyone along, except for my personal maid. Diminutive Tharna cried all night, but there was nothing I could do. I picked my two young slaves, Sonam Tserang and the future executioner, Aryi. Father selected the rest of the group: the crippled steward, a twelve-man guard with a machine gun and ten rifles. There were also a groom, a lama for weather forecasts, a shoemaker to repair footwear, a shaman to test the food for poison, a musician, and two singers. That was all.

If not for this trip, I'd never have known how vast the Maichi territory was. And if not for this trip, I'd never have known how it felt to be a chieftain.

Headmen came out with their people to greet me at each stop. While we were still far off, they would sound the horns and begin singing. Then, once we drew near, the crowds would fall down on all fours amid the dust stirred up by my horses, not rising until I dismounted and waved. But my subjects would stir up the dust again as they rose and shook out their sleeves. At first, it made me choke, bringing servants running up to thump me on the back and give me water. Later I learned to walk past the crowds before telling them to get up. Sonam Tserang acted as my rifle bearer. I must say he really loved weapons. His face would light up whenever he held a rifle in his hand. I could hear his breathing grow heavy behind me. While the attendants and I were enjoying the delicacies presented to us, he preferred to stand behind me with his rifle.

We were always greeted in a grassy area near the headmen's fortresses, where tents were pitched especially for me to receive kowtows, enjoy good food, and watch singing and dancing. The headmen would also take advantage of the opportunity to introduce important members of their entourage: their stewards, the headmen of fortresses beneath them, brave warriors who had performed valiantly in combat, fortress elders, or craftsmen and workers with special talents and skills. Of course, there were also beautiful girls. I uttered a bunch of nonsense that they always found interesting, even if I didn't. I'd say whatever came into my head, whether it was worth saying or not; but the crippled steward made a point of telling me I shouldn't do that. He said it was important for the people living on Maichi land to hear blessings from and aspirations for the Maichi family. This he said in front of lots of people, which showed he didn't really understand me. "Shut up," I said softly. "We may live in the same fortress, but you cannot know what I'm thinking."

Then I turned to those kneeling before me. "Don't mind me. I'm the renowned idiot son of the chieftain."

Their response was proper silence.

Afterward, I told Sonam Tserang to come eat the food we couldn't finish: an entire goat's leg, full pots of wine, and whole strings of sausage. Somewhat more unusual was candy wrapped in colorful paper, imported from the Han area. I told Aryi to put some aside. Happily stuffed with all that food, Sonam Tserang belched and picked up the rifle to stand guard. When he declined my suggestion to get some rest, I said, "Then go take some target practice. Take Aryi with you and let him fire a few rounds too."

Even at something as simple as firing a rifle, Sonam Tserang wore himself out, since he would shoot only at moving targets. Aryi Junior quickly returned. "Sonam Tserang went hunting in the mountains."

I asked why he didn't go along.

He smiled. "Too tiring."

"You're only interested in targets tied to stakes, right?" I teased.

He just smiled.

Crisp gunfire from my rifle resounded up on the mountain.

At night, the headmen sent pretty girls to my sleeping quarters. During the trip, I had a different girl every night, which caused a

116

disturbance in the ranks. But the steward was able to finagle comparable treatment by making people fully aware that the chieftain's son was an idiot. They then treated him as the chieftain's actual representative, an important personage with real power. That worked pretty well, for he got his women and other gifts. I thought he was taking this idiot thing a bit far, so I said to him one day, "Are you afraid of Aryi?"

He replied, "His father is afraid of me."

"Maybe one day you'll fear him."

He hoped to get more out of me, but I changed the subject, acting like a real idiot. All in all, besides being enjoyable, this trip also helped me grow up fast. Now I could tell when I should surprise those who looked down on me by appearing to be the smartest person in the world. Then, once I'd frightened them into treating me as a smart person, I'd act stupid again. For instance, I took full advantage of the girls sent to me at night by the headmen. But when people said that the chieftain's son should be more discreet, one of my attendants would tell him that the chieftain's son, the one by the Han woman, was an idiot. Sonam Tserang, on the other hand, wasn't bothered by the sounds emerging from inside my tent. Carrying the rifle over his shoulder, he stood guard outside, as loyal as ever.

So, too, was Aryi. People always acted as if he were invisible as he roamed the area with that special look and demeanor of his. He always knew what people were saying, but I never asked him to tell me. When we traveled from one headman's land to the next, through long valleys, across high mountain passes, or past riverbanks, and the singers grew hoarse as our entourage stretched out in a long line under a blistering sun, Aryi would come riding up to my side. He'd clear his throat before volunteering that someone had said this and someone else had said that, always in a calm, objective manner, devoid of emotion. I often said to my two young slaves that they must become fast friends.

One evening, I was displeased with the girl sent by a particular headman. She seemed to have suffered some sort of humiliation. I asked why she was unhappy, but she wouldn't tell me. So I asked her if people had told her I was an idiot. She pouted. "Even if it's only for one night, I want the man I'm with to really like me. But you can't."

I asked her how she knew I couldn't.

She shifted her body, and said, "Everyone says you're an idiot."

That night I left the tent and told my slaves to go in and take her to bed. As I stood outside, I could hear Sonam Tserang panting and shouting like a trapped bear cub. The moon was high in the sky when he emerged. Then I told Aryi to go inside, where he made sounds like a fish out of water.

The next morning I said to the girl, "Those two will miss you."

She knelt at my feet, touching my boots with her head. "You may tell people you slept with the young master," I said.

But I realized that my actions might displease the headman, so I had to be on my guard. When the food and wine were brought out, I sent for the shaman to test the food with silver chopsticks and the wine with jade. If it had been poisoned, the chopsticks and jade would have changed color. The headman had a fit, as was apparent by how his neatly trimmed beard twitched. Finally, unable to control himself any longer, he rushed up to the table and stuffed bits of each dish into his mouth, nearly choking when he tried to swallow it all at once. After catching his breath, he said, "May the sun and the moon be my witnesses – no Maichi chieftain has ever doubted my loyalty before. I would rather have the young master kill me than behave like this."

I knew I had committed an unpardonable offense, but my concern evaporated when I was reminded that I was, after all, an idiot.

The crippled steward said, "I won't say anything about how you treat other headmen, but you must not do such things to Headman Songpa."

"Then why did you bring a shaman to test for poison?" I asked.

The steward turned to the headman. "It's all my fault, for not explaining things to the young master."

Headman Songpa did not eat another bite at the meal. He simply could not believe that my actions were those of an idiot. When tea was served afterward, the steward went to sit beside him. They kept looking at me, and I knew what they were saying.

"The young master is an idiot, born to a Han woman and the drunken master."

"Who can guarantee he doesn't have a smart person to help him stir up trouble?"

118

The steward laughed. "What are you talking about? A smart person helping him? That makes me laugh. Look at those two behind him, the one carrying a rifle and the other one who looks like a corpse. They're his trusted servants. Do they look smart to you?"

I was thinking that I had no reason to dislike Headman Songpa, since he was a Maichi loyalist. So, wanting to make him happy, I announced in a loud voice that we would spend an extra day on Headman Songpa's land, to make up for the pain I'd unintentionally caused him. His old face glowed, and I was happy to have made a decision that pleased my host.

But their euphoria quickly turned to astonishment when I announced, "Tomorrow we'll have a hunting party." The tent erupted in a loud buzzing, like a swarm of startled hornets.

Aryi whispered to me, "Young Master, hunting parties are not normally held in the spring."

Then I remembered. My God, this is the season when animals bear their young! If a life is taken, two or even more might follow. That is why hunting is forbidden in the spring. I had forgotten this important rule. Normally, when people treated me like an idiot, I felt the pleasure of having fooled them. This time I knew I was an idiot for sure, but I couldn't back down now, or I'd be seen as worse than an idiot.

As soon as the hunting party set out, I could tell that everyone was humoring me; with a host of people and dogs, we surrounded only a narrow ravine. Although we flushed out many animals, none fell, despite a hail of gunfire. I had no choice but to fire myself; after taking two roebucks, I turned and fired into the bushes. The hunting party ended in a hurry, and I ordered that the roebucks be fed to the dogs.

I did not enjoy the trip down the mountain.

Headman Songpa rode alongside me. Now he was convinced that there was something wrong with my head. A good man, he sought my forgiveness. "How could an old man like me treat you that way? Please don't bear a grudge, Young Master."

I wanted to say I was an idiot, after all, but the sincerity on his face made me swallow my words. Instead I said, "I'm not always like that."

My honesty spurred him to say, "I know, I know." He had some medicine he wanted to give me, which he begged me to accept. I said I would.

He handed me some colorful pills that an itinerant monk had given him. They were made from the wind on a lake and the light of a magic mountain. A strange prescription, to say the least. After leaving Headman Songpa's land, we traveled the whole day under a blazing sun, until my head buzzed like a beehive. I was lonely and I was bored, so, prompted by curiosity, I tossed a pill into my mouth, assuming that the light in it would pierce me like a sword and that the wind would rise in my stomach to send me off into the sky. But all that happened was that my mouth filled up with a fishy taste, followed by the sensation of fish swimming around in my stomach. Then I began to throw up, over and over, until I tasted my own bitter gall. Rubbing my back, the crippled steward said, "Can it be that you were right to be wary of him? Did he really poison the young master?"

"What would he gain from poisoning a cripple and an idiot?" I said, but I tossed the pills into the grass on the side of the road anyway.

16 Flowering Ears ∽

We had inspected only half the Maichi territory by the end of spring.

When summer arrived, we reached the southern border, and now would have to turn north. The steward told me that the inspection wouldn't end until the fall, when harvesting began.

Before us now was the southern boundary, where Maichi land bordered Wangpo's. It was there that I received a message from home. The chieftain told me to stay at the border awhile longer. His intention was clear: he wanted Chieftain Wangpo to attack us, a small band of people led by an idiot son and a crippled steward. But Wangpo was no fool, and did not want to provoke the mighty Chieftain Maichi to give the latter an excuse to destroy him. We had intentionally crossed over to his side, but his people merely followed our movements without showing their faces.

One rainy morning, the crippled steward said, "We won't go out today, since they won't dare take any action. We can rest. Tomorrow we'll set out for the north."

As the rain fell, the groom gave the horses new shoes, while the guards cleaned their rifles. Two singers sang back and forth, one high, the other lower. Unfolding a piece of paper, the steward wrote a long letter to Chieftain Maichi to report the situation at the border, while I stayed in bed and listened to raindrops falling on the tent.

The rain stopped abruptly at about noon. Out of boredom, I ordered everyone to mount up. We crossed the border at the same place as before, just as the sun broke through the clouds to beat down on our backs. Our feet were sodden, so we sat down to dry our wet boots on a patch of low grass.

Chieftain Wangpo's riflemen were hidden in the trees, their sights trained on our backs. Having a gun aimed at you is like being bitten by an insect – it's a prickly feeling, slightly painful. But they didn't dare open fire, and we knew exactly where they were hiding. Our machine gun was loaded and ready; at the slightest movement, a hailstorm of bullets would be upon them. Unconcerned, I was able to take in the scenery around me. The best time to view mountains is when the sky has cleared after a rain. Only at such times are things dressed in the brightest colors, bathed in the most delightful light. Every time I'd ridden past here before, I'd seen bright, beautiful flowers beneath roadside pines, but today they looked especially pretty, so I pointed them out to the steward. "Those are our poppy flowers," he said.

That's exactly what he said: "Our poppy flowers."

It was immediately clear that they were indeed the flowers that had made the Maichi family so powerful. There were three plants, standing tall in the sunlight, with shimmering flowers. The crippled steward deployed our forces before we walked toward the flowers. The riflemen lying in wait opened fire. *Pow! Pow! Pow! Pow!* Four loud shots, like someone beating a cracked gong. The riflemen must have been trembling with fear, for they ought to have done better than merely kill one man and wound another with their four shots. The poison-testing shaman fell facedown, clutching a clump of grass. One of the singers squatted down, holding his shoulder as blood seeped between his fingers. Stillness reigned for a moment before our men returned fire. It sounded like a true hailstorm, after which everything went deathly quiet in the woods, except for the sounds of shattered leaves falling slowly to the ground. All four riflemen lay dead beneath the tall trees, curled up as if afraid of the cold.

I can't recall why, but instead of simply pulling out the poppies, I had my men dig in the ground with their bayonets. Words cannot adequately describe what we found. Beneath the poppy plants were three square wooden boxes, inside of which rested three decomposing heads. The plants were growing from the ears of the heads. If you'll recall, we'd beheaded the poppy thieves and returned their heads to Chieftain Wangpo. Well, the thieves had stuck the seeds in their ears before being caught; Chieftain Wangpo had obtained his seeds from the heads of men who had sacrificed their lives for him.

And he had memorialized his heroes with flowers blooming from their heads.

Canceling our planned northbound trip, we rushed back to the estate. On the way, the steward and I agreed that the news would certainly surprise everyone.

But the extent of their surprise, particularly my brother's, went far beyond what we had expected.

That smart person jumped out of his chair, shouting, "Flowers blooming in dead men's ears! How can that be?"

Up till then, he'd always treated me with kindness. In a word, no brother in the Maichi family history had ever been so kind to a younger brother as he. But that day was different. He raised a disdainful finger to me. "What does an idiot like you know?" Then he ran up to the steward, yelling, "I think you both had a bad dream!"

I couldn't help feeling a little sorry for him. He was the smartest person in the world, his only weakness being that he was afraid that sometimes he didn't come across as smart enough. Though he normally seemed quite blasé, that didn't mean he was uncaring; rather, it showed that he understood and could manage things without really trying. Seeing the pained expression on his face, I honestly wished I'd had a bad dream, one from which I'd awaken to find myself still in bed in a tent at our southern border, with the rain falling outside.

But it was real, all right.

I clapped my hands. Sonam Tserang entered and opened the bundles he carried.

The chieftain's wife quickly covered her nose with a silk handkerchief. Tharna didn't dare do that, but I heard her gag and choke as a stench filled the room. Everyone slowly approached the decomposing heads. My brother tugged at the leaves to prove that someone had planted the flowering poppies in the ears. In doing so, he lifted up the rotting head and shook the plant. A startled shout erupted from the chieftain's wife. Then we watched as the head disintegrated and crumbled to the floor. Now we could trace the roots deep into the ear canals, from where tendrils grew and spread into the gray mass.

Turning to my brother, Father said, "It looks more as if it grew by itself than as if someone had put there."

My brother stretched out his neck as he said with obvious distress, "I think so too."

Monpa Lama, who had been quiet till then, spoke up. We called him "lama" only because he liked the term of address, for he was actually a shaman skilled in incantations and astrology. He asked me which direction the buried heads were facing. I said north, in the direction of Chieftain Maichi's land. Then he asked if they were buried under trees. I said yes. That's it, he said. Our enemy not only stole our seeds, but also cursed us with the most malicious sorcery possible. He turned to my brother. "Don't look at me like that, First Young Master. My livelihood comes from the Maichi family, so I must tell everything I know."

The chieftain's wife said, "Don't be afraid, Lama. Tell us everything."

"What kind of curse did they put on us?" the chieftain asked.

Monpa Lama said, "I cannot say until I've seen what was placed near the heads. Did the second young master bring back everything?"

Of course we'd brought back everything.

Monpa Lama perfumed the room with fine White Cloud incense before leaving to study what we had brought back. My brother left with him. The chieftain then asked the steward how we had discovered the heads. The steward gave a vivid description, saying quite a bit about the important role played by the second young master. The chieftain looked at my mother, then at me in a completely new way. Then he sighed. I understood what that meant: Damn, in the end, he's still an idiot. But all he said was, "You'll inspect the north next year. I'll give you more attendants."

"Aren't you going to thank your father?" Mother asked.

I sat there, saying nothing.

Then Monpa Lama returned to report his interpretation: "Chieftain Wangpo has cursed our poppies with destruction by egg-sized hail at the height of their growing season."

The chieftain let out a long sigh. "All right. If it's a fight he wants, then that's what he'll get. It starts today."

The discussion began, and I promptly fell asleep.

It was nearly dawn when I awoke. Someone had covered me with a blanket. Reminded of something, I waved Monpa Lama over. With a smile, he asked, "What has the young master seen now?"

I told him about the pills Headman Songpa had given me, the ones I'd thrown away. The news elicited a shout: "What sort of magic pills have you thrown away? Who has the ability to make pills with wind and light nowadays?" He added, "Young Master, did you throw away all the pills without trying one first?"

"No, I didn't."

"Then you threw up, feeling as if worms were crawling out from your belly, right?"

"Not worms," the steward said. "The young master said it was fish."

Stomping his feet, the lama sighed. "That's it! That's it! You'd have been cured if you had thrown up everything inside." He was, after all, a lama, and had something to say about everything. "Fine," he said. "It didn't work out for you, but we should have no problem dealing with Chieftain Wangpo."

I asked Father, "Does that mean war?"

He nodded.

"Let's call it the War of the Poppies," I said.

They just glanced at me; too bad there was no one to write that down.

Back when the first Maichi chieftain came to power, a historian had written down what the chieftain said or did. That is how we knew what the first three generations of the Maichi family did, what they ate, and what they said. Then there came a fellow who recorded things he shouldn't have, and the fourth Maichi chieftain had had him killed. From then on, we'd had no historian, so we never knew what our other ancestors had been up to. The hereditary position of historian had begun at the same time as that of executioner; the executioner was still around, the historian was long gone. Sometimes it got into that idiot head of mine that I'd have a historian if I ever became chieftain. It would sure be interesting to read the records every once in a while to see what I'd said or done. Once I even said to Sonam Tserang, "One day you'll be my historian."

That slave of mine immediately cried out, "Then I'll swap with Aryi. He can be your historian, and I'll be the executioner."

If we had a historian now, he'd be standing behind me, licking the tip of his pencil to record that terrific name: War of the Poppies.

17 War of the Poppies ～

Mother said, "The seeds of all plants eventually wind up in other places, so we shouldn't be so concerned. Even if they're not stolen, the wind will blow them or birds will carry them away. It's just a matter of time."

Father asked if she thought we should just do nothing and watch it happen.

The chieftain's wife pointed out that we could use that as an excuse to attack the enemy if we wanted, but it didn't do any good to worry. She also said we should ask for Special Emissary Huang's support if we decided to have a war over the poppies.

For once Father did not object to her idea.

It was also the first time that a letter from the chieftain's family was written by the mistress, and in Chinese. As she was about to seal the letter, my brother, who was going to deliver it, said, "That won't be necessary. I can't read the Han people's language."

"I wasn't worried about you reading it," Mother said cordially. "I just wanted to show him that the Maichi family knows its correspondence etiquette."

Before our messenger returned, we received reliable information that a large group of shamans working for Chieftain Wangpo was gathering at the southern border to prepare curses for the Maichi family.

An extraordinary war was about to begin.

Our shamans built an altar on a small hill near the executioner's house. Led by Monpa Lama, they dressed in colorful clothes and strange-looking hats, and brought over countless ritual vessels and numerous sacrificial items for the gods and spirits. There was every type of weapon used throughout history, from stone knives to stone axes and stone-tipped arrows, from catapults to muskets. The only items missing from the list were our machine guns and rifles. Monpa Lama told me that the spirits he invited wouldn't know how to use new-style weapons. He kept an eye to the heavens as he spoke to me. It was a clear day, with light clouds floating in a sky as blue as the ocean. The lamas paid undivided attention to these clouds to see if they abruptly changed color. White clouds were auspicious. The shamans on the enemy side, meanwhile, were trying everything possible to infuse the clouds with booming thunder, elongated bolts of lightning, and countless hailstones.

One day, clouds just like that actually drifted over from the south.

The shamans' battle was more heated than any waged with knives or guns.

As soon as the dark clouds appeared in the southern sky, Monpa Lama put on a gigantic warrior's helmet and appeared as a character out of a stage play. He was carrying all sorts of triangular and round ritual flags, from which he picked out one to wave, summoning all manner of noisemakers: snakeskin tubes, drums, *suonas*, and bells. The hill was alive with sound. Muskets were fired into the air. The dark clouds stopped above our heads, where they roiled and raged. They were dark in the center and on the edges, colored by the curses, while thunder rumbled overhead. The darkness was finally driven off by our shamans' incantations, by the sacrificial offerings on the altar, and by our weapons, which, though they may have looked like toys, were powerful amulets against spirits and demons. The Maichis' poppies, the estate, and the crowds of people were once again bathed in bright sunlight. Wielding a special sword, sweat-soaked, panting Monpa Lama told Father that the hail in the clouds had turned to rain, and he was waiting for the chieftain's order to send it earthward. The strain on his face made him look as if he were holding up the rain with his sword.

With a stern look, Chieftain Maichi said, "Go ahead, so long as you can promise it's rain."

Monpa Lama let out a long whistle and sheathed his sword, which immediately stopped the noise on the hill.

A wind blew over, but the dark clouds no longer roiled like a tortured stomach. Instead, they spread out across the sky before sending down a torrent of rain. We sat under the sun and watched the rain fall nearby. Monpa Lama, who had crumpled to the ground, was helped into the tent to rest after his helmet had been removed. I ran over to look at the helmet, a hefty thing that weighed about thirty pounds. I was surprised that he was strong enough to leap around in it while waving the sword to display his magic.

The chieftain went into Monpa Lama's tent, where the young shamans and future shamans were wiping sweat off the current shaman's face. "You deserve to sweat," Father said. "My son had no idea your helmet was so heavy."

Monpa Lama was still so weak that he merely said hoarsely, "I only forgot its weight when the gods I summoned arrived."

At that moment, the sounds of Living Buddha Jeeka's monks – those with no magic skills – reciting sutras grew louder. To me that seemed utterly useless. The hail had already turned to rain and fallen to the ground. Monpa Lama said, "I'll bet Chieftain Wangpo's people are also reciting sutras, thinking they have succeeded."

The chieftain said, "We've won."

The lama cautioned, "This was only the first round." Then, in order to maintain the power of his magic, he told us not to go down the mountain and to stay away from women and other unclean things.

The second round began with our turn to send hail their way.

The magic was spectacular, but I was bored – the sky was as clear as if it had been washed, and I couldn't see any meteorological changes. Three days later we received a report that hail the size of chicken eggs had pounded Chieftain Wangpo's land, leveling his crops and sending a flood to wash away his orchards. As a southern chieftain, Wangpo had no pastureland; instead he prided himself on orchards filled with thousands of trees. Now his opposition to the Maichi family had cost him those orchards. But we could not know what had happened to his poppies, since none of us knew how many he'd planted or where. Maybe they had disappeared from his land altogether.

Father announced to all that we would attack Chieftain Wangpo as soon as my brother returned from the Han area.

As we were enjoying a fine meal on the hilltop, the tinkling of brass bells sounded in the wind. The chieftain told us to guess who was coming. We all tried, but with no success. Monpa Lama sighed after throwing twelve white pebbles and twelve black pebbles onto the chessboard before him. He said he didn't know the identity of the newcomer but was sure that he was having a difficult time, since his birthstone had fallen on a bad space. When we walked out of the tent, we saw a pointy head slowly emerge from below the hill, followed by the pointy ears of a mule. It had been a long time since we'd last seen him; people said he was going mad.

He came right up to us.

He was thin and pallid. The worn edges of his sutras peeked out from his mule's back.

The chieftain raised his hat to him.

But he returned the greeting by saying to Father, "I do not want to talk to the chieftain today, except to say that I hope he will not interfere with the internal affairs of our Buddhist faith."

The chieftain smiled. "As you wish, Master."

Of course, Father added, "Isn't the master going to preach the finest religion in the world anymore?"

"No," the young monk shook his head. "I cannot blame a savage chieftain for refusing the wise and benevolent sweet dew, because it is those in cassocks who have ruined our religion."

After that, he walked up to Living Buddha Jeeka and, baring his right arm, placed a yellow cockscomb hat on his head. It was a gesture we knew well: an invitation to engage in a religious debate. In our religious history, many monks had gained the support of powerful people by winning such debates when they first arrived in Tibet from India. The ensuing debate lasted a very long time, until the Living Buddha's face turned as red as cow's liver. Even though it looked as if he'd lost, his disciples all declared the Living Buddha the victor. They also accused the arrogant newcomer of attacking the chieftain by saying that the world did not need chieftains. He said that Lhasa should be the only center for black-haired Tibetans, and there shouldn't be any barbaric overlords who were so cozy with the eastern people.

Chieftain Maichi, who had been listening all along, spoke up.

"Disaster will fall on your head, you who have come from the Holy City."

The man looked up at the sky, his eyes brimming with tears, as if he could see the shadow of his misfortune there. He refused to respond to the chieftain. "You can kill me," he said at last, "but I want you to know that I won the debate."

When Wangpo Yeshi, this monk of the new sect, was bound up, Living Buddha Jeeka looked sad, but that was nothing but a tiny tremor in his conscience. Later, Father repeatedly said that he would have let Wangpo Yeshi go if the Living Buddha had spoken up on his behalf. No one knew if he meant it. But that day, Living Buddha Jeeka, who may well have felt sorry for his opponent, said nothing. That was the day I stopped liking the Living Buddha, who, as far as I was concerned, was not a true Living Buddha at all. When a Living Buddha stops being a Living Buddha, he is nothing. Monpa wasn't really a lama but a powerful shaman who liked to have people call him one. What he said to the chieftain that day was "It's not a good idea to kill anyone at a time like this, especially someone wearing a cassock."

So the chieftain ordered this fellow who claimed that chieftains should be eliminated from the land thrown into the dungeon.

We stayed on the hill.

Monpa Lama performed several divinations, all of which showed that in the final round Chieftain Wangpo would attack someone in Chieftain Maichi's family. The effect of the curse would be achieved by offering menstrual blood and other filthy things to ghosts whose evil deeds had prevented them from rebirth. Monpa Lama and Father even reached an agreement that someone in the family would have to be sacrificed if we could not withstand the attack. I thought it could only be me, since sacrificing an idiot would be the smallest price to pay. My head began to ache that night, and that prompted me to think that the other side had begun its magic work. I said to Father, who stood beside me, "They've found the right person, since I was the one who discovered their evil scheme. They would have focused on me even if I weren't to be your sacrifice."

Cradling my icy hands, Father said, "It's a good thing your mother isn't here, or she'd be in agony."

Monpa Lama worked feverishly to spray clean water blessed with incantations all over me. He said it was a crystal shield to prevent the demons from entering my body. In the second half of the night, the smoky source of my splitting head finally drifted away in the moonlight.

Monpa Lama said, "I'm happy to say I did not perform my magic in vain. The young master can now get a good night's sleep."

But I couldn't. As I lay in my tent, I saw a crescent moon rise higher and higher until it reached the height of the twinkling Venus. Just before dawn, I suddenly saw my own future. It wasn't very clear, but I believed that the blurry sight heralded a good destiny for me. Then I fell asleep. By the time I woke up, I'd forgotten everything.

Rising from bed, I looked down at the estate, enveloped in the morning sunlight. I saw sparkling silver water flowing toward the gate before making a sharp turn as it reached a spot where the riverbed was composed of red rock. I also saw people who had stayed behind moving around on the verandas. Everything looked normal, but I sensed that something was about to happen.

I didn't want to reveal that to anyone. I had been the first to discover the poppies blooming on someone else's land, and that had nearly cost me my life. So I went back inside the tent to go to bed. I couldn't sleep. After all that had happened, I'd grown up a bit. Light was beginning to make inroads into my muddled brain. So I got up and went back outside, where the dew on the grass soaked my feet. I saw Wangpo Yeshi's mule grazing quietly. They were planning to kill and offer it as a sacrifice. I went over and untied the tether, then slapped it on its haunch. It walked leisurely up the mountain, stopping occasionally to graze. I announced to everyone that it was a liberated mule.

Father asked me which I liked better, the mule or its owner.

That was not an easy question to answer, so I squinted to look at the sunlit emerald-green hills. If I liked the mule better, it was because it was such an obedient animal. I couldn't think of a single reason to like that lama, who had never behaved in a likable manner. But I liked him anyway.

Father said, "If you really like the mule, and wish to spare its life, then you should get the Living Buddha to intone a sutra for it. You must also put up a piece of red cloth and drape an amulet over it before you can actually consider the animal 'liberated.'"

"Even a mule wouldn't want Living Buddha Jeeka to intone sutras for it, let alone the lama." That morning I announced loudly to everyone on the hill, "Don't you know that both the mule and its owner have little regard for Living Buddha Jeeka?"

In an unusually good mood, Father said, "If you like the lama so much, I'll let him go."

"He wants to read," I said. "Give him back all his sutras."

"No prisoner wants to read."

"He does."

Yes, at that moment I imagined I could see the proselytizer of the new sect sitting in a bare cell with absolutely nothing to do.

"All right," Father said. "I'll send someone to see if he really wants to read."

It turned out that Wangpo Yeshi was dying for something to read. He sent a message of thanks to the young master, who he said could read his mind.

Father looked at me pensively all the rest of that day.

Monpa Lama said that our opponent had failed in the weather contest, and that if he was not prepared to surrender, we could expect him to move against us. He repeatedly cautioned us to remain clean. What he meant by that was for Father and me not to go down the mountain and have any contact with women. For us that was no problem. My brother, on the other hand, would have presented a major problem, if he'd been around. For him, the idea of avoiding women for even a few days was unthinkable. The world, for all its magnificence, would turn into a pile of dog shit to him. Fortunately, he was off in the Han area. Monpa Lama shared my view. "I can handle the weather," he said, "but my magic isn't up to the task of manipulating people. Luckily, First Young Master isn't here. That makes things easier."

But I already sensed that something was wrong, and I said so to Monpa Lama, who told me that he had similar feelings. So we walked around the area; the important people and things were fine, and so were the less important people.

I said, "Down the mountain, the estate."

From the mountaintop, the house looked strong and impregnable, but I had a nagging fear that something bad had occurred there.

Monpa Lama made a series of strange gestures with his fingers, and was puzzled by something. He said, "Yes, something's wrong, but I don't know who is at the center of it. It may be the chieftain's woman, but not your mother."

"Wouldn't that be Yangzom, the former wife of Headman Tratra?"

"I was waiting for you to say it," he said. "I didn't know what to call her."

"You wanted me to say it because I'm an idiot, right?"

"I guess so."

It turned out that something had indeed happened to Third Mistress, Yangzom.

Back when she discovered she was pregnant with the chieftain's child, she'd taken over the room and told him to spend all his nights with Second Mistress. In this regard, she was a lot like barking hounds in a hunting party, delivering the prey to the hunters. I hadn't seen her once since then, but I knew she was there because I saw servants emptying her brass chamber pot and taking up food on a silver tray each morning. Those were hard times for her, because she was convinced that someone wanted to harm her unborn child. But judging from what was delivered to and taken out of her room, I could tell that her appetite was holding up well. Maybe because her desire to protect the baby was so strong, she felt that her belly was the only safe place for it, and so it had stayed inside longer than normal. Then, during the previous night, as we slept on the mountain, Chieftain Wangpo's shaman found a crack in our security. Yangzom lost her hold on the baby; stillborn, it was said to be black all over, as if poisoned by wolfsbane.

That was the only price the Maichi family paid in this peculiar war.

The baby died at sunrise, and nothing was left on the hilltop by that afternoon, as if it had been swept clean by a whirlwind. Since it was the chieftain's flesh and blood, it was taken to the temple, where Living Buddha Jeeka intoned sutras for it. Three days later it was given a water burial.

Then Yangzom appeared before us, her head covered by a bright scarf.

Everyone said she was prettier than before, but no longer appeared to be walking in a dream, as when she and Father had been madly in love. Dressed in a long skirt, she went upstairs and knelt before Second Mistress. "Mistress, I've come to pay my respects."

"Please, get up," Mother said. "You're cured now, and we sisters have plenty of time to talk."

Yangzom banged her head on the floor. "Elder Sister."

Helping her up, Mother repeated, "You're cured now."

Yangzom said, "It was just like a dream, but so much more exhausting."

Now, finally, she was truly the chieftain's woman. That evening, Second Mistress told the chieftain to sleep with his third wife. But he merely said, "It's no fun anymore, now that the raging fire has died out."

Mother later told Yangzom, "We don't want him to start burning like that again."

Blushing like a bride, Yangzom said nothing.

Mother added, "If he does, it won't be for me, and it won't be for you."

Five ～

18 Tongue ～

I was playing chess in the yard out front.

It was a simple six-piece game. You break off a branch and draw squares in the dirt, then find six small stones. The rules are easy to understand. When you have two pieces in a straight line, and your opponent has only one, you gobble up his piece. Whoever gobbles up all six pieces is the winner. It's as simple as two ants gobbling up one ant or two people killing one person, but it is an ancient truth, and it works in wars between chieftains. We always asked how many people an enemy had deployed. If the number was smaller than ours, we attacked and gobbled them up. If their numbers were greater than ours, we held back until we had greater numbers, then attacked and gobbled them up. But this strategy had lost its effect by the time I was playing the game. During the second stage of the War of the Poppies, the Maichi family used advanced weapons and minimal manpower to create a whirlwind of fire that nearly swept across all of Chieftain Wangpo's land. The small quantity of poppies growing from seeds stolen by Wangpo's people was turned to ashes that floated up into the sky.

Another spring arrived.

Now, let me see, maybe it wasn't the second spring, but many springs later. But what does that matter? The only thing the chieftain's family had more of than silver was time. Lots and lots of time, maybe too much time. We awoke in the morning, and then waited for it to get dark; we looked forward to harvesting as soon we sowed the seeds. Our territory was so vast that time itself seemed never-ending.

Yes, our vast territory gave us the feeling that time was never-ending.

And, yes, the combination of vast territory and never-ending time gave us the feeling that the Maichi empire was unshakable and would last forever.

Yes, everything was unreal. From a distance, it all looked like a floating dreamscape.

Ah, well, let me return to that springtime morning. The sun had been up for a while and the air was filled with a watery fragrance. Distant snowy mountains and nearby trees and crops, moistened by the predawn dew, glistened in the morning sun, looking vibrant and refreshing.

For the longest time, I'd been obsessed with the six-piece chess game, since I'd had so much trouble mastering it.

Normally, I'd get up early and, after breakfast, walk out in the sunlight to sit beneath a walnut tree at the edge of the yard just beyond our gate. After watching the sun climb above the mountain for a while, I'd pick up a branch and draw a chessboard on the damp ground. I'd be thinking about the heated battles with Chieftain Wangpo and all that had happened during the War of the Poppies as servants walked past, busy at work. No one came up to say, "Young Master, let's play a game." These were people resigned to their fate. You could see it in their gloomy eyes, in the way they averted their gaze. I generally played with my young servants. Sonam Tserang liked to work at night, so he didn't have to get up early; a sunrise meant nothing to him. He'd come up to me without bothering to wash up first, the pungent smell of the servants' quarters still clinging to him. Aryi, our future executioner, was just the opposite. He'd get up early and sit on the hill by his house to watch the sunrise after breakfast. Then he'd walk slowly down the hill when he saw me drawing the board in the yard.

But this morning was different.

My young slaves were nowhere to be seen after I finished drawing the board. But Choedak the silversmith, Dolma's husband, walked past, then turned and came back. "How about a game, Young Master?"

I emptied the pieces from a bag, saying, "You play the white ones. That's the color of silver, and you are, after all, a silversmith." I told him to start.

He moved a piece but did not occupy the critical center square. So I rushed forward and, after moving right, then left, quickly won

135

the game. As we were arranging the pieces for another game, he said abruptly, "My woman thinks about you all the time."

I didn't say anything. I was the young master, so she ought to be thinking about me. But of course, that wasn't the main reason I kept quiet.

He said, "Dolma never says so, but I know she misses you. She even dreams about you."

I still didn't say anything, except to tell him that he should treat her well, since she had learned everything from the masters and the mistress. If he didn't, it would be a loss of face for the family. I said, "I think you two should have a baby."

As his face reddened, he said, "She told me to come talk to you. She wanted Young Master to know that we *are* going to have a baby."

I didn't know why she wanted me to know, since it couldn't be the idiot young master's offspring. Not knowing how to respond, I merely said, "Go tell Dolma that the young master wants her to have twin boys." I told the silversmith that if she had twins, I'd give each of them five ounces of silver for their father to make into longevity chains. And I'd have Monpa Lama bless the chains before putting them around their tiny necks.

He said, "Young Master is truly a good person. No wonder Dolma misses you so much."

"You may go now," I said.

Just as I said that, Aryi, our future executioner, came down the hill and stood behind the silversmith, who bumped into him as soon as he got to his feet; Choedak's face paled.

In our land, the chieftain gave the orders and the executioner carried them out. Some people lost an eye, some lost an arm, some lost their lives. But instead of blaming the chieftain, most harbored hatred toward the executioner, whom they all feared. The silversmith had never been so close to an executioner, and this encounter drained the blood from his face. He looked at me nervously, clearly asking, without saying a word, "Have I done anything wrong for you to summon the executioner?"

His reaction amused me, so I said, "You're scared. Why's that? Don't be."

But he wouldn't admit it. "I'm not scared. I've done nothing wrong."

"No, you haven't, but you're still scared."

His face completely devoid of emotion, Aryi said in a calm voice, "Actually, it's the chieftain's rules you're scared of, not me."

The silversmith laughed at Aryi's words, though his face was as pale as ever. "You're probably right," he said.

"All right," I said, "you may go now."

He left.

Aryi and I began to play. He played hard, not giving an inch, and I quickly lost several games in a row. By the time the sun had risen overhead, my forehead was beaded with sweat. "Damn you, Aryi," I said. "You're a slave, so why are you so intent on beating me?"

I had to admit that Aryi was pretty smart. He looked at my face, then straight into my eyes to see if I was really angry. But my mood that day was as good as the weather. "You're the master," he said, "and I must obey all your orders. Does that include losing at chess?"

I reset the board. "Very well. Come beat me again."

"Someone's going to be punished tomorrow," he said.

That caught me by surprise. Normally I knew everything that happened on our land, such as who violated which rules and what the punishment would be. But I hadn't heard a thing about this one, so I said, "Come on, let's play. There are too many people on our land for you to kill them all."

Aryi said, "I know you like this one, so I hope you won't hate my father and me because we have to punish him. Everyone else does."

Now I knew who would be punished.

"Do you want to go see him, Young Master?"

I knew I couldn't hate this pale-faced youngster who spoke in a monotone. It was the Maichi family who had made him that way. "No one is allowed to visit the dungeon without permission," I said.

He held up a wooden tally decorated with a tiger's head. The ebony figure had been seared into the wood by a branding iron. It was a pass to the dungeon cells. Before inflicting punishment, the executioner always went to the dungeon to check on the prisoner's physical and mental condition so he could be sure of himself when the time came. He preferred to do a nice, neat job, unless, of course, the chieftain wanted the prisoner to suffer.

So we went to the dungeon, where the man who wanted to spread his new sect in our land was reading by the window. When the guard opened the cell door for us, I thought the fellow would ignore us by pretending that he was engrossed in his reading. That's what people with a bit of knowledge usually tend to do.

But not Wangpo Yeshi, who put his book away as soon as I walked in. "Look who's here," he said very calmly, the trace of a sarcastic smile at the corners of his mouth.

"Is the lama reading sutras?" I asked.

"I'm reading history." A while back, Living Buddha Jeeka had given him a book written long ago by a crazy lama. Apparently, it was a very interesting book. He said, "Your Living Buddha told me to die in peace, that he would rein in my spirit to serve as the Maichi family temple guard."

I wasn't really listening to him at that moment, for my attention had been caught by the sound of gushing water in the river just beyond the window. It was a sound I liked. The young lama gazed at me silently for a long time. "Before my head bids farewell to my body," he said at last, "I'd like to take this opportunity to thank the young master."

He knew I was the one who'd had the sutras sent to him, and that I'd set his mule free. But rather than fill my ears with praise for me or complaints against others, he handed me a small pamphlet whose inscription was gilded with gold powder that he'd taken as alms. He made a point to tell me that nothing in the pamphlet was unacceptable to the Maichi family. It was simply a record of the Buddha's teachings that every sect must follow. As I held it in my hand, I felt something burn in my heart. I'd heard that such books were filled with wisdom and benevolent thoughts, so I asked this man who was soon to be executed if this book included such things.

"Yes," he said, "it does."

I asked him if those of other sects, such as that of Living Buddha Jeeka, also read this book. His affirmative answer left me even more bewildered. "Then why do you hate each other?" I asked.

That must have cut to the heart of the matter, because he was quiet for a long time. So I turned my attention again to the water beneath the cliff as it raged eastward. Wangpo Yeshi sighed. "Everyone says the young master is an idiot, but I know you are smart. You are smart because you're an idiot." He added, "Please forgive a dying man this lack of respect."

I wanted to say I forgave him, but felt it wouldn't mean much, so I kept quiet, reminding myself that he was about to die. The sound of thundering water rushed into my head again, yet I still managed to commit everything he said to memory. It went something like this: His failure to spread his belief at our place had caused him to ponder many questions all winter long. They were not questions for monks, but he could not help himself. In the end, he no longer harbored any hatred for other sects, although he still had to face the hatred directed at him by followers of those other sects. In the end he asked, "Instead of teaching us to love, why must religion teach us to hate?"

When Aryi and I were back in the yard, I must say how much better it felt out there than in the dungeon, whose long corridors and spiral staircases were unbearably damp and dank.

Aryi said, "Tomorrow the job will be mine."

"It will be your first time. Are you afraid?"

He shook his head as his pale face blushed like a little girl's. "If you're an executioner, such things do not frighten you. They do only if you aren't an executioner."

That was very clever, very philosophical, deserving of being recorded as a saying of the executioner. Within a very short period of time, I'd heard two interesting phrases. The first had come from the dungeon: Instead of teaching us to love, why must religion teach us to hate? Now Aryi had given me another. Both were insightful, worthy of being written down. But many such intelligent phrases have disappeared like scattered dust and dying smoke throughout history.

At dinner, after the candles were lit, and before the servants had brought out the food, I took the opportunity to ask Father, "Are we executing someone tomorrow?"

That must have shocked him, for he belched loudly. He did that only when he'd eaten too much or when he was surprised.

Father said, "I know you like that fellow, which is why I didn't tell you about executing him." He added, "I'm prepared to reduce the sentence if you plead his case."

Dinner was served, so I didn't say any more.

The first course was larded mashed potatoes, followed by

lamb steaks, with honeyed barley cakes called *tsampas*, as the entrée.

The food was piled up before us in small hills, which we slowly chipped away at as the meal progressed. When her turn came, Tharna barely touched her food. Later that night I said to her, "You have to eat more or your hips won't flesh out."

She started to cry, sobbing and saying I didn't like her anymore.

"I'm only talking about your hips," I said. "I wonder what you'd sound like if I started in on your breasts."

At this she cried even louder, which brought Mother into the room. After delivering a loud slap, which shut Tharna up, the mistress told me to go to sleep and ordered the girl to kneel by my bed. We generally didn't care much about girls like her, and whether or not they were unhappy didn't bother us. If she wanted to cry, let her, since she'd stop as soon as she realized it accomplished nothing. But my mother came from a race that cared greatly about women.

I fell asleep amid the tongue-lashing she was giving Tharna. I was soon drenched in sweat, caught up in a dream. I was raising a sword against Wangpo Yeshi, who was tied to the stake. I screamed and woke up, only to discover Tharna still kneeling on the floor. I asked her why she hadn't come to bed. She said the mistress had told her she couldn't sleep until I woke up and forgave her. So I forgave her. She was ice-cold when she climbed into bed. Never very warm to begin with, now she felt as cold as a river rock. Naturally, I warmed her up fast.

When I woke up the next morning, the thought that we were about to kill Wangpo Yeshi came to me. Suddenly, I regretted not pleading for him the night before, when it would have made a difference. Now it was too late.

The long wails of an ox horn sounded on the estate.

People drifted over from fortresses scattered throughout the valley. They led hard, dull lives, and watching an execution was welcome entertainment. From the chieftain's perspective, he needed the people to have an understanding and acceptance of killing; each execution was a form of education. The people quickly filled the yard with their bobbing black heads, talking excitedly, coughing and spitting all over the place.

Then the prisoner was led out to be bound to the stake.

Wangpo Yeshi said to the chieftain, "I don't want your Living Buddha to pray for me."

The chieftain said, "Then you can pray for yourself. But I don't really want to take your life."

The steward added, "Why did you turn your tongue loose in an attack on the religion we have followed for generations?"

The first young master, who had returned from the Han area, then announced the chieftain's decision: "You harbor crazy thoughts in your head, but we find only your tongue to be responsible for the nonsense you've spouted."

This man, who had come to our place to spread his great religious teachings, was about to lose his clever tongue instead. He had been calmly awaiting his execution, but now, after hearing the new verdict, sweat dripped from his forehead. Similar shiny beads of sweat hung from the tip of Aryi Junior's nose, since this would be the first punishment he inflicted. Not a sound emerged from the crowd as the executioner removed some special knives from his leather pouch. They were narrow and curved like a human mouth. Human mouths come in all sizes, and so did the executioner's knives. Aryi Junior held up a few against the proselytizer's mouth to see which one best suited him. It was so quiet in the yard that everyone heard Wangpo Yeshi ask, "What were you doing when you came to the dungeon yesterday? Why didn't you try to find the right knife then?"

I thought Aryi would be frightened, since this was, after all, his first time. His face was a bit flushed, but he was not afraid. "I did, but I was looking at your neck. Now the benevolent master wants only your tongue."

"You'd better keep your hand away from my mouth, because I cannot guarantee I won't bite you."

"There's no point in hating me."

Wangpo Yeshi sighed. "You're right. I shouldn't have so much hatred in my heart."

At that moment, Aryi Senior walked up behind the stake and looped a rope tightly around the prisoner's neck, causing Wangpo Yeshi to stick out his tongue as his body straightened and his eyes bulged. Aryi Junior's knife-work was no less skillful than that of his father and teacher. With a glint of the blade, the tongue sprang out into the space between the prisoner's mouth and the executioner's hand, like a startled mouse. It looked as if it were leaping into the air, but fell after rising no higher than a man's head. Obviously, flesh-and-blood objects can't soar like the spirits. It was falling when people heard Wangpo Yeshi scream. Then it hit the ground, where it was covered in dirt and lost its clever movements and bright red luster. The screams were muffled and meaningless once the tongue was gone. People say that the black-haired Tibetans are the offspring of a man who could not resist the seductions of the demon Nara. Maybe the first scream from the first descendant of our ancestor and the female demon was muffled like that, as he voiced his anger at such a chaotic, disordered world.

Laying down his knife, Aryi took out a small packet of medicine and sprinkled it in the mouth of Wangpo Yeshi, who was still tied to the stake. It quickly stopped the bleeding. Aryi Senior loosened the rope from behind, sending the prisoner sliding to the ground and spewing out large clots of blood. Aryi Junior presented the monk with the tongue, as if to ask if he wanted to keep it as a souvenir. He looked at his own tongue in great pain and shook his head slowly. So with a flick of Aryi Junior's hand, the tongue glided away. Surprised shouts erupted from the crowd as a yellow dog leaped up and caught it in the air. But instead of snaring a piece of edible meat, it yelped as if it had been shot, then fell to the ground with a thud. People were stunned; even Wangpo Yeshi himself stared in a daze at the poor, whimpering dog, hurt by a chunk of tongue. He touched his mouth, and came away only with a handful of clotted blood, which proved only that his body was as vulnerable to violence as anyone's. Still moaning pitiably, the dog spat out the tongue and ran off with its tail between its legs. The onlookers quickly jumped back from the detached tongue as the prisoner, unable to bear the trauma any longer, tilted his head and passed out.

The show was over.

The people slowly dispersed, returning to where they'd come from.

19 Books ～

The proselytizer was sent back to the dungeon to mend before his release.

And that was how the Maichi family acquired another slave.

According to the chieftain's not so complicated laws, whenever a condemned prisoner was spared, he became a family slave. Instead of being embraced by us, Wangpo Yeshi, with a religious belief he claimed to be omnipotent, was now owned by people he considered to be savages.

Aryi Junior daily went to tend to the wound of the first victim of his career.

I didn't go to the dungeon until nearly two weeks later.

Morning was the only time a bit of sunlight dribbled into the man's cell. When we entered, he was staring at the small slice of sky through his window. Turning when he heard the door open, he actually smiled at me. It was hard for him to give a recognizable smile; obviously, it hurt.

I raised my hand. "That's enough. You don't have to do that."

That was the first time in my life I'd raised my hand when I spoke, as my father and brother did. And I quickly discovered its advantages: it lent a sensation of infinite power to my hands and a comfort to my heart.

Wangpo Yeshi smiled at me again.

Finding myself drawn to this fellow, I asked, "Is there anything you want?"

He gave me a look that meant "What can I want looking like this?" Or it could have been understood as "I'd like to speak, how's that?"

But since I'd implied that I wanted to give him something, I had to do it. "I'll send some books over tomorrow. Books. You like books, don't you?"

He slid silently down the rocky wall to the floor, with his head bowed. I'd thought he might like the idea. But my reference to books must have touched a nerve, since he just let his head droop between his shoulders. As we were leaving, Aryi said, "Young Master was trying to be nice, and you should bid him good-bye. Maybe you can't say it, but you can at least use your eyes, can't you?"

Still he didn't look up. His head must have been weighed down by something very heavy. Was it the books he'd read before? I felt sorry for him.

It took a bit of trouble to find books for him, even though I was the chieftain's son.

First of all, I couldn't look for them openly. Everyone knew that the chieftain had two sons, one of whom, the smart one, needed to read, since he would be chieftain one day. As for the idiot son, he knew no more than four of five of the thirty letters in the Tibetan alphabet. When I told the crippled steward to find some sutras for me, he thought I was joking. It was out of the question to look for books in the sutra hall. And as far as I knew, on our vast estate, the chieftain's room was the only place other than the sutra hall where a few books could be found. To be more precise, these weren't books in the usual sense, but records of the first three chieftains, written when the Maichi family still had its historian. I've already told you that one of the historians recorded things he should have avoided, so that now no such servant could be found anywhere under the chieftain's sun. I knew that Father had stored those records in the closet in his room, and that he had stopped sleeping there shortly after recovering from his madness when Yangzom became pregnant. Even when Mother told him to stay there on occasion, he'd spend one night and then return to her room.

When I entered, Yangzom was sitting in the dark, singing. I didn't know how to speak to her; we hadn't had a single private conversation since she entered the Maichi household.

So I asked, "Are you singing?"

"Yes, it's a song popular in my hometown."

Then I noticed that her accent was different from ours. She spoke with a soft southern lilt, a bit slurred, which to a northerner seemed to hold special meaning.

"I've been to the south, during some of the fighting," I said. "You sound like them."

"Who are *they*?"

"Oh, Chieftain Wangpo and his people."

She told me her hometown was farther south. Then we ran out of things to say. I stared at the closet; Yangzom looked down at her hands. I knew what I was looking for. It was wrapped tightly in yellow silk, sandwiched between some important things and some unimportant odds and ends. But I didn't dare walk up, open the closet door, and simply remove the early history of my family. The smell of dust permeated the room. "Um," I said, "this room could use a good cleaning."

"The servants come every day, but they don't do a good job," she said.

Silence returned.

I stared at the closet some more; she went back to looking at her hands.

Then she laughed. "Young Master has come for something, hasn't he?"

"I didn't say that. How did you know?"

She laughed again. "Sometimes you seem smarter than anyone, but now you're acting like a real idiot. How could a clever woman like your mother have a son like you?"

I didn't know if what I was doing fell into the realm of intelligence or idiocy. But I made up a story, saying I'd left something here a long time ago. "Can an idiot lie too?" she asked. When she told me to point at what it was I wanted, I refused. So she moved over to the closet and took out the yellow bundle. After sitting down in front of me, she blew the dust into my face. For a moment, I couldn't open my eyes. "Oh, look what I've done," she said. "I nearly blinded the young master." She bent forward to lick the dust out of my eyes, and that single action told me why Father had loved her so much. The subtle fragrance of orchids wafted around her, so I reached out to hug her. She stopped me. "Remember, you're my son."

"I'm not," I said, then added, "you smell like flowers."

"It was that smell that got me into all this" She told me she'd been born with it.

"Go on now," she said as she placed the bundle in my hands. "Don't let anyone see you. And don't tell me that isn't your family history in the bundle."

The fragrance disappeared as soon as I walked out the door. When I was back out in the sunlight, the wonderful feeling of her tongue on my eyes also vanished.

Aryi and I delivered the books to the dungeon.

Wangpo Yeshi was sitting beneath the tiny window, holding his head in his hands. Strangely, his hair had grown much longer overnight. When Aryi took out a packet of medicine, Wangpo Yeshi opened his mouth noisily to show us that the bloodied scab and powdered medicine had fallen off. His wound had healed and the tongue was a tongue again. Though incomplete, it was a tongue nonetheless. Aryi smiled as he put the medicine back in his satchel and took out a small bottle of honey. Using a tiny spoon, he spread some honey on Wangpo Yeshi's tongue, which produced a look of joy.

Aryi said, "See, he can taste now. His wound is healed."

"Can he talk?"

"No," Aryi said, "he can't."

"Then don't tell me his tongue is fine. If that thing can be called a tongue, I'll have your father cut out yours, since an executioner doesn't need to talk."

Casting his eyes to the ground, Aryi stood aside submissively, not saying anything more.

I took out the books and placed them before Wangpo Yeshi, who had just tasted the honey.

The happy expression disappeared as he frowned at the books.

"Open them and take a look."

He was about to say something when he suddenly realized he didn't have the thing he needed to speak. So he shook his head with a pained look.

"Open them," I said. "They aren't what you think."

He raised his head and looked at me with doubt in his eyes.

"Those aren't the books that got you into trouble. They're the Maichi family history."

He obviously didn't harbor any dislike for books, since his eyes lit up and he reached for the bundle as soon as I said that. I noticed he had long, nimble fingers. The bundle contained handwritten scrolls made of coarse paper. People said that back then the Maichi family had grown its own hemp to make paper. The origin of paper-making was said to have had the same origin as the fortune-making opium – the Han.

When Aryi returned from the dungeon the next day, he passed on a request from Wangpo Yeshi for paper and a writing brush. I saw to it that they were sent to him, only to be surprised the following day, when Aryi brought out a letter. Wangpo Yeshi wanted me to pass it to the chieftain. Not knowing what he'd written made me uneasy.

"They told me you like to go to the dungeon," Father said when I delivered the letter. "Is this why you go there?"

Having no answer, I just smiled foolishly. A foolish smile is very useful when you have nothing to say.

146

"Sit down, you foolish boy," Father said. "I was just telling someone you weren't an idiot, but now you look exactly like one."

As he read the letter, the chieftain's face changed colors many times, like a summer sky. He didn't say a word when he finished. And I didn't dare ask what it said. Many days passed before he ordered Wangpo Yeshi to be brought to him. Looking at the new-grown hair on the monk's head, the chieftain said, "Are you still the man who wanted to spread his new sect in my land?"

Wangpo Yeshi didn't reply – he couldn't.

The chieftain said, "Sometimes I think that maybe this fellow's teachings are good. But if they are too good, how can I govern the land? Things are different here than in inner Tibet, where men in cassocks rule over everything. That can't be done here. Tell me, if you were chieftain, would you be like me?"

Wangpo Yeshi laughed. With a shortened tongue, it sounded as if someone were throttling him even as he laughed.

"Damn!" the chieftain remarked. "I forgot, you don't have a tongue." He sent for a brush and paper and put them before the proselytizer. Their conversation now formally began.

The chieftain said, "You're my slave now."

Wangpo Yeshi wrote, "Did you ever have such a learned slave before?"

The chieftain said, "No, nor did the chieftain before me. But I have one now. Previous Maichi chieftains weren't powerful enough. I am the mightiest Maichi."

Wangpo Yeshi wrote, "I'd rather die than be a slave"

The chieftain said, "I won't let you die. I'll keep you in the dungeon forever."

Wangpo Yeshi wrote, "That would still be better than being a slave."

The chieftain laughed. "You're quite a man. Now tell me, where did you get the ideas you wrote in your letter?"

He had actually mentioned only one thing to the chieftain in his letter: that he would like to be our historian, to resume a tradition that had been interrupted for too long. He said he found the history of the first three chieftains fascinating. At the time, Chieftain Maichi was thinking that he should leave something behind other than silver for later generations, for that way he would be

147

remembered as the most powerful Maichi in history. "Why do you want to record our family history?" he asked.

"Because it won't be long before chieftains disappear from the land." The monk went on, "When that day comes, neither the eastern nor the western neighbors will tolerate the existence of local overlords. And, of course, you yourselves have already thrown a torch onto dry kindling."

The chieftain asked him what he meant by a torch.

He told him it was the poppies.

The chieftain asked, "Are you telling me to get rid of them?"

He wrote, "That won't be necessary. Everything is predestined. The poppies will only make what must happen arrive sooner."

In the end, Chieftain Maichi granted Wangpo Yeshi's request to resume the tradition of recording the Maichi family history. But another argument ensued over the status of the historian. Finally the chieftain told him that he would grant his wish to die if he did not agree to be a slave.

The tongueless one put down his brush and gave in.

When the chieftain told him to kowtow to his master, he wrote, "If it's only this one time."

"Once every year at this time."

Now the tongueless one showed that he indeed possessed a historian's foresight, for he wrote, "What happens after you die?"

The chieftain laughed. "Wouldn't I know to kill you before I die?"

He repeated the question on paper. "What if you die?"

The chieftain pointed to my brother. "Ask him, since he'll be your master then."

My brother said, "You won't have to kowtow to me when that time comes."

Then he walked over to me. I knew he was going to ask me the same question and wanted me to promise I wouldn't ask him to kowtow if I became the chieftain.

"Don't ask me," I said. "Everyone says I'm an idiot and won't ever be chieftain."

But he wouldn't budge. "You really are an idiot," my brother said. "Just promise him."

"All right," I said. "If I do become chieftain one day, I'll make you a freeman."

My brother didn't like the sound of that, but I said to him, "It isn't for real anyway, so what does it matter what I promise him?"

Then Wangpo Yeshi finally knelt before Father and kowtowed.

The chieftain's first order to his new slave was "Write down what happened here today."

20 What Should I Fear? ~

Over those years, the Maichi family waged several wars to ensure its poppy monopoly.

The Maichis' new-style weapons met no resistance, but still we were unable to prevent other chieftains from getting their hands on the plants that had made us rich and powerful. In only a very few years poppies spread like wildfire across all the chieftains' land. Faced with the inevitable, I was not alone in feeling that the wars had been unnecessary; Father and my brother shared that feeling.

If you asked the chieftains how they got their poppy seeds, they'd invariably say they'd been blown over by the wind or carried on the wings of birds.

By this time, the Han person we dealt with was no longer Special Emissary Huang, but a man named Jiang, a regimental commander in the Joint Defense Army.

Special Emissary Huang had been opposed to the Joint Defense Army helping the Central Army fight the Red Army, and was demoted, although with an ostensible promotion to provincial legislator, a post with no real power. He had brought the Maichi family good fortune, so we all felt sorry for him after learning of his setback.

Although not a big man, Jiang appeared to be strong. He wore two pistols on his belt and was fond of fatty lamb and good wine.

Chieftain Maichi asked him, "Do you write poetry?"

Jiang had a booming voice. "I don't write any fucking dog shit poetry. Even after I've stuffed myself and have nothing else to do, I still won't crank out any of that dog shit garbage!"

"Good!"

Jiang wasn't quite done. "If I wrote poetry, you'd sneer at me, and how could I be the chieftain's friend then?"

That brought shouts from my father and brother: "Jiang is our friend! We're Jiang's friends!"

My father and brother liked dealing with the new man more than with Special Emissary Huang; they could not know that Jiang was not only Huang's enemy, but ours as well. Huang had wanted to make one chieftain powerful so he could control the others, but Jiang intended for all chieftains to plant poppies, so he could supply them with silver and machine guns, which they would in turn use against one another. Shortly after he arrived, poppies raged like a prairie fire on other chieftains' lands. The price of opium dropped by more than half that year. The lower the price, the more land the chieftains needed to grow even more poppies. Two or three years later, after the autumn harvest, they discovered they didn't have enough grain for the year to come. For the first time in decades, disaster loomed on the horizon: the chieftains' people were facing starvation. Since we Maichis had plenty of money, we exchanged the cheap opium for Han grain. The Red Chinese were fighting the White Chinese in the Han area, so grain wasn't cheap, and it was very costly to ship to us.

When spring arrived, the Maichi family sent scouts out to see what other chieftains were planting.

Spring came to the south first, where the chieftains continued to plant vast amounts of poppies. Chieftain Maichi smiled at the news, but couldn't decide what to plant this year – more grain or more poppies, only grain or only poppies. It was not an easy decision. Maichi land was centrally located, at a place where spring came later than in the south, but earlier than in the north. It was torment to wait for information on other chieftains' choices. I felt we were more on edge these days than at any time during the War of the Poppies, when we never doubted we would win. Now everything was different. If we waited too long for the northern chieftains, we'd miss the planting season, which would necessitate harvesting barley during the rainy season, and our corn would ripen during a frost. That meant we would have no grain, which was worse than planting just poppies, as the other chieftains were doing.

Our northern neighbors weren't fools either; they were waiting to see what Maichi planted. When we couldn't wait any longer, my brother suggested that we plant poppies. Without indicating whether or not he agreed, Father turned a questioning gaze toward me. At some point – I couldn't say when – Father had begun seeking out my opinion on important matters.

Tharna was standing beside me. "What do you say?" I asked her.

"Poppies."

Overhearing my question, my brother said, "You're not idiotic enough to ask your maid about such matters, are you?"

"You and she said the same thing," I replied.

I don't know when my brother had stopped loving me as before, but at this moment he gnashed his teeth, and said, "Idiot! It was that lowly woman of yours who parroted me"

That incensed me, so I said to Father in a loud voice, "Grain, nothing but grain."

I wanted my brother to know that not everyone in the world took cues from him. To my surprise, Father said, "That's what I was thinking."

"Heh-heh," I laughed, utterly pleased with myself.

My brother stormed out of the room.

Father's decision to plant grain did little to ease his nervousness. If I had been chieftain at that moment, I'd have fallen to the floor and wailed. The concern now was that northern chieftains would follow suit, and the price of opium would skyrocket. The southern chieftains, including Wangpo, would laugh themselves silly over their good fortune. But what worried Father the most was that his heir might scorn him for accepting the harebrained opinion of an idiot. He went up to the second mistress's opium bed, and said to her, "Your son worries me."

She said, "He's right, just as I was right when I told you to accept the poppy seeds from Special Emissary Huang' Mother's maid told me that Mother then said to the chieftain, "Your elder son is the one you should worry about."

Later I went up to Father. " Don't worry," I said. "The northern chieftains haven't start planting not because they're smart, but because of the weather. This winter is coming right on the heels of the last one."

I had gotten this information about winter from Wangpo Yeshi, our historian.

All Father said was, "I see you have loyal friends. We may be the family of the Maichi chieftain, ruler of all the land along the river,

151

but we still need friends, all kinds of friends. I can see you have all kinds of friends."

"My brother said they're just slaves. He laughed at me."

Father told me there could never be any friendship among chieftains, so it was good to have a few loyal slave friends. This was the first time Chieftain Maichi had spoken to his idiot son in such a serious manner, the first time he had rested his hand on my shoulder, not my head.

That afternoon news came to confirm what I'd predicted.

A heavy frost had prevented the northern chieftains from planting grain in time, so they were forced to plant poppies, which have a shorter growing cycle. Everyone in the Maichi family was overjoyed at the news, except for two people. One was Third Mistress Yangzom, who never seemed to care about anything involving the family. The sole significance of her existence appeared to be sleeping with the chieftain once or twice a week. We'd all gotten used to this. The other was my brother, which surprised everyone, since he had always worked hard for a Maichi victory. He wasn't at all pleased to hear the favorable news from the north, because the news showed that he wasn't as smart as his idiot brother when it came to making plans and thinking things through. This wasn't the first time that had happened, which was why he was so stung by the news. One day, I made a point of telling him that I hadn't opted for planting grain that day because of Tharna. "You're right," I said, "she is pretty stupid. She wanted me to say poppies, but since I knew she was stupid, I said grain instead." Unwittingly, that made him even angrier. I hadn't intended for that to happen, and I can attribute it only to brain fever or something.

I was starting to lose control of myself.

The good news from the north had infuriated him. In the past, I'd have dismissed his erroneous prediction as an occasional mistake by a smart person before happily resuming my idiot status. But not this time. I went up to him, my beloved brother, knowing somehow that what I was about to say wasn't right. But I said it anyway. "Don't feel bad. For if you feel bad about good news for the family, people will say you aren't a true Maichi."

He gave me a slap that sent me reeling backward to the ground. That was the day I discovered that my sense of pain was underdeveloped; either that, or I simply didn't know what pain was. I'd felt it before, such as when I fell, or when I was pinched by Dolma in the past or Tharna now. But no one had ever hit me. That is to say, no one had ever hit me with loathing. No, what I mean is, I found that I felt no pain when someone hit me with loathing.

I spent the rest of the day trying to prove that I felt no pain when someone hit me with loathing.

First I looked to Father.

"Why?" he asked. "Why should I hit you? Besides, how could I loathe my own son?"

I couldn't find a single person who would hit me. And I became a laughingstock again, just when I was beginning to show that I could be smart sometimes. I went up and down the stairs, looking for someone, anyone, to hit me. Father wouldn't, nor would Mother. Wangpo Yeshi, the historian, just smiled and shook his head. He wrote something down, which I had Monpa Lama read to me. Here is what he wrote: "I've lost my tongue and have no intention of losing my hands too. Besides, I'm not your family's executioner"

His words cleared my head like a bolt of lightning. So I begged, then ordered Aryi Junior to use his whip on me, but the old executioner rushed up and raised his own whip to his son. I thought the pitiful scream that followed had come from me, but then I saw Aryi Junior rolling on the ground, holding his head. At that moment, the family guards stormed in. Assigned by the chieftain to protect me, they rushed up to see which slave had dared to rebel against authority and offend the powerful.

Sonam Tserang, who had always obeyed my every order, didn't dare do what I asked. So I had no choice but to go back to my brother. He held the whip I forced into his hand, trembling with anger.

"Use this to take your anger out on me," I said. "Mother says I'll have to live under your control in the future anyway."

He threw down the whip and pulled his hair. "Get away from me, you bastard!" he shouted. "You fake idiot!"

That night, I strolled through the orchard, my curiosity unsatisfied.

A sweet-water well in the orchard supplied all the water for the estate. Female slaves drew the water and carried it inside, from dusk till dawn. I met my former maid, Sangye Dolma, that night. After she'd respectfully wished me a good evening, I told her to put down her bucket and sit beside me. Her hands were no longer fragrant, not the soft, smooth hands I'd once known. When she began to sob, I felt like holding her, but she said, "I'm not deserving. I'll only soil you."

"Did you have your baby?" I asked.

Her sobbing intensified, for the child had died shortly after he was born. As she cried under the dim moonlight, her body emitted the pungent odor of dishwater, amid the subtle aroma of flowers.

The silversmith stepped out from behind the bushes.

Startled, the woman asked why he'd come. He said it was taking her too long to carry the water and he was getting worried. He turned to face me. I knew he hated me, so I handed him the whip. Earlier in the day, when I was searching for someone to hit me, everyone said that the idiot was beyond idiocy, that he'd gone absolutely crazy. The silversmith worked in the yard, so he knew all about it.

"Is the young master really crazy, like they say?" he asked.

"What do you think?"

He snickered and knelt down to kowtow before loosing the whip on me; it whistled like the wind. I knew exactly where it hit me, but I felt no pain. This man was hitting me with hatred in his heart, that I could tell. In the past, I'd felt pain even when his wife pinched me lightly. Under the dim moonlight, amid the subtle fragrance of flowers, the dancing whip sheared off blossoms from the apple trees, and I just laughed. The silversmith was gasping as he dropped the whip. Then they both knelt before me.

Overpowered by the miraculous sight he'd just witnessed, the silversmith said, "My woman was once yours. Now so am I. I am your livestock."

"Go on," I said, "both of you, go have a good life together."

Then they were gone. Watching the moon move behind the wispy clouds, I was saddened by an empty feeling. But it wasn't the moon's fault; it was my brother's. As a young master, I had nothing to fear, not hunger, not cold, not even … In any case, I was spared the fears that plagued common people. If there was one thing I feared, it would have to be pain. No one had ever raised a hand to me in my life. Even when I did something really bad, people would simply say, He's just a poor idiot, what does he know? But fear is a part of existence, innate to all humans. Now, today, that fear was gone, vanished without a trace, and that caused me confusion about myself.

The confusion nearly turned me into a true idiot.

I asked Tharna, "What should I fear?"

She looked at me with even greater confusion in her eyes. "Isn't it a blessing not to fear anything?"

But I persevered. "What should I be afraid of?"

She giggled. "Young Master is getting silly again."

I thought that what she meant was, Young Master isn't always stupid, only when something comes over him. So I took her to bed. While we were doing it, I imagined her to be a bird carrying me higher and higher. Then I pictured her as a horse taking me to the edge of the sky. Then the smell from her bottom made me sleepy. That was when I really began to dream.

That doesn't mean my brain hadn't been active in the past when I slept. No, if that were true, it would be a case of slapping my own face. What I mean to say is, I'd never entered a true dream world, never had a complete dream, until then.

During those days, I often dreamed that I was falling, a fascinating experience. I just kept falling, down and down, endlessly. Then I began to fly, as a wind blew in the void. I'd fallen from high places in real life – as a child I'd fallen out of bed, and in later years, from the backs of horses. But that couldn't begin to compare with the fall in my dreams. In real life, I didn't have time to think about anything before landing on the ground. The impact would send a buzz through my head, and I would bite my tongue. In dreams, everything was very different. When I was falling in my dream, my first thought would be, I'm falling. But I could say it over and over, and I'd still never hit bottom. Then I'd sense myself floating in the windswept void. The only problem was, I fell sideways, and could never straighten up. There was nothing I could do about that, not a thing. Sometimes I'd force my body to turn, only to see the earth howl as it rushed toward me. People fear only real things. So, I told myself, if I wake up screaming, my dream must be real. Then a woman's hand would calm me down.

That thought made me feel better, because I'd finally found something to fear, and that is what makes life interesting. Do you know what I feared?

I feared waking up from a dream in which I felt like I was flying, but I was actually falling. If a person must be afraid in order to feel truly alive, then that is what I feared.

21 The Smart One and the Idiot ∼

That autumn, we harvested bumper crops of barley and, later in the season, corn.

Prior to that, First Young Master was always saying, "Just wait and see. We planted so late, the frost will arrive before the corn is ready."

That was what worried the chieftain and everyone else. Waiting for news of the northern chieftains had delayed the planting for more than ten days.

But I told Father that my brother's prediction would not come true.

Father said, "He sounded as if he were cursing his own family."

Luck was with Chieftain Maichi during those years. The autumn weather was warmer than in previous years, so the frost didn't arrive as early as usual. We watched the corn ripen. People were saying that a mild frost would be nice because it adds sweetness to the corn. For people who had little to go with their meals, it was important to have that sweetness in their corn. With it, they could feel that life wasn't all bad and that the chieftain was still worthy of their support.

Father told Monpa Lama to employ his magic and bring a frost, but the lama said that some of the corn on the mountain had yet to ripen. Sure enough, as soon as the corn around the higher fortresses ripened, stars twinkled in the clear sky, and a frost arrived toward dawn. It was a winter frost that hardened the ground, with icy flakes that crunched beneath our feet.

We already had some stored grain and hardly had room for the bountiful harvest of that year; grain-bearing porters lined the roads to the estate. Our crippled steward took up his station in the yard and had the servants weigh the grain before entering the amount in his account book. Suddenly the servants cheered, as the seams of an overflowing storage room gave way, sending golden kernels of corn cascading to the ground like a waterfall.

My brother said, "Before long, all this corn will swamp the estate." I didn't know why, but he'd been speaking in that tone more often lately. We'd thought he spoke in such a cavalier manner only for the girls' sake.

Father said, "Maybe my sons can come up with an ingenious idea about what to do."

My brother merely snorted.

The chieftain turned to me. "Don't keep quiet because you think you're an idiot or because people say you are."

So I made a startling yet simple suggestion. I said we could exempt people from paying taxes for a year. As soon as the words were out, I saw the historian's eyes light up, while Mother looked at me with deep concern. Father didn't say a word for a long time; my heart was in my throat.

As he toyed with the coral ring on his finger, Father said, "Don't you want the Maichi family to become even more powerful?"

I said, "This should be enough for any chieftain. A chieftain is a chieftain; he can never be a king."

The historian copied down my words, so I knew I hadn't said anything wrong. The Maichi family had waged several wars against other chieftains and had grown powerful in the process. If that continued, one day there would be only one chieftain left in the world, which would not escape the attention of Lhasa or Nanking, and neither would be happy with that. But in the valleys beneath the snow mountains, one could not be too weak either, or his neighbors would take turns picking him apart. A bite here, another bite there, and pretty soon he would be nothing but a skeleton. Then, as one of our sayings goes, you could not even find your mouth to drink water. So the Maichi family had to be powerful only to the extent that other chieftains hated us but could do nothing about it. Yet none of this seemed to register with my brother, who should have known that throughout history not a single chieftain had ever succeeded in inheriting the title through wars. In my family, he alone sought constant warfare, since war was the only way he could show he was the chieftain's worthy heir. "Before the other chieftains grow strong," he'd say, "we should gobble them up and everything will be fine."

"Gobbling them up is easy," Father said. "But if we can't shit them out, we're done for."

There was once a chieftain who had tried to gobble up all his neighbors. So the Han emperor sent an army to squash him, and in the end he wasn't even chieftain of his own land. The lack of decent roads to the Han territory made some chieftains forget where their titles came from, and when their brains heated up they forgot all about reality. The Han area, ruled by an emperor in the past and a president now, wasn't simply a place that produced our favorite tea, china, and silk. My brother had been there, but he seemed to be ignorant of the fact that our land was part of a joint defense district overseen by an army commander. He even forgot where our powerful weapons came from.

Fortunately Father had a better understanding of the world we lived in. What puzzled him were his two sons. The smart one loved war and women; obsessed with power, he was short on judgment where important matters were concerned. The idiot son conceived amid drunken passion actually seemed smarter than anyone. Before other chieftains began worrying about their heirs, Father's face was already clouded by concerns. People always said how great it was to be a chieftain, but I thought that was because they didn't know how difficult it was. In my opinion, it was best to be a member of a chieftain's family, not the chieftain himself.

And if you happened to be an idiot, that was even better.

Take me, for instance. Sometimes I offered my views on things. If I was wrong, it was as if I had said nothing. But if I was right, people treated me with respect. So far, I hadn't been wrong on anything important. Mother even said to me, "Son, I shouldn't smoke so much opium. Instead, I should stay alert to help you with your ideas."

I'd rather she stayed with her opium if that was what she had in mind. We had plenty of the stuff, which was the color of cow dung. But I knew I'd upset and disappoint her if I said so. With her, it was always "You hurt my feelings." Father had said, "Your feelings aren't in other people's hands. We can't hurt them whenever we feel like it." My brother said that women liked to say things like that. After sleeping with so many women, he thought he understood them. And after he'd been to the Han area a time or two, he started to say, "Han people like to say things like that," as if he knew them well.

In any case, the chieftain exempted the people from paying taxes for a year. They were so happy that they pooled enough money to hire a drama troupe, which put on four or five days of exciting performances on the estate. The first young master, being a talented man, mingled with the troupe members and satisfied his passion for acting.

Another important decision was made during his absence.

The chieftain said, "Anyone who wants to watch the performances, go ahead."

Then he said, "Let the serfs watch the show. There's something I want to talk to you about."

The "you" included Mother, me, and the crippled steward. While outside the air rang with the sound of drums and gongs, the chieftain informed us of his decision, which we all considered an excellent one. The first young master wasn't there to hear it.

The performances finally ended.

Father told my brother to set out with a headman from the southern border to carry out the decision he'd made during the performances. The chieftain wanted him to pick a piece of land near the main thoroughfare to build a structure; it must face the water and be flat, for horses. My brother asked what the building was for. The chieftain said if he didn't know yet, he'd know by the time it was finished.

"Give it some thought while you're building it," the chieftain said. "How else are you going to be able to maintain the family empire?"

My brother was visibly thinner when he returned to report the completion of the building. He told the chieftain how responsible he'd been and how splendid the building looked. The chieftain interrupted him: "I know all about it. I know you picked an excellent site and I know you weren't with women all the time. I'm pleased with you, but tell me if you've come up with an answer."

His response made me shout inside, Oh, no, First Young Master!

He said, "I know that war is out of the question, since the Republican Government won't allow us to annex other chieftains' territory. So we need to make friends with them. The building will be the Maichi border palace, where we can invite other chieftains to spend the summer hunting."

The chieftain's concern that his smart son would come up with the wrong answer was confirmed. But there was nothing he could do about it. All he could say was, "Now I want you to travel to the north and construct another building. While you're at it, keep thinking about what it might be used for."

My brother sat up till midnight playing his flute. By breakfast the following morning, he'd already left for the north. My poor brother. I'd wanted to reveal the purpose of the building to him, but he'd left before I'd had a chance. In our family, I should have been the one who liked the things he loved, and he should have spent his time observing what the chieftain did and said. In the time of the chieftains, no one ever thought of actually teaching the art of governing, even though lessons were arduous, and only those born with remarkable talent were freed from working hard at them. My brother believed he was one of those, but he wasn't. Battle skills were one thing, as was the charm to attract women. But it was a different matter altogether to be a chieftain, a good chieftain.

Once again it was time for him to return, and Father eagerly anticipated his arrival. He went up to the veranda platform every day to gaze along the northbound road, whose surface sparkled under the winter sun. Birches, their leaves gone, lined the roadside; Father must have felt just as bare as the trees.

On this particular day, he rose early, because the day before Monpa Lama had predicted that visitors would be coming down the northbound road.

The chieftain had said, "It must be my son."

Monpa Lama had responded, "It's a close family member, but it doesn't appear to be the first young master."

22 The English Lady ~

My uncle and elder sister were home!

He'd returned from Calcutta, India, she from England

She had gone first to India to meet up with Uncle, so they could travel together via Tibet.

After dismounting, they went upstairs to wash up and eat. I didn't get a chance to talk to them, but I did get a good look. I liked Uncle's face at once; it was similar to Father's, but rounder, fleshier, and more given to smiles. He didn't look like someone who had to win all the time, and that made him a smart person. Truth is, I was an idiot, but I liked smart people. Who were the smart people? There weren't many, no more than I could count on the fingers of one hand. They were: Chieftain Maichi, Special Emissary Huang, the tongueless historian, and now my uncle, Father's younger brother. See, I needed only four fingers. I couldn't find another person for the fifth, my pinkie, so I just let it stick straight up, looking stubborn.

Uncle spoke in my direction. "The little fellow's playing with his fingers." Then he waved me over and put a gem-studded ring on my upright pinkie.

Mother said, "That's much too good, much too good for him. He'll throw it away as if it were a common stone."

Uncle smiled. "Gems are stones too. It doesn't matter if he throws it away." Then he bent down to ask, "You wouldn't throw away a gift from me, would you?"

"I don't know. They all say I'm an idiot."

"How come I can't tell?"

Father said, "Give him time."

Then my sister spoke to me too. "Come over here," she said.

I didn't understand her right way, so I thought I was getting stupid again. But it turned out that I was fine. Her tongue was stiff when she tried to speak her native language; she knew what she wanted to say, but her tongue had a mind of its own. "Come over here," she mumbled again.

I wasn't sure what she was saying, but I understood what she wanted me to do, since she held out her hand. She'd always sounded very affectionate in her letters. For instance, we learned she'd inquire after me: "How's my baby brother, the one I've yet to meet? Is he cute?" Or "Don't tell me he's an idiot. Of course, it's all right if he is. The neurologists here in England should be able to cure him." Mother had said, "The young mistress is a wonderful person. See, she wants to get you over to England." So now the wonderful person was back. She mumbled something and reached her hand out to me. I walked up to her, but instead of taking me by the hand, as Uncle had done, she stopped me by holding out her hand and giving me a cold stare. The room was very warm, but she was still wearing white gloves. Uncle, who knew what she meant, told me to touch the back of her hand with my lips. Then she smiled as she took out some colored bills from her purse and spread them out like a fan before handing them to me. Uncle taught me to say "*Thank you, Madam.*"

"Does *Madam* mean 'Elder Sister' in English?" I asked.

"No, it means 'Mistress.'"

It turned out that my sister had married a British nobleman, so she was now a mistress, a madam, not my sister.

The *madam* had given me some brand-new foreign money, which she'd collected on her way home. I wondered why she hadn't given me a couple of gold coins instead. Didn't people say that England had beautiful gold coins? That must have meant she didn't really like me. I didn't like her either. I'd always wanted to meet her, because I'd seen so many of her photographs. Just looking at them, I felt bathed in the smell wafting across the Maichi land from the house. But now she was sitting there, emitting a scent that was totally different. We often said that the Han didn't have much body odor and, if they did, it would be the smell of water, which pretty much means no smell at all. People from England had a body odor, similar to the smell of goat that we carried. People who didn't cover that up were barbarians, like us. On the other hand, civilized people like the English, or like my sister, who had returned from England, tried to mask it with other odors. After she gave me the money, she touched my forehead with her lips, emitting a strong, mixed odor that nearly made me throw up. See what that country of England did to our women.

She gave Father a felt hat that was tall and stiff, like an upturned bucket. Mother got some glittering, colorful beads, which she knew were worthless. She could exchange the smallest ring on her finger for hundreds of strands of the things.

Uncle brought his gifts to everyone's room later. In addition to the ring he'd put on my finger, he gave me a real present, a gem-studded Indian dagger. "You'll forgive me for giving you fewer gifts than all the others," he said. "That's the fate of a younger master." Then he added, "Tell me, boy, do you like having an uncle?"

"I don't like the elder sister."

"What about your brother?"

"He used to like me, but not anymore."

*

They hadn't come back just to see us.

On their way home, the Republican Government and the Communists had united to fight the Japanese in the Han area. By then, the Central Government had moved from Beijing, a place our ancestors had visited, to Nanking, a place totally unfamiliar to us. The Panchen Lama had also moved to Nanking, so we believed that the Republican Government was good. The Great Tibetan Living Buddha would not live in a place with no virtue. My uncle's business trips between India and Tibet often took him to Shigatse and the Tashilhunpo Monastery of the Great Panchen Lama, so his business connections extended to Nanking. He even donated an airplane to the Republican Government to fight the Japanese. Later the Republican Government lost Nanking, and the airplane bought with Uncle's money, along with its Russian pilot, crashed into the biggest river in the world. That was how Uncle put it: "My plane and the Russian lad fell into the biggest river in the world."

When the Panchen Lama decided to return to Tibet, Uncle went to meet him with money and supplies, and took this opportunity to visit his family. I could tell that even if Father abdicated, Uncle would not want to become Maichi chieftain. But of course he still voiced his opinions on family matters.

First he said we should withdraw from the quagmire of war and stop growing opium.

Second, even though the Maichi family was stronger than ever, we should not appear to be too powerful. Everything had changed, and chieftains would not last long on this land. Someday the western Land of the Snows would align itself with England, while the eastern chieftains would surrender to the Han government.

Third, setting up a market at the border was the perfect strategy. If future Maichis were to survive, they would have to rely on border trade for their wealth.

Fourth, he had brought his niece back to receive her dowry.

Father said, "I entrusted her to you. Didn't you give her a dowry?"

"When it comes to the dowry, she wants as many wealthy 'daddies' as possible."

"Look what you've turned her into."

Uncle just smiled.

No one in my family appreciated the way my sister behaved.

When she said she wanted to stay in her old room, the steward told her it had been cleaned daily and was exactly the way she'd left it. But she merely scrunched up her nose and sprayed the room thoroughly with perfume.

And she said to Father, "Have someone bring me a radio."

Father snorted, but did as she asked. Uncle was surprised that she had brought batteries all this way. Before long, strange grating noises emerged from her room; that was all she could get, no matter how much she twisted the dial.

"Save yourself the trouble," Uncle said. "No radio station has ever sent signals this way."

"Then I won't have anything new to report when I return to London," she said. "How could I have been born in such a barbaric place?"

That incensed the chieftain. "Didn't you come back for your dowry?" he yelled. "Well, once you've got it, you can get the hell back to that England of yours!"

My brother rushed back from the northern border as soon as he got the news of our sister's visit. What was really strange was that he was the one member of the family who really seemed to like her. He acted as if the English lady were his only true relative. But his dear sister said, "I hear you like to run around seducing village girls. That is beneath the dignity of an aristocrat. You should spend more time with daughters of other chieftains." He didn't know what to say. She obviously didn't realize that the daughters of other chieftains all lived in places that would take several days to reach, not somewhere he could stroll to when the thought occurred to him on a moonlit night.

He turned to me, and said angrily, "The Maichi family is nothing but a bunch of eccentrics."

I wanted to agree, but then changed my mind when I realized that he'd included me.

What my sister got from her trip was enough silver for two loads on horseback and some gemstones. Concerned that something might happen to it, she had the servants move everything from the cellar up to her room on the fourth floor.

Father asked Uncle, "Why is she so concerned? Does she have a hard life in England?"

"Her life is good beyond your imagination," Uncle replied. "But she knows she won't be coming back, and that's why she wants so much silver. She values it so highly because she wants to keep living that good life, unimaginable to you."

"I really don't like her," Father said to Mother. "And she was such a sweet little girl. Maybe I ought to give her some gold."

Mother said, "Sure. After growing opium all these years, the Maichi chieftain believes that he is the richest person in the world."

"She looks so much like her mother," he said.

"After she gets her gold," his wife said, "the sooner she leaves, the better."

"Don't feel bad about how much you're giving her. I've given her much more than you have," Uncle said.

After getting her gold, my sister said, "It's time to go. I really should be getting back."

The chieftain's wife said, "Won't the madam stay awhile longer?"

"No," she said. "Men get ideas when they're away from their women too long. Even an English gentleman."

Before she left, my sister went out with my brother for a "constitutional," while I went out with Uncle. You see, now we had acquired some of the Westerners' habits, even during that brief visit. My brother was acting more peculiar all the time. He felt that he had to pretend to like someone no one else did. I didn't know what they talked about, nor did I want to know. But I had a wonderful time walking with Uncle.

"I'll miss you," he said.

I asked him one more time, "Am I really an idiot?"

He looked at me for a while before saying, "You're a very special boy."

"Special?"

"That means you're different from a lot of people."

"I don't like her."

"Don't waste time worrying about that," he said. "She's never coming back."

"How about you?"

"Will I become an Englishman? An Indian? No, I'll at least come back to die. I want to close my eyes for the last time under this sky."

They left the next day. Uncle kept turning to look back. My sister had changed into a white dress worn by Englishwomen, with a

165

hat and a black veil that covered her face. When saying good-bye, she didn't even raise the veil. She was about to leave her homeland, and us, forever, but Father still worried about his daughter's future. He asked Uncle, "Is silver valuable in England? Is it like money?"

Uncle said, "It's money, even in England."

She kept talking to Uncle about the places they'd see along the way, and I heard her ask time and again, "Are we really going to ride in Chinese sedan chairs?"

"You can if you want," he replied.

"I find it hard to believe that the Han people, in their black clothes, actually walk with a small house on their shoulders."

My brother said, "It's true. I've ridden in one before."

"That doesn't worry me," Uncle said, "What does concern me are the bandits."

"I hear the Chinese are afraid of the English," she said. "I have an English passport."

As we were talking, we arrived at the valley, where we stopped to watch them head down the mountain. She didn't look back once, while Uncle kept turning to wave his hat at us.

After they were gone, my brother began treating me better. He said he'd give me lots of girls once he became the chieftain.

I laughed foolishly.

Patting my head, he said, "So long as you listen to me. Just look at that Tharna of yours. She has no hips and tiny breasts. I'll give you women with big breasts and wide hips."

"Let's wait till you become chieftain."

"A woman like that is a real woman. I'll give you real women."

"Wait till you're chieftain."

"I want you to know what a real woman feels like."

I was getting impatient. "My dear brother, that is *if* you become chieftain."

His expression changed abruptly and he stopped talking.

But I continued, "How many women will you give me?"

"Get the hell out of here. You're no idiot."

"You can't say I'm not an idiot."

Just then the chieftain showed up to ask what his sons were arguing about.

"He said I'm not an idiot."

"If you aren't, then who is?" asked Father.

166

The future chieftain said, "That Han woman has taught him to pretend he's an idiot."

The chieftain sighed, and said softly, "As if it weren't enough to have an idiot brother. Are you turning into one too?"

My brother lowered his head and walked off in a hurry.

Dark clouds appeared on the chieftain's face, but his smile returned after I said some silly things. "I really would like you not to be an idiot," he said, "but you surely are." He reached out to rub my head. I felt something stir deep inside me. A ray of light shone briefly on that very deep, very dark place, but it went out as soon as I tried to take a closer look.

Six ∿

23 Stronghold ∿

Seven or eight roads spoked out from Maichi land to other chieftains' territory; in other words, all roads led to the Maichi estate.

Spring had just arrived, and before the snow had completely melted at the mountain pass, people appeared on the roads in search of food, just as they'd done for poppy seeds several years earlier. They were the chieftains, carrying silver and large quantities of opium to exchange for Maichi grain.

Father asked my brother and me whether we should sell them food.

"They'll have to pay double," my brother said impatiently.

Father glanced at me, but I chose not to say anything. Mother pinched me, and whispered in my ear, "Not double, double double."

But all I said was, "The mistress pinched me."

My brother looked at Mother, Father looked at me. The sharpness of their gazes didn't bother me, but Mother averted her eyes.

The first young master was about to say something to the chieftain's wife, but before he found the right words, the chieftain said, "Double? Did you say double? Even double double, the price would still be like giving the grain away. I'm going to wait till they're willing to cough up ten times the price. That's what they get for fighting over poppies."

Wrong again, my brother was both embarrassed and angry. His head jerked up. "Ten times? You think you can do that? Impossible! Grain is still only food, not gold and not silver."

Stroking the gray beard hanging down in front of his chest, the chieftain held its yellow ends in his hand and studied them with a sigh. "Double or ten times, both are meaningless to me. Look, I'm getting old, and all I want is for my successor to be even stronger." He was quiet for a moment before announcing his decision: "All right, enough of that for now. I want you and your brother to leave for the borders. Take plenty of soldiers and horses with you." The chieftain stressed that he was making this decision for future Maichi chieftains.

He turned to his idiot son. "Do you know why I'm having you both go?"

"You want me to lead some soldiers."

He raised his voice. "I asked you why."

I thought for a moment. "To compete with my brother."

He said to his wife, "Slap your son. He got my meaning all wrong."

So the chieftain's wife slapped me, and not a symbolic slap, either, but a hard one. My brother would have been able to answer a question like that, but the chieftain didn't ask him. I couldn't respond like an idiot all the time, could I? Once in a while I wanted to look smart. The chieftain had clearly intended for his sons to compete with each other, mainly to see if his idiot son was more capable than his brother of becoming the next chieftain. I'd seen through his intent, and boldly said so.

But the words were barely out of my mouth when the mistress turned to the chieftain, and said, "Your younger son is truly an idiot." She slapped me again.

"Mistress," my brother said, "what good does that do? He'll still be an idiot no matter how much you hit him."

Mother walked over to the window to look outside, while I stared at my brother's smart face and smiled foolishly.

He burst out laughing, even though nothing funny had happened. He couldn't help himself. He could be really stupid sometimes. Father had sent him to the south and then to the north to erect buildings. He'd done what he was told to do but was never able to figure out what they were for. It wasn't until we harvested a bumper crop that he realized they were granaries.

The chieftain was sending us to the borders to guard the granaries and wait for people willing to pay ten times the standard price for grain. I was to go north, my brother south.

When other chieftains came to buy food, Chieftain Maichi said,

"I told you opium was bad, but you wouldn't listen. We haven't been able to fill our own granaries with grain yet. We're going to grow poppies next year, so we need to save the grain we have."

They left empty-handed, taking with them a grudge against the Maichi family, which had become rich overnight.

Many years had passed since the last time famine had visited chieftains' lands, and no one ever considered the prospect of facing starvation under such ideal weather conditions.

After the chieftains left, endless lines of starving people filled the roads leading to Maichi territory. "All chieftains must protect their own people," we told them. "Maichi grain is reserved for Maichi people." After being given a meal of corn gruel, they returned to their famine-stricken lands, filled with hatred toward their own chieftains.

It was nearly time for me to head north.

I decided to take a cook with me, in addition to the crack troops and some servants. Needless to say, I chose my former personal maid, Sangye Dolma. I'd wanted to take the tongueless historian, but Father said no. "I'll send him as soon as either one of you can prove you deserve someone like him."

"What if we both deserve it?" I asked. "We don't have two historians."

"That's easy. I'll grab another arrogant scholar and cut out his tongue." Father sighed. "What worries me is that neither of you will deserve it."

I told Sonam Tserang to come with me to the kitchen, where I informed Dolma of the decision for her to accompany me. It came as such a surprise that she kept twisting her greasy apron as she stood before a big bronze kettle, her mouth hanging slack. "But, Young Master ...," she stammered, "but, Young Master ..."

When we emerged from the kitchen, we spotted her silversmith husband working in the yard. Sonam Tserang informed him of my decision. The silversmith's face paled before Sonam had even finished, and he accidentally hit the back of his hand with his hammer. He glanced upstairs briefly, but lowered his head when our eyes met.

Sonam Tserang and I went next to the executioner's house.

The old executioner knelt as soon as we entered his yard. Aryi Junior, on the other hand, stood there with his hands at his sides, smiling like a bashful little girl. I told him to get his execution tools ready so he could accompany me to the border. His face reddened, which I attributed to happiness. He couldn't wait to take over for his father, just as the chieftain's son looked forward to becoming a real chieftain one day. The old executioner's face also reddened, because he didn't want his son to start using his knives so soon. I raised my hand, signaling him to keep silent, but he said, "Young Master, I wasn't going to say anything. I have to belch. I do that a lot."

"Do you have an extra set of execution tools?"

"Young Master, I prepared a set for the Maichi's young slave on the day he was born. But, but …"

"But what?"

"But your brother, the future Maichi chieftain, will be unhappy with me."

Without another word, I turned and walked out of the executioner's yard.

Aryi showed up with a complete set of tools on the day of departure anyway.

Father also told the crippled steward to accompany me.

My brother was smart enough that he didn't need to take so many helpers with him. He often said that the Maichi estate would have lots of empty rooms when he became chieftain, meaning that many people would lose their jobs and positions under him. He limited his retinue to a squad of soldiers and a master brewer. He figured it was only natural for me to take the steward, the future executioner, and a cook who'd slept with me, because I was an idiot. When he learned that I wanted to take Tharna as well, he laughed at me. "Where there's a crowd, there are women. Why take that girl? Do you see a single woman among my attendants?"

I said foolishly, "But she's my personal maid," which made him laugh out loud.

So I said to Tharna, "All right, that's enough crying. You wait here for me."

On our way to the border, starving people who had been turned away at the estate surrounded us. I told the servants to give them some food when we stopped to eat. That had them all saying that the second young master of the Maichi family was a kind and generous man.

The crippled steward said to me, "It won't take long for these people to come after us like hungry wolves."

"Really?" I said. "Would they do that?"

He shook his head. "Why is it that I can't see any future with either young master?"

"You can't? Really?"

"But we'll do better than the first young master, that's for sure, because I'll do my best to help you."

Sonam Tserang, who was walking in front of my horse, said, "We'll do our best to help the young master too."

The steward's whip landed on his back, making me laugh so hard I nearly fell off my horse.

"Young Master," the crippled steward said, "you treat the servants too well. That's not right. A chieftain would never do that."

"Why should I act like a chieftain? The next chieftain will be my brother anyway."

"If that were true, the chieftain wouldn't have sent you to the northern border." When I didn't respond, he flicked the reins to catch up with me, and said softly, "Young Master, you're right to be cautious, but you should let us know what you have in mind. I want to help, but I have to know what you're thinking."

I smacked his horse on the rump with my whip; it reared up and nearly threw our loyal crippled servant. Then I whipped the horse again, and it shot ahead like an arrow, trailing wisps of yellow dust on the roadway. As for me, I reined back until the servants had caught up with me. All the while, my former maid, Dolma, who carried a kettle and a small bundle of dry kindling on her back, and whose face was lightly streaked with soot, avoided me. In a word, she was no longer the Dolma who had taught me about what happens between men and women. Her appearance filled my heart with sadness as I comprehended the transience of life. I ordered a servant to carry the wok for her and told her to wash her dirty face in the creek. She walked briskly ahead of me. I said nothing, nor did she. I couldn't say what I had in mind. Since I didn't want to sleep with her anymore, what exactly did I want from her? My idiot brain wouldn't tell me. Then her shoulders began to convulse; she was crying.

"Are you sorry you married the silversmith?" I asked her.

She nodded, then shook her head.

"Don't be afraid."

What she said then took me completely by surprise. "Young Master," she said, "some people say you'll be the next chieftain. I say the earlier the better."

Her sadness swelled my heart. Dolma wanted me to be the next chieftain so I could release her from the bondage of slavery. At that moment, I honestly thought I should be the next chieftain.

"You've never been to the border," I said, "so take a look around, and then you can return to your silversmith."

She knelt on the springtime road and kowtowed, smudging her forehead with dust. You see how futile it is to seek out memories from the past? Just look at what happened to this woman who had been so neat and clean when she was waiting on me. I spurred my horse forward. Its hooves kicked up more dust, enshrouding everyone behind me.

Spring was deepening. As our journey progressed, it was as if we were walking into the heart of the season. When we reached the border, azaleas were blooming all around us. The number of starving people had increased. Their faces were beginning to take on the tinge of spring grass and raging, emerald green water.

My brother had built a terrific granary. What I mean is, it would be an impregnable stronghold if we were to be attacked.

Of course, I must tell you that he wasn't the least bit creative. I know it's hard to believe that such a clever future chieftain, one to whom so many girls were drawn, was not creative. But as his architectural achievement rose in front of us when we approached the border, the steward exclaimed, "Would you look at that, it's another Maichi estate house."

It was almost an exact replica.

A three-story building surrounded a courtyard, finished with fine yellow clay. Large windows and doors faced inside, while gun portholes that also served as windows faced out. The bottom floor was a semibasement storage space; the top two floors served as living quarters that could be quickly converted into defensive positions to return fire against attackers. You could even shoot from bed. Too bad for my brother. If he'd been born at a time before the chieftains' borders were settled, he'd undoubtedly have been a true hero. But my understanding was that Father hadn't sent him to the border to build an estate.

Father was getting older, and frequently lamented, "The world has certainly changed." But lately, more often than not, instead of using a definitive tone, he'd ask with a puzzled look, "Has the world really changed?"

My brother, incapable of understanding the pain this puzzlement had caused Father, said nonchalantly, "The world has to change, but the Maichi family is so strong it doesn't matter whether it changes or not."

Father knew that any chieftain, even one with unprecedented might, who could not adapt to these changes, was headed for disaster. So the chieftain turned his bewildered face to his idiot son. As I sensed the pain hidden in his heart, a similar look of pain appeared on my face. Seeing his own pain reflected on his idiot son's face, the chieftain felt that father and son were united as one.

When he said the world had changed, the implication was that many things on our land should change accordingly. In days past, our ancestors had built a solid fortress in the center of our territory. But that didn't mean we had to do the same thing at the border. Naturally, we would continue to fight other chieftains, but we'd already won battles fought with guns and cannons. This spring we'd fight one with barley, and for that we didn't need a stronghold.

But for now, we'd have to move into the stronghold.

It was a year of famine, but we walked, talked, and dreamed directly over mounds of grain. Vast stores of barley and corn filled the dark storage area. The fragrance floated up and entered our dreams. Green-faced, starving people wandered outside in the warm spring fields; many of them could not imagine having a decent meal before they died, while we were virtually sleeping on top of food. The servants knew that, and they looked proud to be slaves in the Maichi family.

24 Barley ∼

At this point, I should mention our neighbors.

Chieftain Lha Shopa had been very powerful over a century ago. But powerful chieftains all misused their power and abused their weaker neighbors. Their family had once forced a Maichi chieftain to marry their daughter, making Lha Shopa an uncle to Maichi. Later, when our mutual neighbor, Chieftain Rongong, defeated Chieftain Lha Shopa, the Maichi family took advantage of the situation by giving the current Chieftain Lha Shopa a niece to be his third wife, which now made Chieftain Maichi the paternal uncle.

I was hoping our relatives would show up soon after we reached the border.

But the Lha Shopa family disappointed me.

Each day, the starving people, their faces the color of grass, circled our grain-filled stronghold in a dizzying cycle. It would be absurd for them to think they could wrest the stronghold from us that way, but it was an annoying sight nonetheless. One group would come and circle for two days, followed by another group that circled for three days; there was no end to it. In the meantime, our former uncle and current nephew had yet to show his face. His people were dropping like flies; they circled and circled, then fell to the ground for the last time. Maybe Chieftain Lha Shopa was trying to appeal to my sympathy. But if that's what he thought, he was no chieftain, for no chieftain on this land would place his hopes on another's kindness. Only the miserable commoners were that naive.

The signs of spring grew more pronounced daily. One day, I summoned the cook, Dolma, and told her that instead of preparing our meal, she was to take ten servants and set up ten cauldrons in the yard to roast barley. Fires were quickly lit, and tongues of flames, blown by the wind, licked the bottoms of the cauldrons, making the barley crackle.

Our steward gave me a puzzled look. "I'm not doing that just to hear the crackling," I said.

"Of course not," he said. "If that's what you wanted, we could have frightened them off with the machine gun."

Our steward was very smart. He crinkled his nose, and said, "It smells wonderful." Then he slapped his head as a realization hit him: "Young Master, won't the smell kill those people outside?"

He took me by the hand and led me up one of four sentry towers on the stronghold corners. It was about five stories high, so we could see a great distance. The starving people were still circling, which meant that the aroma of roasted barley hadn't yet reached them.

"This was your idea," the steward said, "so don't get impatient."

I said, "I *am*, a little."

From where she was supervising the roasting, Dolma looked up at us. The sight of all that barley burning up obviously pained her. I waved, and saw that she understood what I was doing. Most of the people around me understood too. She waved to the other servants so they'd pour more grain into the scalding cauldrons. From where I stood, I could see that she no longer looked like a lowly cook, though she hadn't completely reverted back to being the woman I'd slept with.

Fire is a wonderful thing; it not only burned the grain, but enhanced its aroma by ten- or even a hundredfold, releasing it before the life inside the kernels was extinguished. A mouthwatering fragrance rose up from the center of the stronghold and was carried out to the fields by the wind. Starving people raised their heads, hungrily flaring their nostrils at the sky and stumbling like drunks. Has anyone else ever seen hundreds and thousands of people, men and women, young and old, all drunk? I doubt it. I was touched by the sight of so many people looking up at the same time. They stumbled because they were looking at the sky and not at the ground beneath them. Finally they slowed down and began to turn in circles. Then they stopped and fell to the ground.

The starving people passed out from the overwhelming aroma of barley.

I had just witnessed with my own eyes that barley was more powerful than guns.

And I immediately understood why Father believed that the value of barley would increase tenfold.

I ordered that the stronghold gate be opened.

I don't know where my brother had found the craftsmen to build such a wonderful gate – sturdy and impregnable when closed, but easy to open. The wheels rumbled like thunder as the gate was pulled open. The servants inside swarmed out and placed a handful of fragrant roasted barley in front of each fallen individual. The sun was setting behind the mountain when they were finished. The people on the ground regained consciousness as cool evening breezes blew, and they discovered the barley, as if it had dropped from the sky. That little bit of food gave them enough strength to stand again. In the dimming light I watched as, one by one, they forded a small river, crossed a low hill, and disappeared from view.

The steward coughed behind me, but I wasn't foolish enough to think he had a cold. "Do you have something to say?" I asked.

"If I were with the first young master and not you, I wouldn't say what's on my mind."

I knew he was telling the truth, but I asked him, "Is that because I'm an idiot?"

He shuddered. "I want to be perfectly honest with you. You might be an idiot, or you might also be the smartest person in the world. But no matter what, I'll follow you."

I wanted to hear him state that the young master was indeed smart, but he disappointed me. So I was really an idiot. But I was comforted by his expression of loyalty. I said, "All right, let's hear what you have to say."

"Tomorrow, certainly no later than the day after that, our guests will be here."

"Then prepare a reception."

"The best preparation is for them to think we've prepared nothing."

I smiled.

Now that Chieftain Lha Shopa was coming, I went hunting on the mountain with a large group of attendants and enough advanced weaponry to frighten many chieftains. That day, our relative, Chieftain Lha Shopa, approached the border amid the sound of rapid gunfire. We stood on the mountain firing into the air as we watched him and his people advance toward the stronghold. They walked in through the gate, but there was no reason for us to rush back. I had my servants make a fire to roast rabbits for lunch.

I even took a nap in a field of blooming azaleas. Imitating seasoned hunters, I pulled my hat down over my face to keep out the bright sunlight. At first I was only putting on an act, but I fell asleep before long. They waited until I woke up before eating the rabbits. We all stuffed ourselves, and no one felt like getting up from the carpet of grass. We were even more reluctant to leave when people from a nearby pasture brought over some yogurt.

This was the best season of all for people with a full stomach.

A gentle breeze blew across the pasture as tiny, brilliant white strawberry buds surrounded us, making the occasional yellow dandelion appear even brighter and more eye-catching than usual. Then came the sounds of cuckoo birds from trees so green that they seemed to be dripping wet. The cuckoo birds sang and sang, each call louder than the one before, each one lasting longer. My servants, who were lying in the grass, began to mimic the cuckoos. The birds' songs were a good omen, since everyone believed one's situation would remain the same from the first time the cuckoo sang until the next time. At this moment, our situation couldn't have been better. At the foot of the hill, people were staring wild-eyed at our full granary. Meanwhile, we were high above them, killing rabbits with fine weapons that had never been used in battle. We ate the rabbits and the delicious yogurt, and, as we lay in the grass, the cuckoos sang.

It was wonderful.

"This is wonderful!" I shouted.

Then others, led by the steward, knelt before me.

Believing that I was someone blessed with unfathomable good fortune, they knelt to show that they would be loyal to me from now on. I waved them to their feet. "Get up, all of you," I said, which meant that I accepted their loyalty. Their kneeling was more than a simple gesture; it was a ritual, and that made everything different, totally different. But not wanting to bring up this change, with a wave of my hand, I said, "Let's head back down."

The people cheered as they leaped onto their horses and galloped down the hill.

I was sure our guests were watching our awesome procession.

I was pleased with what Dolma had done.

She had placed a mound of food before each of our guests, so much they couldn't have eaten it all if they'd had three stomachs to burst in the process. They weren't shy about it either. The foolish looks they wore could appear only on the faces of people who had stuffed themselves until they couldn't eat another bite.

Sangye Dolma said, "They won't be hungry again for three days."

"A job well done," I said.

She blushed. I wanted to tell her again that I'd free her one day, but I was afraid it wouldn't mean much. From behind me, the steward walked over to where the guests were staying. Seeing that I was watching her, Dolma blushed again. After roasting the barley and treating the guests so properly, she seemed to have regained the confidence she'd felt when she was with me. "Young Master," she said, "don't look at me the way you used to. I'm no longer that Dolma. I'm an old hag now." She giggled.

Women can also look foolish when they laugh. Maybe, I thought, I should say something to her, but what? I would never sleep with her again, but I couldn't just tell her that what she'd done today was exactly what I'd wanted. As I pondered my dilemma, the steward walked up with a fat fellow who dragged his feet, making a loud nose as his boots scraped against the floor.

Dolma whispered, "Chieftain Lha Shopa."

I'd heard that Chieftain Lha Shopa was only in his forties, but he looked older than my father. Maybe that was because he was so fat; he was panting hard from just walking across the floor, and he kept wiping his sweaty face with a towel. The sight of someone so fat that a few steps had him breathing hard and forced him to constantly mop his sweaty face amused me.

I felt like laughing, so I did.

From the look the steward gave me, I knew I'd laughed at just the right moment, since now I wouldn't have to greet our uninvited guest.

Chieftain Lha Shopa spoke in his guttural voice. "Is that my nephew laughing?"

He hadn't forgotten our one-time relationship. With all the difficulty he had moving, he still managed to make his way over to me quickly. He grabbed my shoulders and shook me, as if to wake me up. Then, in a tear-choked voice, he said, "Dear Maichi nephew, I'm your uncle Lha Shopa."

Rather than acknowledge his greeting, I turned to look at the magnificent sunset.

I had no real interest in the sunset; I just didn't want to look at him. That's how I was: I'd look up at the sky any time there was something I didn't want to see.

Chieftain Lha Shopa turned to the steward, "My God, what they say about my nephew is true."

"You can tell?" the steward replied.

Chieftain Lha Shopa said to me, "My poor nephew, don't you recognize me? I'm your uncle Lha Shopa."

He must have thought that his idiot nephew wouldn't dare speak to someone he didn't know, so I caught him by surprise when I said, "We roasted lots of barley."

He dropped his towel.

"Lha Shopa's people didn't have food," I went on, "so I roasted some barley for them, and now they've all returned home. If I hadn't, they wouldn't have been able to eat it after the kernels fell to the ground and began to sprout."

The powerful aroma of roasted barley lingered above the stronghold as I talked with him, attracting birds from all over. Now that dusk was falling, they were singing cheerfully and soaring in the dying rays of sunlight that signaled the end of day.

I turned and went up to my room.

From upstairs I heard the steward bid Chieftain Lha Shopa good night. The chieftain, who had thought he could easily manage the Maichi idiot, stammered, "But, but we haven't finished our discussion."

The steward said, "Didn't the young master mention grain? He knew you hadn't come on a family visit. Get up early tomorrow and wait for him."

I told my young servants, "Go tell Dolma to get up early tomorrow and feed the birds."

Then I went to bed and quickly fell asleep. They put a towel under my chin, so I wouldn't be drenched in my own slobber.

The next morning, I was awakened by the sounds of more birds than I'd ever heard in my whole life.

To tell the truth, there really was something wrong with my head. During those days, I often woke up in the morning not knowing where I was. When I opened my eyes and looked up at the patterns on the wooden ceiling, like ripples on the water, and saw dust motes floating in the rays of sunlight streaming in through the window, I'd ask myself, "Where am I?" Then I'd sense a sour taste from the previous night's dinner. I'd answer my own question: "I'm at such and such a place." Once I'd finally straightened that out, it would be time to get up. I'd never been afraid of people saying that I was an idiot, but I didn't want anyone to know about this particular problem. So I made a point of asking myself silently, although sometimes the words slipped out of my mouth.

I'd never had that problem before. I'd always known exactly where I was, under which roof and in which bed, the moment I woke up. But back then I hadn't proved myself to be so smart about so many things, so the problem never arose, not once. I assumed that instead of diminishing, my stupidity had merely moved in new directions; that is, I was stupid in regard to some things, but not others.

I didn't want people to know that I'd become smart in certain areas, and definitely didn't want them to know the areas in which I was still stupid. But the situation had worsened lately. Most of the time I had to ask a question, and sometimes two, before my head cleared completely.

The second question was "Who am I?"

This second question was torture for someone who had lost himself in a dream.

Fortunately, I needed to ask myself only the first question that morning.

Softly I answered myself, "You're on the northern border of Maichi territory."

The sun was high in the sky when I walked outside. Chieftain Lha Shopa and his servants were standing downstairs, waiting for me to appear. Dolma was supervising the servants as they roasted more aromatic barley in the yard. Flocks of birds circled the area. I called out to Dolma, who stopped and sent someone up with a big sifter filled with roasted barley. The servants stood there with handfuls of the stuff, and as soon as I flung mine toward the birds, they threw theirs into the air. Our yard was immediately aswarm with all kinds of birds. Then Dolma swung open the heavy gate and, with a line of servants behind her, walked out, flinging handfuls of barley ahead of her.

The sight dumbfounded our guests.

"The birds are starving on Chieftain Lha Shopa's land, so give them some more," I said as I handed the sifter to Aryi. Normally as pale as a corpse, he flushed as he ran downstairs and began flinging handful after handful of barley all over the yard.

Then I invited our guests to breakfast.

Chieftain Lha Shopa no longer referred to me as his nephew. Instead he said, "We are related. The Maichi chieftain is Lha Shopa's uncle."

I burst out laughing, which made them happy.

Now, finally, it was time to talk about food.

And as soon as we did, the second young master of the Maichi family became an idiot again. "What's inside the Maichi granary isn't grain," I said foolishly, "but silver that weighs the same as grain."

Lha Shopa stopped wheezing like a bellows. "Are you saying that the grain is as valuable as silver?"

"Maybe."

Chieftain Lha Shopa said adamantly, "No grain in the world is that costly. No one will buy your barley."

"The Maichi family will sell every kernel," I said. "It was precisely to make it easy on buyers that the great Chieftain Maichi, with his foresight, built this granary at your doorstep, so that starving people wouldn't have to walk so far to reach food."

Chieftain Lha Shopa tried to reason patiently with the idiot: "Grain is grain. It's not silver. Sooner or later it will rot, and what's the point of keeping so much rotten barley in a granary?"

"Then we'll just let it rot, and your people can starve to death."

Our northern neighbor's patience gave out at that point. "If worse comes to worst, we'll just let a few people starve. But members of the chieftain's family won't die of hunger, that's for sure."

I didn't respond.

In an attempt to provoke me, Chieftain Lha Shopa said, "We'll just wait and see. The barley is already sprouting in the field and will be ready for harvest in three months."

The steward piped up, "Let's hope your people don't all starve before that."

"Has Chieftain Lha Shopa invited a shaman to turn the poppies into barley?" I asked him.

He nearly drowned in his own sweat.

We treated the chieftain and his party lavishly before sending them back across the border. When seeing them off, we took care not to step onto their land, since I'd promised our neighbor that our people would never cross the border. As we were parting, I said to Chieftain Lha Shopa, who was my uncle and was also my nephew, "You'll be back."

He opened his mouth, but couldn't throw down the gauntlet. That's right, he didn't dare say "Never."

After panting heavily a time or two, he rode down the mountain ridge without a word.

We watched until he and his entourage disappeared into the blue mountains on the other side of the border.

25 Female Chieftain ∼

Chieftain Rongong arrived a few days after Chieftain Lha Shopa's departure.

Rongong was also a northern neighbor, whose territory lay to the west of Lha Shopa's.

Any mention of Chieftain Rongong leads to a discussion of an interesting phenomenon on our land. We all knew that chieftains were, to a certain degree, emperors, regional monarchs. They all had more than one woman, but none of them had many children. Siring eight or ten kids was unheard of. Mostly they married one woman after another, without producing a male heir to their title. Every chieftain experienced the same fateful problem, and the Rongong family was no exception. For generations, no matter how many women the Rongong chieftains married or how hard they tried in bed, they could sire only one son. To remedy the situation, they traveled north to Lhasa and east to Mount Emei, but to no avail. Eventually, even that one son was denied them.

And that was how a fearless and clever woman became head of the family.

Initially, the female chieftain was to be a transitional figure. Her first duty after assuming the title was to bring a husband into the family and produce a son who would then assume the title. At the time, any chieftain with more than one son saw this as an opportunity not to be missed.

But even after the first female chieftain assumed power, neither she nor any of her successors was able to produce a son with one of the Rongong sons-in-law. I was told that the female chieftain who came to see me was the fourth. She was said to be so good in bed that her first man wasted away within three years. The one who followed lived longer, eight years, long enough to give her a daughter. She then decided not to remarry, which caused an uproar among the other chieftains, who said that a woman must not head the Rongong family permanently. By threatening to attack her land, they forced her to marry a man they had chosen. Her new husband was as strong as a stud ox.

"Now she's finally going to have a son," they said.

Then came news that the man had died.

I heard that this female chieftain was in the habit of bedding some of her more powerful headmen, her military officers, even lamas. She lived the carefree life of an emperor, which, in my eyes, made her a smart woman. But she too had planted only poppies, which had plunged her people into famine during a time that was free of natural disasters.

As my anticipation swelled to the bursting point, she showed up.

My servants spotted her and her entourage as soon as they appeared on the horizon, which was dotted with old cypress trees.

All afternoon I stood in the sentry tower, but the procession halted not long before reaching us. They climbed down off their horses in a beautiful meadow near a creek that wound through the cypress trees, close enough for me to see them, but too far to satisfy my powerful desire to meet the female chieftain. The horses were unsaddled so they could graze freely. Then dark blue smoke curled into the sky above the meadow; and I could see that they were going to eat before they crossed the border.

I said to the steward, "Who says that a female chieftain isn't the equal of a male one?"

"I doubt that they've brought along enough food to keep them going till winter," he replied.

That made sense, so I went down to eat. After dinner, nothing was happening out on the road. Unable to contain myself, I went back up to the sentry tower, only to find that they'd pitched a circle of tents in the meadow, where they clearly intended to spend the night. Upset by this development, I commanded the steward, "Don't give them a single grain of barley."

He laughed. "Was the young master actually planning to give them some?"

I knew I wouldn't sleep well that night, so I asked for a woman.

"We didn't bring any pretty girls along," Sonam Tserang said.

"I want a woman," I insisted.

And so they devised a plan. After I turned out the light and went to bed, they sent me a girl they thought was lacking in beauty. Well, she was like a leopard. With a howl, she leaped on top of me, and as

I was enjoying this special treat, I wondered if the female chieftain of Rongong was anything like this in bed. I thought about lighting a lamp to see if this fierce woman, who snorted like a mare, looked anything like the female chieftain, who was said to possess masculine qualities. But I didn't wake up till morning, when the sun shone through the window onto my bed. Before I could ask myself that special question of mine, Aryi stormed in.

"They're here!" he whooped. "Young Master, they're here."

I heard people running around upstairs, which proved that I wasn't alone in my excitement over the arrival of the female chieftain. After dressing and washing up, I walked out, just in time to see four horses trotting toward us – one red, one white, and two black – each carrying a female rider.

The one on the red horse had to be the female chieftain. Her slightly masculine bearing only made her prettier, more chieftain-like. She was first to dismount, followed by the armed, red-clad maids on the black horses. One of them grabbed the reins of the white horse while the other knelt on the ground as the rider raised her veil.

"Oh, my God!" I heard myself exclaim.

My God! The girl on the white horse was gorgeous!

Up till that moment, I hadn't known what true beauty was, but now I knew.

I nearly tripped on the veranda floor and, if not for the railing, would have fallen to the ground, at the feet of that fairylike beauty. The steward smiled, and whispered, "Young Master, just you wait and see. That girl has the power to make a man a hundred times smarter or to turn him into a complete idiot."

My feet carried me down the stairs, one step at a time, but I was unaware of their movements, for my eyes were fixed on the stunningly beautiful girl on the horse, who was just now dismounting by stepping on her maid's back.

Somehow I arrived at the foot of the stairs. I wanted to get a closer look at the girl, but her mother, the female chieftain, stepped up and blocked my view with her broad figure. I'd completely forgotten she was the famous female chieftain.

"You're in my way," I said to her. "I can't see that beautiful girl."

The steward coughed behind me, snapping me back to reality. Knowing that I was the idiot son born to the Maichi chieftain and his Han wife, the chieftain smiled as she removed the rifle strapped to her chest and handed it to one of the maids in red. Then she gave me a modest bow.

"The second young master looks as exactly as I had imagined," she said.

That may not have been the proper protocol for two chieftains, but I appreciated it. It was so casual that it seemed exactly the way two chieftains ought to meet.

So the second young master of the Maichi family smiled. "Everyone says that the female chieftain is like a man, but I think she's all woman."

"Does the Maichi family always make their guests stand in the yard?" she asked.

Finally the steward shouted, "Prepare to greet our guests!"

A long red carpet was rolled all the way down the steps with such precision and practice that it stopped right at the guests' feet. Following our rise to power, we had hosted a steady stream of visitors, which had given the servants ample opportunity to perfect the greeting ritual.

"Let's go upstairs," I said.

So we climbed the stairs on the red carpet. I tried to hang back behind the chieftain to get a better view of her beautiful daughter, but her maids took me by the arms, and said, "Young Master, watch your step." They pushed me up alongside the chieftain.

As soon as the wine was served, the steward spoke up: "The young master was unhappy that you decided to spend the night outside after reaching our territory."

The chieftain said, "The young master doesn't seem to be the worrying kind."

I didn't like her cocksure attitude, but all I said was, "The Maichi family wants its guests to feel at home."

She smiled. "The Rongong family is run by women, and women prefer to attend to their appearance before seeing people. Me, my daughter, and my maids wanted to look as presentable as possible."

Not until that moment did her daughter smile at me. It was not the ingratiating smile of someone in need of help, but that of a girl who knew how beautiful she was. On the other hand, her mother smiled like a woman who took satisfaction in the knowledge that she was the only female chieftain anywhere in the world. Both smiles showed that they assumed they were dealing with a young fellow who wasn't quite right in the head.

In a loud voice I said to the steward, "Let's ask our guests to discuss the matter at hand."

"Yes," he said, "let's discuss the most pressing matter first."

But Chieftain Rongong was still acting as if she didn't really need help. "My daughter ..."

I interrupted her. "Let's talk about barley."

She blushed, her dark skin turning red. "Let me introduce my daughter to you."

"When I introduced myself and my steward a while ago," I said, "you did not mention your daughter. The time for that has now passed. You may talk with my steward about barley."

I stood up and left the table with my two young servants. The female chieftain would regret being dismissive of me. She had made a mistake common to smart people: underestimating an idiot. At a time like this, underestimating the Maichi idiot amounted to underestimating the value of barley. As I was leaving, I heard the steward say to her, "The young master is in a good mood today. He ordered the servants to roll out the red carpet to welcome you and immediately told me to discuss barley with you. When Chieftain Lha Shopa was here, he had to wait three days before we discussed barley, and it took them three more days to realize that they couldn't buy it at the usual price."

On my way to my chambers, I confided in my servants, "He's a terrific steward."

But they didn't catch the significance of my comment, so I asked Aryi, "Will you be a terrific executioner for me?"

Embarrassed, as always, about having to kill people, he hesitated, and before he could reply, Sonam Tserang weighed in. "I'll be a terrific leader of your army, the best."

"You're a family slave," I said, "and no family slave has ever become a military leader."

But he wasn't discouraged. "I'll make great contributions and ask the chieftain to set me free. Then I'll make even more contributions so I can become a military leader."

The same old question resurfaced: Who would be the chieftain, the one who held the power of life and death?

"With me, neither of you will get anything," I said.

They laughed, and so did I. We were still laughing when Sonam Tserang straightened up, and said, "Young Master, that girl is truly beautiful."

Yes, she was the sort of beauty who came around only once every few hundred years. I sort of regretted not letting Chieftain Rongong introduce her to me. But now that I'd left, I couldn't turn and shamelessly head back, could I?

The steward entered my room and came up to me. "The chieftain hoped to influence you with her beautiful daughter. That was her strategy, but you didn't fall for it. Young Master, I was right. You are not an ordinary person, and I will do anything you ask me to do."

"But I already regret leaving," I said with a moan. "I began thinking about her the moment I walked out."

"Of course you did," he said. "You would be the idiot they say you are if you weren't enchanted by such a beautiful girl."

I could only say, "I'll force myself to stay in my room while you talk to them."

He noticed my pitiful appearance. "Young Master, your father won't be upset if you make a mistake or two."

"You may go now," I said.

He left and sent me a girl. But if I were to compare the Rongong chieftain's daughter to a flower, then the one he sent wasn't even the equal of a leaf. I sent her away. Then he sent another. The steward's idea was to send me someone who could take my mind off the young beauty whom I found so tempting. But it didn't work. No one could take the place of that girl. Besides, I didn't want to take her straight to bed; I just wanted to talk to her. I had the idea that everything would clear up in my head if I could only talk to her. Then the second young master of the Maichi family would no longer be a hopeless idiot.

26 Dolma ∽

The steward's earnest efforts on my behalf that night only made me angry. He even sent people out looking for girls. It was nearly midnight by the time I finally managed to drive away the image of the Rongong girl and fall asleep. But I was awakened by the sound of a galloping horse. Sonam Tserang and Aryi were standing by my bed. Gnashing my teeth in anger, I said to Aryi, "Go kill that rider and cut off his horse's hooves."

Sonam Tserang laughed. "You can't do that. The steward sent him to find you a girl for the night."

Another girl came and stood before me. I looked at the area beneath her belly, not even feeling like raising my head. "Take her away. Whoever found her can enjoy her company."

When the two servants walked out with the girl, a wind blew in, carrying the fragrance of grass. I called her back and, still not looking at her face, held her lapel against my nose. The smell of grass was indeed coming from her. "Are you from the pasture?" I asked her.

"Yes, Young Master," she answered. Her mouth gave off the aroma of tiny meadow flowers. So I ordered the servants away and kept her there to talk to me. After they were gone, I said to her, "I'm not well."

She smiled.

Many girls would have shed tears at a moment like this, and they all tended to act coy and reluctant in bed, even though it gave them pleasure.

I said, "I like you, girl from the pasture."

"But the young master has yet to take a good look at me."

"Blow out the lamp and talk to me about the pasture."

As the light went out, I was quickly bathed in the smell of grass and the subtle fragrance of meadow flowers.

The next day, I told the steward to keep our guests company while I went out to the pasture with the girl from the night before.

The people in the pasture set up a lovely tent for me by a warm spring. As I soaked in the water, I gazed up at clouds floating in the sky and forgot all about the daughter of the female chieftain. After

189

preparing food for me, the girl came to the spring, where I sat stark naked.

"Come eat something, Young Master. I can't fight off the gnats much longer."

She was so strong and yet so natural. A few years back, I'd had a maid named Dolma. I never dreamed that another Dolma was hidden in this pasture, one who radiated the smell of flowers and grass. "Are you called Dolma?" I asked her.

"No," she said, "My name is not Dolma."

"Dolma!" Many years before, I could take the hand of a Dolma as soon as I awoke in the morning. So I shouted for the cook, Sangye Dolma, who was busy preparing food for the large contingent of people I'd brought along. "Dolma, there's someone with the same name as yours."

The girl from the pasture looked at Sangye Dolma and quickly understood. "I don't want to be a cook in the estate," she said. "I want to stay here. This is where I belong."

I said, "I promise you won't become a cook. You'll stay here and marry the man you love. But for now your name is Dolma."

She took off her clothes and lay down on the soft sandy bed of the warm spring. I said, "The water has engulfed your fragrance."

Rolling into my arms, she began to sob. "Whatever is going to happen, let it happen quickly."

I climbed on top of her, and called out, "Dolma, Dolma," which excited both of us. She knew I was calling out to two people, to my teacher and to her. Even her body was much like Dolma's. A grown-up now, I was no longer swallowed up by a girl's robust body; rather it was like riding a strong, fast steed. Riders on galloping horses always shout joyfully, so I cried out as her body trembled like rippling water. Hearing me shout like that, the cook Dolma rushed over to the spring, thinking I wanted her for something. She saw her youthful self making love to me. I was still shouting, "Dolma! Dolma!" The horse ran to the very end, where a steep cliff rose. I flew up off the horse and fell at the base of the cliff. A long time passed before I came to amid the buzzing of bees. I saw the cook kneeling before me. "What are you doing here?" I asked her.

"Young Master," she said, "I heard you call my name. I thought you wanted something from me, so I came running and saw what you were doing."

I got dressed without telling her to get up, and said to the Dolma I'd just possessed, "She was like you before."

That's right, her breasts, her hips, her thighs, and the smell coming from her private place were exactly the same as the Dolma of years past.

I turned to the aging Dolma. "She's just like you when you were younger."

The cook was still kneeling on the ground, weeping. "Master, I didn't intend to see it."

"What does it matter if you did?" I said with a laugh.

"According to the penal code," she said, "they'll gouge out my eyes. I don't want to be a blind woman. You might as well have Aryi kill me."

I said to the teacher who had initiated me into the secrets between men and women, "Get up and take a good bath."

She said, "I'll wash myself very clean, so I can die with dignity."

The cook was actually preparing to die.

She sang in the warm spring, songs from when she was with me, but her voice had never been so loud that it pierced the passing clouds. With her wet, dripping hair hanging down, she lay in the water, her still firm breasts seemingly floating on the surface. She was singing as if she were drunk or dazed. Before getting into the water, she had sprinkled the area with flower petals, and the Sangye Dolma before marrying the silversmith and becoming a cook was resurrected. She flashed me a brilliant smile.

"Don't worry," I said. "I forgive you. I won't have you killed."

The dazzling smile quickly disappeared from her face as she stepped out of the water naked. Covering the place between her legs with her hand, she sat on the ground and began to cry. I knew I'd done a stupid thing. Of course I had to forgive her, but I should have waited until she'd bathed and finished singing before telling her. Only when thinking she was about to die, and without her husband around, could she return to the past, briefly reliving sweet moments. But now I had ruined the one and only romantic period in the cook's life. I ought to have waited until she returned to reality after bathing and kneeling before me to await death before saying "I forgive you."

That way, she would have felt that the young master had not forgotten their past and that she had not served him in vain. But I hadn't waited for the right moment. So now she was out of the water, weeping as she said, "I hate you! This is worse than death."

Stunned, I just stood there, not knowing where to put my hands.

"Let me die!"

"No," I said. "No."

She clutched a handful of grass, pulling it out, dirt and all, and smeared her face with it. I watched in agony as she returned to being a cook. Her breasts had been erect in the water, but now they sagged, reminding me somehow of the silversmith's hands. Now it was she who was in the wrong. She should have put her clothes on after crying. Instead, she'd shouted, "Let me die!"

I walked off as the young Dolma said to the aging Dolma, "You should not have done that. The young master has so much on his mind. How can you make him unhappy like that?"

Apparently, the cook came to her senses then, for the crying stopped. But it was finished. Our relationship and my concern for her snapped like the strings of a lute on that day. In life, we must sometimes cut ourselves off from some people and things. So fine, Dolma, my maid, I shall no longer be concerned about you. Go be a cook, go back and be the silversmith's wife. Accompanied by these thoughts, I headed toward the edge of the meadow, with my two young servants and the Dolma from the pasture following at a distance. When I tired, I lay down to watch clouds float above me. Then I got up and headed back. The meadow was wide, but I walked straight through the three of them standing there. By not stepping out of the way in time, Sonam Tserang received a slap on the face. It was loud and crisp. "It's okay," he said to Dolma. "Everything's fine. He's happy now."

I stopped and turned around. "I'd be happier if I slapped you again."

My two servants rushed up and squatted down, one on my right and one on my left, then carried me back to camp on their shoulders. The people all ran out of their tents to greet me. Our legend says that the first king of the Land of the Snows was carried this way to his throne when he descended to the human world. A crowd of people knelt before me. Back then I didn't know that the one who had used human shoulders as a sedan chair was our very first king. So when I saw so many people kneeling so properly, I thought that

Father or someone even more important than he had arrived. I looked behind me, but saw only a brownish yellow road cutting through the emerald green meadow. Clouds hovered at the far end of the road, where heaven and earth met.

The wind raised surging waves deep inside a sea of grass.

Seven ∽

27 Fate and Love ∽

With her beautiful daughter in tow, Chieftain Rongong came out to the meadow.

I was dreaming when they arrived, a very noisy dream. It sounded as if flowers blooming in profusion beside the water were making a racket. I nearly woke up a time or two, but then I heard someone say softly, "Let him sleep. It's exhausting to be the young master of a powerful chieftain."

Vaguely I thought to myself, "It would be even more exhausting to be a powerful chieftain."

Around midnight, I woke up and heard a loud wind whistling outside. Still too sleepy to open my eyes, I asked, "Is that the wind?"

"No, it's the water."

"They say that if the water is loud at night, the next day's weather will be good."

"That's right. The young master is very smart," said a strange voice.

I went back to sleep and slept very well that night, which was why I didn't want to open my eyes right away the next morning. Since I often felt lost when I first awoke, not knowing where I was, I knew that my brain would be shocked into emptiness by the bright morning light if I opened my eyes before I was ready. I would be like a wine decanter that contained nothing but sound. So that morning, I shifted a little, feeling each body part before sending my consciousness toward the center, approaching my brain, and asking the questions: Where am I? Who am I?

I asked myself, "Who am I?"

I was the second young master of the Maichi family, the one whose head wasn't quite right.

Then a perfumed hand touched me carefully as a voice asked, "Is the young master awake?"

"I'm awake," I answered in spite of myself.

The voice shouted, "The young master is awake!"

I sensed two or three more fragrant people come up to me. One of them said sternly, "Open your eyes if you're awake."

Normally, after I opened my eyes, I'd stare at something for a while before getting a fix on where I was, which was how I could make sure not to lose myself. There were times when I'd been awakened before I was ready, and for the rest of the day I was at a loss as to where I was. That was what happened this time. People around me started laughing before I had time to pose my important question and figure out where in the world I was. Someone was saying, "Everyone says that the second young master of the Maichi family is an idiot, but he sure knew where to find a good place to rest."

A hand fell on my shoulder and shook it. "Get up. I need to talk to you about something."

Without waiting for me to get up, several hands dragged me out from under the blanket. Amid women's taunting laughter, I quickly saw myself, a stark-naked fellow with that thing between his legs standing up proudly. Their hands reached out and quickly dressed me. Now I really couldn't recall where I was. The arrangement in the tent was familiar, but the seat of honor was taken by the female chieftain. As several hands dragged me over to her, I asked, "Where am I?"

She laughed and said, not to me but to the maids who had pushed me forward, "I wouldn't know where I was if I awoke to find strangers all around me either."

They giggled. It was impossible to stop those women from tittering at a moment even I found bizarre.

"Laugh if you want," I said. "But I still don't know where I am."

Instead of answering my question, the female chieftain asked, "Don't you recognize me?"

How could I not? But I shook my head.

Gnashing her teeth, she flicked a whip in her hand and opened a hole in the top of the tent.

"Where are my people?" I asked.

"Your people?"

"Yes, Sonam Tserang, Aryi, and Dolma."

"Dolma? Was that the girl who shared your bed?"

I nodded. "She has the same name as my cook."

She laughed. "Take a look at the girls around me."

They were all very pretty. "Are you giving them to me?" I asked.

"Maybe, if you do as I say. But let's eat first."

I discovered that none of the servants who delivered the food was mine. After a few bites, I could tell that it hadn't been prepared by Dolma. So while the female chieftain was occupied with eating, I racked my brain trying to figure out where I was and where my servants had gone. But I couldn't, so I held my head and fell backward, only to land in the arms of a girl. The chieftain wasn't upset by that.

"We'll manage just fine if you stay like that," she said.

Still holding my head in my hands, I said to the girl, "My head's about to explode."

She began to massage my temples with her perfumed hands.

When the chieftain finished eating, she asked, "Can you sit up now?"

I sat up.

"Fine, now let's get down to business. You know you're my prisoner, don't you?"

"No, I don't."

"You don't?"

"Where am I?"

"Stop acting stupid. They say you're an idiot, but I don't believe it. Now I want to know, are the rumors wrong or are you not really the second young master of the Maichi family?"

With all the sincerity I could muster, I told her I wouldn't be able to remember anything, not a single thing, if she didn't tell me where I was.

"All right," she said. "Didn't you come out to the warm spring pasture to avoid me?"

With a slap to my own forehead, I felt my head fill up with things, with everything. It all came to me. "I slept yesterday," I said.

She snickered. "What nonsense is that? You slept yesterday and you woke up today."

As the conversation progressed, I realized that I'd been kidnapped by the female chieftain. She had gotten nothing from the steward, who said he had no authority over the grain belonging to the Maichi family.

"Shall we take a walk?" she suggested.

"All right," I said, "let's take a walk."

Armed women were guarding my servants. You see, that's the difference between masters and slaves. Even under such circumstances, the young master was in the company of beautiful women. I could tell that my poor servants were hungry by the looks on their faces as I walked past.

"They're hungry," I said to the chieftain.

"My people are hungrier than they are."

"Give them something to eat."

"After we finish our discussion."

"There'll be nothing to talk about if you don't feed them."

"Would you look at this?" she said. "I'm having a tug-of-war with an idiot."

But she told her people to bring them food, and my servants looked at me like dogs seeing their master. After strolling through the meadow, the chieftain and I returned to the tent. When she cleared her throat, I knew we were about to get down to business, so I spoke up first: "When do we leave?"

Caught off guard, she asked where we were going.

"To the Rongong dungeon."

She laughed. "My God! You're frightened. Would I do something like that? Of course not. All I want from you is some grain. You see, owing to my stupidity, my people are starving. You must lend me some grain. That's all I came for, but then you decided to avoid me."

The sun was directly overhead, turning the tent hot and stuffy. I was uncomfortable, but I could tell that she was much worse off than I. I told her that Chieftain Lha Shopa had mentioned grain as soon as he arrived, but she hadn't said a word about grain until now. "As far as I can see, you came to introduce me to some pretty girls."

She interrupted me. "But Lha Shopa went away empty-handed."

"We had a disagreement. He said he was my uncle, and I said I was his, and that led to an argument."

My comment amused her. "Yes, he's the type who remembers

every detail about family relationships, going back many years."

"But he didn't bring any money. Father said the Maichi grain is worth at least ten times the usual price."

"Ten times?" she cried out. "I tell you, I only want to borrow some, just borrow it. You won't get an ounce of silver. Do you hear me? Not a single ounce!"

I smiled. "It's stuffy in here. I feel like going outside."

Like it or not, she got up and followed me as I wandered among the tents. I was secretly treating her like one of my personal maids. When she grew impatient with walking, she said, "I've never walked like this with an idiot. I'm tired. That's enough for me."

We had, as it turned out, reached the warm spring, so I took off my clothes and slipped into the water, where I began to float. She turned her back to me, as if she'd never seen a naked man before. "Did you bring plenty of silver with you?" I said to her back.

"Is this how you discuss serious business?"

"Father says we can't sell it for less than ten times the usual price. He knew that you planted only opium, so he built our granary at your doorstep. If he hadn't, you'd finish it off before you even got home."

She turned toward me, desperation written all over her face. After sending her servants away, she said tearfully, "I've come to borrow food. I don't have much silver, and that's the truth. Why are you doing this to me? Everyone knows that the Rongong family is run by women, which is why they never turn down one of our requests. Why are you rebuffing a poor woman now?"

"No one in the world takes advantage of an idiot. Why should a woman be any different?"

"I'm old. I'm an old hag."

She then summoned two of her maids and asked me if they were pretty enough. I nodded. But when she told them to get into the water with me, I shook my head. "My God!" she exclaimed. "What else do you want? I have nothing left."

I smiled foolishly. "Yes, you do. You have a daughter, don't you?"

She cried out in pain. "But you're an idiot!"

Without another word, I took a deep breath and buried my head in the water. That was a game I'd played in the river every summer since I was a boy. I could stay submerged for a very long time. I surfaced after holding my breath as long as possible, but she pretended she didn't see. So I kept at it, going under, then coming up, snorting like a horse after a long ride. The water was soft and satiny, and as I tumbled around, I stirred up a strong sulfur odor, which the people on the bank could barely stand. I was having so much fun that I forgot what we'd been talking about. Women were only women; they couldn't begin to compare with the water. If the historian had been there, I'd have told him to take note of my feelings. Instead, I'd have to tell him when I got home – if I remembered it that long. I'd have him write: On a certain day in such and such a year, the second young master experienced such and such feelings, and stuff like that. I was sure that the tongueless one could make my feelings sound a lot more significant than I could. But maybe, since his vision had gotten so much sharper after losing his tongue, he'd just smile and ask sarcastically, "How significant can that be?" But I'd still make him write it down. That's what I was thinking as I bobbed up and down in the water, which pounded my eardrums like thunder.

By then the chieftain was so angry that she tore a string of coral beads from her neck and threw it at me. My forehead swelled up immediately. "If Chieftain Maichi knew you'd hit his idiot son," I said as I stood up, "you couldn't buy a kernel of our barley even at ten times the price."

Immediately realizing the gravity of her rash action, she moaned. "Young Master, please get out. Let's go see my daughter."

My God! I was actually going to meet the most beautiful girl in the world!

The heart of the Maichi's second young master was thumping so wildly that he experienced sharp pains under his ribs, pains that filled him with happiness.

When we reached a particularly handsome tent, she turned somber. "Are you sure, Young Master? Are you sure you want to meet my daughter?"

"Why not?"

"Men are all the same, smart or stupid." She gave me a long look. "Great misfortune falls to unlucky people who get what they do not deserve. No ordinary man should have a girl like Tharna."

"Tharna?"

"Yes, that's my daughter's name."

My God! The name made me hot all over. I'd already met a Dolma who was more wonderful than the former Dolma, and now here was a girl with the same name as my personal maid. Without even waiting for a servant to raise the flap, I rushed forward and was immediately caught up in the soft material. The more I struggled, the more tightly it wound around me. At last I got free. Panting heavily and holding onto the ripped flap, I stood before Tharna like an idiot. At that moment, even my fingernails were burning, let alone my heart and my eyes. It was as if a shout sent forth at Earth's creation had traveled all that time before finally obtaining a response here, at this moment, from an unsurpassingly beautiful girl. Now she was sitting in front of me at the far end of the tent, smiling brilliantly, her sparkling white teeth showing between red lips. The clothes she wore were intended not to cover her body, but to suggest, to spark the imagination.

Unable to control myself, I shouted, "It's you! It's really you!" That first shout was loud and filled with joy. But when the second shout emerged from my mouth, I went limp and nearly keeled over. Somehow I managed to steady myself.

The Maichi's idiot son was stunned by the girl's beauty.

Startled by my entrance, Tharna looked at her mother. "Is this the one you came to see, Ah-ma?"

The female chieftain nodded gravely. "He's here to see you, my dear daughter."

Tharna said in a soft whisper, "I see."

Then she closed her eyes, which should have aroused my sympathy. I was a kind person, but this was Tharna's fate, the fate of meeting her man. I was rendered powerless when her long, curving, rainbowlike lashes fluttered.

Feeling that even my bones were blistering, I cried out, "Tharna!"

And she responded. A tear rolled out of the corner of one eye. But the smile returned as she opened her eyes, and said, "You know my name. Now tell me yours."

"I'm the idiot of the Maichi family, Tharna."

I heard her laugh. I saw her laugh!

"You are an honest idiot," she said.

"Yes," I said, "yes, I am."

Laying her hand, so soft yet so cold, on mine, she asked, "Have you agreed?"

"Agreed to what?'

"To lend my mother some grain."

"Yes."

At that moment, my head was gurgling like boiling water. How could I have known the difference between yes and no? Her hand was as cold as jade. Once she received the answer she sought, she laid her other hand in mine. This one was scalding hot, like fire. She smiled before turning to her mother again. "Would you excuse us, please?"

Her mother and the maids left.

Now there were only the two of us inside the tent.

On the ground, tiny yellow flowers peeked out from between two rugs. Since I didn't dare look at her now, I fixed one eye on the flowers and the other on the two pairs of clasped hands.

She suddenly cried out, "You don't deserve me. You really don't deserve me."

I knew that, which was why I had trouble looking her in the eye.

But she merely wept a bit before leaning against me and saying, "I'll not fall in love with you. You cannot capture my heart, and you cannot earn my faithfulness. But I am yours now, so hold me."

Her words filled my heart with ecstasy and searing pain at the same time. I held her tightly, as if clasping my own fate. And at that moment, I realized that, even from the point of view of an idiot, this is not a perfect world. Everything in it is the same: When you don't want something, it is complete and pure. But when you take it in hand, you find it is only partly yours. Yet I was delighted to be holding this beauty in my arms, gazing into her eyes, my lips close to hers. I was the happiest man alive. "You see," I said. "You've turned me into an idiot. I don't know what to say."

She surprised me by laughing. "Turned you into an idiot? Aren't you the idiot known far and wide?" She reached up to block my lips, which were drawing up to hers, and muttered, "Who knows? Maybe you're a fascinating man after all."

Then she let me kiss her. But when I reached for her supple breasts, she stood up and straightened her clothes. "Get up," she said. "Let's go get the grain."

At that moment, my blood and marrow, and not just my brain, were bubbling over with love. In a daze, I walked outside with her.

There's something between us now, I told myself, but I wasn't sure what that something was.

After the female chieftain released my servants, we headed toward our fortress, the border granary. Tharna and I rode side by side ahead of everyone, followed by the Rongong chieftain, then her maids and my two young servants.

The steward's mouth dropped when he saw us.

I told him to open the granary; his mouth dropped even lower. Pulling me to one side, he said, "But, Young Master, surely you remember the master's orders."

"Open the granary."

Flames of madness must have shown in my eyes, for the steward, who believed that his absolute loyalty to the master gave him the right to insist upon certain things, said no more. He removed the key tied around his waist and tossed it to Sonam Tserang. When I turned around, I heard him mutter that, when all was said and done, I was no different from my smart brother, who could lose his wits over a woman. The old steward was a good man. As he watched Sonam Tserang walk downstairs to open the granary, then load sack after sack of barley onto the backs of Rongong's horses, he said, "Poor Young Master, you have no idea what you've done, do you?"

"I got the most beautiful girl alive."

"They never expected to get so much grain. You see, they didn't bring enough pack horses."

They were forced to use riding horses for some of the grain, and even then, with fewer than thirty horses, they weren't able to transport a quarter of one storage room's contents. We had twenty-five such rooms, each brimming with grain.

The chieftain walked over from the laden horses and told me that her daughter was returning with her to wait for Chieftain Maichi's marriage proposal. She added, "You'd better send someone soon."

Before they sent more horses for grain, that was.

Tharna disappeared beneath the clouds as their caravan moved into the distance.

"Why is that lovely girl going too?" the steward asked.

The inquisitive look on his face told me what he was thinking. He believed I'd fallen into Chieftain Rongong's beauty trap, and I began to regret letting Tharna go. What if she didn't return? What good would all that damned grain be then? None, none at all. An empty feeling in my heart stayed with me that night as I lay in bed listening to a high wind blow across the sky. Look at me, losing sleep over a woman.

My heart – now I felt your existence. You were filled half with longing and half with torment.

28 Engagement ∽

Chieftain Maichi came to inspect the northern border.

He'd already been to the south, where my brother had had a run-in with our habitual enemy, Chieftain Wangpo, who was up to his old tricks. He had launched a surprise attack to steal barley and corn, but had been beaten back in an ambush. My brother never lost a fight. But Chieftain Wangpo lost a son in the battle, and he broke an arm when his horse fell.

"Your brother is doing fine," Father said. "How about you?"

The words were barely out of his mouth when the steward knelt before him.

Chieftain Maichi said, "It appears I won't be getting good news here."

The steward then told him how we'd sent Chieftain Lha Shopa away empty-handed, but that the female chieftain had easily gotten the grain she'd come for. Dark clouds gathered on Father's face. He glared at me before saying to the steward, "You didn't do anything wrong. You can get up."

He did.

Then Father took a look at me. Ever since we'd taken on a tongueless historian, everyone had learned to talk with his eyes. Chieftain Maichi sighed, spitting out what was weighing on his heart. Well, the second young master's actions proved that there was indeed something wrong with his head. As chieftain, he no longer had to worry about deciding which of his sons was to be his successor. After the steward left, I said to Father, "Now Mother can't say anything."

Shocked by my comment, he was silent for a moment before saying, "I really don't know what's going on with you."

"I know I'll never be the chieftain."

Father didn't plan to scold me for giving our grain away. "Tell me about Rongong's daughter," he said.

"I love her. Please quickly arrange a marriage proposal for me."

"Son, you are lucky indeed. You cannot be Chieftain Maichi, but will wind up being Chieftain Rongong. They have no sons, so as son-in-law you'll become chieftain." He smiled. "Of course, you'll have to get a bit smarter."

I didn't know if I had the brains for it, but I knew I had too much love to forget Tharna.

My dear father said, "Tell me, what is love?"

"Love is bones filling up with bubbles."

It was a foolish answer, but my smart father understood. He laughed. "You poor little idiot. The bubbles will burst someday."

"They'll keep coming."

"All right, son. As long as Chieftain Rongong really wants to give you her daughter, she can have more barley. I'll send a messenger at once."

He said he was going to send a messenger at once! Then he asked me, "Are the Rongong maids prettier than ours?"

I answered with an emphatic yes.

"Could the chieftain have substituted a maid for her daughter?"

"She's Tharna, whether or not she's the chieftain's daughter, and I love her."

Father immediately changed the messenger's orders. Instead of delivering a letter, he was to find out if Tharna was indeed Chieftain Rongong's daughter. Now everyone was saying that I'd fallen into a real beauty trap, infatuated with a lowly maid of the Rongong family. I didn't care. I'd love her even if she were a maid. Her beauty was real, and it didn't matter if she was a chieftain's daughter or a maid. I climbed the sentry tower every day to wait for the messenger's return. Standing alone against the wind, I knew I'd lost the last thread of hope of ever becoming the Maichi chieftain. The blue sky was high and empty, not a single thing in sight. The ground was a vast carpet of green as far as the eye could see. To the south, deep mountains, and to the north, an expansive meadow, filled with roaming people, the hungry subjects of Chieftains Lha Shopa and Rongong. No one gave them food after Father's arrival, but they kept circling the granary. When they could no longer hold out, they filled up with river water, then returned to roam the area like wandering ghosts.

One day, lightning flashed and thunder rumbled. I was in the sentry tower, staggering under a strong wind, when a bolt of lightning sliced through the sky. I saw something, something I couldn't describe. So I yelled down at Father to tell him that something big was about to happen, and that I wanted to see what it was. My two young servants helped him up to the tower, where he shouted into his idiot son's ears, "What shitty big thing are you talking about? If you were struck by lightning, that would be something big!"

The wind took the words out of his mouth and blew them away. I had to turn my head to hear what he said.

But something *was* going to happen. I felt my heart leap out of my body. I screamed at Father, "You should have brought the historian with you. He ought to be here at a time like this."

Lightning struck one of the other sentry towers, creating a ball of fire, followed by the collapse of the soaring structure. It turned into a pile of rain-soaked yellow dirt, with charred logs and a solitary sentry sprawled on top.

The idiot son struggled when people tried to drag him down from his tower. Chieftain Maichi was seething. "Is this the big event you were talking about? Do you want me to die up here with you?"

He slapped me. It hurt, so I knew he loved me. I wouldn't have felt the pain if I'd been hit by someone who hated me. It actually hurt so much that I fell to the floor. Luckily, the steward restrained the enraged chieftain. A torrential rain fell as the thunder died out. No, actually it didn't die out; it just rolled off into the distance like a gigantic wheel. I wanted to lie there and drown in my own tears. But then I saw everyone's ears prick up, and I heard a sound too: horse hooves pounding the ground. Not one horse, but not a hundred either. It sounded like twenty or thirty. Father glanced at me, and he knew that my premonition had come true. He ordered the servants to pick up their weapons. But I jumped to my feet and cried with joy, "Tharna is back!"

Then came a series of rapid knocks on the door.

The door was opened and the female chieftain burst in with her entourage. By the time I'd run downstairs, everyone but Tharna had dismounted. They were all soaked, as if they'd just been plucked out of water. But the only one I saw was Tharna, still on horseback, dripping wet, as if she'd brought all the rain in the world with her, as if she were the goddess of rain.

I was the one who lifted her down off the horse.

With her arms around my neck, she fell with her full weight against me. She was so cold that my body temperature wasn't enough to warm her up; she needed a fire and she needed wine.

We didn't have enough women's clothes for them all to change into.

The female chieftain, her face ghostly white, managed a light comment for Chieftain Maichi. "What's this? I thought Maichi was a wealthy chieftain."

Father smiled at her before leading the men out. He closed the door and called out, "Dry your clothes first, then we can talk."

Complicated rituals were the norm when two chieftains met, so complex that both parties were made keenly aware of the distance between them. But this timely rain had brought the drenched chieftain to us and lightened the mood. This time a relaxed atmosphere attended the meeting of the two chieftains. She was inside, he was outside, and the two of them carried on casual banter through the window. I didn't say anything. Amid the pattering of rain, I could hear the women take off their wet clothes and shriek among themselves. I knew that Tharna had undressed, and I could tell that she was now sitting on a bearskin rug as heat from the fire caressed her body. But to my dismay, my mind filled up with such a dense fog that I could not picture what a beautiful woman like her looked like naked. Father tapped me on the head, and we went into another warm room.

Looking up at the darkening sky, the chieftain said, "You've done well."

The steward and I exchanged glances, not knowing what the chieftain was referring to.

The chieftain looked away from the rain-filled evening sky and repeated to himself, "You've done well. I can tell you will get the beautiful girl you desire."

The steward said, "I believe the master means more than that."

"Yes," the chieftain said, "I do. Something happened to them on the road. It doesn't matter what, because the female chieftain must now rely on our aid. But I wonder what it was."

The chieftain raised a finger as the steward opened his mouth to speak; understanding the signal, he said instead, "The young master knows, and I wouldn't be surprised if he planned the whole thing."

Meanwhile, I was trying to envision the sight of Tharna's naked body. Father cast me a questioning look, and I could tell he wanted me to say something. So I blurted out what was on my mind: "When the chieftain was here a few days ago, she changed clothes three times, but today she must strip down and dry her clothes by the fire." I asked, "Who took their clothes away?" I found that puzzling, but Father and the steward thought I was giving them a hint.

"Yes," Father said, "they were robbed. Is that what you're trying to tell us?"

The steward added, "They have enough guns and people to fend off common bandits. Yes! Yes, yes! Lha Shopa!"

"Lha Shopa's gone too far this time." Father patted me on the head. "Your barley has earned us more than ten times its value."

To be honest, I didn't quite understand what they were saying. Father clapped his hands for some liquor, and we each drank down a big bowlful. Then, with a hearty laugh, Father threw his bowl out the window; it smashed when it hit the ground. The liquor quickly set my body on fire.

At some point the rain stopped, and a brilliant sunset filled the sky. I told myself to remember this day and the gorgeous sunset that followed the rainstorm.

With the smell of liquor on our breath, Father and I returned to the women who were by then dressed. Wind, fire, dry and warm clothes, and delicious food had calmed the panicky female chieftain. She had wanted to renegotiate the distance between her and us as a buffer to regain a sense of security, but her attempt had failed. Now, when she tried to start over with the greeting ritual, Father said, "There's no need for that. Our initial meeting has already taken place. But look, your hair isn't dry yet. Why not just sit quietly by the fire?"

His words sent her reluctantly back to the fire with an ingratiating smile. She had lost her chieftain's airs. Chieftain Maichi was pleased with his tactic, but wasn't prepared to stop there, even though he was dealing with a woman. "Lha Shopa has tarnished his reputation. How could he not even leave you with a change of clothes?"

This unerring comment hit its mark, for a look of astonishment appeared on the female chieftain's face. After leaving here, they had indeed been robbed by Chieftain Lha Shopa, who had relieved them of all the barley I'd given them. Rongong tried to look stoic, but, being a woman, she could not keep tears from welling up in her eyes.

"Don't worry," Father said. "The Maichi family will set things right."

She turned her head to dry her tears, which lowered her status even more. And I hadn't even mentioned the kidnapping. If I had, she'd have been in a real bind. Tharna looked at me before getting up to leave.

I followed her out, pursued by hushed laughter.

The night air, washed by the rain, was fresh and clear. The moon had risen and was shining down on the rippling river. Those bright, silvery rays lit up my heart and the love it contained. Tharna kissed me.

Stupefied by her kiss, all I could say was "What a wonderful moon!"

Her smile was like the clear, cold moonlight. "We barely have time for important matters," she said, "and all you can talk about is the moon."

"The river is so bright!"

She softened her voice. "Are you trying to irritate me?"

"My father is going to present a marriage proposal to your mother." I felt like kissing her, but she blocked my mouth with her hand, while allowing my legs and chest to touch her body.

"You won't tell your father, will you?" she asked.

I knew what she meant. "All I told Father," I said, "was that I found you in the pasture."

She fell into my arms. I wanted to take her to my room, but she asked to return to her mother. So I just held her for the longest time, bathing in the moonlight.

Tears glistened in Tharna's eyes when she told me how they'd been robbed, and my heart filled with anger and pain. "Did they do anything to the women?" I asked.

She knew I was asking if she'd been raped. Covering her face and shuffling her feet, she said softly that she and her mother had fled under the protection of their guards. The necessity of marrying a virgin had never occurred to me, since that concept is not part of our education. But I'd asked anyway. After giving her answer, she too thought it was a bizarre question. "Why do you ask?"

I said I didn't know.

The robbery had nothing to do with me, but Father and the steward believed I had set a trap by giving grain to the female chieftain. When the chieftain asked the steward whose idea it had been to give her the grain, he was told that it was the young master's idea. So Father asked what we should do next. Whatever is necessary, I replied loudly, because I was very upset. For even though the chieftain's protocols allowed me to be with the beautiful Tharna, I could not take her to bed, like a lowly maid, not until we were married. That was why I'd said impatiently, Whatever is necessary.

Father clapped his hands and laughed heartily.

The two chieftains held the engagement ceremony at the border. Extravagant rites were the norm for the children of chieftains, but since these were extraordinary times, at an even more special place, everything was simplified. In fact, my engagement ceremony entailed only a grand feast. We ate and we ate, consuming a vast quantity of delicious food. Sangye Dolma, who was in charge in the kitchen, came upstairs and placed before Tharna and me a large platter of food she'd made herself. "Congratulations, Young Master," she said softly.

After the meal was finished, Tharna and I were separated. We were not to see each other again until the marriage ceremony. Prior to parting we exchanged personal items: rings from our fingers, necklaces, and pieces of jade from our sashes. I couldn't sleep that night, my mind filled with thoughts of Tharna. Then I heard soft footsteps coming up the stairs from one of the guest rooms below. Not long after that, animal-like panting sounds emerged from Father's room next door. Then I heard Chieftain Maichi say, "It's not often that two chieftains do this."

The female chieftain laughed. "You're not so very old."

"I can still manage."

"But not that young either."

Even though the steward had assigned the two women separate rooms, the female chieftain had chosen to share a room with her daughter instead. Now, with the two chieftains having such a merry time together, it was too good an opportunity to miss. So I groped my way downstairs to the guest room. But not a trace of her smell on the bed, let alone the girl herself. It turned out that she'd been sent back to the Rongong estate after the engagement feast, in the company of Maichi guards, who carried machine guns to protect the large amount of grain we'd given to the Rongong family. If Lha Shopa's people showed up this time, they would pay a heavy price.

I asked Father what was going on.

"Didn't you say we should do whatever is necessary?" He answered with a sort of petulant look. Fascinating, absolutely fascinating! It was as if I had become the chieftain and he was now the idiot son.

"Well, then," I said, "that's fine."

He told me he'd kept the female chieftain around to trick Lha Shopa's people. But how will they know if she stayed inside the fort the whole time? he added. I knew he liked wide-open spaces, so I said, "If you two ride out on your horses, they'll see her."

So the two chieftains left in the company of guards. I wasn't sure if Father had some sort of plan or was simply going out for some fun in the wild with the female chieftain. So I went up to the sentry tower to find out. It had rained the night before, and now the sky was so clear that I could see for miles. The starving serfs knew they should seek food from their own chieftains, not from us, but they kept returning to our place, which they knew was the source of grain. When they turned back, those who had lost all hope could barely stagger; but none of them had died anywhere near our fort, not yet. That would have been more than I could bear. They simply came to see the place that was said to have plenty of grain, then turned and headed back home. Like pilgrims visiting a holy site, they braved hardships to lay their eyes on a spot close to heaven before returning to their own dusty homeland, where people starved even in the absence of natural disasters. Compared to them, the Maichi subjects were heaven's chosen people, the favored children of Buddha.

More and more birds of prey circled the skies above the distant blue mountains, where many people must have died.

I knew that valley like the back of my hand: this was the season when water in the creeks rose daily, and wild cherries bloomed. People were dying of hunger under trees on the road home, and I wondered if the fragrance of the blossoms might guide them to

210

heaven. Since their masters couldn't help them enter heaven, they may as well ask the flowers for help.

I watched Father and the female chieftain ride among the dazed crowds. They stopped by a river, where their reflections spread across its calm surface. But they were looking into the distance, not at their own images in the water.

They took the same route every day.

And every day I climbed the sentry tower to watch. More and more I found myself wishing they'd keep going until they reached the blue mountains in Lha Shopa's land, where they would be killed. I couldn't shake the feeling that Lha Shopa's people would kill the two chieftains the minute they entered the blue valley. The thought amused me at first, but I began to feel guilty when it persisted. The fact that Aryi followed me silently like a dog only increased my guilt feelings.

So one day I said to Father, "Don't go out there anymore."

He turned and looked triumphantly at Chieftain Rongong, the woman who had now been sharing his bed for many nights. What that look meant was, I was right about my son.

They had already decided not to go out again.

For years, good fortune had followed the Maichi family, me included. Now I had said something that mirrored Father's thoughts. I just smiled. A foolish person's smile is always profound and mysterious.

29 It's Happening ∾

I had a wonderful sleep that night. Most nights, thoughts of Tharna kept me awake. But not that night. And thoughts of her were usually the first to pop into my head in the mornings. But this morning, before I had time to think of her, I heard people shouting and horses whinnying in the yard.

More horses had arrived to transport grain for the Rongong family. Then the horses and the female chieftain were gone. Looking exhausted, Father went up to his room to sleep. But before he climbed into bed, he said, "Wake me when it happens."

I didn't ask what was going to happen. For me the best thing was to wait quietly. Out on the southern border my brother was accumulating victories, using grain to attract the other chieftains' people, who then became his subjects. By the time Father died, he would control more people and more territory than ever. But while my brother was conquering the south, we were simply handing over vast amounts of barley to Chieftain Rongong. "Those two have been duped by the Rongong women," he said. "One of these days, the female chieftain will be sitting in our estate and giving orders."

To him, both Father and I were idiots.

We quickly got wind of this comment, which he had made to those closest to him, but Father said nothing until he and I were alone. "Is your brother smart," he asked, "or is he just someone pretending to be smart?"

I didn't answer.

To be honest, I couldn't tell the difference. If someone knew he was smart, of course he'd want everyone else to know. Father's question reminded me of the other question he asked so often: Are you an idiot or just someone pretending to be stupid? "Your brother would find it impossible to believe that you had done a better job than he," he said. "But you're right, we must do whatever is necessary. I'm going to bed now. Wake me when it's happening."

Since I didn't know what was going to happen, I turned and gazed blankly at the wide-open spaces outside.

There was no change in the green covering the ground, not anywhere. It was as if summer had settled on the land without change for centuries. I yawned, and so did my two young servants, before I'd even closed my mouth. I should have kicked them, but I didn't want to take the trouble. I was too busy wondering what was about to happen, but no answer came. So I simply imitated Father, and yelled, "Stop yawning! And call me when it happens."

"Yes, Young Master."

"What's going to happen?"

"Something, Young Master."

So they had no answer either. Then my head started to get all muddled. I thought I saw something, but not clearly. I didn't realize I'd fallen sleep until I opened my eyes. I was still leaning against the veranda railing. Once I was awake, the deep blue sky began to turn gray. The windblown tattered clouds were moving faster than a snake slithering along the base of a wall. It was past noon, so I must have slept a long time.

"Is it happening yet?" I asked.

But my two servants were long gone.

I panicked a bit when no one answered. Then I heard footsteps behind me. I knew it was the chieftain, my father.

"You are indeed blessed," he said when he was standing beside me. "I couldn't sleep a wink in bed, but you can fall asleep standing up."

Now it was my turn to ask him, "Is it happening yet?"

Father shook his head, slightly bewildered. "It should be, since the place isn't far from here. They should have arrived by now."

He pointed to the distant undulating mountains, where so many people had starved to death.

Finally realizing what was about to happen, I yawned grandly.

"Go get some sleep," Father said. "I'll wake you when it happens."

I went inside and lay down. I was in the habit of sticking my head under the blanket when I went to bed, though I didn't care if it was still covered after I'd fallen asleep. I couldn't do anything about it then, anyway. Well, I'd barely entered the darkness under the blanket when there was a loud boom somewhere. The noise was like blazing light, illuminating everything. I threw back the blanket and ran out of the room shouting, "It's happening, it's happening!"

At that moment, the fort was basking in the last and the warmest sunlight of the day. Having nothing to do, people lounged under the sun, as if trying to milk every last drop of enjoyment from life. My two servants were playing six-piece chess. They were the only two people in the world who never showed an inkling of surprise, no matter what I did. Aryi didn't even look up when I shouted, while Sonam Tserang flashed me a silly grin before returning to the game.

But what really surprised me was that Father and the steward were sitting cross-legged, also engaged in a game of chess. The slanting sun was sprinkling its remaining light on them. My shouts had no effect. I think they were pretending they hadn't heard me, so as not to embarrass me. They all knew that something would happen that day and were waiting. At a moment like this, all those pricked-up ears would have heard me, even if I'd whispered "It's happening," let alone shouted.

My image had changed in Father's eyes, from that of an idiot to someone with superior intelligence who only acted like a dullard. But with my stupid shout, all that vanished like a puff of smoke. The servants were looking up at me to determine the source of the shout, shielding their damned eyes from the blinding sun with their hands. Neither Father nor the steward so much as twitched.

My shout vanished in the afternoon sun, which illuminated everything as far as the eye could see.

I was hopeless. A hopeless idiot. All right, then I'll just act like one. Let the whole world – the chieftain, the steward, the servants, men and women everywhere – laugh behind my back and spit in my face. Let them say, Ha, ha, you idiot! You bloody idiot! Go to hell, all of you! The idiot was about to sing. And that's what I did, to the tune of the ballad "King Bende Is Dead."

It's happening, it's happening.
What was planned didn't happen.
What was unplanned is happening.
It's happening.
It's happening.

As I sang, I paced back and forth on the veranda, kicking at the railing as if taunting them all. I wanted to mask my disappointment and anger at myself. At that rate, the Maichi's idiot son would soon be wailing over his stupidity.

But, wait, let me take back my tears.

Why? Because it was happening as I sang. Me, I was so immersed in hopelessness that I wasn't even aware that it was happening. I sang and I sang, and I saw people throw their game pieces into the air and I saw the servants running around. My mouth was busy singing while my eyes were fixed on the chaos downstairs. Maybe, I was thinking, those people thought I might leap out of sadness. Father ran over to me, waving and pointing toward the distant valley. Then I heard it too – gunfire in the direction Father was pointing.

I stopped singing.

Father yelled at the steward, "He knew it. He knew it before any of us. He's the smartest idiot in the world."

"Long live the Maichi family," the steward shouted back. "He's a prophet."

They were shouting as they ran up. I had nothing to say to them. Maybe I'd used up too much energy singing. "I'm tired," I said. "I'm going back to sleep."

They followed me into my room as fierce gunfire continued in the distant valley. Only the Maichi weapons could lay down such dense, happy sounds. As I climbed into bed, the steward said, "Go on, sleep well, Young Master. There's nothing the Maichi weapons can't handle."

"You may go now," I said. "You take care of everything."

They left the room.

Chieftain Maichi had told his men to lie in wait for Chieftain Lha Shopa when he came to rob the female chieftain. Now that the strategy was working, I was ready to fall sleep. I had no desire to know what the world would be like when I woke up in the morning.

I … just wanted … to sleep …

Our two northern neighbors were fighting over grain.

On this land of ours, whenever a battle erupted between two chieftains, there would always be one or more other chieftains who, unwilling to remain idle, skittered back and forth mediating.

This time, the Maichi family was considered to be the provocateur of a grain war between two northern chieftains. When the self-appointed mediators came, Father told them rudely, "You want my grain too, so I advise you to say nothing."

The Maichi's idiot son said, "If what you held in your hands was grain and not that shitty opium, you could say whatever you wanted."

The steward, on the other hand, ordered a sumptuous feast for our uninvited guests.

What could any of them say? Nothing, and they knew it.

After sending the mediators off, Father prepared to return to the house. But before setting out, he said to me, "Let them fight."

His meaning was crystal-clear; there could be no misunderstanding.

"All right," I replied, "let them fight."

The chieftain patted me on the shoulder and set out with a few of his guards.

They'd gone quite a ways when the horses began to trot. Then

215

he abruptly reined in his horse, which reared up on its hind legs. He turned to shout to me, "Do whatever is necessary!"

"Why does that sound so familiar?" I asked.

Sonam Tserang answered, "That's what you said to him."

I asked the crippled steward, "Did I really say that?"

"I think so."

He always grew evasive when we touched upon the relationship between Father and me. I couldn't blame him. He'd done so much for me. Like now, for instance. Since both Father and I felt we had to do whatever was necessary, I told him to feed the Rongong people and horses so they could launch a surprise attack on Lha Shopa's starving subjects. I also sent the female chieftain a few machine gunners and grenade throwers, which meant that I had decided who would win and who would lose this battle before it even started.

30 New Subjects ∾

Let the female chieftain be the victor. That's what was necessary, and that's what I did.

Then I started making preparations for something else.

I mentioned before that my brother should not have built a fort on the border. The Maichi estate was a fortress, but it had been built at a time when the family was under constant attack, when there were no machine guns, grenades, or cannons. Now times had changed, and what went around came around. The Maichi family no longer lived with the constant fear of attack, as before, not even when we settled at the borders. Now it was the other families' turn to fear us. All I had to do was meddle in others' battles, and I could decide the outcome beforehand. Of course our northern neighbors couldn't know that they were fighting a war whose outcome was already determined.

It took no effort on my part; I just had to wait for the female chieftain to send her people so I could load their horses with grain and supply bullets for the machine gunners. When the prospects were that good, so was the mood; even an idiot was smarter than usual at such times, his every action a stroke of genius.

216

All right, then, let me get down to what I was planning to do.

I told Dolma to set up five cauldrons along the river, then pour in some barley, add a bit of salt and some aged butter, and roast the grain at a high temperature, spreading the salivating aroma into the distance under a clear sky. I was sending the hungry people a feeding signal. Within half a day, the famine victims who had faded away returned. When they reached the nearby creek, they lay down on the ground, as if content just to confirm the source of the aroma. Dolma waved her ladle, and shouted, "Get up. Anyone who's lying down won't get any."

They got to their feet and forded the creek like sleepwalkers.

Each of them received a big ladleful of barley roasted in butter.

Now Dolma had gotten a taste of power. I think she liked it; otherwise, she wouldn't have kept wielding the charitable ladle even after she was tired and drenched in sweat. If she'd stayed on the estate, she'd never have experienced such a wonderful feeling. Only with me could she wave her ladle with such style in front of a mob of starving people who were staring hungrily at her hand.

"One ladleful each, no more, no less," she repeatedly yelled with gusto. "Those who want another meal will have to work. Work for our benevolent and generous young master."

Lha Shopa's people, after eating the buttery barley, were now coming to work for me.

Following my instructions, the steward had them tear a wall down from our boxy fort.

I wanted to take down the row of rooms facing east, so the morning sun would shine its glorious rays on us unhindered. In the meantime, the building, now with its open yard, would be connected with the vast fields. The crippled steward asked if he should build a wall somewhere with the rubble, but I told him that wasn't necessary. I believed I'd seen the future, in which it made no difference whether there was a wall by the gate or not.

"Can't you see what lies in the future?" I asked him.

"Yes, I can," he said.

"Okay, then, tell me what you've seen."

"We are using machine guns to wipe out an attacking force, like a cavalry charge, in the open field."

I had to laugh at that. Yes, machine guns could easily repel an attack, like slaughtering sheep. But that wasn't what I had in mind.

Opium had enriched Chieftain Maichi and brought him machine guns, while wreaking havoc on the other chieftains. It was all a matter of timeliness. So why should we box ourselves in?

It took no more than four or five days to demolish one side of the fort, which was now a mansion, a magnificent edifice.

Dolma asked if she should continue to cook. I told her to keep it up for five more days, during which time the famine victims hauled adobe blocks and rocks over to the creek; as it soaked in the water, the adobe slowly disintegrated, turning the water muddy for several days, until there was nothing left but exposed rocks that shone in the water. Those that settled to the bottom created sprays and ripples on the surface. Yes, with those rocks, the creek was now more like a river.

On that day, I told myself that river water ought to be clear.

But I was amazed by what I saw before I even had a chance to go down to look at the water.

The compound facing the open fields was filled with starving people who had torn down the wall. After the demolition work was completed, Dolma led servants down to the creek to retrieve the cauldrons. The famine victims then left the area and stayed away for several days; I assumed they wouldn't return. But no, they had just gone home to summon their families; they now spilled out of the compound and filled the meadow between the house and the creek.

They fell to their knees as soon as I appeared.

I'd never seen so many people at one time. They neither did nor said anything, but such a huge mob of people exerted tremendous pressure by its presence alone.

The steward asked me what we should do.

I told him I had no idea.

So they spread out and sat outside, a sea of black. When I wasn't around, they sat or stood doing nothing; when I made an appearance, they fell to their knees. Now I regretted taking down the wall.

One day had passed, and the second day was nearly over, but they were still out there, getting hungrier by the minute. When their hunger grew unbearable, they went down to the creek to drink. Normally, people don't drink that much water. That's what cows and horses do – bury their heads in the water and drink until they can hardly breathe, until their bellies swell up with all the water sloshing around inside. Now these people were drinking like cows and horses. Even in my dreams, I could hear them gasping for air after nearly choking themselves, and I could hear water sloshing around in their bellies. I knew they weren't intentionally disturbing someone as kind as I; if they had been, they wouldn't have wrapped their arms around their bellies when they walked.

On the third day, when they went down to the creek, some of them toppled into the water. Unable to pick themselves up, they drowned in the shallows. It took the better part of a day for them to swell up like sacks and be carried off by the flowing water. People who didn't go down to drink died too; they were picked up and dumped into the creek to float off to the edge of heaven.

Just look at how well behaved Lha Shopa's people are: even in the grip of hopeless misery, they don't utter a sound of protest, pinning what hope is left on a kind person who isn't even their master.

I was that kind person.

Not a single grain of barley had seeped through my fingers during those three days, but the people didn't complain. How could they, since I wasn't their master? When they first appeared, I often heard the buzzing of muted prayers, but that had stopped. Now they simply died, one after another. They died by the creek and were baked by the sun, swelled up like bloated sacks that were carried on the water to the edge of heaven.

On the third evening the nightmares began. Before I even opened my eyes on that fourth day, I knew the people were still outside, their hair damp from early-morning dew; none of them had left. The stillness enshrouding such a vast collection of humanity was decidedly not tranquil; rather, it exuded tremendous pressure.

"I can't stand it!" I screamed. "I can't stand any more of this!"

Since I'd never missed a meal in my life, the force of my shout carried my words far into the misty morning. The famine victims raised their heads from between their knees, as the sun leaped above the horizon and drove away the mist. Yes, I was overcome by their patience and by the might of their hopelessness, which was more powerful than all the other forces of the world combined. Too weak to get out of bed, I moaned, and ordered the servants, "Cook something, cook something for them to eat. Make them talk, make them cry, let them do whatever they want."

My servants, the steward, Dolma, my two young slaves, and many others had already made those very preparations, without telling me. They were just waiting for my order before lighting the kindling under the cauldrons.

My people cheered when the fire was lit, but the starving people didn't make a sound. They remained quiet even when the food was being distributed. I couldn't say if I was fond of these subjects or afraid of them.

So I shouted again, "Tell them only this one meal, just this one. After they've eaten, they'll have the strength to get on the road and return to where they came from."

My words were relayed to them by the servers.

Tears streamed down Dolma's face as she said to them, "Don't trouble our kind master. Go back to your homes. Return to your own masters. Didn't heaven give each of us a master?"

Meanwhile, their masters weren't having such an easy time either.

Now that they had been fed, Chieftain Rongong's people were running down Lha Shopa's people. One could say that I had found people to fight for the Maichi family at the northern border. My brother, who was more competent than I, personally led his people in attacking the enemy in the southern mountains, which were hotter and more rugged than here.

More and more people were thinking that while he was the smart one, good luck was always on the side of his idiot brother. That's how I felt too. Good fortune followed me like a shadow. Once or twice, when I sensed that that mysterious thing was close by, I turned and stomped my foot. But it was a shadow, not a dog that could be frightened off. You can't shoo away your shadow.

Aryi asked me what I was trying to frighten off when I stomped my foot.

"A shadow," I said.

He smiled, and said, "Not a shadow." Then my future executioner's bloodless face began to glow, and I knew what he wanted to say. As an executioner, he was keenly interested in the netherworld. Sure enough, he said excitedly, "You can't scare away ghosts by stomping your foot. You have to spit at them."

He showed me how to do it by spitting behind me. "Like that."

I couldn't let an executioner spit like that. If good fortune were indeed following me day and night, wouldn't his exorcism scare it off? So I slapped him. "I'd let you sear my mouth shut with a

220

red-hot branding iron if *I* spit behind me. What makes a slave like you think he can do it?"

The light in Aryi's face went out.

I said, "Go down there and work a ladle for a while."

Even the poorest of my servants experienced the sweet taste of dispensing charity that day. In this world, people who give to others are the lucky ones. So I made sure that everyone had a chance to ladle out food and feel how wonderful it was to give. I could hear their silent shouts: Long live Second Young Master.

But those other people continued to occupy the open field, even after they were fed.

"It's time to wrap it up," I shouted to the smiling steward, who walked up dragging his gimpy leg. "Tell them to leave. Send them away."

He had waited until the last person had slurped down the final ladleful of barley congee before coming upstairs, looking contented. With my shout still hanging in the air, he said, "They're going to leave now. They promised me they would."

At that very moment, the mob began to move. Although they were silent, their feet had regained enough strength to make the ground speak. The combined sound of each faint footstep, given the magnitude of the crowd, caused the earth to tremble slightly. A billowing cloud of dust followed them; by the time the dust cleared, they had already walked to the opposite bank of the creek.

A long sigh of relief escaped from my mouth.

But then they stopped in the field across the creek, where the men left their women and children to form a separate group. What were they doing? Were they planning to attack us now that their bellies were full? If so, I hoped they'd start right away, because I really didn't have anything to do between sunset and bedtime. If they attacked now, we'd open fire, and it would all be over in time for me to go to bed. That way, a situation no chieftain had ever encountered before would be quickly wrapped up. Yet there must have been a chieftain sometime who'd faced a similar situation!

The men sat down and stayed put for a long time, until a minor disturbance erupted among them. With the afternoon sun shining in my eyes, I could see only the center of the disturbance, like a tiny eddy that disappeared as quickly as it had come. A few of the men emerged from the crowd and waded back across the creek, heading toward us. Behind them, the others stood up to watch.

It took a long time for them to cross the open field.

They came and knelt before me. They had killed the headmen and fortress leaders who were loyal to Lha Shopa and brought their heads to me. Staring at the heads lying at my feet, I asked, "Why are you doing this?"

They said that the Lha Shopa chieftain had lost his benevolence, as well as the intelligence and bearing necessary to judge a situation, a common trait among earlier Lha Shopa chieftains. So his subjects were deserting him. Chieftain Maichi would now rule an even vaster territory with many more subjects. It was destiny; it was also what the people desired.

I summoned Aryi and introduced him to these people, who had decided to pledge allegiance to us. Not every chieftain had an executioner, and even among those who did, none had such a long family line of them. They all gazed with curiosity at this long-limbed, pale-faced youngster.

"Who took the lead in killing your masters?" I asked them.

They all knelt down again; shrewd and brave, they shouldered the responsibility together. I liked them already, so I said, "Get up. I won't kill any of you. There are so many of you, my executioner wouldn't know where to begin."

They laughed.

And so, several thousand of Chieftain Lha Shopa's people came over to the Maichi family.

People said that Lha Shopa's land was like a big tree, formed by many mountain ridges. A river that kept getting bigger and bigger washed down the mountain to create a widening valley, and that was the trunk. The roots were the area near the mouth of the river, which roared down like thunder, while the branches were the mountain ridges created by upstream tributaries. That night the steward brought me a map, which I studied under a lamp for a long time, finally discerning the vague shape of a tree from the twisting lines. Now I had lopped off two of the thickest branches. I anointed the people in front of me as new headmen. They asked me to give them a new leader, but I told them I would give them only barley, not a leader.

"You'll be your own leaders," I said, "and then I will be your leader."

The next day was a busy one. I distributed enough grain to tide the people over for the year, and gave them seeds for the years to follow. But instead of leaving that night, they built bonfires by the creek. People who had stared death in the eye now displayed incredible passion; their cheers rumbled between heaven and earth like spring thunder when I waved to them from a distance. And when I went down among them, they knelt, stirring up so much dust that I choked. I still couldn't believe that all those thousands of people had become mine so quickly. I really couldn't. When the dust rose, my two slaves came up and stood by me, one on each side, afraid that someone might harm me. But I pushed them away; there was no need for that. We couldn't begin to supply enough bite-sized pieces for all those people if they decided to turn on us. But they wouldn't, for the simple reason that they were now part of the Maichi family. I was lucky, in that heaven was watching over me, as were the gods of fate, so no one could hurt me.

I wanted to say something, but was still choking on the dust stirred up by all the people; they were not fated to hear their new master's voice. I simply waved them to their feet. Their foreheads, all of them, young and old, were smeared with dirt. They had deserted their master, but that did not mean they desired no master. That idea would never cross their minds. Even if someone tried to force it into their heads, they would simply frown and push it away with little effort. Look at those blank faces around the bonfires: their eyes shine, bright and lively, as they gaze at me, as if witnessing the miraculous appearance of a god. When they saw me off, it was as if they were watching a god returning to heaven.

They departed the next morning, leaving behind only the vastness of the creek banks. I felt an emptiness inside as things quieted down after all those hectic days. I also sensed a problem. But I didn't bring it up; since, sooner or later, others invariably sensed any problem that worried me, it was always better to let them mention it first.

Sure enough, at breakfast, the steward said, "I hope those people weren't sent by Chieftain Lha Shopa to trick us out of our grain. First Young Master would have a good laugh at our expense."

Sonam Tserang said, "If you don't believe in the second young master, go serve the first young master. We can take care of things here."

"Just who do you think you are? What gives you the right to speak to me like that?" The steward raised his hand, but let it drop when he saw my face. Sonam Tserang smirked triumphantly.

The steward turned to Aryi. "Give him two hard slaps."

Aryi slapped his friend twice but clearly not hard enough. So the steward was forced to punish the executioner. Yes, executioners punish others when they make mistakes, but when the executioners themselves are in the wrong, people above them mete out punishment to them. The steward hit him so hard that his hand stung. Sonam Tserang laughed again. I did too, but quickly changed my expression, and commanded Aryi, "Hit him."

This time Aryi put everything into it. He may have looked frail, but one slap sent the brawny Sonam Tserang to the ground. Now everyone laughed. After the laughter died down, I told the steward to write to Chieftain Maichi and tell him that his territory had increased and that he had gained several thousand more subjects on the northern border. The steward wanted me to wait awhile before sending the letter, but he knew I'd been right so far, so he had the letter delivered.

The situation on the northern border was looking excellent, since the female chieftain, with my support, had Chieftain Lha Shopa's army in complete disarray.

"What else can Chieftain Lha Shopa do?" I asked the steward.

"Chieftain Lha Shopa? I think he'll have to come here again." I laughed as the image of the fat Chieftain Lha Shopa, constantly wiping his sweaty face with a towel, came to mind.

Eight ⁓

31 Border Market ⁓

Chieftain Lha Shopa returned.

He thought he'd come to the wrong place when he saw a wide-open, magnificent building instead of an enclosed fortress.

This time there was no talk of being my uncle.

Although the gate had been taken down, he still rolled off his horse at the spot where the gate had been. "Rolled off" is not meant as an insult, because Lha Shopa was so fat that he couldn't lift his leg to dismount. The single most important thing to remember in order to mount and dismount with style is to raise your leg to the proper height. Obesity had caused our one-time horseback warrior to lose his vigor and agility; now he had to shift his body to one side, lift his rear end off the saddle, and, with the help of gravity, drop into the arms of his slaves.

He walked toward me with obvious difficulty. I could hear him panting heavily even from a distance. He must have caught a cold, for his voice was hoarse as he announced, "Most clever and benevolent Young Master of the Maichi family, your nephew Lha Shopa has come to see you."

"I told my people that Lha Shopa would bring us wonderful gifts."

"Yes, yes. I have."

His hands shook as he removed some things from inside his shirt and thrust them into my hands. I told the steward to unfold them and show me. They turned out to be a thick stack of old documents and some bronze seals. His subjects had deserted him, so now he had no choice but to hand over to me the legal documents and seals for the fortresses belonging to his people, thus acknowledging his acceptance of the new reality. The papers and seals, all awarded by emperors of past dynasties, were proof that I now truly owned his fortresses.

I was about to say something but held back, knowing that someone else would say it for me. Sure enough, the steward offered, "Our young master said that anyone who wanted our barley would have to pay ten times the usual price, but you wouldn't listen. Now you're paying more than ten times."

Lha Shopa agreed wholeheartedly. "Can we have the barley now?" he asked, adding that the backs of his horses were weighed down with silver.

I said, "I don't want that much silver. I'll sell you the barley at the usual price."

He had, of course, been expecting me to refuse. And when I didn't, the poor, desperate man nearly wept. "My God!" he sobbed. "The Maichi family has nearly ruined its nephew Lha Shopa."

"Everyone can use a lesson."

From the logic of the victors, the Maichi family had paid an even higher price.

Isn't that right? Would we have had to put up with so much trouble if they hadn't insisted on growing poppies like us? Anger rose up inside me with this thought. "We charge everyone the same price for the barley," I said. "Three times the usual cost. That goes for you too."

"But you just said you only wanted ..."

He stopped when he saw the icy look on my face and said with a pitiful smile, "I'll shut up. I'll be in even worse shape if Uncle Maichi changes his mind again."

"Now that we're clear on that," the steward said, "you may proceed to the guest room. We have prepared food and drink for you."

The next morning, Chieftain Lha Shopa's animals were loaded down with barley, but I didn't really charge him three times the usual cost.

When he was leaving he said, "You've given food to my people. Please also spare them from being attacked."

I knew what he was referring to, but I simply gave his horse a whip on the rump, sending the animal shooting forward with him in the saddle. I shouted at his receding back to come buy more barley when he needed it. For what the Maichi family had built on the border wasn't a fort, but a market for trade.

Yes, now I could finally say that it was a market, not a fort. The open spaces along the river would be an ideal place for traders' stalls and tents.

The steward said, "We should be hearing from the female chieftain soon."

I told him to write a letter and tell her what we expected from her.

But she didn't respond at once, since her people were now fed, and she had defeated Chieftain Lha Shopa. Finally a letter came, in which she said she was still getting her daughter's dowry ready, that she herself had been engaged in the man's work of leading an army on the battlefield. She even asked me, "Would my future son-in-law please tell me if Chieftain Rongong should get a man to do a woman's job for her? Something like preparing a dowry for her daughter?"

Having eaten the Maichis' barley and won a minor battle with the protection of Maichi machine guns, the female chieftain was now acting like a mare in heat with her tail raised.

She was quite a capable woman, but not a very smart one, and should have realized that the world was changing. Whenever new things appeared, old rules had to change. But most people could not see that, and I felt sorry for them. She, unfortunately, was among those who aroused my sympathy. On the other hand, she'd said exactly what I was hoping she'd say. When Tharna was here, my love for her had caused me to lose my head. But over time, I found I couldn't even recall what she looked like. Which meant that the female chieftain's most lethal weapon had lost its power. I was quite pleased with what she'd told me.

It took only two days for all the machine gunners and grenade throwers I'd lent her to return. She sent people to chase them back, but they fell on the road amid the cackling sound of machine-gun fire. It's hard for an arrogant man to realize his own mistakes, let alone an arrogant woman.

She didn't know that Lha Shopa had gotten barley from me.

Whenever Lha Shopa's long procession of horses reached a mill, they unloaded some of the barley, and by the time they reached the center of his territory, it was all gone. So they turned and headed back to the border. Recalling what I'd said about setting up a market at the northern border, Lha Shopa brought along a large group of servants and threw up some tents on the riverbank so he could trade items from his land for our grain.

After filling their stomachs with the processed barley, Lha Shopa's soldiers had regained their morale and it would be fool-hardy to go up against such soldiers without machine guns. The Rongong army, not used to fighting without the protection of machine guns, quickly retreated, all the way back beyond the front lines of the first battle.

Instead of returning to his land, Chieftain Lha Shopa settled down near the border market, where he often invited me to his riverside tent to drink with him. On clear days, it was wonderful to sit and drink next to the river by the open field.

Lha Shopa and I soon got down to doing some real business.

He paid for what he bought not only with silver, but also with medicinal herbs, furs, even fine horses. The steward told me that these things would command high prices in the Han area. So he put together a large team of horses to take the stuff to the east and sell it to the Han Chinese, from whom he then bought more grain. Very quickly a prosperous market grew up on the northern border. More and more chieftains came to pitch tents across the river, bringing all sorts of good things to exchange for barley. And although the Maichi family had plenty to sell, there is a limit to everything. We were close to the Han territory, which made things difficult when the Han courts were strong. That was the main reason the Maichi chieftain could never be all-powerful. But then the Han people had a revolution, followed by a war, and the poppy seeds turned our luck around. Poppies made the Maichi family strong and impover-ished the other chieftains. Now we sent the stuff we received in exchange for the barley to the Han area, where we bought more grain to exchange for other things back at the border. A single round trip turned a tenfold profit. The steward made a careful cal-culation: even when the famine was over and normal times returned, we could still double or triple our money by trading things other than grain.

In the history of chieftains, I was the first to turn a defensive fortress into a market. And whenever I pondered that, I was reminded of our tongueless historian, who, if only he had been there, would surely have understood the significance of such a beginning. Out here, the people around me said something like this had never happened before, not ever. That's all they could think of to say. I'm sure the historian would have had much more profound thoughts on the subject.

32 News from the South ∼

I was uneasy.

What had things come to when someone like me was telling people what to do? A strange world, indeed. Yet I wasn't convinced that the strangeness was limited to the fact that an idiot was thinking for everyone else. On the other hand, I couldn't tell you exactly what it was that made this world so strange. For nights I lay in bed pondering this question, oblivious to the woman sleeping beside me. This particular one had been sent from the fortress of recent defectors from Chieftain Lha Shopa. I'd been so wrapped up in a question that wasn't really mine to worry about that I hadn't even asked her name during the several nights she'd been sleeping in my bed. It's not that I didn't want to ask; it simply hadn't occurred to me, not once. Luckily, she was a good-natured girl and didn't complain. She'd come to pay a debt for those who had been pulled back from the brink of death. But I had no desire for her, because I was consumed by questions about the world we live in.

Finally, one morning, the desire awoke in me. As I've said before, I almost always felt lost first thing in the morning and had to ask myself where and who I was. But not that morning. Forgetting the questions, I woke the soundly sleeping girl, who smelled like a young mare, and asked her, "Who are you?"

She woke up slowly, and as I looked into her sleepy eyes, I figured she didn't know who she was either at that moment. But once she was awake, her face blushed the same color as the nipples on her firm breasts. I smiled when I told her that, which made her blush even more deeply. She reached out to hold me, pressing her strong body against mine.

"Do you know who I am?" I asked her.

"They say you're a kind idiot, a smart idiot, if you're really an idiot at all, that is."

You see, everyone had formed an opinion of me. "Forget other people," I said. "Tell me what you think of me."

She laughed. "I think you're an idiot who doesn't like girls."

My desire was immediately aroused. She struggled, moaned, and moved like a small cow as she covered my face with full breasts that smelled strongly of milk. But she resisted opening that moist, dark place I really wanted to enter. Her body spread out for me like cowhide, but she held her legs tightly together, refusing to let me in. When she finally relented, I exploded as soon as I entered.

She smiled. "It seems you haven't had a woman for a long time."

It had indeed been a long time.

It occurred to me then that my brother, who was still fighting in the south, would never go that long without a woman. If someone were to tell him that his brother had slept with a girl two or three nights before having sex with her, he'd have laughed, and said, "Now, that's an idiot!"

But that was the only thing he could laugh about. At last, news of his defeat came from the south. He appeared to have won a battle nearly every day, while in fact the enemy troops avoided those battles they knew they could not win. So he pushed deep into Wangpo's territory without having much to show for it. No matter where he went, he saw few cows or sheep, let alone people. And, of course, no gold or silver or other treasures. Even with his powerful, sophisticated weapons, the first young master of the Maichi family, the future chieftain, could find no one to kill. Most of the people he encountered had already starved to death, and the live ones were too weak to fight against their fate. His soldiers cut off their ears as fake trophies, and the first young master's reputation as a ruthless man began to spread.

My brother had moved too far inside enemy territory. He never saw the enemy troops as he forged ahead, but they sniped at him at every opportunity. A man one day, a gun the next, and within a few months, he had helped arm the enemy with Maichi weapons. As a result, Chieftain Wangpo, using weapons handed over by my brother, had taken the lightly guarded fortress on the southern border. By the time my brother fought his way back, more than half of the grain was gone. He wanted to launch a new attack against Wangpo, but Father stopped him.

Chieftain Maichi said to his heir, "You gave them guns and

grain, both of which they didn't have and desperately needed. There will be time to attack again when you know what else he needs."

My brother fell ill.

Father told him to rest.

My brother remained in the border fortress, recuperating and waiting for Chieftain Wangpo to wage another attack. He was gearing up to deal his enemy a mortal blow this time.

But the new Chieftain Wangpo, who had just succeeded to the position, took the long way around, arriving at my new market to engage in trade.

You see, it was all because of me that peace came to our vast land. People knew about me even in faraway territories where no chieftain's influence had ever reached. Within a short period of time, I'd given a new and much broader meaning to the word *idiot*. Now, because of me, the words *idiot*, *fate*, *good fortune*, and *destiny* had all become synonymous.

There were only minor skirmishes between Chieftains Lha Shopa and Rongong, and even those would be over soon. I hadn't expected to pull the firewood out from under the female chieftain's cauldron, but I did. I'd always treated her like a mother-in-law, but she seemed unwilling to have me as a son-in-law. Without my support, she was soon unable to sustain any attack at all. She wrote to ask for help from her future son-in-law. I said nothing after the steward read the letter to me, so he replied on my behalf. "Something isn't quite right with our young master's head, and he isn't sure why he is to be your son-in-law."

Another letter arrived, this time tinged with bitterness, stating that the future son-in-law of Rongong would also be its future chieftain.

The steward smiled, but not I. I had too much time on my hands those days and had begun thinking about Tharna again. So the steward sent another letter in which he reported that the young master could not recall what Tharna looked like.

At such extraordinary times, an idiot was actually in a position to decide the fates of many smart people. No longer able to insist upon proper protocols, Chieftain Rongong sent her daughter over without even waiting for a formal wedding ceremony.

Tharna arrived in the morning. When the servant came to report her arrival, I was in bed with the girl whose blushing face was the same color as her nipples. I don't mean to say that we were doing anything. No, we'd done enough of that recently at night. But, as usual, I woke up late, and then only because Sonam Tserang was standing by my bed, coughing discreetly. I opened one eye and saw his mouth move, but mention of Tharna's arrival didn't register. "All right," I said sleepily, "all right."

That would not have been a good time for Tharna to barge in. Luckily, the steward was up, and had already shown her into another room when Sonam Tserang went to relay my silly response. I shook the girl next to me, who stirred, then sighed and went back to sleep. Anxiety set in. Fortunately, she woke up soon after that, as if she'd rolled over not to sleep, but to wake up slowly. "Where am I?" she asked with a giggle.

I told her and then asked, "Who am I?"

She told me.

Just then, Sonam Tserang came in looking somber, and said, "Your fiancée is growing impatient."

"Who?"

"Tharna!"

I leapfrogged off the bed and nearly ran out naked. Sonam Tserang stifled a laugh, but not the girl in bed, who was giggling as she knelt on the bed to dress me, even though she herself was still naked. Her laughter turned to sobs, as sizable teardrops rained down on her breasts.

She stopped crying when I told her that Tharna, my wife-to-be, was Chieftain Rongong's daughter.

Then I added that the tears hanging on her breasts were like dewdrops dangling from apples. She laughed through her tears.

The moment I saw Tharna, her beauty struck me with the force of a red-hot bullet. My skin and my veins, my eyes and my heart, were all lacerated by its power. It never took much to turn me back into a real idiot – the sight of a beautiful girl usually did the trick.

When a person turns stupid, the skin on his face tautens. Look at someone's smile, and you'll know if he's an idiot or not. When an idiot smiles, his facial muscles won't obey orders from his brain, which is why the face of a smiling idiot wears the expression of someone who has died in a snowstorm. You can see all his teeth, but not a ripple of luster.

Tharna spoke first. "I'll bet you didn't expect me to be here so soon."

I said I hadn't, and as soon as I opened my mouth, my facial muscles relaxed, which in turn cleared up my head.

But I still didn't know what to do. Up till then, I could sleep with any woman I wanted just by asking for her. Even if I had feelings for a woman – emotions as lofty as the mountains and as mighty as the streams, as it were – I wouldn't feel comfortable revealing them until I'd slept with her a few times. But that wouldn't work with Tharna, who would soon be my wife. So what was I to do? Fortunately, I had a steward who'd thought things through for me. He whispered, "Call the servants in, Young Master."

Given my complete trust in him, I waved grandly, and before I knew it, a bunch of servants entered and placed a pile of jewelry before Tharna. Now that I'd become a businessman, jewelry was easy to come by. I waved some more, summoning a stream of servants, who placed before Tharna all sorts of precious objects from other chieftains' lands and the Han people's place. I kept my hand busy waving all that morning. Even though Tharna fought to remain calm, I figured that amazement would set in sooner or later. But she just giggled, and said, "I couldn't possibly use all these things, no matter how long I lived. Right now I'm hungry."

That sent the servants scurrying between the downstairs kitchen and the upstairs guest room. What a fine steward I had. He had all these splendid gifts ready the moment Tharna arrived. I also had the best cook in the world; she had prepared a sumptuous feast for my guest. Again Tharna giggled. "I can't eat another bite. I'm full just looking at so much food."

I waved again, this time for the servants to clear the table. Then the thought struck me that if I waved my hand again, the servants might take the jewelry away, as they had done with the food. I was still thinking when my hand rose into the air and waved, which sent everyone out, starting with the steward. Only the two maids in red who had escorted Tharna remained standing behind her.

Tharna turned to them. "You may go too."

Now there were only the two of us in the large room. I didn't know what to say; apparently, neither did she. The room was blindingly bright, partly from the sun, and partly from the jewelry piled in front of her.

She sighed. "Sit down."

I sat down beside her.

She sighed again, ripping my heart to shreds. It would have killed me if she'd kept sighing like that. Luckily, she did it only twice before leaning over and falling into my arms. Then our lips met. Now it was my turn to sigh, like a traveler who has finally reached his destination after a long journey.

Although her lips were icy, the kiss loosened my tongue.

"Your lips are as cold as ice. They'll give me frostbite."

"You must save my mother," she said. "You promised you would. Please send your machine gunners back to her."

"If not for that, you wouldn't be here, right?" I asked.

She thought a bit before nodding, with tears glistening in the corners of her eyes.

The sight of her gave rise to a dull pain in my heart. I walked out to the veranda to gaze at the distant green mountains. The sun had just risen, and the mountains were barely visible behind the silk screen of sunlight, mirroring the sadness in my heart. The sorrow of not getting what you desire is nothing compared to the pain of having what you want. The steward, who was standing beyond the door, sighed deeply when he saw the look on my face. I could tell from his eyes as he came toward me that he wanted to ask if Tharna had consented to me. "Stay where you are," I said. "I want to enjoy the early-morning mountains alone."

The incomparably beautiful Tharna had hurt me deeply.

I stood on the upstairs veranda gazing at the mountains.

My servants stood downstairs looking up at me.

The sun came up, driving away the screen created by the slanting light to expose the mountains. There wasn't really anything to see now. It was quiet in the room, almost as if a pretty girl weren't sitting in front of a pile of jewelry. I'd come out on my own, and now I had to return without being asked.

Sunlight streaming in the window shone on the jewelry, its dazzling light reflecting off of Tharna, which made her even more beautiful. Not wanting to ruin such a sight, I said, "Why don't you have your maids put those things away."

Her maids came in, and said, "This isn't our place, and we don't know where to put them."

So I told my servants to find them two large trunks. Then,

smacking my boot with my whip, I said to Tharna, "Let's go see Chieftain Lha Shopa and rescue your mother, Chieftain Rongong."

I kept smacking my boot, not daring to look at Tharna. When we reached the horses downstairs, Sonam Tserang said, "Young Master, you've chipped the polish on your boot."

The steward rewarded him with a slap. "Young Master's spirits are low, so what does it matter if he ruins a pair of boots? Bring him a new pair."

The steward's order was relayed from one mouth to another, until it reached the shoemaker, who rushed out of his workshop with a brand-new pair of boots, a fawning smile on his face. After our market opened for business, he had done quite a bit of work on the side. His boots may not have been the best-looking ones around, but they held up well. Since traders had to travel far to get here, that is exactly what they needed. The soles of his own boots, on the other hand, were so loose they flapped as he walked.

Kneeling by my horse, he removed one old boot and replaced it with a new one. Then he moved to the other side.

"Look at your feet," I said to him. "How can a shoemaker not own a pair of good boots? Are you trying to make me lose face in front of the people who come and go around here?"

He just laughed and wiped his coarse, dark hands on his leather apron. It turned out that someone had wanted a pair of new boots in a hurry the night before, so he'd given the man his own boots, and was now wearing the ones left behind by the man.

I rapped his head with my whip and granted him the chipped pair he'd just taken off my feet.

We then rode across the river to Chieftain Lha Shopa's tent.

He came out before I even had time to raise the tent flap. He was so fat and was layered in so many clothes that he looked as if he'd rolled out of the tent. The sight of Tharna took his breath away.

I guarantee you, that fat pig had never seen such beauty before, not even in his dreams.

Tharna, who was used to the effect she had on other people, sat on her horse and giggled. My God! After giving her such a pretty face, you had to add a lovely voice!

Chieftain Lha Shopa was flustered by her laughter. As his face reddened, he said to me, "A girl as beautiful as that would be a demon if she weren't a fairy."

"She's the future chieftain of Rongong," I said.

That took his breath away for the second time.

I poked her willowy waist with my whip handle. "Tharna," I said, "greet Chieftain Lha Shopa."

She was still laughing when I poked her, which caused her to choke. She belched, loudly, as if answering me: "Eh."

Chieftain Lha Shopa whispered to me, "Tell me, is she a fairy or a demon?"

Once everyone had sat down on layers of rugs in the tent, I replied, "Neither. Tharna is my fiancée."

Again he laughed. "You are indeed destined to be a chieftain. The Maichi family doesn't have a vacancy, so now the Rongong family has made one for you."

I laughed too. "But Tharna says your people are about to take over her land. Where will I go if that happens? Will I become the Lha Shopa chieftain then?"

Now he understood. The Rongong land and subjects were like a big chunk of fatty meat, a large portion of which he'd bitten off. Now he'd have to open his mouth and spit it out. I smiled. "You're fat enough already and shouldn't eat any more. If you do, your gut will pop."

He nodded as his eyes reddened. "All right, I'll order my troops to withdraw."

Would you look at that! Ever since opening and taking control of the market, my words suddenly carried a great deal of weight.

"Now that you have acquired my important promise," Lha Shopa said, "let's have a drink."

"No, thanks," I said. "A bowl of tea will be fine."

While we were drinking tea, Lha Shopa said to Tharna, "Do you know who's the biggest winner here? Not you, and not me. It's him."

I nearly spoke, but I had a mouthful of hot tea. And after I swallowed it, I no longer felt like saying anything.

After leaving the tent, Tharna surprised me by asking, "Is that fat pig really Chieftain Lha Shopa?"

With a hearty laugh, I smacked my horse on the rump, sending it, and me, tearing toward a small hill. Anytime I whipped my horse, it headed for high ground, which I found fascinating. I'd never seen any other horse that would gallop until it reached the highest hill in sight. Now the river, the open field, and the marketplace I'd set up spread out around me. Tharna's horse, also a fine animal, followed mine to the top of the hill, where her laughter was carried on the gentle wind, sounding like the cooing of a spring turtledove about to lay her eggs in the bushes.

It was happy laughter.

That proved I could make the woman I loved happy.

She came up to me on horseback, laughing the whole way. The red tassel on the tip of her whip twirled in the air. I shouted at her, "Are you really the Rongong chieftain?"

She laughed loudly, and shouted back, "No, I'm not."

As she shouted, I rose up on my horse and leaned into the path of hers. A terrifying scream tore from her mouth when I reached out and swept her off her horse. She wrapped her arms around me, her horse shot out from under her, and we hung in the air for a moment before starting to fall. I had just enough time to turn in midair and hit the ground first, followed by my beautiful Tharna. I saw her eyes and teeth glitter in midfall.

My God, how soft and spongy the summer grass was!

Our lips met as soon as we touched the ground. Now we were both in a kissing mood. With my eyes closed, I felt our lips kindle a bright, searing flame, igniting in us moans of pleasure.

After a long while, we separated and lay in the grass to gaze at white clouds in the sky.

Tharna muttered, "I didn't love you before. But I fell in love at the sight of your back as we stormed uphill." She kissed me again.

Lying on the hill in a refreshing breeze and gazing up at a sky roiling with clouds, I felt as if I'd fallen into an ocean whirlpool.

I told Tharna how much I loved her.

She covered my eyes with yellow petals that were silky soft, as if covered with antler down, and said, "Everyone who sees me falls in love with me."

"But I'm just an idiot."

"Could there really be an idiot such as you in the world? I'm afraid. You're strange, and I'm afraid."

33 Family Feud ~

The famine wasn't over yet.

Although the chieftains all believed that their land was the center of the world, where they received special favors from heaven, they endured their share of the same sorts of disasters suffered by places where there were no chieftains. Flood, fire, wars, plague, and famine – they were all unavoidable; there were no special dispensations. And now famine even in the absence of natural disasters. It seemed as if their lands were being pushed to the edge of the world by some mysterious power.

The people all believed the famine would be over by autumn.

But that belief was based on past experience, which had taught them that when autumn arrived, something to fill their stomachs would appear in the ground, like corn, barley, potatoes, broad beans, and peas. Those who hadn't starved to death in the spring or summer figured that their lives had been spared. But the problem now was that in most of the chieftains' territory, there was nothing to harvest but poppies that danced in the wind as far as the eye could see. A few chieftains, Lha Shopa among them, had come to their senses and destroyed the sprouting poppies. Although the season had passed, and they could plant only greens normally used for animal feed, and a few beans, at least they could count on a harvest that might ease the minds of their subjects.

I asked Lha Shopa if the rumors that he had wept when he dug up the poppies were true.

Rather than answer directly, he said that some of the chieftains had laughed at him when he'd uprooted the plants. But now that the Republican Government was waging a war against Japan and had banned opium, it was their turn to shed tears over the increasingly unprofitable crop.

The Maichi family enjoyed another abundant harvest, with corn and barley piling up like mountains on the drying grounds. The Maichi subjects were in luck, even if they didn't know where their good fortune had come from. The sky was as blue as ever; the river still flowed through the widening valley, sending sprays skyward on its southeastern journey.

I was starting to get homesick. Since the steward took care of everything, I had nothing but time on my hands. Anything he couldn't handle, Sangye Dolma was there to manage.

"Sangye Dolma is a very capable woman," he said to me one day.

"You're very capable too," I said, "but of course you're a man."

Not long after that, he said to me, "Sangye Dolma is a very good person."

"So are you," I said.

He was hinting that he wanted to take her to bed. Of course, he'd want to sleep with a cook who, after being separated from her husband for so long, wanted to sleep with him too. I watched her closely and could see that she didn't miss her silversmith the way she had when she first came.

"I'm getting old," the steward said. "My legs don't work so well anymore."

He said it as if he weren't a cripple, as if his legs had been just fine up till now.

But I knew what he meant. "Then go find yourself an assistant," I told him.

"I've found one."

"Tell her to do a good job."

So he promoted Sangye Dolma to the position of personal assistant. After being a steward for over two decades, he was now displaying his authority. That was partly accomplished by looping a large enamel snuff bottle on a silver chain around his neck. Whenever he pondered something, or after giving orders to the servants, he'd take a pinch of snuff and inhale deeply. That would be followed by a loud sneeze and a red glow in his face; he looked exactly like a steward ought to look. I mentioned that to him, and he rapped softly on the bottle's slender neck with his fingernails. Instead of responding when I finished, he laid his snuff-laden fingernail against his nostril and inhaled. By holding his breath before producing a loud sneeze, he excused himself from saying anything.

On the northern border, our barley was sold at a tenfold profit. But more importantly, I'd expanded the Maichi territory. And even more important than that, I'd taken the most beautiful woman in the world as my wife and would become the chieftain of Rongong when my mother-in-law passed on. Of course, that didn't come without danger, since all the men who had hoped to become the Rongong chieftain were dead.

But that didn't scare me.

I told Tharna what I was thinking.

"You're really not afraid?" she asked.

"The only thing I'm afraid of is not having you."

"But you have me now."

Yes, I did, if having someone meant lying on top of a girl, cupping her breasts in your hands, thrusting inside her, and making her bleed. But that's not all there is to having a woman, nor to having a future with her. Tharna made me understand all that a woman could be, and what was meant by a future.

"You hurt me," I said. "You hurt my feelings."

"I wouldn't be alive if I couldn't do that to a man."

Then an evil thought occurred to me: I'd be at peace if she no longer existed in this world.

"You'll live in my heart after you die," I said.

She lay in my arms, and said, "You idiot. What's the point of living in your heart?" That led to tears. "Isn't it enough to live in your eyes? Now you want me to live in your heart too?"

"Let's go for a stroll," I said.

I loved her, but often didn't know what to do with her. And whenever I felt that way, I suggested taking a stroll. Most of the time, she preferred to stay inside, giving me an excuse to wander off alone. I could go see what the steward and his assistant were doing, or what Chieftain Lha Shopa was up to, or who had come to trade, or what new store had opened on the market street.

Chieftain Maichi had closed down the fortress on the southern border and sent all the grain to me. It slowly disappeared in all directions, replaced by all sorts of good things from here and there.

But that day, Tharna said, "All right, let's go for a stroll."

So we went downstairs. All beautiful women are like that, crying one moment and smiling the next.

My two young slaves had gotten our horses ready for us.

We saddled up, followed by Sonam Tserang and Aryi. "Look at your two shadows," Tharna said. "People will know what sort of person you are just by looking at them."

"They're the most loyal servants in the world," I said.

"But they're not presentable."

You see, people who think they're smart, pretty, and respectable care only about appearances, not loyalty. Later that day, Tharna, who was now my wife, even though we hadn't had a wedding ceremony, also said spitefully, "Your steward's a cripple and has a cook as a mistress. Don't you have a single presentable person around you?"

"I have you. That's enough."

We'd gotten used to talking to each other that way. That's how our conversations went, and we weren't terribly concerned about what we said. Most of the time, at least. I knew exactly what to do when we were in bed, but wasn't sure how to deal with her once we were dressed and out of bed. As a smart person, she should have been the one to take the initiative. But I could tell she didn't know what to do with me either. Should she respect me, as most women respected their husbands? But I was an idiot. So should she treat me like an idiot instead? But I was her husband, and not your average idiot. I might be an idiot, but I knew that a man mustn't simply submit to his woman. Besides, I realized there was no need to be submissive when I reminded myself how she had fallen into my hands and gone to bed with me without a proper ceremony. Those were the circumstances that led to our brusque conversations once we were dressed and out of bed. Give me a jab, and I'll give you one right back.

Constantly being hurt by a woman cannot be a permanent state of affairs.

We arrived at the creek, where the water was clear enough to see ourselves. How beautiful those two horses were, one red, the other white. And how young and pretty their two riders!

That day, using the water as a mirror, I took a good look at myself for the very first time. If there had been nothing wrong with his head, the second young master of the Maichi family would have been seen as a handsome young fellow, with black, wavy hair, a strong, broad forehead, and a firm, high, straight nose. It would have been even better if the eyes had been brighter, and not glazed over, like those of a sleepwalker. But still, I was happy with how I looked.

Out of the blue, I turned to Tharna, and said, "You don't love me, so get lost. Go find the man of your dreams. I won't ask your mother to return the grain."

She was dumbstruck.

Biting her lip, she stared silently at my reflection in the water. "Giddap!" I shouted. My horse stepped into the water, shattering the reflections of the man and the woman.

Tharna, I'll bet no one had ever said anything like that to you.

I crossed the river. With no one to help her, Tharna slid off her horse and sat by the river in a daze.

Tharna had me confused too. Unable to think of anywhere to go once I crossed the river, I let the horse take me around the market.

The tents there were disappearing, gradually replaced by flat-roofed adobe buildings, where all sorts of things from various chieftains' territories accumulated, including a bunch of worthless stuff. A long, narrow street had formed among the buildings. The grass, trampled by people and horses, had been crushed out of existence, the surface turning to mud on rainy days. But on clear days like this one, dust and human noises filled the air. What a scene, and all because of me! So when I showed up on the street, the people broke off their transactions, bargaining phrases frozen on the tips of their tongues, their signals perched on flittering fingers inside their loose sleeves. As they watched the creator of the first fixed market on any chieftain's territory ride by, they were puzzled by how an idiot could have produced something so innovative. I rode around aimlessly amid the dust, human noises, merchandise, and adobe houses, feeling empty inside. Most of the time my heart was full, but now there was a void. Chieftain Lha Shopa was sitting outside an adobe building, watching me wordlessly. After I'd ridden up and down the street a dozen times or so, he finally stood up, walked over, and grabbed my horse's bridle.

He looked behind me. "Has the young master gotten himself a new servant?" he asked.

"Maybe he *wants* to be my servant," I replied.

Someone had been tailing me like a shadow ever since I entered the marketplace, following me up and down the street. I felt his presence but hadn't gotten a good look at his face. This was clearly a pattern, the pattern of an avenger. He was letting me know that the Maichi enemy was here. It must have seemed to him that I'd intentionally left Tharna and my two young slaves on the other side of the river just to await his appearance. In the past, thoughts of an enemy of Father or some other member of the family settling on me as the target of revenge had always frightened me. But now that he'd finally come, I felt no fear at all.

I asked Chieftain Lha Shopa how business was going. Not bad, he said. I spun around, hoping to see the man's face, but all I saw was a broad-brimmed hat and a pair of sheathed swords, a long double-edged one on the left and a wide single-edged one on the right.

Lha Shopa smiled, his eyes sinking into the creases in his face. "Does the young master have enemies too?" he asked.

"Only if you hate me."

"That can only mean that you're a surrogate for your father."

"Or for my brother, who knows?"

He jerked his fleshy chin upward, and two strapping servants materialized next to him. "Want me to catch him for you?" he asked.

I considered that for a moment, and then said, "No."

A coolness caressed the nape of my neck; it felt good. It was the sensation of a blade pressing against my skin. I flicked the reins and rode out of the marketplace, not stopping until I reached the river. Once I was in the water, I turned to look behind me. He was getting closer. He wasn't very tall, and I knew he couldn't reach my neck from the ground. So when he was close enough to hear me, I said, "I'm sitting too high for you. Would you like me to climb down off my horse?"

The words were barely out of my mouth when he did a reverse somersault, drew his swords, and waved them in the air until their glint covered his body. His hat had flown off, and now I saw who he was.

"Get up," I said. "I knew your father."

It was the son of Dorjee Tsering, who had killed Headman Tratra for the Maichi family, who had in turn killed him.

He flipped up onto his feet, but said nothing.

"Didn't Dorjee Tsering have two sons?" I asked.

He approached my horse, holding the glinting swords in his hands. Then I heard a woman's scream from across the river. It was Tharna. When I turned to look at her, the avenger walked up next to me. By standing on his tiptoes, he managed to press the double-edged sword against my throat. The chilling sensation was soothing. I needed to get a good look at my killer's face. If he was going to kill me, he'd have to let me do that, or he wouldn't be much of a killer. But he forced me to look at the sky with the tip of his sword against my throat. Maybe he thought I'd never seen the sky before. Staring heavenward, I waited for him to speak. It was time for him to say something, I told myself. But he didn't. What kind of killer won't say even a word or two? The spot where the sword touched my skin began to heat up, as if the tip had turned into a small flame. I figured I was about to die, but still he wouldn't snap his wrist to force me off the horse.

I heard myself laugh. "Let me down," I said. "This is really uncomfortable."

Finally he spoke up. "Damn you aristocrats! You want to feel comfortable even when you're about to die."

At last I'd heard his voice. "Such a deep voice," I said. "That's what a killer ought to sound like."

"It's my voice," he said.

This time it wasn't as deep, and that must have been his real voice. It was hatred that had made it so low and so tight at first. Apparently, he didn't have enough hatred for me, which was why his voice had loosened up after his first comment.

"What's your name?"

"Dorjee Norpu. My father was Dorjee Tsering. He was killed like a dog in the poppy field by Chieftain Maichi. My mother burned herself to death."

"I'd like to see if you look like Dorjee Tsering."

He let me dismount, but placed the sword back up against my neck as soon as my feet touched the ground. Now I could see his face. He didn't look like his father *or* a killer. One thrust of his sword would have solved everything: No one would have to worry about me anymore, and no one would have to hate me. My brother wouldn't have to guard against me, and Tharna would no longer have to feel sorry for herself for falling into the hands of an idiot.

But then he pulled his sword back. "Why should I kill you? It's your father and brother I want. Back then, you were a just a kid, like me. Besides, I'd ruin my reputation if I killed an idiot."

"Then why are you here?"

"Go tell your father and brother that their enemy has come."

"Tell them yourself. I won't do it for you."

Before I could say any more, he vanished.

That's when my mind began to wander. I looked up; the clouds, the wind, and the birds were all still there. Then the ground: the soil, the grass in the soil, the flowers on the grass, and my feet among the flowers were all still there. Hordes of summer insects were busily crawling around. I looked at the river and saw splashes of water, and I saw Tharna in the splashes. I was thinking, Tharna is wading through the river. Then she emerged from the splashes and came up to me. "Idiot," she said. "Blood! Blood!"

I didn't see any blood. All I saw were the splashes settling back onto the surface of the water after she had climbed out of the river. She walked up, grabbed my hand, and held it in front of my eyes. "Idiot! Look, blood."

There was in fact a bit of blood on my hand, but she was exaggerating. That little bit wasn't worth getting excited about.

"Whose blood is that?" I asked her.

"It's yours!" she screamed.

"Whose hand is that?"

"It's yours!" Now she was shouting in my face. "He nearly killed you!"

Yes, it was my hand. He had nearly killed me, and not the other way around. So how had I gotten blood on my hand? When I let it fall to my side, a trickle of blood fell from my loose sleeve like a little bug. I took off my jacket and, following the trail up along my arm, found the source. It was dripping down from my neck. Dorjee Norpu, the Maichi enemy, had cut me as he was pulling back the sword. I washed my neck and hand in the water, and the bleeding stopped.

What annoyed me was that the blood didn't change the color of the water, not a bit.

Tharna was clearly upset, not knowing what to do.

She took hold of my head and pulled it toward her. I was able to find breathing space by tucking my nose between her arching breasts. It was a long time before she finally let me go.

"Why did that man want to kill you?"

"You're crying," I said. "So you do love me."

"I don't know if I love you or not," she said. "But I know that my mother didn't grow barley and that I was turned into the wife of an idiot."

She took a deep breath and held my face as she would a child's. "Was that man here for barley too?"

I shook my head.

As if coaxing that child, she said, "Tell me all about it."

"No."

"Tell me."

"No!"

"Tell me!" She raised her voice to frighten me.

She really was treating me like an idiot. She had married me for the barley and didn't love me. But that didn't matter, since she was so beautiful, and since I loved her. But still, I couldn't let her treat me like that. If even an avenging killer couldn't harm me, what could she do? So I slapped my pretty woman – hard. She squealed and looked at me with shock in her eyes. Now what should I do?

Luckily, my people had seen from a distance that someone was trying to kill me and ran over as fast as they could. But when they reached me, instead of encountering an enemy, they were just in time to see me hit my wife. The steward stopped me from doing more. He was the only one among all these people who knew at once what had happened. He asked, "Has he come?"

I nodded.

The entire group stormed toward the newly paved street, where they ran screaming and shouting from one end to the other several times. Since they hadn't seen the killer, naturally they came up empty-handed. I noticed one man who resembled the man who'd nearly killed me, except that this one was slimmer and taller. And he'd been around for some time, running an inn on the street. Steam rose from the big Russian-style kettle outside his inn all day long. Inside, meat stewed in a large cauldron and large vats of liquor lined the wall.

This inn was the very first on Maichi land, so I feel I should mention it. I once heard someone say that history is composed of many "firsts." Before he came along, we'd had to take food along when we traveled. If it was to be a long trip, we'd take a wok for boiling tea in the morning and making noodle soup in the evening. This fellow didn't have much business, since he only steeped a bit of tea, cooked a bit of meat, and sold a bit of liquor.

While my servants were running around outside, I went in and sat down. The innkeeper poured a bowl of liquor and placed it before me. When I told him he looked familiar, he just gave me a noncommittal smile. I drank the liquor.

"This is good stuff," I said. "But I don't have any silver to pay for it."

Still silent, the innkeeper brought over a jug and refilled my bowl.

I nearly choked on the liquor. After catching my breath, I said, "I have the feeling I've seen you someplace."

He said, "No, you haven't."

"I don't mean you, I mean a face like yours."

"I know what you mean," he said as he stood beside me with the jug, refilling my bowl every time I drained it.

Starting to get tipsy, I said, "They've never seen the killer's face, but they're out there trying to catch him." Then I laughed.

The innkeeper stood there silently, filling and refilling my bowl. Soon I was so drunk I didn't realize that the steward had entered. I asked why he and the servants were running around like that. He said he was trying to catch the would-be killer. I laughed out loud again. But he was unfazed; tossing down a few pieces of silver for the liquor I'd drunk, he started back to resume his search. But when he reached the door, he said, "I'm going to find him, even if I have to turn that street upside down, like turning intestines inside out to make sausage."

With that gimpy leg of his, he didn't look like much when he walked, but he presented an awesome sight on horseback.

"They won't find him," I said to the innkeeper.

He nodded. "No, they won't, because he left already."

"Where do you think he's going?"

"To find Chieftain Maichi."

When I looked at him again, my drunken eyes saw everything I needed to see. I said, "Your face is the same as his."

He smiled, looking sad and a bit embarrassed. "He's my younger brother. He said he wanted to kill you, but in the end he didn't. I'd told him that our enemy is Chieftain Maichi."

I asked if he'd laced the wine with poison. He said no. "I won't kill you unless your father and brother are no longer alive."

"Will you kill me if your brother doesn't return?"

247

He poured me another bowlful, and said, "No, not even then. I'll try to find and kill them. If they're dead, but not by my hand, then I'll kill you."

On that day, I made a promise to our family enemy: I'd pretend I didn't know his true identity so long as he followed the rules of revenge.

That night, Tharna, whom I'd slapped earlier, was unusually passionate. She said, "Just think. An avenger wants to kill you, a killer. You have an enemy."

I said, "Yes, I have an enemy. I met up with a killer."

I guess I hadn't done badly. Otherwise, she wouldn't have moaned and groaned under me.

"Hold me tight!" she cried out. "Hurt me! I'm disappearing! I'm gone."

She was gone. Then I was gone too. We turned into fluffy clouds and flew off into the sky.

She awoke before me the next morning. Propping her head up with one hand, she studied my face. I had to ask her, I knew I had to, "Who am I? Where am I?"

She answered with a giggle. "You don't look foolish when you're asleep, but you do once you're awake."

What could I say, since I couldn't see myself when I was asleep?

A messenger brought word from Father that my brother had returned home and that I should too.

The steward said he'd stay behind to take care of things for me, so I left the armed servants for him. Sangye Dolma wanted to go home with me. "Do you miss the silversmith?" I asked her.

"He's my husband."

"Go home and take a look. Then come back here. The steward needs someone to help him."

She didn't say anything. I could see she didn't know if she should come back here or not, or if she should be the silversmith's wife or the steward's assistant. But I wasn't going to waste any words on the subject. It was the steward's business. Now that Dolma was sleeping with him, it was his problem, not mine.

I'd been away so long that I needed to bring everyone a gift. I chose things for Mother, Father, and my brother, of course, but I also selected a pair of gem-studded earrings for Yangzom. Then there was Tharna the maid. To help me gather all these gifts, the steward took me to one storage room after another, and that was when I first realized how rich I was. It took two or three days to select everything and to load silver ingots and bullion into crates. On the last day, I felt like taking a stroll, so I went out into the street. I'd nearly put Chieftain Maichi's enemy out of mind. I walked into the inn and tossed a silver dollar down on the table. "Liquor."

The innkeeper brought over a jug.

I drank two bowlfuls. He didn't say a word until I was leaving. "There's still no news from my brother."

I stood there, momentarily at a loss for words. Finally I said, "Maybe he doesn't know who to kill, the current Chieftain Maichi or the future one."

The innkeeper muttered, "Maybe that's it."

"I know it's hard, but there's no other way. You made a vow when you ran away, so he has to kill at least one of them."

"But why would a mother make a vow through her sons?" he wondered aloud.

It was a simple question that grew complicated once you thought about it. I had no answer, but was happy that I was able to be so calm in the presence of an enemy. "I'm going back there tomorrow," I said.

"Will you see him?"

"Your brother?"

"Yes."

"It'd be better if I didn't."

34 Going Home ∾

We made fast time on our way home. That was the servants' idea, not mine. I wasn't a demanding master, and didn't tell them to slow down.

Anyone who has made a name for himself away from home should return at a leisurely pace, knowing that people are waiting expectantly for him.

On the morning of the fourth day, we reached the last mountain pass, where we could see the Maichi estate in the distance.

Looking down from the mountain, we saw cypress trees scattered here and there, making the riverbank appear wide and empty. Beyond the cypresses was a vast field of barley swaying in the wind; the estate house stood quietly amid the barley waves like a large island. When the horses galloped down the mountain, the silver on their backs and the copper bells around their necks rang out crisp and loud, filling the spacious valley. The house was still off in the distance, quiet, with an indulgent, dreamlike quality. We passed some fortresses, whose people, led by the headmen, followed us cheering thunderously.

More and more people joined us, and their cheers grew louder and louder, waking the people in the houses from their afternoon naps.

Even knowing that it was his son coming home, Chieftain Maichi was nervous when he saw so many people and horses tearing down the spacious valley. We saw family guards scampering to the towers.

Tharna smiled. "They're afraid."

I smiled too.

When I left, I'd been an unimportant idiot, but now I frightened them. Even when we were close enough for them to see that we were family, the chieftain still would not let down his guard. I must really have worried them, created a fear that I might attack the estate.

"How could your father act like that?" Tharna asked.

"It's not my father," I said. "It's my brother."

That's right, I could smell my brother's presence amid the clamor and chaos. His disastrous defeat down south had made him skittish.

Tharna turned to me, and said sweetly, "Even your father is on guard against you; it looks like they're treating you as a member of the Rongong family already."

We drew nearer to the house, which was shrouded in an ambiguous silence behind its heavy stone walls.

It was Sangye Dolma who broke the awkward silence by opening a large sack on the back of her horse and taking out some candy that had come from the Han area. She threw handfuls into the air, the adept benefactor, a dispenser of favors from the second young master of the Maichi family. My two young servants followed her example.

In days past, we'd so seldom seen candy that even members of the Maichi family rarely tasted it. But once I'd begun trading on the northern border, such candy was no longer a rarity.

It fell onto the crowd like hailstones. Waving the colorful wrappers and sucking on candy as sweet as honey, the people shared in the taste of my remarkable successes on the northern border; they surrounded us and cheered loudly for me and the beautiful Tharna in the yard outside the house. Dogs chained to the gate barked like mad. "Is this how the Maichi family welcomes its daughter-in-law?" she asked.

"This is how smart people welcome an idiot," I yelled back.

The cheers drowned out her reply and the barking of dogs. Amid the thunderous cheer, I heard the heavy gate creak open. The people fell silent. Through the opened gate walked the chieftain and his wife, followed by a contingent of women, including Yangzom and the other Tharna. My brother was nowhere in sight. He was still in the tower with the family guards.

Life didn't seem to be treating them very well. Father's face looked like a turnip after a frost, and Mother's lips were parched. Yangzom, on the other hand, had retained her beauty, though still with that sleepwalker look. As for the maid Tharna, she looked truly stupid as she stood amid a group of maids and stared at my beautiful wife while gnawing on her fingernails.

The chieftain's wife broke the ice, as she walked up and touched my forehead with her lips; they felt like dry leaves falling on my head. She sighed and walked over to Tharna and put her arms around her.

"I know that you're my daughter. Let me look at you. The men can take care of their business. I want to take a good look at my beautiful daughter."

The chieftain smiled and shouted at the people, "You see that! My son's back. He brought back untold riches and the most beautiful woman in the world!"

The crowd shouted, "Long life!"

I felt that it was the sound of the cheers, not our feet, that carried us into the compound.

While we were still in the yard, I asked Father, "Where's my brother?"

"In the guard tower. He said you might be an enemy force coming to attack us."

"No wonder, since he was defeated down south."

"Don't say his defeat threw fear into him."

"You're the one who said that."

"Son, I think your illness is cured."

At that moment, my brother appeared atop the tower, looking down on us. I waved to show I'd seen him. Since he couldn't hide anymore, he came down. The two brothers met on the steps.

He scrutinized me.

In front of him stood a renowned idiot who had accomplished what smart people could not. To be fair, he was not someone who cared so much about fame and power that he had to be the chieftain. What I mean is, if his younger brother hadn't been an idiot, he might have yielded to him the title of chieftain. The business at the southern border had taught him a lesson, and he didn't want to trouble his head too much. But his brother *was* an idiot, so things could only be the way they were now. Even though he had suffered defeat, he patted my shoulder with a haughty air, before his gaze fell on Tharna.

"Look at you," he said. "You can't even tell if a woman is pretty, yet you wind up with a true beauty. I've had many women, but none as pretty as she."

"Her maids are all very pretty too," I said.

So that's how my brother and I met, not at all the way I'd imagined. But at least we met.

From where I stood upstairs, I waved to Sangye Dolma, who had the servants unload the crates of silver. When I ordered them to open the crates, shouts of astonishment rose from the crowd. The Maichi estate owned plenty of silver, but most people – the headmen, our subjects, and family slaves – had never seen so much in one place at the same time.

As we walked toward the dining room, I heard the rumble of the warehouse door being opened in the basement. Once inside, Tharna whispered to me, "This is exactly how things are in the Rongong family. How come?"

Mother overheard her. "Chieftains are all the same," she said.

"But things are different at the border."

"That's because your husband isn't a chieftain."

"He will be someday."

"I'm glad you think so," Mother said. "But it makes me sad to think that he'll be living with your family, and not ours."

That ended the conversation between Tharna and Mother.

I then summoned my two young slaves and Tharna's two pretty maidservants to place a lavish gift in front of everyone. The jewelry sparkled, and they had trouble believing that all this could have come from a desolate place like the border region.

"There'll be even more in the future," I said.

I omitted the second half of that sentence: If you don't treat me like an idiot, that is.

At that moment, our maids shuffled their way into the room and knelt behind us. The Tharna who was a groom's daughter was on her knees behind the Tharna who was the daughter of a chieftain, and I could sense her trembling. I couldn't understand why I'd ever slept with her. Yes, back then I hadn't known what kind of woman could be considered beautiful, so they had sent any woman they wanted to my bed.

Tharna looked at the maid out of the corner of her eye. "You see," she said to me, "it's your family who has treated you like a hopeless idiot, not me. You can see that by the sort of woman they gave you."

Then she laid a string of pearls in the maid's hand and said loudly enough for all to hear, "I'm told your name is the same as mine. Well, from now on, you can't use that name anymore."

The maid answered in a tiny voice, like that of a mosquito, "Yes."

Then I heard her say, "Won't you give me a name, Mistress?"

Tharna laughed. "Everyone around my husband is so sensible. He's a lucky man."

The now nameless maid continued in her mosquito voice, "Please give me a name, Mistress."

Tharna turned her radiant face to Chieftain Maichi and smiled. "Father." That was the first time she'd spoken to him. And by doing so, she confirmed their relationship. "Father, please give our slave a name."

"Ermy Gyami."

So that was how the groom's daughter got her name, one that wasn't really a name at all, since it meant "nameless." Everyone smiled.

Ermy Gyami smiled too.

Then my brother spoke to my wife for the first time. "A beautiful woman shows up," he said with a snicker, "and other women lose their names. Fascinating."

Tharna snickered too. "Beauty is there for all to see. It's much the same as how the existence of smart people shrouds the future of those who are considered stupid."

My brother's smile vanished. "That's how the world is."

"Everyone knows that," Tharna said. "It's the same logic as 'There are only victorious chieftains, no vanquished ones.'"

"Chieftain Rongong is the vanquished one, not Chieftain Maichi."

Tharna replied, "Yes. Elder Brother is a smart man, and all the other chieftains hope for you to be their opponent."

The second round went to Tharna as well.

As we were leaving, he took me by the arm, and said, "That woman will ruin you one day."

"Shut up," Father said. "Ruin can only come at one's own hand."

My brother left. But now that Father and I were alone, he was at a loss for words.

"Why did you order me back?" I asked.

"Your mother missed you."

"The Maichi enemy has come," I said. "Two brothers. They plan to kill you and my brother. They chose not to kill me. One of them gave me liquor but wouldn't kill me."

"They probably didn't know what to do with you either. I'd like to ask them if it was because everyone says you're an idiot," Father said.

"Father doesn't know what to do with me either. Is that it?"

"Are you a smart person or are you an idiot?"

"I don't know."

So that was how my homecoming went. See how they treated the person who had made the Maichi family more powerful than ever?

Mother and Tharna were inside talking about things only women would find interesting.

On my first evening home, I stood alone, leaning against the railing and watching the moon rise.

Once it was high in the sky, it threaded its way through the flimsy clouds.

Somewhere in the house, a woman was plucking a bamboo mouth lyre. The sound was dreary, bewildering, and forsaken.

Nine ~

35 Miracle ~

I took a walk around the estate. Sonam Tserang, Aryi, and Sangye Dolma were surrounded by servants, all looking as proud as if they were no longer menials.

The old executioner bowed deeply. "Young Master, my son has a future with you."

Sonam Tserang's mother pressed her forehead against my boots, and said tearfully, "That's how I feel about my son too, Young Master."

The old woman's snot and drool would have soiled my boots if I hadn't walked off quickly.

People in the yard greeted me with fervent shouts, but I didn't feel like handing out candy today. Then I spotted the historian. During all the time I'd been away from home, I'd thought more about our tongueless historian than about anyone in my family. He was sitting beneath a walnut tree at the edge of the yard, smiling at me. I could tell from his eyes that he'd missed me too.

"Well done," he said with his eyes.

I walked up to him, and asked, "Did they tell you about me?"

"News travels fast."

"Did you write it all down in your notebook?"

He nodded earnestly, looking much better than when he'd first become the historian after getting out of the dungeon.

I removed a gift from under my billowy robe and laid it in front of him.

It was a rectangular, hard-shelled briefcase, commonly carried by Han military officers. In studying them carefully, I'd seen that they put their notebooks, pens, and eyeglasses in briefcases like this, and I had told someone in the trading team to get one from the Han

255

military. Inside were a pair of eyeglasses with crystalline lenses, a fountain pen, and a stock of pretty notebooks with plastic covers.

Normally, the sight of such lavishly delicate objects ruffled lamas, since they detracted from the study of Buddhism and life's vicissitudes. But our historian was no longer a zealous monk interested only in spreading his faith. Neither of us knew how to fill the pen with ink. We uncapped it and screwed the cap back on several times, but were still unable to get ink into the pen. In the face of such an ingenious object, even the wise Wangpo Yeshi turned into an idiot.

He smiled. "In the past," his eyes said, "I'd have refused this ingenious object."

"But now you want it to work."

He nodded.

In the end, it was the chieftain's wife who came out and filled the pen with ink. As she was leaving, she kissed me and smiled at the historian. "My son brought back wonderful things for all of us. He gave you an American fountain pen. Use it well."

The historian wrote a line on a piece of paper. My God! It was blue. We'd only seen writing in black before. As he gazed at his writing, the color of the sky, he moved his lips.

I was amazed to hear a sound.

Yes, it was a sound from a man with no tongue.

No, he didn't simply make a sound, he actually said something. He was speaking!

Although the voice was muffled, he was clearly speaking. He heard it too. With a surprised look on his face, he pointed to his wide-open mouth, and asked with his eyes, "Was that me talking? Was I speaking?"

I said, "It *was* you! It *was*! Say something else."

He nodded and spoke again. It was halting, and muffled, but I understood what he said. "Those ... words ... are ... pretty."

I shouted into his ear, "You said the words are pretty."

He nodded. "Your ... pen ... my ... hand write ... beautifully."

"My God! You're talking!"

"I ... am ... talking?"

"You are!"

"I ... talked?"

"You did!"

"Really?"

"Really."

Wangpo Yeshi's face was twisted with rapture. He tried to stick out his tongue to examine it, but it was only half there, not long enough to reach his lips. When he couldn't see it, teardrops splashed out of the corners of his eyes.

I shouted at the crowd, "The tongueless one is talking again!"

The people in the yard quickly spread the word.

"The tongueless one is talking again!"

"The tongueless one is talking again?"

"Yes. He's talking again!"

"He's talking again!"

"Talking again?"

"Talking again!"

"The historian is talking again."

"The tongueless one is talking again!"

They pressed up to us, while swiftly relaying the startling news to those behind them. It was a miracle; their faces glowed and their eyes sparkled, as if they were part of the miracle. Living Buddha Jeeka came as soon as he heard the news. I hadn't seen him for some years. He had aged noticeably; the pink glow was gone from his face, and now he walked with a handsome cane.

Either because he was too excited or too anxious, Wangpo Yeshi was trembling, and sweat beaded his forehead. Yes, a miracle had occurred on Maichi land. A tongueless person had spoken! By now, the chieftain's entire family had joined the crowd, looking very apprehensive, unsure if this sign portended good fortune or bad. Every time something unusual happened, someone was quick to provide an interpretation. Everyone now waited quietly for that someone to do just that.

The Living Buddha walked out of the crowd and announced to Chieftain Maichi and everyone else, "This is a sign of the gods' favor, brought to us by the second young master. Wherever he goes, the gods will send down a miracle."

To hear him talk, you'd have thought I was the one who had spoken without a tongue.

The taut faces of the Maichi family members relaxed as soon as the Living Buddha made his pronouncement. Except for my brother, the members of my family felt they had to display something to the miracle maker. They all fell in behind Father as he walked up to me solemnly, so slowly that I nearly burst with anxiety.

But before he reached me, a pair of strong men lifted me onto their shoulders, and suddenly I was riding above hundreds of bobbing heads amid deafening cheers. I towered over the crowd, drifting on an ocean of human heads and tossed by raging waves of human voices. Then the two men began to run, whisking me past one upturned face after another, including those of the chieftain's family. But only briefly, for they quickly floated off like leaves and disappeared in the crowd. Even so, I saw Father's fear, Mother's tears, and my wife's dazzling smile. And I also saw the one who could speak without a tongue, standing quietly just beyond the sudden whirlwind in the yard and becoming part of the dense shade beneath the walnut tree.

After the excited crowd made several turns around the yard carrying me, they turned and rushed off toward the barley field like floodwaters crashing through a broken levee. Sunlight washed over the ripe kernels of grain, wave after wave. I was swept into a sea of gold along with the crowd.

I wasn't afraid, but wondered where all that exhilaration had come from.

Kernels of ripe grain kicked up by so many feet pelted my face, stinging it so badly that I began to scream. But the people kept running, as if crazed. The kernels turned into red-hot sparks. The Maichi barley field, of course, didn't go on forever, and finally the crowd emerged from the far end, at the foot of a mountain, where vast patches of azalea bushes blocked their way. The waves crested a few times before the crowd stopped, reluctantly, their energy spent.

When I looked behind me, a large patch of the barley was gone. On the other side of the trampled field was the estate house, Chieftain Maichi's magnificent house. It looked lonely, as if it didn't know what to do with itself. An unknown sadness rose up inside me. The flood of serfs, the people, had swept me away, leaving other members of the Maichi family behind. I could see them still in the yard. They must have been wondering what had happened or they wouldn't have been standing there in a daze. I didn't know why it had all happened either, but I sensed that something serious had occurred to put such a distance between them and me. It took so little time to widen the distance that I'd had no time to think about it, and now it was going to be hard to draw close to them again. The people around me lay in the meadow after collapsing from exhaustion. I was pretty sure they had no idea why they'd done what they'd just done. Even if there were miracles in this world, the common people could not share in them. That sort of madness was a lot like sleeping with a woman – the climax is also its end. Excitement, elation, running wild, only to wind up sprawled on the ground, like clumps of wet mud.

My two young servants were also sweat-soaked, their foolish mouths hanging slack like beached fish. They wore the same foolish smile that so often adorned my own face.

The sun was warming up, so the people got to their feet and walked off in twos and threes. By noon, only the three of us were left – Sonam Tserang, Aryi, and me.

We turned and headed back to the house.

The barley field was so vast that I stank from sweat by the time we reached the end.

The yard was deserted, except for Wangpo Yeshi, who was still sitting where we'd met earlier that morning. The estate was deathly silent. I wished someone would come out to look around, or make a noise, or something. The bright autumn sun reflecting off the massive stone wall made it look like iron. Now that the sun was overhead, shadows curled around my feet like thieves, not willing to unfold and show themselves.

Wangpo Yeshi looked at me, his expression changing constantly.

Ever since losing his tongue, he had developed a rich repertoire of facial expressions. In that brief moment, his face revealed all four seasons, as well as wind, rain, thunder, and lightning.

He didn't speak this time; instead he continued to talk with his eyes. "Young Master returned, just like that?"

"Just like that." I'd wanted to say that the people had swept me away like a flood, then disappeared from the vast field. But I didn't, because I couldn't express the significance behind the event or of other things I really wanted to say. The flood was a metaphor, but what's the meaning of a metaphor? A metaphor is meaningless if it's nothing but a metaphor.

"Don't you know that a miracle has occurred?"

"You spoke."

"You're a true idiot, Young Master."

"Sometimes."

"You were carried off like water by the miracle."

"They were like a flood."

"Did you sense the power?"

"An overwhelming, uncontrollable power."

"Because it had no direction."

"Direction?"

"You didn't point the way for them."

"My feet weren't on the ground and I was dizzy."

"You were up high, and the people need someone up high to point the way for them."

I believed that I was starting to see the light. "Did I miss an opportunity?"

"Do you really not want to be a chieftain?"

"Let me think. Do I want to be a chieftain?"

"I mean the Maichi chieftain."

Standing beneath the scorching noonday sun, the second young master of the Maichi family racked his brain while the estate remained silent. Finally, I shouted toward the house, "Yes, I do!"

The blindingly white sunlight quickly absorbed my shout.

Wangpo Yeshi stood up, and said aloud, "Miracles ... do ... not ... occur ... twice."

Now I understood. Had I but waved my hand, the flood would have swept away everything blocking my path to becoming the chieftain. The flood would have washed away even the estate house if I had simply waved my hand. But I was an idiot and, instead of pointing the way, I'd let them spend their powerful energy in the vast barley field until the final cresting wave crashed into the azalea bushes at the foot of the mountain.

I dragged myself back to my room, and still no one came out to meet me, not even my wife. I lay down on my bed, and heard one boot drop to the floor, then another. The sound reverberated in my ears and in my heart. I asked myself, "Was it a miracle or was it a flood?"

Then, with my ears ringing with the echo of the flood, I fell asleep.

I woke up to dim lamplight.

"Where am I?" I asked.

"Don't ask me." It was Tharna's voice.

"Who am I?"

"You're an idiot, a complete idiot." That was Mother.

The two women stood beside my bed, their heads bowed, as if unwilling to look at me. I didn't dare look them in the eye either. A tremendous sense of sorrow rose up inside me.

Tharna was the one who understood what I was asking. "Do you know where you are now?" she said.

"I'm at home."

"Do you know who you are?"

"I'm an idiot, the Maichi family idiot." Tears flowed when I said that. Teardrops slipped down my face. I heard them fall and I heard my explanation. "We can't hurry things. I know we can't, but events are moving too fast."

Mother said, "You two had better return to the border. That's where you belong." She added that she'd come to live with her son when the current chieftain was "gone." Knowing that a sleepless night awaited me, she filled the oil lamp for us before leaving.

My wife began to cry. I'd heard women cry before, but none had ever made me feel so miserable. The hours crawled that night. Never before had I been so keenly aware of the existence of time. Tharna cried herself to sleep, and continued sobbing as she dreamed. The sad look on her face excited me, but I sat still under the lamplight. The heat left my body after a while, and a chill set in. Then Tharna woke up. At first she was very gentle. "Idiot, are you just sitting there?"

"I'm just sitting here."

"Aren't you cold?"

"Yes, I am."

Now that she was completely awake, she shrank back under the blanket as she thought about what had happened during the day. Her eyes turned cold, and tears began to flow again. After a while, she fell back to sleep. I didn't feel like going to bed – I wouldn't be able to sleep anyway. So I went for a walk.

I saw a light in Father's window. The estate was shrouded in silence, but I knew something was happening somewhere. Earlier that day, there was a moment when I could have settled things, but night had fallen, and everything was different. Now others would do the deciding.

The moon traveled leisurely in the sky; with events now moving

261

so slowly, time followed suit. Who said I was an idiot? I felt the passage of time, and that is not something an idiot can do.

Back inside, the lamp oil ran out. Moonbeams lit up the room. Then they too disappeared. Sitting in the dark, I tried to find something to think about, such as what I'd do when another day arrived. But I couldn't think of a thing. The crippled steward had once said that thinking about things was the same as talking to oneself. But it was hard for me to do that without making a sound. How can you talk without making a sound? Yet that might have been interpreted to mean that I'd never thought about things before, even though I had. It's just that I'd never focused on anything in particular; I'd just thought. When I tried to focus my mind, which was the same as talking softly to myself, my mind went blank. So I sat in the dark, listening to Tharna's deep, steady breathing, interrupted from time to time by sobs. Then even the darkness thinned out.

For the first time in my life, I watched how dawn arrived.

Tharna was awake, but she pretended she was still sound asleep. I sat there. A while later, Mother came in with a gloomy look on her face, which meant that she hadn't slept either. "Dear son," she repeated, "go back to the border region. Either that or go to Tharna's place, and take your things with you."

Now that someone was talking to me, I was able to think. "I don't want those things."

Tharna got out of bed. Her breasts didn't seem as if they were part of her body; they looked more like bronze sculptures that had been affixed to her. They shone like the bronze pigeons we kept in our dining-room cupboard. As she dressed in a long satin robe, the morning sun flowed over her. You never saw that on other women. Sunlight would shine on them, but never flow over them.

Even the troubled chieftain's wife said, "No woman is as beautiful as your wife."

Rather than respond, Tharna looked at herself in the mirror. "Given the way my husband is, one day someone might steal his wife away from him."

The chieftain's wife sighed.

Tharna laughed. "When that happens, you'll be an idiot to be pitied."

36 Abdication

Many decisions were made at the Maichi breakfast table. On this particular day, the atmosphere was strained. We kept stuffing food into our mouths, as if competing to see who could eat the most. Except for my brother, that is. He was observing everyone with bright, darting eyes, and I realized that most of the time he was looking either at Father or at my beautiful wife. Breakfast was nearly over when the chieftain's wife let out a timely belch. "Urp."

The chieftain said, "If you have something to say, say it."

She straightened up. "Urp. The idiot and his wife are going back to the border."

"Going back? Isn't this their home? But, of course, I know what you mean." He went on, "But he should know that the border region doesn't belong to them. My territory has not been divided in half. The chieftain is the true king of all this land."

"Let me go take care of the king's business there," I said.

My brother, the heir to the title of Chieftain Maichi, the family's smart person, spoke up. But to my wife, not to me. "Why do you want to go there? Is it fun?"

Tharna snickered, and said, "So everything you do is just for fun, is that it?"

"I can be fun sometimes."

He was trying to seduce her, plain and simple.

Father looked at me, but I said nothing, so he turned to Tharna. "Do you want to leave?"

Tharna looked at my brother and thought awhile before saying, "I don't care."

The chieftain said to his wife, "Let the two youngsters stay home awhile longer."

Everyone continued sitting, clearly not intending to move. The chieftain coughed once, then several more times before looking up. "We can leave now."

We all got up from the table and left the room.

When I asked Tharna if she wanted to go for a stroll, she said, "Were you expecting something good to happen? You were so forceful in handling my mother. What's going on now?"

"That's right," I said. "What is going on now?"

"You're finished," she said, snickering again.

The yard was deserted when I stepped outside. Normally, there'd be people around, but today it was as if a wind had swept everything away.

I ran into the old executioner but didn't speak to him. He knelt before me, and said, "Young Master, please release my son. Don't keep him with you. One day he will be your brother's executioner, not yours."

I felt like kicking him in the teeth, but I turned and walked away instead. A while later I saw his son. "Your father doesn't want you to serve me anymore," I said.

"Everyone says you won't be the chieftain."

"Get out of my sight."

But he didn't. He just stood beside the path, those long Aryi arms of his hanging at his sides, watching me beat the shrubs and burdock bushes with a stick as I walked slowly off.

Next I went to see Sangye Dolma and her silversmith. He smelled like a furnace, while the odor of dishwater clung to her once more. I filled her in on what was happening. With tears in her eyes, she said, "When I came home I told the silversmith we'd have a good life with you, but ... but ... Young Master!" Unable to finish, she spun around and ran off. I heard the silversmith say, "In the end, your young master is still an idiot."

I felt lost as I looked at their retreating backs. And at that moment, someone put words to the thought in my head: "I'm going to kill that silversmith."

It was Sonam Tserang. He was right behind me. "I'm going to kill all these people for you," he said. "After I kill the silversmith, I'll kill First Young Master."

"But I won't be chieftain. Never."

"Even more reason for me to kill them."

"They'll kill you too."

"Let them."

"And they'll kill me. They'll say I ordered you to do the killing."

He opened his eyes wide, and shouted, "Young Master, we know you're an idiot, but are you afraid of dying too? If you can't be chieftain, then let them kill you!"

I wanted to tell him that I was already in agony, as if I'd been stabbed. I'd once thought that whether I became chieftain or not concerned only me, but now I realized that it concerned others as well. But it was too late to say anything now. I took a long walk around the estate and returned to the yard, where Wangpo Yeshi was once again sitting in the shade of the walnut tree. His face still displayed a rich variety of expressions, and he appeared unperturbed by what had happened the day before. I sat down beside him, and said, "Everyone says I won't be chieftain."

He didn't say anything.

"I want to be."

"I know."

"I didn't realize until now how much I want to be."

"I know."

"But is there still a chance I will be?"

"I don't know."

All of the preceding was what I did on the day after the miraculous event.

The chieftain came to breakfast much later than anyone else the following morning. Seeing that we were all waiting for him, he covered one of his eyes, and said, "Don't wait for me. Go ahead and eat. I think I'm sick."

So we began to eat.

I was a little slow in picking up my bowl, and he gave me a savage look. I'd thought there was something wrong with his eye until I saw the glint in the look that he gave me; no diseased eye ever looked like that. He quickly covered it with his hand again. He was trying to frighten me, but it hadn't worked. "Father's eye is fine," I announced.

"Who said there was anything wrong with my eye?"

"It's your hand. When a person is sick, he puts his hand on the spot that bothers him."

I thought he was going to fly into a rage, but he managed to control himself. Removing his hand, he looked me up and down, and said, "All things considered, you're still an idiot." Then he laid his hands in his wife's hands, maybe to keep him from covering his eye again. The look he gave her was more that of a son gazing at his mother than a husband looking at his wife. "Should I call in the historian?" he asked her.

"Go ahead, if you've made up your mind."

When the historian entered, large teardrops fell from Mother's eyes and splattered loudly on the floor. The chieftain's wife said to Wangpo Yeshi, "Write down everything the chieftain is about to say."

He opened one of the notebooks I'd given him and licked the nib of his pen. We all laid down our bowls. Very somberly, the chieftain looked at each of us in turn before moaning softly. "I'm ill and I'm old," he said. "For many years I've worked hard for the Maichi family. Now I'm tired, and I won't live many more years."

I asked myself how someone could change like that overnight. "How did Father get tired, old, and sick so quickly?" I asked. "And all at the same time?"

He raised his hand. "Let me finish. If you weren't such an idiot and if your brother weren't so smart, I wouldn't have gotten tired, old, and sick so quickly. Your father has not slept for many nights." With his head hanging low and his hands covering his eyes, the chieftain spoke rapidly, as if he wouldn't have the energy to resume once he stopped. His voice was low, but it rang in our ears.

"Anyway, in a word," he said, "I want to step down before I die. I will therefore bestow the position of chieftain on my legal heir, my older son, Tamding Gonpo."

The chieftain had announced that he was going to abdicate!

He said he wanted to hand the title over to his older son for reasons well known to everyone as well as for reasons known only to himself. He slowly raised his head as he talked on and on. In fact, he was talking mainly to himself – the chieftain about to abdicate speaking to the chieftain who did not want to. Sometimes your heart splits in two, with one half wanting to do one thing and the other wanting to do something else. With two voices sounding in his head, the chieftain tried to drown out one with the other. In the end he said his choice was the right one, because the chosen son was older, not younger, and because he was smart, not an idiot.

Then Chieftain Maichi tried to console his younger son. "Besides, the young son of the Maichi family will be the Rongong chieftain one day."

"Can someone not qualified to be the Maichi chieftain become the Rongong chieftain?" Tharna asked.

The chieftain had no answer to that.

To everyone's surprise, the historian, who had just learned to talk the day before, spoke up. "The chieftain is right about the older son becoming the chieftain. But he is wrong too, because not a single important event proves that the second young master is an idiot, or that the first young master is smart."

The chieftain's wife looked at the historian, her mouth hanging open.

"Everybody knows that," the chieftain said.

The historian continued, "A while ago, you told me to record that your idiot son was not stupid, and that what he has done is beyond the imagination of smart people."

The chieftain raised his voice. "Everyone says he's an idiot!"

"But he's smarter than all the smart people."

The chieftain snorted. "Have you grown another tongue? Are you talking again? You're going to lose your new tongue if you're not careful."

"If you are willing to lose a good chieftain, then I won't feel bad about losing half a tongue."

"Then I'll take your life."

"Take it, then. But I see the Maichi family foundation crumbling because of your stupidity."

"What business is it of yours what this family does?" the chieftain bellowed.

"Didn't you make me the historian? A historian is history, history!"

"Stop arguing," I said. "Just write down what you observe. Won't that be history?"

Wangpo Yeshi's face turned red as he yelled, "What do you know about history? History must tell people what is right and what is wrong. That is history!"

"You have half a tongue left," my brother, who was about to become the Maichi chieftain, said to the historian. "When I am chieftain, I'll need a historian to write down everything I do. But you shouldn't be in such a hurry to let me know you have half a tongue left. Now you'll lose it all."

The historian looked grimly into my brother's face, then my father's, and he knew he would lose his tongue again. He glanced over at me, but not as if it were my fault. His face turned as white as paper as he said to me hoarsely, "Young Master, who loses more, you or I?"

"You. No one becomes a mute twice."

"Nor does any man whom everyone considers an idiot lose out because of his smart father's foolishness, when everyone else thinks he'll be the chieftain," he replied.

I had nothing to say to that.

"Of course," he added, "if you were to become chieftain, that would also be the result of a smart man's foolishness. I'm talking about your brother."

The executioner was waiting downstairs even as we talked. Since I didn't want to see the historian punished again, I said good-bye upstairs. In a voice loud enough for everyone to hear, he said to my beautiful wife, "Mistress, don't worry about your husband and don't lose hope. Sooner or later, those who consider themselves smart will make a mistake."

This he said on his way downstairs to be punished. He said something else after that, but the wind carried it away, and no one heard it. My brother followed him downstairs. When the wind died down, we heard my brother say to him, "You could choose to die."

The historian stopped, turned, and looked up at this fellow who was dizzy over his success. "I don't choose to die. I want to see you die with my own eyes."

"I'm going to have you killed."

"Are you the Maichi chieftain now? The chieftain said he was going to abdicate, but he hasn't yet."

"Very well. I'll take your tongue now and have you executed as soon as I become chieftain."

"By then, I may not be the only one you want to kill."

"Yes."

"Tell me who you want to kill, Master. I'm your historian."

"You'll know when the time comes."

"Your younger brother?"

"He's an idiot who isn't content with being an idiot."

"The chieftain's wife?"

"By then she'll know who's smarter."

"And your brother's wife?"

My brother smiled. "Damned if she's not a true beauty, lovelier than a demon. I dreamed about her last night."

The historian laughed. "None of the things you, a smart person, want to do is unexpected."

268

"Go on talking, if that will make you feel better before your punishment is carried out."

The genteel, refined historian cursed for the first time, "Damned if I'm not a little scared."

Those were the last words we ever heard from him.

Tharna had never seen a professional executioner at work, and had never seen anyone have his tongue cut out, so she went downstairs to watch. The chieftain's wife said to her husband, "You've never seen another chieftain punish someone. Don't you want to go watch?"

He shook his head, a look of torment on his face. He wanted everyone to comprehend the noble pain of someone who had decided to abdicate.

But his wife paid him no heed. "I'll go if you won't. I've never seen someone who has yet to become chieftain exercise the rights of one." She went downstairs.

The upstairs was all but deserted in an instant.

The chieftain looked at his idiot son with an even more tormented look on his face. But my torment was ten times, a hundred times, greater than his, even though it didn't show on my blank face. I looked up at the sky, where cottony white clouds were quickly blown across the small square of blue framed by the window. I didn't want to stay with a chieftain who would soon be a former chieftain, so I got up to leave. I'd barely taken a step when Father abruptly said to my back, "My son. Don't you want to spend a little more time with your father?"

"I can't see the clouds in the sky."

"Come back and sit by me."

"I want to go outside. I want to see the clouds in the sky."

The chieftain had no choice but to follow and stand with me on one of the estate's many verandas. We watched the floating clouds for a while. Unlike other times, when someone was being punished, the yard was quiet. The sun blazed down on the silent crowd like a shiny metal shield. There wasn't a sound.

"It's so quiet," the chieftain said.

"As if the Maichi family didn't exist."

"You hate me, don't you?"

"I hate you."

"You must hate yourself for being an idiot."

"I'm not an idiot."

"But you appear to be one."

"You're more stupid than I, and he's more stupid than you."

Father started to quake. "I feel dizzy. I don't think I can stand."

"Fall down, then," I said. "You'll be useless once we have a new chieftain."

"My God, how heartless you are! Can you really be my son?"

"Are you really my father?"

He steadied himself and sighed. "I didn't want it this way. But your brother would start a war if I let you succeed me. You've done things a hundred times smarter than he, but I'm not sure if you'll be smart forever. I don't know whether you're an idiot or not."

Something in his voice touched me. I wanted to say something but didn't know how.

Overhead, a dark cloud drifted over and blocked out the sun. At that moment, the crowd below sighed in unison, which made me feel as if the entire estate were shaking.

I'd never heard so many people sigh so loudly as when the executioner flicked the knife in his hand. Neither had the chieftain, I was sure. He was frightened. I thought he was going to change his mind, so I walked down the steps, with him on my heels. He wanted me to state honestly whether I was smart or an idiot. I turned and smiled, happy to have a chance to smile at him like that. He ought to treasure that smile, I told myself. Standing three steps above his idiot son, the chieftain said emotionally, "I know you'll understand my feelings someday. You heard it yourself, the sigh from the people that seemed to rock the earth. When they carried you over their heads, leveling the barley field, I was afraid, truly afraid. Even your mother was afraid. That was when I decided to abdicate, so I could see him enjoy a solid reign and you live a peaceful life under him."

An idea suddenly occurred to me, accompanied by a sharp pain in my tongue. I knew that the historian had lost his tongue once more and that the pain had come from him. So I said, "I don't want to talk anymore."

The pain in my tongue disappeared as soon as I spoke.

37 I'm Not Talking

I abruptly decided not to talk anymore.

My friend, Wangpo Yeshi, lost his tongue for the second and last time. All because of me. He would not speak for a third time, even if another miracle occurred, for this time the executioner had removed his entire tongue. When I reached the yard, the dark cloud had disappeared, returning the sun to light up the earth. The historian lay beneath the walnut tree with Aryi's blood-clotting medicine in his mouth, looking up at the sky without moving. When I walked up to him, I saw that he was sweating, so I moved him deeper into the shade, and said, "It's good not to talk, so I'm not going to talk anymore."

He looked at me, two large teardrops welling up in the corners of his eyes. I reached out and touched one. My finger had a salty taste when I put it in my mouth.

The two Aryis were putting away their tools. On the far side of the yard, my brother and my wife were talking beneath a giant shadow cast by the house's stone wall. The first young master was lashing out at the flourishing hemps at the base of the wall. Tharna, too, seemed uneasy, for she kept wringing her hands. Were they exchanging views over watching someone lose his tongue? Since I wasn't going to talk anymore, I wouldn't join their conversation. The chieftain's wife, possibly interested in what they were talking about, walked toward them, but before she reached them, they headed upstairs separately. My wife didn't even look at me on the way. But Mother did, in much the same way that I was looking at Wangpo Yeshi.

Just then I glimpsed a face sticking out furtively from around a corner of the wall. I spotted something in that face. Yes, one look told me that this person had not spoken to anyone for a very long time. Not even to himself. And when that face, seemingly more lonesome than the moon, peered out again, I saw hatred hidden beneath the lonely surface. I knew at once who it was; it was the enemy of the Maichi family, come to avenge his father. He had set out when I was still at the border, but for some reason, he hadn't shown up until today. Mother turned to take another look at me when she reached the gate. Since I'd decided not to speak again, I felt no need to tell her about the arrival of the killer, who posed no danger to women anyway.

Sitting beneath the walnut tree, I watched as the estate house cast deeper and deeper shadows in the afternoon sun, and gazed out at the bright autumn scene before me. Wangpo Yeshi sat with me for a while, but then the executioners came to carry him away. Finally, the sun went down behind the mountains. A wind blew noisily across the field as flocks of homeward-bound birds flapped their wings like rags. It was time for dinner, so I went straight to the dining room.

Everyone was there, and everyone smiled at me warmly. I told myself that was because I'd once again become a harmless idiot. They vied to talk to me, but I'd made up my mind not to speak. My brother was looking at Tharna when he said to me, "If my younger brother continues to keep his silence, even Tharna will think he's an idiot." This statement was intended for the ears of his beautiful sister-in-law. "All idiots let their anger fester inside, unlike the rest of us, who say what's on their mind."

A green glare emerged from Tharna's eyes; I thought it was directed at my smug brother, but she turned to me, and said, "You can no longer say you're not an idiot, can you?"

I thought back as far as I could go, but couldn't recall ever saying that to her. But I'd decided not to speak again.

Father said, "If he doesn't want to talk, don't force him. He's a Maichi man, and he's done for us things that the rest of us could not have accomplished. It makes me sad to see him like that."

I remained where I was after the others had left.

Father stayed with me. "My wife left the table without a word to me," he said. "Your wife left the table without a word to you."

I didn't say anything.

"I know you want to return to the border, but I can't let you. If you really are an idiot, it will serve no purpose. And if you aren't, that's even worse. One day the Maichi brothers might use our fine weapons in a war against each other."

I didn't say anything.

"Our crippled steward sent people here to escort you back," he said, "but I dismissed them." He went on, "I can't entrust you with everything. You've done wonderful things, but I'm just not sure if you're really smart. I'd rather believe they were all miracles, with the gods' help. But I cannot base my decision on miracles."

I got up and walked out, leaving him alone in the dining room, where he buried his head in his arms, buried it deeply.

My beautiful wife was combing her long hair in front of the mirror in our room. Her hair glistened faintly in the lamplight. I tried hard not to appear in the mirror with her lovely face.

She was smiling and sighing at her reflection. Quietly, I lay down on the bed. Then she spoke to me: "You didn't spend a minute with me the whole day."

Wind howled beyond the massive stone wall, sending fallen leaves and dry grass swirling in the air.

She said, "No one would believe that a beautiful woman like me would not have her man at her side even once all day."

The wind blowing across the river warmed the water. But when sprays rose out of the warm water, they turned icy. That was how the water got colder each day, until one night the splashes would fall back into the river in the form of ice, and winter would arrive.

"I chatted with your brother awhile. Even though he was defeated in battle, he's still an interesting man."

Tharna hadn't stopped admiring herself in the mirror, turning this way and that. I lay in bed thinking about the coming winter scenery. The fields had been picked clean in the harvest. Red-beaked black crows and white pigeons soared in the sky, cawing and cooing as they circled. But winter days are too quiet, even with the birds calling, for the river is sealed up by ice. It is the river's raging water that gives the world its vitality.

Tharna laughed, and said, "I didn't expect you to actually stop talking."

Finally she left the mirror and came to sit on the bed. "My God! One of the world's idiots isn't talking anymore. What are we going to do now?"

There was a knock at the door. Tharna drew her clothes together and returned to the mirror.

My brother pushed open the door and came over to sit by my bed with his back to me. Tharna sat with her back to both of us, so my brother said to her reflection, "I came to see my brother."

That comment started up a conversation in the mirror.

"You're wasting your time," Tharna said. "He's not talking anymore."

"Do you want him not to talk, or is that his idea?"

"I don't know what goes on inside the heads of Maichi men."

"I'm different."

I fell asleep, during which they must have talked about many things. They were saying good night when I woke up. Tharna was still facing the mirror, her back to the first young master. He stopped at the door, and turned to say, "I'll come see my brother often. I've been fond of him ever since we were boys. He began to hate me when he decided he wanted to be chieftain. But I'll keep coming to see him."

Tharna was untying the braids she'd made from her loose hair.

Then the first young master spoke to her again through the window. "Go to bed. This is a big house, and you're so pretty; you needn't worry about not having anyone to talk to."

Tharna laughed.

So did he, from the other side of the window. "My brother is really an idiot. There can't be another girl as pretty as you anywhere, and he refuses to talk to you."

Amid the sound of his retreating footsteps, Tharna blew out the lamp, letting moonlight stream into the room. It was late autumn, and there was a chill in the air. But that didn't faze Tharna, who stood by the bed and undressed. She remained standing there until the footsteps died out, then slipped under the covers. "Idiot, I know you're awake, so stop pretending you're asleep."

I didn't move.

She laughed. "If you're still not talking tomorrow morning, I'll know it's for real."

I woke up later than usual the next morning. Tharna was already dressed and made-up when I opened my eyes. Clad all in red, she sat amid rays of sunlight that shone in through the door. My God, she was beautiful, sitting there like a fresh flower that blooms only in dreams! She walked up to the bed and bent over me when she saw that my eyes were open. "I've been waiting for you to wake up," she said. "I'm told it's a wife's duty to wait for her husband to wake up. Besides, you have those same old questions to ask, don't you? Otherwise, you'll look even more like an idiot."

I kept my lips clamped shut while the beautiful woman bent down over me.

She said, "You really will be an idiot if you don't start talking, since you won't know who or where you are. I think you should say something."

My mouth stank after I'd slept through the night, especially since I hadn't opened it to talk for a while. The foul smell that emerged when I finally did open it forced her to cover her nose; she turned and walked out. Like a dying animal, I opened my mouth wide and spewed out mouthfuls of putrid breath. I didn't start thinking about my questions until my mouth no longer stank. Who am I? Where am I? I thought as I lay in bed, staring at dusty, smoky gray spiderwebs in the corner, which, after a while, seemed to enter my head.

I walked around with a dreamy smile the whole day, looking for a place to remind myself where I was. But everything seemed to have come from a previous life, familiar and yet strange. From a distance, the towering, magnificent chieftain's estate house seemed to lean a little. When I got closer, I saw that even the foundation stones had begun to crumble from decay. I recalled a story about a wise man named Aku Tonpa. One day he came to a sacred place, also located in a square. Wanting to play a trick on a serious monk, he told him to embrace a flagpole in the center of the square to steady it. Even though the monk didn't believe that the pole would fall, still he wrapped his arms around it. The monk held on to the tall pole and looked deep into the sky, where clouds billowed just like flags. In the end, the pole seemed to move and the monk strained to keep it from toppling over. He would have died from exhaustion if the clouds hadn't floated away, revealing that the pole was intact after all. Now as I looked up at the sky, I felt the estate's stone wall falling down on me. But I didn't try to steady it, because I was an idiot, not a wise man. The clouds kept drifting, and the stone wall above me kept pressing down. But in the end, nobody was hurt, and I burst out laughing at the sky.

The Maichi enemy, the fellow who had nearly killed me at the border, stuck his head out from behind the wall again. The furtive look on his face did not help clear my head. He walked slowly up and sat down beside me, where he hiked up his clothes to show me the swords he'd brandished at me before. "I'm going to kill your father and brother," he said.

I smiled.

The killer gnashed his teeth and slipped away unnoticed.

Mother came out to take me to her room. My muddled head cleared up a bit after she blew some opium smoke in my face. Tears streamed down her cheeks as she said, "Don't be afraid. You're with your mother, my idiot son."

She blew some more smoke at me. Opium is wonderful stuff; I fell asleep almost at once. Not only that, I dreamed I was flying leisurely the whole time. It was morning when I woke up. "Son," Mother said, "talk to me if you don't want to speak to other people."

I gave her a foolish smile.

The chieftain's wife started crying again.

"At least talk to me, even if you don't want to talk to them. I am your mother, after all."

I got up, put on my clothes, and walked out of her room. She slid to the floor holding her hand over her heart. I felt a pain shoot through my heart too, so I stopped and waited for it go away. No pain lasts forever; this one would disappear too. It pierced me like a razor-tipped arrow, pausing at my thumping heart before flying out through my back like a bird. I walked down one level, turned the corner, and arrived at my own room. My two young servants, who had come to stand behind me, suddenly spoke, making me leap up in surprise. The sun was just rising in the east, and I nearly stepped on my own shadow when I landed on the floor.

"Why didn't the second young master sleep with Tharna?" Sonam Tserang asked. "The first young master went to see her last night, and she sang for him."

"Hush!" Aryi held up a finger.

Inside the room came the sound of Tharna getting up and putting on her robe, the sound of silk scraping against her skin, and the sound of her bare feet walking on the rugs. Tharna began to sing again amid the sounds of her ivory comb slipping through her hair. I'd never heard her sing before.

I led the two servants downstairs. Instead of stopping in the yard, we continued on to the executioners' house on the hill. The aroma of herbs in their yard was very comforting. My head began to clear and I recalled the time I'd been there before, which had included a visit to the room where they stored dead people's clothes. This time, when we walked up under that lonely room, my servants brought over a ladder. Aryi told us he came here often and had become good friends with some of the clothes.

Sonam Tserang laughed. Since his voice was changing, he sounded like a night bird that exists only in the jungle. "Is there something wrong with your head too," he asked Aryi, "like the young master's? How can anyone make friends with clothes?"

Aryi was outraged, his normally hesitant voice turning assertive as he said, "My head, just like the young master's, is fine. Those aren't ordinary clothes. They belonged to executed people who left their souls behind."

Sonam Tserang reached out to touch the clothes, but stopped in midair. He was breathing hard.

Aryi laughed. "You're scared."

Sonam Tserang grabbed a purple garment, sending dust flying all around the room. Who'd have thought that a simple garment could have accumulated so much dust? We all keeled over coughing, while the clothes, with their bloodstained collars, began swaying, as if they really were inhabited by spirits.

"They're unhappy because I brought strangers along," Aryi said. "Let's get out of here."

We came out of the dusty room to stand in the sun. Sonam Tserang was still clutching the garment, a very handsome one. I didn't recall ever seeing such a pure purple; it was still very bright, as if it had been made only yesterday. But before we had time to memorize the color, it faded in the sun and turned into a different shade. It was now even more marvelous, for the purple had become the same color as the bloodstains on the collar. I couldn't control the urge to put it on; even after Aryi knelt down to beg me not to, I wouldn't change my mind. But then I felt my body tighten, as if someone had me in a vise. Yet even that didn't make me take it off. Aryi boiled some herbs, which I drank, and that dispelled the pinched feeling. My body was one with the clothes.

The garment didn't want to talk either. Or maybe I should say that I'd satisfied its need to move around again in the world, and so it followed my desire to remain silent.

Now everything before me was tinted with shades of purple. The river, the mountains, the fields, the estate house, the trees, and dry grass were all shrouded in a film of purple, with a tinge of slightly fading, aging blood red.

When I returned from the executioners' house, the chieftain's wife was reclining on her opium bed.

"What a strange garment!" she said. "When did you have that made?"

As soon as Tharna saw me, the vitality in her face drained away like mist in the sun. She wanted me to change into something else and rummaged through a big closet. But I trampled on everything she took out. Finally, she fell on the pile of fancy clothes, her face as ugly as sun-blanched bedrock. She said over and over, "I can't stand it. I can't stand it anymore!"

She ran out of the room.

I sat in my room in that purple garment, staring at the heart of a golden flower woven in the rug. Suddenly I saw Tharna pass along a quiet, deserted veranda and enter the first young master's room, where he sat cross-legged on a rug, just like me. His younger brother's beautiful wife stumbled toward him and fell into his arms, almost as if she were unable to stand. She hit the future chieftain in the nose with her elbow; blood began to drip the moment the beautiful woman fell into his arms. The future chieftain had always been a romantic, but he never anticipated starting up a romance with the loveliest woman in the world this way.

"You made me bleed."

"Hold me, hold me tight. Don't frighten me."

The future chieftain held her tightly. The blood from his nose dripped onto her face, but she paid no heed. The future chieftain repeated himself: "I'm bleeding, thanks to you."

"You're bleeding? You *are* bleeding. You're real. I'm not afraid anymore."

"Who's not real then?"

"Your brother."

"He's an idiot."

"He frightens me."

"Don't be frightened."

"Hold me tighter."

At that moment, the old chieftain was also in his room. He had been thinking about when he should formally step down and hand over the title to his older son, the defeated warrior. Having grown tired of thinking, he drank himself into oblivion. All of a sudden, he was seized by an uninvited desire. He'd been alone over the past few days, since no one had come to see him. So he took that uncontrollable desire into his wife's room; it would likely be the last outburst of sexual desire of his life. She lay smoking on her opium bed, her face seemingly cut out of paper behind the misty smoke. The face smiled up at him. Unable to stand, the old chieftain knelt by the opium bed with a pained look on his face. Thinking he'd changed his mind, she said, "Having second thoughts?"

The old chieftain reached out for her lapel, making an animal-like noise; that and the smell of alcohol on his breath awoke painful memories in her. She pushed the old man away, and grumbled, "You old bastard. This is how you gave me that son. Get away from me!"

Tormented by the burning desire, the old chieftain could say nothing, so he went straight to Yangzom's room. She was meditating, each breath deeper and longer than the one before. The old chieftain rushed toward her.

At that moment, my wife was pressed beneath my brother's body.

The agony returned, like an arrow piercing my chest, then pausing at my heart before exiting through my back like a bird, chirping as it flew away.

In broad daylight, two couples tore at each other, shaking the estate. I closed my eyes, my body swaying with that shaking, which turned even more violent when the rumble of thunder rolled in from a distance. I swayed at first like a tree in the wind, then bounced up and down like barley in a sifter.

When the shaking stopped, Sangye Dolma and her silversmith stormed in. With little effort, the silversmith hoisted me over his shoulder and carried me out into the yard. Before everyone's eyes, the two couples, my father and his third wife, my brother and my wife, ran out of their rooms nearly naked, as if to announce to all that their maniacal actions had caused an earthquake. The people's shouts of "Ahhh!" were like the rumbling inside the earth before the quake. They were deep and low, but their power was impossible to ignore.

The two couples, brought up short at the top of the stairs by the shouts, realized they were standing nearly naked in front of everyone. With the chieftain, it didn't matter, since he had been with his third wife. But my brother was different – he was with the beautiful

279

wife of his younger brother. A second, more violent, shaking rose from inside the earth just as they were wavering between turning around to get dressed and fleeing downstairs for their lives.

The earth shook yet again, sending dust flying and flinging the two couples to the floor. Then, like a cascading waterfall, a section of the Maichi estate's tall sentry tower crumbled. Chunks of stone and pieces of wood rained down like a broken dream. The clay that had bound the stones and wood together turned to dust amid the shaking before rising again. People lay on the ground watching the column of smoke and dust rise into the sky. I think they felt they were seeing something of the Maichi family disappear into the air. When the dust settled, the sentry tower was missing a corner, but it still dominated the blue sky. Its exposed, smoke-charred inner wall would surely collapse if the earth shook again.

But the rumbling had moved off to someplace far away.

The dust flying over the earth finally settled.

Chieftain Maichi and the first young master were once again standing before us, this time fully dressed. The two women were gone. The men told the people on the ground that they could get up, that the earthquake was over.

My brother even helped me up. "Look at you," he said. "You're always mingling with the servants. And now you have dirt all over your face."

He took out a silk handkerchief to wipe his idiot brother's face. Then he opened the handkerchief to show me. Yes, it was smudged with dirt.

His idiot brother raised his hand and slapped him.

A purple mark in the shape of a hand slowly materialized on his smart face. He sucked in cool air as he covered his cheek.

"Idiot. I was feeling sorry for you a moment ago because your wife was unfaithful. But I'm glad, I'm glad I fucked your woman!"

He desperately wanted to hurt this younger brother who had been such a huge threat to him. Normally, even a smart person (let alone me, an idiot to begin with) would flirt with idiocy after being hurt like that. But today everything was different for me. Today I was wearing that purple garment and I could feel its power turn me around and escort me upstairs, ignoring the maniac. I walked straight to my room, where Tharna was sitting at the mirror, as always, but without the dreamy look she'd worn before the earthquake. She shuddered. "My God! Where did that chill come from?"

I heard myself say, "Get out of my room! You're not my wife anymore. Get the hell out and go to him!"

When she turned around, I was happy to see the look of surprise on her face. But she tried to compose herself and smile. "Why are you still wearing that strange garment? Let's get you into something else."

"Get the hell out of here!"

Now she was sobbing. "Take off that garment. It frightens me."

"Weren't you frightened when you were sleeping with your husband's brother?"

She fell onto the bed, watching me out of the corner of one eye and crying with the other. I didn't like that; I wanted her to cry with both eyes. So I said, "Write to your mother and tell her how you felt when you were standing naked in front of everyone during an earthquake."

She didn't love me, but she lacked the courage to stay with the first young master. Even if she'd had the nerve, I couldn't say the same about the smart first young master. When I sent for the historian, she finally cried with both eyes.

"How cruel you are! How can such cruel words be the first ones out of your mouth?"

Yes, I was talking again. And once I started, I said things I'd never have said before. How happy that made me.

Ten ~

38 The Killer ~

Tharna tried to climb into bed with me, but I kicked her to the floor.

Curled up like a cat on the rug, she gave me a particularly pitiful look as she said, "I don't want to think about anything. I don't want to think at all. I want to sleep."

But she didn't. And the fellow who would soon be the new Maichi chieftain didn't come to see his lover either. The buzz of chanting lamas in the sutra hall upstairs was like a gloomy current flowing above my head. The sound of leather drums and brass cymbals rose and fell, like undulating waves on the river. The monks got busy any time something happened on this land. The clergy would cease to exist if nothing bad ever occurred in this world; but they had no need to worry about their livelihood, since there was always something that required their effort.

I said to Tharna, "Go to sleep. The chieftains are busy tonight, so he won't come to see you."

She was curled up on the rug and raised only her head to look at me, reminding me of a snake. Now this lovely snake was saying, "Why must you always hurt a woman, a beautiful woman?"

She looked so pathetic that I was tempted to believe in her innocence. I had to stop talking to her, or it would be I, not she, who was the guilty one.

It had been a mistake not to keep my mouth shut. I'd enjoyed some power when I wasn't talking, power I lost as soon as I opened my mouth. I quickly learned my lesson and covered my head with a blanket, not talking anymore. After I'd been asleep awhile, I think I dreamed that I had become the chieftain. Then I dreamed about the earthquake. The house, shaken by the rumbling earth, was shrouded in a gigantic cloud of dust, and when the dust settled, it was gone. I woke up in a sweat.

I went outside to pee. In the past, I'd always had a maid help me with a chamber pot, but I stopped relieving myself in the room when I began sleeping with the beautiful daughter of the Rongong chieftain. She wanted me to use the toilet outside. I found it didn't feel bad at all to get up in the middle of the night and walk outside, listening to myself make the sound of rain and watching the moon and stars in the sky. Even when there was no moon or stars out, a dark glimmer shone on and off from the river.

But I stopped using the toilet on the day Chieftain Maichi announced his intention to abdicate. As an idiot I didn't have to follow smart people's rules. So that night I walked out of my room and pissed through a gap in the railing. It took awhile for the flagstones below to send back the sound of someone clapping. My urine was still making the sound when I pulled up my pants. I didn't go right back to my room, but walked up and down the stairs in the dead of night.

It wasn't me, but my purple garment, that felt like walking. Then I saw the killer who had been sneaking around the house for days. At that moment, he was standing outside the chieftain's window. My footsteps startled him, and his panicky, fleeing footsteps in turn woke up the chieftain, who ran out with a pistol and fired at the killer's back. Seeing me standing nearby, he then aimed the gun at me. I didn't move, giving him a perfect target. He surprised me by letting out a terrified scream and falling to the ground. Lights quickly came on in many windows as people opened their doors and ran out to see what was happening. The first young master also ran out with a pistol. After the chieftain was helped up, he pointed a shaking finger at me. I thought that he and his smart son were about to kill me, but it appeared that my brother hadn't even seen me. More and more servants swarmed out of their rooms and surrounded the terrified chieftain.

To make a long story short: Father had mistaken me for one of the men executed on his order because of the purple garment I was wearing.

The purple garment I'd taken from the executioners' house had caused him to mistake me for someone dead all these many years, a ghost. You see, many of the condemned had gone meekly to their deaths, but whoever had worn this purple garment had not. Instead of departing to await reincarnation, the dead man's soul had stubbornly remained on the Maichis' land, waiting for its chance for revenge. The man in purple was lucky, because the Maichi chieftain's idiot son had given him that chance, a very good chance indeed. For it was not I whom the Maichi chieftain had seen, but the man he'd killed. The Maichi chieftain was never afraid when he ordered someone executed, but had been scared out of his wits when he saw someone who had been dead for years standing there in the moonlight.

Once all the fuss died down, everyone went back to sleep.

Tharna was truly no ordinary woman. With all that was going on outside, she didn't come out even for a brief look. Instead, she had climbed into bed. Now it was my turn to wonder whether I should get into bed with her. Seeing my indecision, she said, "It's all right. Climb in."

So I lay down beside her as if it were in fact all right.

And the night was nearly over.

The dining room was the only place where everyone gathered together in the morning. So I went down. Father had a silk kerchief wrapped around his head, which he had injured the night before. He was saying to his smart son, "Tell me, why are so many strange things happening all at once?"

The first young master, focusing his attention on his food, didn't answer.

The chieftain turned to his two women. "Have I done something wrong?"

Yangzom said nothing; she never said anything.

Mother thought awhile, then said, "I don't know about that. But you should tell your son that being a chieftain doesn't mean he can do whatever he pleases."

Tharna, realizing that Mother was referring to her and my brother, choked on her food. She was surprised that the Maichi family would air its dirty laundry so openly. "Please, Mistress," she said.

"I've placed a curse on you. Now we'll see if you can be the wife of the new chieftain." Mother turned to me. "Don't you want to take some action, my son?"

I shook my head.

284

Father groaned. "Stop it," he said. "I'm old and getting worse every day. Do you want me to die before my abdication?"

My brother smiled, and said, "Why not transfer the power to me now, if that's what worries you?"

The chieftain groaned again. "Why do I see dead people?"

My brother said, "Maybe they like you."

I said to Father, "It was me you saw."

He smiled at me, a bit embarrassed. "Are you laughing at me for not recognizing you?"

It was a waste of time to talk to people who thought they were always right. So I got up, intentionally straightening the purple garment in the chieftain's presence. He ignored me. "Help me back to my room," he said to the servants. "I want to go to my room."

After everyone was gone, the historian stood up in the corner and said to me with his eyes, "Remember this day. The chieftain won't come out again."

"You've recovered," I said. "That was fast."

He still had a pained look on his face, but his eyes said, "You can't leave now. This is the time when major events will take place."

He gave me another look when he reached the door, holding the notebook and pen I'd given him. "Remember. Today is a very significant day."

The historian was right. From that day on, the chieftain did not leave his room.

When Wangpo Yeshi still had his tongue, I'd asked him what history was. He'd said that history means learning about today and tomorrow from yesterday.

"Isn't that what the lamas do?" I'd asked him.

"No. That's divination. History doesn't mean asking for signs from gods."

I trusted him on that. Sure enough, Chieftain Maichi did not take another step out of his room. He slept during the day. His window was lit night after night, with maids going in and out all night long. His two wives went to see him occasionally, but I didn't go at all, nor did his heir. Sometimes when I got up to pee at night, I'd stand under the starry sky, watching the maids go in and out. I believed that Father was ill. But what a strange illness to require so much water. The maids would bring one basin after another of hot water from the kitchen downstairs. But the water cooled quickly, and they'd have to dump it out. On a quiet night, it was heart-stirring to hear basins of water splash down from upstairs and splatter on the flagstones below.

I was glad to see that my unfaithful wife was afraid of that noise. She shuddered, even in her sleep, when a basin of water splattered on the ground. I told her not to be afraid when that happened, and she replied, "What am I afraid of? I'm not afraid of anything."

"I don't know what you're afraid of, but I know you're afraid."

"You're such an idiot," she cursed, but somehow sounded coquettish.

I was wearing the purple garment worn by the executed man when I went out to pee. If you asked why I was so fond of that garment, I'd say it was because I'd begun feeling that life was very hard, as if I too had fallen into the hands of an executioner.

Once I got used to the sound of the maids dumping water from upstairs, the noise I made pissing through the railing was nothing.

Many days passed and winter was coming to an end. Spring was nearly here again. One night, when I got up, the Milky Way was shifting its position, like a waking dragon. The dragon always turns its body in a slightly different direction during seasonal changes. The movement of the Milky Way is so slow that you cannot detect the change within just a few nights.

I began to pee, but couldn't hear a sound, which made me wonder if I'd actually urinated. I couldn't go back to sleep if I wasn't sure I'd peed.

The towering estate house blocked the light from the sky downstairs. I sprawled on the ground, searching out the smell of urine, like a sniffing dog. The difference was that dogs flare their nostrils to sniff out other dogs, whereas I was seeking out my own smell. I finally found it. I had indeed peed, but the sound had been camouflaged by the splashing of the servants caring for the sick chieftain. With a sigh of relief, I got up to go back upstairs. Just then, a basin of water came crashing down on my head. I felt as if I'd been thrown to the ground by something warm. Then I heard the stirring splatter.

I screamed as I fell to the ground. Servants rushed downstairs from the chieftain's room. But my room remained pitch-dark – not a single lamp was lit. Maybe my unfaithful wife had gone to the first young master's room again.

The servants helped me up to the chieftain's room and took off the purple garment. This time I couldn't fight them, because a film of ice had formed on it. I was surprised when Tharna walked in.

"I've been looking all over for you," she said. "What were you doing?"

I flared my nose like a dog, and said, "Peeing."

Everyone laughed.

But not Tharna, not this time. She rolled up the purple garment and threw it out the window. I thought I heard the desperate cry of a dying man, whose soul unfurled like a flag, just like that purple garment, in the chill wind on a cold late-winter night. Tharna said to everyone in the room, "He was never this stupid. It's that garment that made him seem that way."

My love for her rose up again in my heart. Yes, I'd known that from the very beginning; she was so uniquely beautiful that I could forgive her for any mistakes so long as she was willing to change.

"My children," the chieftain said abruptly, "I'm so happy to see you like this."

Just think. I hadn't seen him since breakfast on that other morning. He still had not abdicated in favor of my brother and didn't look all that old and sick either. Sure, he was aging, and his hair was turning gray, but that was all. His face was fuller and paler than before. His once firm, decisive, manly face had taken on the appearance of a granny. The only overt signs of illness, though, or the only way he could convince himself that he was sick, were the hot towels covering his body. He wore little, since he was covered from head to toe in steaming towels.

Father said in a voice more sickly than a truly sick person's, "Come over here to your father's bed."

I went to sit by him, and discovered that his bed had been altered. It was now much shorter than before, after servants had sawed off sections of the legs. It had also been moved from the corner of the room to the middle.

Father raised his hand, sending two or three towels to the floor. He laid his spongy fingers on my head, and said, "I've made things hard for you, son." He waved Tharna over; she knelt before him. "You may return to the border whenever you want. That's your place. I'm giving it, plus ten fortresses, to you as a wedding gift."

He then asked me to promise that after he died I would not attack the new Maichi chieftain.

"What if he attacks us?" Tharna asked.

Father removed a towel from his forehead. "Then that will depend upon whether or not my younger son is indeed an idiot." He turned to Tharna. "And it depends even more upon which of my sons you prefer."

Tharna lowered her head.

Father smiled, and said to me, "There's no woman in the world more beautiful than your wife."

Then he sneezed loudly, since the towels had turned cold while he was talking. Tharna and I backed away to let the maids go to him. Father dismissed us with a wave of his hand. After returning to our room, we were about to climb into bed when the loud, stirring sounds started up again downstairs.

Tharna rolled into my arms, and said, "Thank God! That eerie garment is finally gone."

Yes, the purple garment was gone, and I felt as if I'd lost something.

"You don't hate me, do you?" she asked.

I really didn't. Maybe that was because I'd given up the possessed garment. It had been a long time since the chieftain's idiot son had been intimate with his wife, so the sense of loss was quickly replaced when Tharna rolled into my arms. I took her, with all the strength and violence born of love and loathing. I detected no sense of unease over what she'd done as she screamed with gratification. She then curled up, still naked, and fell asleep in my arms, as if, when I was at my most vulnerable, she hadn't flown into the arms of another man, who just happened to be my brother and my adversary. She was breathing evenly almost at once.

I tried hard to figure out women, but my head was so full that nothing else could get in. I shook her. "Are you asleep?"

She laughed, and said, "No."

"When shall we go back?"

"Before Chieftain Maichi changes his mind."

"Do you really want to go back with me?"

"You really are an idiot. I'm your wife, aren't I? Didn't you insist upon marrying me?"

"But you . . . and . . ."

"And your brother, right?"

"Yes," I said with difficulty.

She laughed again, and asked naively, "Am I not the most beautiful woman in the world? Men cannot keep their eyes off me. There will always be men who touch my heart."

What could I say to such innocent honesty?

She added, "Don't I still love you?"

What could I say when such a beautiful woman wanted me even after sleeping with a smart man who would soon be the chieftain?

"Aren't you sleepy?" Tharna said. "I'm really going to sleep now."

She rolled over and fell asleep. I closed my eyes, only to see the purple garment before me. It was there when I closed my eyes and it was still there when I opened them. I watched it billow in the wind like a flag when Tharna threw it out the window. It was soaked, and so it froze as soon as it unfolded. It, or he, or she, fell down stiffly. Someone was waiting down there, or maybe someone just happened to be there, and the garment fell and covered his head. The man struggled, but the frozen garment was on him now.

I saw his face, and it was a face I knew.

It was the killer.

It had been months since he'd arrived at the Maichi estate, yet he still hadn't made his move; maybe he lacked the courage.

I saw that face, which had become paler than the moon and more sensitive than a wound, after being tormented by hatred, by his cowardice, and by the chilly weather.

When the purple garment fluttered down from the window, he was standing by the wall, watching the light in the chieftain's window. His teeth were chattering. It was so cold that he would not reject a garment that fell from the sky. Especially since it possessed the remaining will of another person. Yes, I could see many things, even though they didn't actually take place before my eyes.

The purple garment, though frozen stiff, softened up as soon as it fell onto the killer, whose name was Dorjee Norpu. Even the ice on it melted. He was not much of a killer. He had not carried out his plan since arriving here not because he lacked the opportunity, but because he was agonizing over why he had to kill in the first place. Now everything had changed, thanks to the purple garment, which focused the combined hatred of two families on him. The night was so cold that both his sheath and sword had frosted. As he stood on the grounds of the Maichis' seemingly impregnable estate, he unsheathed his sword, making such a loud, crisp clang that my bones seemed to freeze. The killer climbed the stairs and took the path I wished him to take, a cold glint flickering on the blade of his weapon. His choices were my choices. If I had been the killer, I'd have taken the very same path. Since the chieftain was dying, the killer's target had to be the potent, aggressive man who would soon be the next chieftain. The killer came to a door and flicked open the latch with the tip of his sword. The door opened with a creak, like a startled woman. The lights were out in the room; he crossed the threshold as if entering an abyss of darkness. Standing there motionless, he waited for his eyes to grow accustomed to the dark. Slowly a hazy mass of whiteness rose out of the dark. Yes, it was a face, the face of the Maichi first young master. The purple garment held no hatred for that face; that was reserved for another face. It wanted to turn and leave. The killer, who didn't know any of this, felt a mysterious force pushing him out. He steadied himself and raised his sword, knowing he might never have the courage to raise it again if he let this opportunity pass. There was not enough hatred in his heart, but the customs of the land required someone like him to avenge a relative. There had been plenty of hatred while he was hiding out in that faraway place. But when he and his brother returned, that hatred had slowly disappeared once they learned that their father's death had been the result of his own betrayal of his master. But he had to raise his avenging sword against the Maichi family and let the cold glint of revenge shine on their terrified faces. You see, revenge did not mean only killing one's enemy, but also revealing to the enemy the avenger's identity.

But on that night, Dorjee Norpu did not have time to awaken the first young master and tell him whose son had returned for vengeance. As the purple garment kept pushing him in the direction of the old chieftain's room, the killer's sword descended on the shadowy figure in bed.

The person in bed let out a sleepy, muffled moan.

The hatred in the purple garment vanished with the soft slurp of steel cutting into flesh. This was the first time the killer, Dorjee Norpu, had ever murdered a man, and he hadn't known that the blade of a sword would make a slurping sound as it entered a body. Standing there in the dark, he sensed the smell of blood permeate the room as the slain man made another sleepy, muffled moan.

The killer ran out of the room, the bloody sword in his hand no longer glinting. He ran down the stairs in a panic, his coattail fluttering behind him. The estate was as quiet as if everyone had been killed – all but the idiot young master, who screamed from his bed, "Murder! The killer's here!"

Tharna woke up and clamped her hand tightly over my mouth. I bit her savagely, and screamed again, "Murder! The killer Dorjee Norpu is here!"

My shouts were so loud that anyone who said he didn't wake up would have been a liar. One by one, lights went on behind windows in the house, but the people went back to bed once they realized that it was I who was screaming. One by one, the windows went dark again. "Are you happy now?" Tharna said angrily. "As if being an idiot's wife weren't enough, now you want me to be a madman's wife too."

Tharna would never have made a great lover. She didn't feel a thing when someone buried a sword deep inside the first young master's belly. "Someone stabbed my brother in the belly," I told her.

"My God!" she said. "I didn't know you hated him that much. He didn't mean to take your wife from you. It was your wife who went to him. Didn't you say girls all like him?"

"He was stabbed in the belly," I insisted. "He's not only bleeding; he's also shitting in his pants."

Ignoring me, she turned over.

At that moment, the killer, who had run out of the house, lit a torch and stood in the yard, shouting out the name of his father, who had died at the hands of the Maichis. Then he shouted his own name and how he had returned to avenge his father. "Take a good look at me. This is my face, and I have come to exact revenge!"

This time, everyone ran out to look at the man in the yard. He sat astride his horse, shining the light of the torch on his face. Then he flung the torch away and disappeared in the dark, accompanied by the clatter of his horse's hooves.

The torch slowly went out on the ground before the chieftain shouted for people to go after the killer.

"You'll never catch him," I said, "so don't try. Go save a life instead. He's not dead yet."

"Who?" The old chieftain sounded utterly terrified.

"Not you," I said with a laugh. "It's your elder son. The killer stabbed him in the belly, and blood and shit are flowing onto the bed."

He asked, "Why didn't he kill me?"

He hadn't needed to ask, nor did I see any need to answer.

"Yes," he said, "I'm too old for them to kill me."

"He thought so too," I said.

"How can an idiot like you know what others are thinking?" Father asked.

Tharna whispered in my ear, "You're scaring him."

"It's precisely because I'm an idiot that I know what others are thinking."

The chieftain was helped to his heir's room. Everything before him was just as I'd said. The smell of blood and shit filled the first young master's room. His intestines had oozed out of his body. Covering the wound with his hand, he was moaning sleepily, his eyes closed. He sounded as if it were immensely agreeable to be stabbed. People shouted his name in his ear, but he didn't respond.

The old chieftain's gaze swept the room before falling onto my wife.

I said to her, "Father wants you to try calling his name."

Father said, "Yes, maybe you'll be able to awaken him."

Tharna blushed. My head swelled as she looked at me, but I muttered something about the urgency of saving a life.

So Tharna walked over to give it a try. "Open your eyes if you hear me."

But he kept them shut and had no intention of opening them. Monpa Lama, who knew only how to cure disorders that the eye could not see, was helpless in the face of such a horrifying wound. In the end, the executioners were summoned to treat the wound. They stuffed my brother's intestines back in before tying a medicine-filled bowl upside down over the wound. He stopped moaning. Aryi Senior wiped the sweat from his forehead, and said, "The first young master isn't feeling the pain, which means the medicine is working."

"Good," Chieftain Maichi said.

The night was nearly over. My brother fell into a deep sleep, with a childish look on his face, which was as white as paper.

The chieftain asked the executioners if they could heal my brother.

Aryi Senior said, "Only if he didn't lose control of his bowels."

Aryi Junior was more straightforward: "What my father means is that the first young master could die of poisoning from his own excrement."

The chieftain's face turned paler than that of his older son. He waved them away. "You may all go now."

Everyone filed out of the first young master's room. Aryi Junior looked at me with an excited glow in his eyes. I knew he was happy for me. Tharna clutched my hand, and I knew what she meant too. Yes, when my brother died, I would naturally become the legitimate Chieftain Maichi. I didn't know whether to be happy for myself or sorry for my brother.

I went to his room two or three times every day, but not once did he wake up.

Spring arrived quickly that year. Within two or three days after the wind changed direction, the willow branches by the river turned green. After a few more days, wild peaches on the mountain and in the gullies were in full bloom.

The dusty air was quickly suffused by a moist fragrance in a matter of days.

My brother was getting thinner each day, but Father had recovered his own vitality. He no longer required heat pads throughout the night. "You see," he said, "I won't be free of the burden I must shoulder until the day I die."

He said that as if he had only one son, who was rotting away before he died.

At first, the foul smell from my brother was masked by a special medicine blended with aromatic herbs administered by the executioners. Later, even the pungent smell of the herbs could not overcome the stink emerging from beneath the wooden bowl on his belly. The two odors together were so repugnant that no one could stand them. Women gagged when they went in; only Father and I managed to remain in the room for a short while, and I was always able to stay longer than he.

One day, after Father went outside, the servants fanned odor-repelling cypress smoke over him. He was choking on the smoke when I saw my brother's eyelids quiver. He'd finally awakened.

"Am I still alive?" he asked as he slowly opened his eyes.

"You're still in your own bed."

"What happened?"

"An enemy and a sword. The sword belonged to the Maichis' enemy."

He sighed and smiled weakly as he groped for the wooden bowl placed upside down on his belly.

"He wasn't very good at it," he said.

He gave me that frail smile, but I didn't know how to respond to him, so I said, "I'll tell everyone you're awake."

The people streamed in, but the women couldn't help gagging, which put a faint blush on the face of the Maichi first young master.

"Do I stink?" he asked.

After the women left, he said, "I stink. Why's that?"

Holding his son's hand, the chieftain forced himself to stay awhile, but it was too much for him. So he hardened himself and said, "You're not going to live, my son. Go quickly so you won't suffer." Tears were raining down the old chieftain's face when he finished.

The son looked at his father resentfully. "I could have been chieftain for a few days had you abdicated earlier, but you didn't want to. You know what I wanted most was to be the chieftain."

"All right, son," Father said. "I'll grant your wish immediately."

My brother shook his head. "I no longer have the strength. I'm going to die." He closed his eyes, and even though the chieftain called out his name several times, he did not respond. The chieftain walked out of the room in tears. When Father was gone, my brother opened his eyes again, and said to me, "You know how to wait. Unlike me, you are patient. Do you know that I fear you more than anyone else? That fear was the reason I slept with your woman. But I needn't fear you any longer." He paused, then added, "I can't help thinking about how much I loved you when we were young, my idiot brother." He was right. At that moment, memories of the past came flooding back.

"I loved you too," I said.

"I'm very happy," he said before he passed out.

The first young master of the Maichi family never woke up again.

A few days later, he departed quietly while we were all asleep.

Everyone wept.

But no one's tears were more genuine than mine. I felt saddened by his last words, even though there hadn't been much feeling left between us by then. Tharna wept too. In the middle of the night, she'd roll into my arms and hold me tight. I knew it didn't mean she loved me that much; she was afraid of the ghost of the newly deceased member of the Maichi family, which proved that she didn't love him as much as I loved him.

Mother dried her tears, and said to me, "I'm very sad, but now I don't have to worry about my idiot son anymore."

And Father had regained his vitality.

He personally took care of all his son's funeral arrangements. His hair was as white as the snowy mountains, but his face glowed red by the pyre cremating his son's body. The huge fire burned all that morning. By noon, the ashes, now cool, were placed in an urn, which was carried to the temple by monks playing musical instruments. The ashes would stay in the temple to receive sacrificial rites, and could not be buried until Living Buddha Jeeka declared that the soul of the deceased had settled. Yes, the bones of a once living person were kept in an urn, turning cold amid the buzzing sound of the monks' recitation of the "Reincarnation Sutra." With the red glow still on his face, the chieftain told Living Buddha Jeeka, "Do a good job raising the soul of the dead. I have to worry about the living. It's time for planting, and I need to take care of spring business."

39 Looking Northward ∾

That year, poppies were planted on one-third of the Maichi land and grain on the remaining two-thirds. The other chieftains did the same; everyone did what was best after that record famine.

I stayed home for another year, until my brother's ashes were transferred to the Maichi family cemetery.

Father showed more passion than before toward things that required the chieftain's attention. He was old, and women had lost their power over him; he didn't smoke opium and he didn't drink much. He even exempted the people from most of their taxes. The Maichi estate overflowed with silver, and Chieftain Maichi was more powerful than ever. No other chieftains would be so ignorant of their own inferiority as to try to compete with us. The people had never had such a peaceful, bountiful life; it was the first time the subjects and slaves on any chieftain's land actually felt proud to be living there.

One day I asked Father if we should recall the crippled steward from the border. Without thinking, he said, "No, let him stay there. If he comes back, I won't have anything to do."

That day, the family was drinking tea. When we had finished, he said, "Who says an idiot son is no good? I can say anything I want to you. I couldn't do that with your late brother."

"That's right, you don't have to be on your guard with me."

A look of concern suddenly clouded his face. "My God!" he said. "But you've got me worried about what will happen after my death." He added, "Powerful as the Maichi family is, it doesn't have a proper heir."

Tharna asked, "How do you know my husband isn't a proper heir?"

The chieftain's expression changed. "It would be best for him to be Rongong chieftain first, to see if he is qualified to be the Maichi chieftain."

"That will depend upon who dies first, you or my mother."

"See what I mean, idiot," Father said. "You can't even rein in your wife, let alone govern so many people."

I thought for a while before saying, "Will the chieftain let me leave to return to the border now?"

Father said, "So long as we make it clear beforehand that I'm only lending you the border region, and that you'll have to give it back to me when the female chieftain dies."

The chieftain's wife laughed. "Did you hear that? Chieftain Maichi will never die. He wants to live ten thousand years, like the silver in the storeroom."

"I can feel myself getting stronger each day," the chieftain said.

"If word of your recovery leaks out," Tharna said, "the avenger will return. He killed your son instead of you because you acted as if you were about to die."

The chieftain was now looking forward to our departure. He'd agreed to let me take the same group of people with me. My two young servants, Sonam Tserang and Aryi, had no trouble with the arrangement, but Dolma seemed reluctant to leave her silversmith. So I summoned the silversmith and told him to come with us, but he refused. He said the chieftain wanted to hire more silversmiths and had already promised him the position of head silversmith. I didn't want Dolma to be a cook forever, so I told them they would have to be separated. I asked Dolma if she wanted to be a lowly cook for the rest of her life. She just cried, without answering. I knew she didn't. On the day we were to leave, I was gratified to see her among the departing people with a small bundle of possessions on her back. I told Aryi to give her a dark horse. Father also gave me the historian.

As our convoy moved off slowly, I turned to take one last look at the Maichi estate house and was struck by a feeling that the towering building would not be there long. A wind carried the voice of the chieftain's wife's from behind us, but no one could make out her shouts. I asked the historian whether she would live on if the old chieftain did not die.

The historian answered with his eyes, "How can flesh and blood live forever, Young Master?"

We all knew that our souls would continue to reincarnate. What we meant by death was obliteration of the body in the present incarnation. Who really knew what happened in previous and future lives? "Why does my father think he'll never die?" I asked the historian.

"Power," he said with his eyes.

You see, with the historian by my side, I became a smart person. On the road, the historian wrote a poem for me. It went like this:

A mouthpiece will cover your mouth,
Scars will appear at the corners;
A saddle will be placed on your back,
With a load on the saddle;
Someone will sing to you,
Singing the wounds in your heart.
Someone will sing to you,
Singing the sunshine in your heart.

The crippled steward met us halfway.

He welcomed me with the formalities befitting the arrival of a chieftain.

"Let me take a good look at you, Young Master. You've been gone for two years."

"Yes, it has been that long."

"Is everyone well?"

"I brought Sangye Dolma with me."

His eyes reddened slightly. "Young Master is truly a good man. It's wonderful to have you back. And it's wonderful that everyone is fine."

Tharna said, "What good is that? Everything here is the same as when we left."

The steward laughed. "Don't worry, Mistress. The young master will be chieftain one day."

The moon was bright outside the tent on that night we spent on the road. After Tharna fell asleep, I got up to walk in the moonlight. A cold glint flickered from the sentry's bayonet behind some rocks not far from me. I coughed as I walked by the steward's tent, then moved off a little way. Soon someone came out and headed in another direction. From the back, it looked like Sangye Dolma. I smiled. I'd been very sad when she married the silversmith, but I didn't feel that way anymore. I liked her and I liked the steward, so I was happy to see them together.

Then the steward walked up to me.

"I thought I heard the young master out here."

"I got up to look at the moon," I said.

He laughed. "Enjoy yourself, then."

So I did. We were on a northern plateau, where the moon was much larger than it was at the Maichi estate. Here, it seemed, I could reach out and touch it as it flickered amid the watery sounds of a creek. The steward's voice seemed to descend from the moon. "Every time news came from the Maichi estate, I worried you wouldn't be able to come back."

I didn't have to look at his face to know that he was sincere. Besides, no one would pick a night when moonlight flowed like water to lie.

"I'm back," I said.

Yes, I was back, but I'd brought a dull pain in my heart with me. Since leaving the border, my wife had betrayed me, and my brother, who was also my adversary, had died. The old chieftain felt that life was getting more interesting now that he was solidly back on his throne. I'd placed my hopes on the chieftain's wife, since she had always wanted me to be chieftain. But after my brother died, her attitude had become more ambiguous. She said that her son shouldn't worry, because Father would not take another woman and that was good for everybody. But I saw nothing good in the situation. On the day I left, she told me that she was not opposed to my becoming the Maichi chieftain but was afraid of my wife becoming the wife of the Maichi chieftain. She herself planned to live many more years, and had gotten accustomed to being the chieftain's wife.

The steward called out to me.

"Go ahead, say what's on your mind."

He took a letter from his pocket, a letter from Tharna's mother, the chieftain of Rongong. Since I couldn't read, the steward told me that the female chieftain asked that her daughter and son-in-law not hurry back to see her. Then he said, "Don't feel bad, Young Master."

"I'll feel bad when they're all dead," I said.

I walked back to my tent, letter in hand, thinking I'd have to stay in the border region now. When I looked up at the moon, I thought about my uncle, living in a distant land. I missed him terribly that day, as if he were my only relative. From behind me, the steward said, "I'm going back to bed."

I heard myself reply, "Mm."

The steward walked off, stepping on moonbeams.

I raised the tent flap, letting in rays of moonlight to shine on Tharna. She laughed. Her laughing face dazzled even when she'd just awakened. I let down the flap, returning her face to darkness. But though I couldn't see her anymore, her laughter continued to echo in the dark.

"Out looking for girls?" she asked.

I shook my head; the letter crackled in my hand.

"Speak up, idiot. I know you're shaking your head. But don't you know I can't see you when you do it in the dark?"

I raised the flap again to let the moon light up the interior. Now she not only knew that I was shaking my head, but could see it too. On that deep night, with its watery moon, Tharna laughed.

299

"You're an intriguing man."

I waved the letter in my hand. Since she could read, she said, "Light the lamp." She took the letter and said, under the light of the lamp, "It's from my mother."

I lay down and covered myself with the blanket. She didn't say anything after reading the letter.

"She doesn't want us there either," I said.

"She doesn't want us to worry about her."

"If anyone worries about a chieftain, it's the position he worries about, not the person."

"Mother says I belong with the Maichi family, so we needn't concern ourselves with Rongong matters."

In the letter, the female chieftain of Rongong had also written, "Enough has happened in the Maichi family to occupy you both. You must help share the old chieftain's burdens, since he has suffered the loss of a son. My son-in-law may be an idiot, but he's no ordinary idiot, and occasionally he does something truly wise. I heard you were coming to the north. Why don't you stay on the chieftain's estate? What are you going to do at the border?"

At the end of the letter, my mother-in-law wrote, "Don't worry about me, now that the famine is over."

Tharna had thought she'd be the apple of her mother's eye forever, that she would always be Chieftain Rongong's uniquely beautiful daughter. With tears in her eyes, she said to the letter, "Mother, don't you want your daughter anymore?"

The letter crackled in her hand. She wanted to read it one more time, but the lamp oil had burned out, leaving only the pungent odor of animal fat in the dark.

Tharna leaned against me, and said, "Idiot. Where are you taking me?"

"To our own place."

"Will you make your wife, the most beautiful wife in the world, suffer?"

"You'll be the wife of a chieftain."

"You won't bring harm to me, will you? I'm the prettiest girl in the world. Have you ever heard me sing?"

I had, of course. And now that song sounded in my ears. We then did something we hadn't done for a long time. Afterward, as her fingers played on my chest, I asked her if she was thinking about how to respond to the female chieftain. A teardrop fell on my chest. It burned my skin and made me tremble.

"I hurt you when I slept with your brother, didn't I?" she said.

Such a woman! I never expected her to ask a question like that. Not even an idiot like me would ask that kind of question and remind others of their pain. Back then I'd wanted to kill my brother. Later, the killer, with the help of the purple garment, took care of him, even making the handsome playboy stink terribly. That thought made me feel as if I'd killed him with my own hands. But that was only how I felt inside. With the sense of guilt buried deep, I heard myself say coldly, "It's a good thing you don't have that disgusting stink on you."

"My body is redolent. Smell me. I have a wonderful fragrance even without perfume."

I smelled her.

"Idiot," she said. "Don't ever let me fall for another man again."

Pretty women are never short of men who have their eyes on them, I knew that. If someone tried to take her by force, I could do my best to protect her. But there was nothing I could do if she willingly went to another man's bed. She probably guessed what I was thinking, so she said casually as her fingers played on my chest, "All right, don't be angry. I'll get the steward to find you a girl when we reach the border. As for you and me, we are bound together, inseparable."

I was sad that it had taken her so long to realize that.

Once we were back on the road again, I kept thinking about what she had said. The steward told me I should be happy that such a pretty woman had thoughts like that about me. I agreed with him. Now that I'd mulled things over, my steps were lighter.

I was back at the border.

I went out looking for a suitable room for the historian. "It must be close to mine," I told him, "and quiet, so you can think, with fresh air and lots of light. How does that sound?"

He nodded his head vigorously, his face aglow. I don't think he'd been this excited in all the days since his tongue was cut out the first time. He hadn't quite believed that what stood at the border was a huge open market and not an enclosed fort, especially one that attracted all the wealth of the world. As a recorder of

301

history, he had written that Chieftain Maichi had announced his abdication, and then not followed through with it; that the two brothers had carried on both an open and a veiled rivalry for the chieftain's position; and that the chieftain's heir had been slain by an enemy of the family. All this he considered to be history repeating itself. But now at the border, he was seeing something he'd never seen before. His eyes shone bright, and I knew he would write down everything in minute detail.

First I showed him around the bustling market, then the inn run by the enemy of the family, a place I'd gotten to know well. The innkeeper smiled when he saw me walk in, as if I hadn't been away for the past two years, as if I'd sat there getting drunk only the day before. I asked him if his brother had returned. When he glanced at the historian, I told him that the man had no tongue. He replied that anyone who had carried out such a deed needed to hide out for a while, or would not be considered a true killer. Every trade has its rules.

Streets are such wonderful things. We could sit at the inn and watch people ride or walk past, filling the air with dust. Even though I had to cover my bowl with my hand to keep the dust out, the liquor tasted good. As I was talking with the innkeeper, my two young servants came in to say that the steward was looking for me. I ordered a bowl of liquor for each for them and told them to take their time drinking it.

40 Guest from Afar ∽

Walking north down the street, I reached a river, where the steward had erected a lovely little wooden footbridge. The far end faced my open compound, where the steward was waiting.

"Guess who's coming to dinner?"

I had no idea. So he smiled and led us to the dining room. Sangye Dolma, dressed in nice, new clothes, was standing there to greet us.

"Well, well," I said. "I've yet to become chieftain, but you've already been promoted."

Hiking up her skirt, she began to kneel, but I stopped her.

"The steward asked me to guess who was coming to dinner," I said.

She laughed, and whispered, "Don't mind him, Young Master. You're not an idiot if you can't guess and it won't make you smart if you can."

My God! It was the Maichis' old friend, Special Emissary Huang who stood there before me.

His face was still gaunt, and he still sported a pathetically scraggly yellow beard. The only change was in his eyes, which seemed calmer. I said to our guest from afar, "There's no more weariness in your eyes."

His answer was quite direct: "That's because I don't have to worry on behalf of others anymore."

I asked after Regiment Commander Jiang. He told me that Jiang had drowned in a river after being sent to a remote spot to fight the Red Chinese.

"He didn't stink, did he?"

Special Emissary Huang opened his eyes wide, not knowing why I'd asked a question like that. Maybe he'd finally realized that he was talking to an idiot, so he laughed, and said, "It was a hot day on the battlefield, so of course he stank. When a person dies, there's nothing left but flesh and bones. We're no different from dogs or cows."

We sat down at the table, with me at the head. I clapped my hands and Dolma relayed the clap at the door to summon a parade of maidservants.

Rectangular wooden crimson platters decorated with gilded fruit in strange shapes and giant flowers said to be popular in India had been placed before us. They contained porcelain from the Han area and silverware made by our silversmiths. The wineglasses were made of blood-red Ceylonese agate.

I waited until we had downed three glasses of liquor before asking Special Emissary Huang what he had brought us this time. Years back, of course, he had brought the Maichi family modern weapons and opium. In our experience, every time Han people came to our land they either brought us something or took something away with them.

Huang Chumin said, "I have brought nothing but myself. I have come to stay with the young master." He was very candid in telling me that he was no longer welcome in his homeland. When I asked him if he couldn't stay in his homeland anymore because of the Red Han Chinese, he shook his head. "You might say it's because of relatives of the Red Han Chinese."

"Han people all look the same to me. I can't tell the Reds from the Whites."

"That's a distinction only the Han themselves make."

"I'll give you a room."

He tapped his head, his beady eyes shining. "Maybe something in here will be of use to the young master."

"I don't like to communicate through an interpreter," I said.

"I'll start learning your language today," he said. "It won't take more than half a year before we can speak without an interpreter."

"What about girls? I don't plan to give you any."

"I'm too old."

"You're not allowed to write poetry."

"I don't need any more posturing."

"I never liked how you acted before. I'll give you a hundred taels of silver every month."

Now it was his turn to show what he was made of. "I don't want your silver. I might be old, but I still can find ways to earn my own keep."

So that was how Huang Chumin came to live with us. I did not ask why he'd come to me instead of to Chieftain Maichi. I figured that would be a tough question to answer, and I didn't like to ask people tough questions.

One day, I went for a drink at our enemy's inn. The innkeeper blurted out that his brother had returned the night before. I asked where the killer was. The innkeeper looked at me, studying my expression, which told me that his brother was there with us. I had only to pull back the door curtain to see him sitting by the tiny window with a bowl of liquor in his hand.

"It would be best for him to be gone from here. Rules are rules, and I can't violate them."

"My brother spared you once," he said, "so you ought to spare him this time."

He was tempting me with a new rule. When a person is born into this world, he quickly discovers that others have set up many rules for him. Sometimes these rules are a form of bondage, but sometimes they can be used as weapons. Take the rules of revenge, for example. Chieftain Maichi killed the innkeeper's father after exploiting him, so it was only natural for his family to avenge him. The rules require it. The innkeeper's brother had not killed me by the river because I wasn't the Maichi chieftain. He would have violated the rules of revenge and been mocked by everyone if he had.

I said, "He didn't kill me because he shouldn't have. Now I must kill him because he killed my brother. I would be a laughing-stock if I met up with him and didn't kill him."

The innkeeper reminded me that I should thank his brother for giving me the opportunity to become a chieftain.

I then reminded him that he and his brother did not kill just to give me that opportunity. "I don't know about you," I said, "but your brother is a gutless killer, and I prefer not to see him."

A sound emerged from the window inside the room, followed by the echo of horse hooves as they headed toward the edge of the earth.

"He's gone now," the innkeeper said. "I set up a little nest here, a place for us to stay once the unavoidable deed was carried out. Now the young master has forced him out of his home."

I smiled. "That's the rule."

"I was wrong to think you don't follow rules. We were all wrong."

The tabletop in front of me was covered with all sorts of images carved by knife-carrying customers. There were mysterious signs and incantations, hands, birds, the figure of a head on silver coins, even something that looked like a mouth. I said it was a woman's private parts, but the innkeeper insisted that it was a wound. He was actually telling me that I had wounded him. My fist landed on his face the third time he mentioned the so-called wound. When he got back up to his feet, his face was smeared with dust and flames were shooting from his eyes.

At that moment, Huang Chumin swaggered in and ordered liquor. Then he said he wanted his personal bodyguards to join my soldiers.

"I don't want anything of yours."

"Should I be concerned with my own safety when I'm here, then?"

Talk about smart people – Huang Chumin was definitely one of them. After his situation turned ugly, he put his fate in my hands, knowing full well that a few bodyguards would not make any difference if someone really wanted to kill him. By passing them on to me, he wouldn't have to worry about his own safety. That would now be my responsibility. All he would really give up was the grandeur of walking on the street surrounded by bodyguards. But what did that matter, if he no longer had to keep looking over his shoulder or cocking an ear when he slept? He drank down a bowl of liquor and laughed, a few drops of wine hanging on his scraggly yellow beard. I told him that this inn was the place to come for a drink, and he asked if that meant he'd lost his freedom, that he was to drink at an assigned place. I told him he'd get free drinks here, and he asked if the inn was exempt from paying taxes.

"No," the innkeeper answered him. "I write down the amount, and the young master pays."

"Are you his friend?" Huang Chumin asked. "The young master has many strange friends."

"I'm not sure, but I think it's because my brother is a killer."

Huang Chumin choked on his liquor, and his yellow face paled.

He was stumbling like a drunk when I escorted him out of the inn. I told him that the killer was someone who had avenged a wrongful death in the family, and that put his mind at ease. I, on the other hand, was feeling the liquor's effects, which got worse when a wind blew off the river as I was crossing the bridge. Huang Chumin told me to lean on his shoulder. "Is his brother really a killer?" he asked.

"That I know for sure. What I don't know is what you have in mind."

After a thoughtful pause, he said, "My situation is so bad, I have no idea. What do you say to this? I'll be your *shiye*." He used the Chinese word, *shiye*, for adviser. That idiot head of mine was buzzing, as if a swarm of bees were singing inside. "Then who will I be?" I asked him.

He thought about that for a moment. "You're nobody now, but you can be whomever you want to be," he finally shouted into my ear.

He was right. You're nobody if you're a chieftain's son but not his heir. After my brother's death, Father gave no indication that he wanted me to be his heir. Then my mother-in-law wrote to say I needn't go and see her. She said she couldn't snatch away

Chieftain Maichi's only son to be her heir in light of the chieftain's heartrending experience. But the steward hinted that someday I might be chieftain of both families. Now Adviser Huang had made that possibility seem even more likely.

And, of course, they both told me that I had to wait patiently for all this to happen.

All right, then. I told them we'd wait. I was in no hurry.

So the days passed, with spring flowers being replaced by autumn moons. The steward and my adviser took charge of the affairs at home and the business at the market, while my two young servants and Sangye Dolma took care of odds and ends. Within a few years, the idiot son of the Maichi family became the wealthiest person on this land, or so the steward said when he brought over the account books.

"Even wealthier than my father?"

"Much wealthier," he said. "The young master knew that opium had long since become worthless. Business at our market, on the other hand, is starting to take off."

That day, I rode out with Tharna and gave her the good news while we were on the road. After returning to the border, she hadn't been with any other men, and that made me feel good.

"Are you really wealthier than any chieftain?"

"Yes."

"I don't believe you," she said. "Just look at the people around you."

I took a look at the people closest to me. Tharna raised her eyes to the sky, and said, "My God, just look at the kind of people you've handed the world to."

I knew she said things like that only when she was happy.

Yes, just look at them. My steward was a cripple and my adviser was an old man with a scraggly yellow beard. As for my two servants, possibly because they'd been with me so long, each was reduced to a single trait: Aryi's shyness and Sonam Tserang's fierceness. Sonam Tserang had become my tax collector, and was extremely pleased with the uniforms I'd had made for him and his underlings. Dolma, who was in charge of the maids and cooks, had grown heavy; men were no longer important to a woman her age. Gradually she had forgotten all about the silversmith and, it seemed, the time when she'd been my personal maid.

Tharna asked me, "Why hasn't Sangye Dolma ever been pregnant? She has slept with you, the silversmith, and the steward."

It was a question I couldn't answer, so I turned it back on her. Why hadn't *she* given me a child yet?

She answered by saying she still wasn't sure if I was worth getting pregnant for. "What if you really *are* an idiot? Am I supposed to give birth to an idiot too?"

My beautiful wife still wasn't sure if her husband was an idiot. "I am an idiot," I said, "so your belly will be barren all your life."

"On the day I'm sure you're an idiot, I'll find someone else to give me a daughter."

I found it hard to believe that someone could choose whether or not to have a child. So she showed me some pink tablets that she said came from India. Now, India already had many wondrous things, and the English had taken even more wondrous things there. So when someone said that a thing beyond our comprehension came from India, it immediately earned our trust. That was the case even with the poppies, since Adviser Huang had said that the English had brought them to the Han from India decades before. And so I believed that the pink tablets could help Tharna decide whether and with whom she could have a baby, sort of like deciding which cook would make our meals. Tharna and I had always been frank with each other, something I preferred; I admired her ability to set the tenor of our relationship. She was good at controlling things and knew how to pick the right moment for a discussion.

With the wind at our backs, we ran our horses for quite a distance before stopping at the crest of a hill, where the broad plains rose up majestically below us. Hawks were poised high up in the sky, their outstretched wings keeping them virtually motionless. At such moments, real things became abstractions. Even matters that normally caused a searing pain in the heart were turned into burning bullets that could have been fatal but merely scraped the skin and scorched a few hairs. My wife said, "Listen to what we've been talking about."

My heart could tolerate anything because of the panorama before me. I said, "So what!"

Tharna laughed, showing her white, even teeth. "It will cause you heartache after we go back," she said.

That woman, she knew everything!

Yes, what we talked about would cause me heartache when I woke up at night back at the house; it would turn into a slow poison. But now, as the wind pushed masses of clouds across the sky and caressed the boundless green grass below, words meant nothing. We talked of many other things, but they were all blown away by the wind, leaving not even a shadow on my heart.

All of sudden, Tharna flicked her reins, turned, and galloped off. She was going to relieve herself. Sonam Tserang took that opportunity to gallop up alongside me. He had grown into a big fellow over the years, with a thick neck and a large Adam's apple. Avoiding my eyes, he said, "I'm going to kill that demon one of these days." His brown tax collector's uniform made his face look especially dark and somber. "Rest assured, Young Master, that I'll kill her for you if she acts the whore again."

"I'll kill you if you kill my wife," I said.

He didn't reply, since he often didn't take the master's words seriously. Sonam Tserang was the dangerous type. The steward and my adviser both told me that someone like him could be valued only by a master like me. I asked them what kind of master that was. Stroking his yellow beard and observing me closely, my adviser nodded, then shook his head. The steward said that Sonam Tserang felt at ease following orders. He also said that a servant needn't worry about a master's suspicions about betrayal if the master isn't a chieftain.

Tharna came riding back.

That day, I seemed to see, however vaguely, a glorious future: I am spurring my horse through the fields, with the others straining to keep up. Startled birds fly up before my horse, and each undulation of the earth produces exquisite scenery.

I received a letter from a Han place called Chongqing that day. It was from my uncle. The purpose of his last visit, in addition to negotiating a dowry for the wife of an impoverished British aristocrat, had been to escort the Panchen Lama on his return to Tibet. But the great lama had passed away on the journey, so Uncle returned to the Han area.

There were two copies of the letter, one in Tibetan, the other in Chinese, but both said the same thing. That way, Uncle said, no one could convey the wrong meaning to me. He knew of my successes at the border and wanted to borrow some silver, now that I had become so wealthy. The Japanese were on the verge of defeat, he said, and everyone must pull together to finish the job, in answer to the Panchen Lama's prayers. It was critical for everyone to bear down for the final push to crush this cruelest of all demons. He said he'd repay me with gemstones when he returned to India after the war was won. Everything he owned would be mine, once he changed his will, replacing the English lady's name with mine. He also said he'd be immensely proud, especially for the Maichi family, if his nephew could treat the money as a personal contribution to the country.

I ordered horses prepared to transport silver to Chongqing, the place Uncle mentioned in his letter.

But Adviser Huang said we didn't have to go to all that trouble. Transporting silver back and forth like that would get in the way of continuing our business, and it would be better to open an account. So that is what we did. Adviser Huang wrote out a note, stamped it with the red seal of our account, and had one of my servants deliver it to the city of Chengdu. My uncle could then withdraw a hundred thousand silver dollars anywhere in China. At least that's what Adviser Huang told me. Later Uncle wrote to say he had received the money. From then on, our people no longer needed to travel with piles of silver when doing business with the Han people. Likewise, they had only to bring a note from an account we could honor when they came here. Adviser Huang took charge of all our banking affairs.

The historian said this was a momentous event.

"Is anything that happens for the first time momentous?" I asked him.

"Momentous events are momentous on their own terms."

"What you just said doesn't sound momentous in my head."

My historian laughed. He had become more serene over the years, just recording things he observed. When he was free, he liked to sit in the sun and savor a bowl of liquor with a bit of honey added. Once some of the poplar trees we'd planted were tall enough, he moved his chair from the veranda out into the shade.

He was sitting under a tree that day. "Young Master, the days are passing slowly."

"Yes, they are," I said. "They're barely creeping by."

My lamentation was overheard by the steward, who said, "Young

Master, what are you talking about? Time is passing much faster than before. So many unimaginable things have happened. In the past it would have taken at least five hundred years for all of them to happen. Are you aware of that? My dear young master, even five hundred years might not be enough, and here you are, saying that time is passing too slowly."

The historian agreed with him.

With nothing to say and nothing to do, I went to the inn for a drink.

By then, the innkeeper and I had gotten to know each other pretty well, but I still didn't know his name. I'd once said to him that our relationship was unlike that of mortal enemies. He said that his family's enemy was the Maichi chieftain, not the young master who had opened up business on the border, collected taxes in the market, and ran a bank.

"One of these days I'll be a chieftain."

He smiled. "Then you'll be our enemy, but that belongs to the distant future."

People here liked to place imminent events in the distant future. I asked him if he felt that time was passing faster and faster.

He laughed. "Well, well. Time. The young master is now concerning himself with time."

He said this so sarcastically that I had no choice but to bathe his face with my liquor. He sat down, lost in thought for a while; he clearly wanted to speak but held back, as if something had gone wrong with his head and prevented him from saying what was on his mind. In the end, he wiped the liquor off his face, and said, "Yes, time is passing faster than before, as if being driven by a whip."

41 Fast and Slow ∼

Life on the border passed in a relaxed fashion.

I lived in the same room all those years, seeing the same ceiling every morning when I woke up. The swirling patterns of the grained wood would be right there in front of me, even if I didn't open my eyes. And the land outside the window always had the same undulating lines. The sun rose for the thousandth time and set for the thousandth time. I woke up every day in the same shaft of light streaming in through the window, and those two everlasting questions no longer bothered me.

I can't recall if this occurred in the second year or the third.

That morning, Tharna, her arm propped against the pillow, was studying me closely. When she saw me wake up, she bent down to fix her searching eyes on mine. Her breasts rubbed against my face, sending a strong feminine aroma into my nostrils. She kept staring into my eyes, as if trying to see inside me, but I was preoccupied by the smell of her body. We had been sleeping in the same bed for many years, but this was the first time I realized that her body had such a tantalizing fragrance when the morning light streamed in. She smelled good, even without perfume. Normally, though, she used lots of perfume, so I'd thought she stank like other women.

The smell from Tharna's body made me giddy and I began to gasp, as if being smothered. Tharna laughed and then blushed as her hand snaked its way down my chest, brushed past my belly, and held my burning erection, which I thought seared her hand because she shuddered. "Ah!" Her body was on fire. Tharna was a good rider, and now she mounted me deftly, as if climbing into a saddle. Her body rose and fell, carrying us – horse and rider – to the far end of the sky.

Something flew past my eyes – maybe it was scenery or maybe it was just colorful bubbles. I heard myself whinny like a stud horse.

My rider also screamed from the saddle.

Finally, horse and rider crashed down, stuck together by sweat. Then the sweat dried, and I heard the tinkle of bees hitting the window glass.

Tharna put her lips to my cheek, and said, "We forgot to ask your questions."

"I know where and who I am," I said.

She sat up in bed, her face and breasts glowing bewitchingly in the morning light. She asked loudly, "Do you know who you are?"

I jumped out of bed, onto the rug, and answered her in a commanding voice.

"Where are you?" she asked.

"In the place where I'm waiting to be the chieftain."

With the blanket over her back, Tharna joined me on the rug, where we lay naked, wrapped in each other's arms. It was on that morning when she promised she'd stop taking the tablets that kept her from getting pregnant. I asked what she'd do if I turned out to be a real idiot. I wasn't trying to be funny.

"I'm not afraid," she said. "Anyone who's waiting to be chieftain of two places cannot be an idiot."

I had always considered those around me to be smarter than I, especially the beautiful Tharna. If intelligence were the ultimate affirmation of a person, I would not have hesitated to declare her the smartest person in the world.

But great sex between husband and wife when time was passing so slowly is not what I want to talk about. Yes, my nose was filled with the tantalizing fragrance of a woman, but there's something I want to say, and since I find it hard to start right in talking about an important matter, let me use a metaphor. I am by a lake watching swans fly through the sky. They try to fly high, but they must frantically flap their wings while dragging bodies that are so heavy they worry me. They paddle fiercely across the surface of the water before finally rising into the air.

What I want to say is, one day I began to notice how slowly time passed on this land.

I'm perfectly happy to talk to people about things I notice, a desire that was likely caused by the fact that I rarely noticed anything. The historian, Adviser Huang, and the crippled steward were all good discussion partners. The historian was the best. It was during this period that time began to speed up. After our discussions, I found myself agreeing more with the historian, who now believed that time passed faster not because the sun had quickened its pace in the sky. (The sun never changes, even if we judge the speed of time with its rising and setting.) The speed of time is different only if we compare it against events. He said that the more events that occurred, the faster time passed.

As time quickened, I began to feel giddy, like riding a fast horse. I'd first become aware of things during the year when the Maichi family began growing opium and had gotten used to the abnormal rate of bizarre occurrences.

In the years following the death of my brother, I lived on the border, collecting taxes and running a bank, a time when nothing seemed to happen on the other chieftains' lands. After the madness of the opium planting and the longest and most widespread famine in our history, an extended period of anxiety, the land relaxed, like a woman who has just given birth, and fell into a dazed slumber. The chieftains were like hibernating bears, hiding out on their own estates and not showing their faces.

Not a single chieftain came to see me on the border, where so many people were forever coming and going. There was a lot they could have learned there, but they were afraid to come after the catastrophe they'd met when they followed Chieftain Maichi's example of growing opium. Once the famine had passed, they simply hid away, unwilling to meet us.

But that wasn't worth worrying about. My servants told me what a bright future I had: one day I'd be the chieftain of both the Maichi and Rongong families. They said that I'd used intelligence to win the hand of Chieftain Rongong's only daughter, and that it was my good fortune that the killer had slain my brother.

But what made me happiest of all were the frequent letters from my uncle. I'd sent him one silver draft after another from my account.

Uncle sent me two photographs.

One showed him with the late Panchen Lama. He sent the other, showing him with a group of White Chinese generals, when he received my first money draft. They were standing on a flat, barren land, with several large objects in the background. Adviser Huang identified them as airplanes, or iron birds, which could shoot from the sky at the people below. I asked him how many airplanes a hundred thousand silver dollars could buy. He said maybe a wing. So I told him to send another hundred thousand immediately. I liked the idea of having two iron wings in China's sky. Uncle said that the Chinese emperor had once been our emperor, so the Chinese government was now our government. Adviser Huang told me that the country would be strong again after it won the war.

I asked if there was some way for Uncle to see me.

He said all we had to do was buy a camera. Time passed even more slowly while I waited for the camera to arrive. One day now took longer than three. But finally, the camera came. Adviser Huang also found a photographer. Then time started to pass more quickly. We took many pictures, at all sorts of places and at all times; we went mad over it. Since the photographer did not want to stay at the border permanently, I told Aryi to learn the man's skills. Among the servants I liked, the young executioner was the only one with any sort of skill. So who else should learn photography, if not him? I rejected the historian's request to learn photography, which he said also recorded history. For me, photography was just a skill, and his hands were meant to hold pen and paper, not a camera.

Let me relate a funny thing that happened.

One day Aryi came running and shrieking out of the photographer's darkroom, his face twisted in terror.

Sonam Tserang asked him if the photographer had made a move on his warm rear end. Our photographer had never shown any interest in women, which had people saying that he liked boys. For some strange reason, Aryi had always appealed to men who liked men. But that sort of encounter could not have produced such awful shrieks, any more than they could have come from a woman who encountered a man she'd rejected. And that is not what happened that day. As he ran out of the darkroom, Aryi shouted, "Ghost! A ghost came out of a piece of paper the photographer put in water."

With a laugh, the adviser told him it wasn't a ghost, but an image developed from the film. So I went in to see how the photographer developed his film. The images materialized slowly on the paper under a special light, and even though they looked a little strange, I couldn't say they were particularly scary. But it scared the piss and a few loud farts out of my future executioner, and people laughingly called him a scaredy-cat. When he was carrying out his duties as executioner, he'd never acted anything like that. After a while, the photographer left and Aryi took over. But he never went into the darkroom alone.

Now that we had a camera, our days flew by. I sent the first picture to Uncle at Chongqing.

I don't recall the year, but it was an unusually hot summer when Uncle wrote to invite me to visit him in the fall, once the days got cooler. Adviser Huang said that victory in the War of Resistance was in sight, and that the newly unified country would be stronger than ever. During the decades after the fall of the emperor, the chieftains felt abandoned; now things would be different. The steward told me that Uncle wanted me to meet some high officials who had traveled to places near us during the war. Now that the war was coming to an end, they'd soon be leaving. Once they did, I would have to travel great distances if I wanted to meet them. The historian said that I could guess my uncle's intentions by combining the interpretations of the steward and the adviser. Time slowed as I waited for fall to arrive.

Tharna's passion for photography was intense; that, combined with her constant dealings with the tailor, kept her so occupied that she left me alone most of the time.

People said that the young master was getting stupid again when they saw me staring at the edge of the sky, not knowing that I hoped to be the first to see fall arrive. I wanted to see when the first frost turned the trees a shiny gold, since that would be the time for me to get on the road.

Chieftain Maichi sent me a letter. We had not communicated since I left the estate. The letter, a short one, asked what I'd been up to at the border. Since everyone thought it unnecessary to mention my planned trip to Chongqing, I wrote back, telling him only about photography. There was no need for me to send a long letter, since his was so short. Another letter quickly followed. After saying that Mother missed me, he asked why the chieftain's son hadn't thought about sharing the novelty item with his father.

"To hell with him," Tharna commented.

Everyone knew that she was a willful woman. But I was different. I wanted to hear the rest of the letter. Following a bunch of meaningless nonsense, the chieftain asked if I could return to the estate sometime to take pictures of the mistress.

"While we're at it" – that's how he ended the letter. "While we're at it, we can discuss the future. I'm beginning to feel my age."

Once before he had felt himself getting old, but had later recovered his vigor.

So I decided not to go, and sent Aryi back with the camera instead.

Aryi stayed a few days, taking lots of pictures. When he was about to return to the border, the chieftain repeated that he was getting old and that his vitality and wisdom were waning. Aryi said, "Master, the young master told me to ask if you'd be young again if he died."

Soon afterward, Aryi returned with the camera and that bashful look of his.

He also brought back a letter filled with complaints and bitterness. Father said that he'd have discussed plans for the Maichi chieftainship with me had I gone back myself. But I hadn't, which meant that I, not he, didn't care about the family's future.

On that same day I received another letter, written not by Uncle, but by a Han general.

This letter said that my uncle, a great Tibetan patriot, had been on a trip somewhere when his boat was bombed by a Japanese airplane, and that he was now missing.

I realized that the Han people weren't all that different from us. Instead of delivering bad news directly, which could bring only sadness, they'd couched it in terms that struck a less painful nerve. Rather than say that my uncle had been killed by a Japanese bomb, and that his body had not been found, they'd used the nicer-sounding word – *missing*.

Maybe because of that word, my pain was not as great as it might have been.

I said to the servants, "He gave himself a water burial."

"Don't be too sad, Young Master."

"Now we don't have to go to Chongqing."

"We don't know who Uncle wanted us to see."

"The general who wrote the letter didn't extend an invitation."

"I don't want to give them any more silver for airplanes."

Not long after that, the Japanese surrendered.

I heard that the stumpy Japanese accepted their defeat on some ship, and that the Red Chinese and the White Chinese had begun fighting each other. Adviser Huang's face now turned even more yellow, and he began to cough, often bringing up blood. He said that was all because of his love of country. I wasn't sure I believed him, but I knew the sorrow of losing someone. Sometimes, when I looked at Uncle's picture, I felt my eyes turn hot and tears well up. I'd call out, "Dear Uncle!" My insides were burning up.

But he never answered me, except to stare at me blankly with the smile of a rich man. He never made it back to India. He'd told me that after returning to India he would change his will so I would inherit the jewels he kept in a British bank in Calcutta. Tharna had told me more than once that she dreamed about those jewels. But that didn't pan out, and the original will left everything to the wife of the impoverished British aristocrat.

My wife deeply resented the fact that we hadn't gone to

Chongqing when we could have. It was the heat in the Han area that had kept us from going to see Uncle. One of our Maichi ancestors had set out for Nanking once, and had died of heat stroke on the way. After that, any chieftain who sought an audience with the Han emperor left in the fall and returned in the spring, avoiding the lethal summers there. All right, that's enough talk about such things. All I want to say is, time began to fly after Uncle's death. One thing would happen, only to be quickly followed by another. Time speeded up, and events occurred faster and faster, as if they'd never slow down again.

Eleven ~

42 About the Future ~

Throughout the winter, I sank deeper and deeper into the sadness of losing Uncle. As I faced the wind, tears streamed down my face, and my head was weighed down with gloom and sadness.

Father and Mother continued to send letters filled with complaints. People ignorant of the realities might have thought that the idiot son had abandoned his father in the old estate, rather than being driven out by his father.

I didn't feel like paying any attention to him.

Lying in bed and looking at the sky through the window, I'd think about Uncle, and that would send tears coursing down my cheeks. One day he appeared to me suddenly, telling me that his soul had followed a big river into a vast ocean. On a moonlit night, he could go anyplace his heart desired. I asked him if he'd grown wings, like the airplanes, and he said the soul could go anywhere it wanted without them. He also told me not to grieve for him, because no one in the Maichi family had ever been as happy as he was now. From that day on, grief disappeared from my heart. When the beautiful summer arrived, thoughts of Uncle no longer saddened me. I merely wondered what that vast ocean looked like.

Tharna wanted a child, something we had been working hard at for a long time.

When we were first married, she had swallowed those pink Indian tablets because she was afraid of carrying an idiot son. Now she was worried, frightened even, that she could not have a son by me, which took the pleasure out of sex. She was always trying to get me to do it, and the more reluctant I was, the harder she tried. Whenever we were in bed, I'd lose interest at the sight of her desperate, frightened look, but she held on to me like a writhing snake.

She didn't love me any more than before; at most, she felt more keenly that I wasn't such a big idiot, and she wanted to carry my flesh and blood in her belly. Her private parts, scorched by anxiety, had become rough and dry, like a hermit's cave, no longer the site of pleasure. No one likes to go to a place scorched by the flames of anxiety.

One day, she led me out into the field, where, to spark my desire, she performed a seductive belly dance, tossing her clothes all over the place. I entered her, but she was so dry that I withdrew before spewing the rain and dew of life. I said that her anxiety and those Indian tablets had scorched her.

She cried as she retrieved her clothes and put them on haphazardly.

The sight of a haphazardly dressed beautiful woman in tears can arouse pity and love in a man. Even though I could still feel the burning sensation in my crotch, I held her face, and said, "Tharna, it isn't your fault. It's mine. I'm useless. Go find a young man and give it a try, what do you say?"

Loosened hair covered her face, but I saw a glint in her eyes. She sat blankly for a long while before finally saying softly, "Idiot, wouldn't that upset you?"

I touched my chest; the hurt I'd felt when she'd slept with my brother wasn't there. I whistled, summoning our horses, and we set out. I'd heard that a man will die young if he sleeps with a woman with dry private parts. I didn't know if that was true, but she was wearing me out.

"Why do you want a son?" I asked as we rode. "Look at my father and mother. They wish they'd never had one."

"That's because they're old and dying. They're afraid that the title of chieftain will be taken from them before they live out their days."

We were silent for a while, listening to the leisurely sound of the horses' hooves. Then Tharna asked again if it upset me when I told her to sleep with someone else. I said I didn't feel the same pain as when she'd slept with my brother.

She began to sob piteously. She cried for a long time. Enveloped in her soft sobs, the horses slowed down. Swarms of bees and dragon-flies followed us – maybe her sobs reminded them of their own sounds.

The insects dispersed and returned to the fresh flowers in the field when we entered town.

Yes, people now called the market a town, a town with one street. In the winter there were only adobe buildings, but the street grew longer in the summer, when tents were set up at both ends. The street was usually dusty, but that day it was different. Gentle rains a few days before had turned it flat, like the surface of a mirror, with clear imprints of horse hooves the size of little bowls.

The people on the street all bowed to me.

"Idiot, you don't love me anymore," Tharna said.

She said that as if she'd always been the one who loved, not the other way around. Women are like that; you can't expect them not to turn things upside down, if that's what they need to do.

Looking at the imprints of hooves on the street, I said, "You want a son, don't you? Well, I can't give you one. I can't give you an idiot son."

See there: what I said wasn't what I believed, and that's how men are. But I was an idiot, after all, so I added, "People say a man will die young if he has sex with a woman who's dry down there."

Tharna looked at me, tears welling up in her eyes again and moistening her long, black lashes. She whipped her horse and stormed back home. At that moment, I felt a sharp pain in my heart.

Tharna wouldn't let me into our room. I knocked for a long time before she finally told me to sleep somewhere else. Both the steward and Sangye Dolma said she'd open the door if I pleaded with her a bit. But I didn't; instead, I told Dolma to prepare a room for me. We were not a poor family with no extra rooms or bedding. The room was quickly made ready, with everything new: silver objects, rugs, bed, silk coverlet, incense burners, and paintings. It sparkled. Seeing that I didn't know what to do first, Dolma lit the pungent Indian incense. The familiar fragrance covered the strange smell of new objects, but I still felt out of place. She sighed. "The young master never changes."

Why should I change?

Dolma said she'd find me a girl, since I wouldn't know where I was if I woke up in the morning in a strange room. I said no. When she asked what I'd do if no one were there to answer my questions when I woke up, I told her to go away.

321

"This is a critical moment," she said. "Don't get silly on us again, Young Master."

I told her I didn't want a woman.

"My God," she remarked quietly, "what has that beautiful demon done to our young master?"

She sent for the steward and Adviser Huang, with whom I reached an agreement. No woman, but my two young servants would sleep on the rug to be nearby if I needed anything. Adviser Huang stroked his beard and smiled, while the steward threatened to have the two servants killed if anything upset the young master. He spoke to them as if they were children, even though they were adults by then. I didn't know how old they were, just as I couldn't tell you what my age was. But we were all adults. Sonam Tserang laughed at the steward's admonishment, but Aryi said, "How are you going to kill me? *I'm* the executioner."

The steward laughed. "What makes you think I can't do it myself?"

Sonam Tserang said, "Those aren't the Maichi family rules."

"There's Aryi Senior, isn't there?" the steward said.

When they were with me, my servants always displayed total nonchalance toward others.

That night, they tried not to fall asleep before me, but their necks could not support their droopy heads. In the end, I was the only one awake, listening to their thunderous snores and worrying about whether I'd be troubled by the same old questions, whether I might not know who and where I was when I woke up in the morning.

My servants slept on the floor fully dressed; I lay fully dressed in bed. When I awoke in the morning, they were standing properly before me.

"Ask us your questions, Young Master."

But I knew who and where I was, which greatly disappointed them.

I'd dreamed about Father, Chieftain Maichi, during the night.

After lunch, I went back to bed, and just as I was falling asleep, I heard footsteps on the stairs. Maybe, I said to myself, the person in my dreams has come. When the noise died down, my door creaked open. Light filled my eyes, but the room quickly returned to darkness. Chieftain Maichi's stocky body stood in the doorway, blocking out the light. He was the person in my dreams. I said, "Please get away from the door, Father. Otherwise, my day will turn into night."

He chortled, and from that laughter, I could hear the phlegm blocking his throat. He walked up to me, and I could tell from how he walked that he'd gotten much heavier. Soon he wouldn't be able to walk at all if he kept putting on weight.

He walked so slowly that the chieftain's wife quickly slipped in front of him and bent down to place her lips on my forehead. My woman had dried up down below, and Mother's lips, which had once been soft and moist, were also dry. Teardrops fell on my face as she said, "I miss you so much."

My eyes were getting moist too.

"Are you happy your parents are here?" she asked. I leaped off the bed and held the gaunt old woman tightly in my arms. But the old chieftain pulled us apart, and said, "My son, I'm here to spend the summer at the Maichi summer palace."

By calling a place that had taken me years to build up his summer palace, the chieftain agitated the servants. They thought he was going to force me to go away again. Sonam Tserang muttered that he'd kill the old man for me. And Tharna said she'd return to her mother's home if her husband couldn't stay here.

The chieftain was glad to see that his arrival had disturbed the peace, like tossing a rock into a placid lake.

"You're my son," he said. "You represent the future of the Maichi family." That could only mean that he was formally recognizing me as his legal heir, which quieted the servants down.

Still, I had nothing to do, even after being recognized as the Maichi heir, so I went drinking in town.

The innkeeper told me that his brother had run off to the Han area to join the army. He had written to say they would soon set out to fight the Red Chinese. The two brothers, during their years of wandering, had been to many places where the Han and other peoples lived. He boasted that they were fluent in at least three languages and knew six or seven more. All I said was "What a waste."

"Sometimes I think we would serve you if you weren't a Maichi. Now I don't know if my brother will be able to return. He doesn't seek revenge; he just wants to kill people openly and for a cause.

That's why he became a soldier." He then said, "Now it's up to me to kill Chieftain Maichi."

I told him that Chieftain Maichi was here.

"All right, let me kill him and be done with it." Sadness clouded his face.

I asked why he looked so sad.

"If I kill your father, then you'll kill me. That will end it."

"What if I don't kill you?"

"Then I'll have to kill you, since you'll be Chieftain Maichi by then."

The innkeeper wanted me to bring the chieftain to his inn for a drink.

"Are you in such a hurry to end it?"

"I just want to have a closer look at the man who killed my father."

But I knew he really wanted to end it then.

A few days later, after the chieftain and his two wives had enjoyed Aryi's photographic skill, I took the chieftain into town to watch Sonam Tserang and his men collect taxes, and to see how someone could obtain silver from Adviser Huang's bank just by showing a piece of paper. Then we went to the inn, where the innkeeper placed a bowl of dark liquor in front of Father. I knew it wasn't the normal color, so I tossed a dead fly into the bowl. Naturally, the chieftain asked for a new one, and when the innkeeper brought it over, I dumped the first bowl on the innkeeper's foot. The liquor scorched his leather boots.

Father left after drinking his liquor.

The innkeeper groaned as he touched the foot burned by the poisoned wine. "Is the young master afraid I'll kill you after I poison your father?"

"I was afraid I'd have to kill you right away. Then who would avenge your death, since you have no son? Go find yourself a wife who'll give you a son to avenge your death."

He smiled. "But that wouldn't end it. I want to end it now. I told you that's what I want." Then he asked me, "Do you know how much my brother and I have suffered over our father's mistake? I won't have a son, if it means that he too will suffer over this."

I began to feel sorry for him.

As I was leaving, he said to my back, "You're forcing me to kill you after your father's death, Young Master."

I didn't look back. To me that was just the idle talk of a pitiable man. Years ago, his brother could not have killed my brother without the help of the purple garment possessed by the ghost of a wrongfully executed man. Killers of olden times would not have entertained all those thoughts when they carried out their revenge, powerful proof that the world and the people in it had changed over the years.

As I was falling asleep that night, Father came to my room to say that I had saved his life that day. He told me that when morning came, he'd send someone to kill that man and torch his inn, even though there wasn't much to burn. I explained to the old chieftain why that wouldn't be necessary.

After hearing me out, he said, "You could have taken the title of chieftain from me, but you didn't. The reasoning here is pretty much the same, isn't it?"

I pondered for a moment and came to the realization that there was truly nothing to prevent me from usurping his position. But I had no intention of forcing him out.

"Your brother would have done it," Father said.

But my brother had been slain. I didn't point out the obvious, that Father hadn't really wanted to abdicate. Instead, I said, "I'm a different son from a different mother."

"All right," Father said. "I'll spare the man. This is your place, after all."

"The summer palace belongs to you, Chieftain Maichi. I'll leave if you don't want me here."

Moved by my comment, Father grabbed my arm. "Son, do you know why I came? I know my days are numbered. Come back with me when autumn arrives. You'll be Chieftain Maichi when I die."

I started to say something, but he covered my mouth.

"Don't tell me you don't want to be chieftain. And don't tell me you're an idiot either." Tharna was singing in her room as Father spoke. Her voice carried far in the evening sky. After listening to her sing for a while, Father asked, "What do you want to do when you are chieftain?"

I racked my brain but could think of nothing. A bewildered look appeared on my face. Yes, all I'd wanted was to be chieftain; I'd never given any serious thought to what I wanted to do. So I tried hard to imagine what I'd get by becoming chieftain. Silver? Women? Vast territory? Numerous servants? I had all those without even trying. Power? Yes, power. But it wasn't as if I didn't have any now. Besides, power could get me only more silver, more women, vaster territory, and more servants. Which was to say, being chieftain didn't mean much to me. But strangely, I still wanted it. I thought there must be some advantage unknown to me; otherwise, why did I want it so badly?

Father said, "You know all the advantages. What's left is losing sleep at night, since you have to be wary even of your own son."

"I'm not afraid of that," I said.

"Why not?"

"Because I won't have a son."

"No son? How do you know you won't have a son?"

I wanted to tell him that Tharna was dry down below and couldn't give me a son. But I heard myself say instead, "Because your son will be the last chieftain."

Father was stunned.

I repeated, "It won't take long before all the chieftains are gone."

I told him a lot more, but can't remember just what I said. In our place, spirits that had no idols often attached themselves to people and predicted the future through them. These were spirits of prediction that had emerged from people who had been considered rebellious when they were alive. People like our historian, Wangpo Yeshi. After those people died, their spirits had nowhere to go, so they became prophets. I didn't know if I was talking now, or if a spirit had entered my body.

Chieftain Maichi knelt before me. "Where does the prophetic spirit come from, if I may ask?"

I said, "There's no spirit. It's just your son and his ideas."

Father got up, and I brushed his knees as if they were covered in dust, even though the floor was spotless. Servants cleaned the room with a white oxtail duster every morning. But I brushed the non-existent dust off his knees anyway. The idiot's trick worked, as a smile reappeared on the chieftain's face, replacing the gloomy look of knowing he'd been tricked. He sighed. "I really don't know if you're an idiot, but I'm sure that what you've said is rubbish."

But I had seen the future, one in which all the wrangling chieftains disappeared overnight. Their estates crumbled, sending mushroom clouds of smoke and dust into the air; nothing was left on the earth when the dust settled.

Chieftain Maichi had said that his son was spouting rubbish, but deep down he believed me. He just didn't want to admit I was right.

He told me that Living Buddha Jeeka had cast a divination that said that Father's end would come this winter. "Tell the old Living Buddha to cast another divination," I said. "The chieftains will be gone soon, and if you live just a little longer, there'll be no need for you to step down."

"How much longer do you think?"

"Ten years or so."

He sighed. "I could probably hold out for four or five years, but ten years is too long."

It might be only four or five years, I was thinking. But however long it was, that day I felt the end coming – I didn't see it, I sensed it. I sensed that not just Chieftain Maichi, but all the chieftains, would be gone in the world of the future.

Before the chieftains, there had been local lords here, but they had disappeared with the arrival of the chieftains. Who would come after the chieftains? I couldn't see that; what I did see was the chieftains' estates crumbling to dust, leaving nothing behind after the dust settled. Yes, nothing was left. I didn't even see the footprints of birds or animals. The earth was covered by dust, as if shrouded in loosely woven silk.

I looked at the people around me. They were engrossed in what they were doing, all except for my Han adviser and the tongueless historian, who were staring at the sky, lost in thoughts that had nothing to do with what was before them. They were contemplating the future, so I described my feelings to them.

The historian said that everything would disappear one day. In his eyes all he saw were my blank face and clouds floating in the sky.

Adviser Huang closed his eyes. "Could it really be that soon?" he asked, obviously surprised. "That's sooner than I expected." He opened his vacant eyes and stroked his scraggly beard. "When China was powerful, many chieftains were enfeoffed. The chieftains would have been destroyed the next time China grew powerful. But it remained weak, which allowed the chieftains to survive another hundred years or two." His vacant eyes sparkled. "Is the young master saying that it will take only ten years for China to be powerful again?"

"Maybe, maybe not even ten years."

"Will I, with my old bones, live to see that?"

I didn't feel like answering him; instead, I asked why a powerful country would not keep the chieftains. He said he'd never thought that the Maichis' young master was an idiot, but even the smartest person in this land would appear to be a moron as far as such issues were concerned, because not a single chieftain had ever really wanted to know what nation and nationality were. After pondering his words, I figured he might be right; I'd been with many chieftains, but I'd never heard them talk of these things.

All we knew was that we were the kings of the mountains.

The adviser said that a strong, unified country can allow only one king, who will never permit anyone else to call himself king, not even a minor local king. He added, "The young master need not worry about changes, since he is no longer living in the age of chieftains."

I didn't believe him, because I knew I was surrounded by chieftains, which meant I must still be living in the age of chieftains. Besides, even *I* was waiting to sit on a chieftain's throne.

More importantly, I saw only the disappearance of the chieftains, not the future itself.

No one is happy about a future he can't see clearly.

43 They're Getting Old ∾

As a matter of fact, many people believed my prediction that the chieftains had no future.

That was not because the prediction had emerged from my mouth, but because the historian and Adviser Huang agreed with me. Now everyone was convinced.

The first to embrace that conviction was Chieftain Maichi.

He pretended he didn't believe me, but the steward told me that the old chieftain was a die-hard believer in mysterious prophecies. Sure enough, Father said one day, "I've got it all figured out. You're not an idiot, you're an immortal. Why else did the gods send you down to the human world?"

Chieftain Maichi was convinced that I'd been sent on a mission to bring an end to an era.

During this period, Father sighed constantly. Humans are strange creatures. He believed that everything involving the chieftains would turn to dust in the end, but deeply resented the fact that he could not sit on his lofty throne up to the last moment. Once he stared at me, and muttered, "How could I have a son like you?"

It wasn't a question I could answer, so I asked him why he'd sired an idiot son.

My father, who was truly starting to show his age, screamed in my face, "Why can you see the future, but not the present?"

The chieftain's wife, who had given him an idiot son, had also lost her beauty, but she still looked much younger than the chieftain, who was growing old fast. She said to her husband, who now looked old enough to be her father, "The way you're always hovering over him, what else but the future could my son see?"

I heard myself say, "Honorable Chieftain, take your wives, your servants, and your soldiers home with you tomorrow."

I told him that the border town was not his summer palace, that it belonged to a future no one could see clearly. In that future, all the estates would be gone and this would be a new place, one that would grow bigger and more beautiful, belonging to an age without chieftains.

Chieftain Maichi was speechless.

Of course I didn't mean for him to leave the next day, after all. I'd already had invitations written and sent servants on fast horses to invite the neighboring chieftains to meet with him. I called this meeting the Chieftains' Last Gala. I had dictated what was written on the invitations: "I respectfully invite Chieftain So-and-so to such-and-such a place for the Chieftains' Last Gala." Strangely, none of them interpreted the word *last* as a threat, and they all showed up.

First to arrive was my mother-in-law. She still looked young and was still followed by four pretty maidservants, each carrying a sword and a pistol. In accordance with proper etiquette, I had the welcoming carpet rolled right up to her feet, and I came downstairs with her daughter to greet her. The minute she dismounted, she repeatedly called out her daughter's name, giving me only the briefest of glances before walking upstairs with Tharna. In hardly any time, my wife's heartrending cries poured down on us. Chieftain Maichi was incensed and urged me to do away with my mother-in-law. That way, he said, "You'll be the Rongong chieftain, and nothing can stop you then."

I told him that I was the one stopping myself.

He breathed a long sigh and said that my only concern was waiting to become the chieftain of Maichi. It was as if I'd been sitting there like an idiot all these years instead of expanding the chieftain's territory, instead of building a bustling town in a desolate border area, one that did not belong to the age of chieftains.

The crying upstairs had stopped by mealtime, but my guest showed no intention of coming down. So I told Dolma and a large group of maidservants to send up a sumptuous meal. For three days, not a word from the female chieftain, except to say that I was to take good care of her horse. The pretty maid with bright eyes and sparkling teeth who delivered that message told me that her mistress had spent a huge sum of silver on the Mongol horse.

I sat in the sun squinting up into the light and ordered that the Mongol horse be brought to me.

Knowing what I had in mind, my two young servants took out their pistols. A couple of gunshots later, the female chieftain's Mongol horse fell to the ground and lay in its own blood. The spent cartridges rolled noisily down the stairs. The steward then went to the upstairs guest room with servants carrying silver twice the value of the horse.

The maidservant messenger was petrified. Sonam Tserang caressed her hands, and said, "If I kill that senseless chieftain of yours, I'll bet the young master will give you to me."

She glared at him.

"By then," I said to her, "you'd consider yourself lucky if my tax collector wanted you."

Her legs buckled as she knelt before me.

I ordered her to go back up to her mistress, then said, loudly enough for everyone in the house to hear, "Tell your mistress not to worry. She'll get an even finer horse when she leaves."

That was not something I'd planned, but it worked like a charm.

That evening, the female chieftain came down with Tharna to

eat. She still wouldn't condescend to speak to me, but she mustered up enough patience to chat with Chieftain Maichi and his wife for a while. Tharna looked at me the whole time, first stealing a glance and then staring at me boldly. Her gaze was intended to be taunting, but there was fear behind it.

After dinner, the female chieftain ordered her maidservants to bring in the servant whom Sonam Tserang had taken a fancy to. They'd already whipped her. The female chieftain turned her brilliantly smiling face to me, and said, "The bitch sent the wrong message, so now I'm going to kill her."

"How did she get the message wrong?" I said. "She told me to have your horse fed. Do you mean to say that your message was really intended for me to let your valuable horse starve?"

Enraged, the female chieftain ground her teeth and ordered three maids to take their friend out and shoot her.

Sonam Tserang, my tax collector, rushed up and knelt before me. I told him to get up, but he refused. "The young master knows what I want," he said.

I turned to my mother-in-law. "This girl is promised to my tax collector."

The female chieftain snickered. "Tax collector? What kind of position is that?" She added that she neither understood nor liked a great many things at the border.

"These things and the world being created for them don't require everyone to like them."

"I don't give a damn what kind of horseshit position it is. It's just a title, after all." She turned to Chieftain Maichi, who had once shared her bed. "Your son knows nothing about rules. This little bitch is a maidservant, a slave."

Chieftain Maichi didn't like that comment one bit.

The female chieftain had been doing everything within her power to cross me. I'd asked her over so the chieftains could enjoy one final festival, but she had made up her mind to oppose me. Over the years, the chieftains had lived a worry-free life, and maybe they believed that a new era of good times was just beginning. Now I wanted to embarrass the female chieftain, who had made it through the famine and retained her position thanks to my barley. So I told her that everyone around me, except for Tharna, who was of noble birth, a chieftain's daughter, was a servant. I summoned the head of the maidservants, Sangye Dolma, the executioner-photographer Aryi, and my personal maid, a groom's daughter, and described their backgrounds to the chieftain. Each of my servants gave these masters the dignified smile due those of the upper class. Outraged, the female chieftain asked her maidservant, "Do you really want to be with this man?"

The maid nodded.

The female chieftain said, "What if I pardon you and forgive all your mistakes?"

The maid walked steadfastly over to Sonam Tserang, stood behind him, and interrupted her mistress: "I didn't make any mistakes."

Aryi held up his camera; a loud pop was followed by a blinding light. Even my mother-in-law was scared witless; her terrified expression was captured by the camera. She then announced that she was leaving the next day.

I reminded her that the other chieftains hadn't yet arrived.

She said to Chieftain Maichi, "I thought I could have a nice chat with you, but you're old and listless. If other chieftains are coming, I'll wait around and enjoy myself with them."

She spoke as if the other chieftains were her closest friends.

In fact, every one of those lofty chieftains was a very lonely person.

They had silver, but that only made them lose sleep, and even when they did manage to sleep, they dreamed that someone was stealing their silver. They had women, but in the end, good women want to control you, while the bad ones could not arouse the desire deep down in those fat bodies. The chieftains were old, and the thing that filled men with confidence had long since died. Chieftain Maichi, now encased in rolls of fat, could only gaze helplessly at Chieftain Rongong, with whom he had once enjoyed sexual congress. They were all getting old.

Night fell.

The female chieftain looked much older than she had that morning; so did Mother and Father. Cosmetics had helped in the morning, but even more important, they had seemed full of life then. Their faces grew dusty in the afternoon, and the fatigue of old age revealed their true ages.

Both chieftains were eagerly anticipating the arrival of the other chieftains. Servants laid out soft cushions in the sunniest spot upstairs, where they sat to gaze off into the distance. Chieftain Maichi's wife was enjoying opium in her room. She had once told me that people in her hometown in the Han area had lost everything over that little addiction. But in the Maichi family, she didn't have to worry about dying on the street over a few puffs of opium smoke. She took pleasure in her good fortune. I asked Adviser Huang to sit with Mother so the two Han Chinese could chat about their homeland in their own language.

Every day at noon, when the weather was nice, a wind blew across the river. Now it was blowing toward Chieftain Maichi's summer palace. The servants stood up to block the wind with their bodies. Guests began to arrive on a daily basis, and nearly every invited chieftain came. That, of course, included Chieftain Lha Shopa, a relative of ours. During the famine years, when I first built the town, he had spent quite a bit of time here. I must admit that, of all the chieftains, he had the keenest business sense.

When Lha Shopa's entourage appeared on the horizon, all the chieftains came downstairs. Seeing that the earlier chieftains had soiled the red carpet, I told the servants to put out a new one. Lha Shopa passed through the drowsy, midday town and rode up onto the wooden bridge. He was even fatter than before, so what everyone saw first was an inflated sack on horseback. When his horse got closer, I saw my friend's cordial face between his sacklike body and broad-brimmed felt hat.

See there, most of the chieftains of this land stood before him, but he only tipped his hat to them. But he embraced me as soon as he dismounted, even though I had wrested a large chunk of land from him. We touched foreheads and cheeks and rubbed noses. Everyone heard him say, nearly sobbing, "Ah, my friend, my friend."

Chieftain Lha Shopa could no longer walk upstairs without help.

Adviser Huang sent for a handsome chair of his, which the servants used to carry Lha Shopa up the steps. He wouldn't let go of my hand. "See there," he said, "with the strength of my waist I can still ride a horse, and with the strength of my hand, I can still hold on to my friend."

I want you to know that this chieftain could have served as an example for the others.

The last chieftain to come was a young man unknown to any but me – the most recent Chieftain Wangpo. He had set out from the southern border and followed a circuitous route, which had taken him longer to get here. The shortest route would have been to cross Chieftain Maichi's territory, but he lacked the nerve to take it. After hearing his explanation, Chieftain Maichi burst out laughing. But his laughter quickly turned into violent coughing. Chieftain Wangpo paid him no attention, because he believed that Father was the late Chieftain Wangpo's adversary, not his.

The new Chieftain Wangpo said to me, "I believe we have something to talk about."

I poured him a bowl of liquor as a sign for him to go on.

"Let's bury the hatred in the earth, not inside us," he said.

The steward asked if he wanted something from the young master.

He laughed and asked for a piece of land in town, where he could do business. Chieftain Maichi shook his head vigorously, but I granted his request, and he in turn indicated that he would pay taxes regularly.

"What use do I have with so much money?" I said. "If the Chinese were still fighting the Japanese, I would follow my uncle's example and buy airplanes. But the Japanese have been defeated, so what use do I have for so much money?"

"Aren't the Han Chinese fighting among themselves?" someone asked.

I said, "Adviser Huang says that this is China's last war."

The chieftains asked Adviser Huang who would win, the Red or the White Chinese.

"No matter which side wins," the adviser said, "the chieftains will never be the same. They will no longer be the lofty kings they think they are."

"Are you saying we can't beat a single Han king even if we join forces?" the chieftains asked.

Adviser Huang laughed and said to his compatriot, Chieftain Maichi's wife, "Mistress, did you hear that? Are they living in a dream world?"

The chieftains were not convinced. The female chieftain drew her sword and stood up to use it on my adviser. The other chieftains held her back as she shouted, "Is there a man among you? The male chieftains have all died!"

44 The Chieftains ~

The chieftains sat around chatting day in and day out.

One day the steward asked me what I wanted to do with all the chieftains I'd invited.

It wasn't until then that I began to think about that. Had I really invited them over just so they could get together one last time with their friends and enemies before they died? If I said yes, no one would believe that such a kind person existed, even if that person was an idiot who sometimes did very smart things. But if I said no, then I couldn't come up with the real purpose of inviting these people here, no matter how hard I tried.

Since I couldn't find a purpose, I asked the people around me, but no two answers were the same.

Tharna smiled coldly, saying that all I wanted was to show off in front of the two women of the Rongong family.

That wasn't the right answer.

I asked Adviser Huang, who responded with a question: "Do you know why I've fallen so low, Young Master? Like them, I believed I was clever. That was the cause of my downfall."

My question had rekindled thoughts of his sad past, and he recited an elegant phrase: "One has a home but cannot go back. One belongs to a nation but cannot serve." He had seen his own future. He said he could find no role to play, no matter which color won among the Han Chinese. This is exactly what he said: "There'll be no role for me to play."

He opposed the war between the Red and White Chinese, but it had occurred nonetheless. If the Whites won, well, he had once been a Red. But if the Reds won, he had no share in the glory, since he could not think of a single thing he'd done for them. I never expected Adviser Huang to be so distraught. I asked him which side Uncle was on when he was alive.

He said the White Chinese.

"Fine," I said, "I like the White Chinese too."

"That makes sense, but I'm afraid you'll wind up on the wrong side."

A chill ran down my spine as he spoke. I could not afford to shiver in front of everyone, not with the sun so bright overhead.

"Don't be in a hurry to pick a color, Young Master," the adviser said. "You're still young. I'm old, so it doesn't matter if I choose poorly. But your career has just started to take off."

But I'd already made up mind. Since I'd liked my uncle so much, I would be on his side.

I then approached the historian, who was burying his head in his writing. After hearing my question, he looked up slowly. I could see what he meant to say in his eyes. He was a mystic, and I knew he wouldn't give me a straight answer. Sure enough, his eyes said only: "Destiny cannot be explained."

Sonam Tserang was unhappy that I hadn't gone to ask him, so he sought me out.

"Don't tell me the reason you brought these people here wasn't to kill them."

I said firmly, "No."

"Do you really not plan to do that, Young Master?"

My answer this time was the same, "no," but I sounded somewhat hesitant.

If Sonam Tserang had insisted, I might well have ordered the chieftains killed. But he just snorted and said nothing. Instead he took his unhappiness out on his underlings. My tax collector was very hot-tempered. Since killing was always on his mind, he was envious of his best friend, Aryi, who had been born to kill. Sonam Tserang had once complained that Aryi was born to be an executioner, and said that it was unfair for anyone to be born to be one thing and not something else. Someone then asked him if it was also unfair that someone had been born to be the chieftain. That stopped him. The steward had even suggested that I have him killed, but I didn't go along with it because I trusted his loyalty, which would be further demonstrated that day. Seeing the disappointment on his face, I was tempted to pick a chieftain for him to kill just to satisfy his urge.

After this minor interlude, I stopped asking myself why I'd invited the chieftains.

One day, I joined them while they were drinking. Everyone came up to toast me, except for Chieftains Maichi and Rongong. After two rounds, I began pouring and drinking on my own, without waiting for their toasts. Lha Shopa and Wangpo, who were closer to me than the others, tried to get me to stop, complaining that the host was getting drunk.

Father said, "Let him be. You can't tell whether my son is drunk or sober anyway."

He wanted to show everyone that he was the real host.

But that was only what *he* thought; the others didn't agree, except for the female chieftain, who flashed him an approving smile.

In fact, Father and the female chieftain had already drunk too much. "His son is an idiot," she said. "My daughter is a rare beauty, but he won't go near her. Now, don't you think that makes him an idiot?" Covering her face with her wine cup, she grabbed the young Chieftain Wangpo by the arm. "Let me marry my daughter to you." Then, holding the young man's arm tight, she asked him, "Have you ever seen my daughter?"

"Please let me go," Wangpo said. "I've seen your daughter, and she is indeed a rare beauty."

"Then why won't you take her? You can marry her if you feel like it, or you can just show her a good time." This she said in a wanton tone, keeping one eye on Wangpo and the other on Chieftain Maichi. "Everyone knows I like men. Well, so does my daughter."

My new friend Wangpo said in a slightly altered tone of voice, "Please let me go. My friend will see you."

I lay on the carpet with my head in a maidservant's lap, gazing up at the sky. I knew that my new friend was about to betray me. But that caused me no pain; rather, I was afraid that things would stop then instead of moving forward. I wanted something to happen; something should happen when so many chieftains got together.

Chieftain Wangpo was breathing heavily and nervously.

"All right," I said to myself, "betray me then, my new friend."

It appeared that heaven was going to grant my wish; otherwise Tharna would not have picked that moment to begin singing on the veranda. Her loud, melodious voice floated between the white clouds and the blue sky. I wasn't sure if she was singing to the crowd or to the open field, but I knew she wore an alluring expression. Her very existence was a temptation. A sage once said that a woman like that was either an abyss or a poison. That, of course, could hold true only for someone with the mind of a sage. I was an exception – I wasn't afraid of betrayal. I wondered if someone would slip and fall into that abyss or stick his neck out to swallow the sweet poison. I stole a glance at Wangpo, whose face did indeed display the terror of someone who was falling into an abyss or faced with poison.

And now someone was leading him on – my mother-in-law.

"That girl you hear singing is my beautiful daughter," she said, "but this idiot won't stay in the same room with her or share her bed."

I wanted to tell them that was because her spring had dried up, but I clamped my mouth shut.

"My God!" Wangpo muttered to himself. "Why would my friend do that?"

"Your friend? I don't understand why a lofty chieftain like you has to treat him like a friend. He's not a chieftain, he's an idiot." The female chieftain's voice was still as alluring as a young woman's. With that sort of allure, a voice has the power to sway, no matter what it says. In this case, even the words were tempting. "The title of Chieftain Rongong will go to her husband after I die. I lie awake every time I think about that idiot becoming Chieftain Rongong. Prolonged loss of sleep has caused me to age fast. My face is covered with wrinkles, and no man wants me anymore. But you're still so young, like the early-morning sun."

I wanted to hear what else they had to say, but I fell asleep under the balmy sky.

It was afternoon when I woke up.

The female chieftain snickered. "Aren't we chieftains supposed to be your guests? Then why did you fall asleep?"

I wanted to apologize, but instead I said, "Why don't you go back to your own land, where you can kill someone who falls asleep in front of you."

"See how this idiot treats his own mother-in-law," she said. "He doesn't know how pretty his wife is, nor does he know that he should show respect to his mother-in-law." In the same incendiary tone, she addressed the chieftains, "He wants me to go back, but I won't. He invited me here. He invited us all. He must have something planned; otherwise, it borders on the criminal to ask us here, when we have vast lands and numerous subjects to manage."

All the chieftains' liquor-saturated heads rose at these words.

Chieftain Wangpo turned away, not daring to look at me.

It was Lha Shopa who said, "Me, I have nothing to do. And I don't think the rest of you have either."

They all laughed, saying that since he wasn't qualified to be a chieftain, he should quickly hand over his position to someone more suitable.

Neither ashamed nor angry, Lha Shopa smiled and said he'd never had much to do from the day he became chieftain. "What's there to worry our heads over?" he said. "The limits of our territory were set by our ancestors, and the crops are planted by the people, who then send their rent and taxes to the estates in the fall. That too was determined by previous chieftains. They set all the rules, which means that today's chieftains have nothing to do."

Someone objected, saying that Chieftain Maichi had found something to do when he grew poppies.

Lha Shopa shook his flabby head, and said, "Ah, opium, now that's bad stuff." He shook his head at me, and repeated, "I mean it, opium is bad stuff." Then he turned to the female chieftain. "Opium caused us all to lose many good things."

"I didn't lose anything," she said.

Lha Shopa laughed. "I lost land and you lost your daughter."

"I married my daughter off."

"Whatever you say," Lha Shopa replied. "Everyone knows that for the female chieftain, beauty is the most lethal weapon."

Rongong sighed, but didn't reply.

So Chieftain Lha Shopa continued, "I followed your example and used my head once. In the end, many good subjects starved to death, and I lost a huge piece of land."

"I'd like to know what you people want to do while you're here," I said. "Something other than relive the past."

The chieftains asked me to leave them alone for a while so they could talk about what they wanted to do. Since I didn't know what *I* wanted, I agreed to let them decide. "But be careful," I said. "It seems to be getting easier and easier for the chieftains to make mistakes."

With that I turned and went downstairs to take a walk around town with the historian, so I could tell him what had happened. I was of the opinion that it should be recorded.

He agreed, his eyes saying, "When the chieftains first appeared on this land, every one of their decisions was correct. Now whatever they decide is meaningless, if not totally wrong."

I stayed away as long as possible. But the chieftains still hadn't reached agreement. Some wanted to do something, while others wanted to do nothing. And those who wanted to do something could not agree on what that might be. Those who wanted to do nothing said, "Things are fine back home. This is where the action is. Let's stay a while longer and have a good time."

A glint of excitement showed in the peaceful, sincere eyes of Chieftain Wangpo; he had made up his mind to do something.

I sent the servants to fetch a performing troupe and build a stage.

Then I had tents erected on a grassy field, where I laid out machine guns, all sorts of rifles, and some pistols for anyone who cared to do some shooting.

But I still didn't know why I'd invited the chieftains over.

I racked my brain for an answer; I thought and I thought but couldn't come up with a thing. So I stopped worrying about it.

Meanwhile, my beautiful wife was singing in that melodious voice of hers again.

45 Syphilis ～

My guests continued to complain that I hadn't found anything for them to do.

I felt like telling them that they need not look, that something would happen by itself sooner or later. All they needed was patience. But in the end I said nothing.

Finally my servants located a performing troupe.

I must say that it was a very strange troupe; it wasn't Tibetan or Han. The performers were girls of many different nationalities. I had a huge stage erected for them, but I never expected them to run out of plays in only three days. They even took a pug dog up onto the stage, where it walked around in circles picking flowers from under the girls' skirts. That too lasted only three days. The owner of the troupe said that she and the girls had nowhere to go during turbulent times like this, and would like to settle down in this peaceful place. I didn't say no. I even had a large tent set up for them. Meanwhile, construction began on an adobe house at the far end of the street. The owner supervised the work, and construction progressed quickly. In less than ten days, they had completed the framework of a large house with a waiting room and a wide staircase leading up to a deep, dark hallway lined with small rooms.

The girls idled all day long, sending their tinkling laughter flowing up and down the street. Their clothes didn't quite cover their bodies, so I told the troupe owner that I'd have some made for them. The woman, already past her prime, burst out laughing. "My God! I love this place. It's like a dream world. And I like you, an idiot who has yet to see the real world."

We were chatting inside the big tent when she gave me a kiss, and not just anywhere, but on the lips. I jumped to my feet as if burned by a fire.

The girls laughed, and amid the laughter, the one with the darkest brows and biggest eyes came to sit on my lap.

The owner sent the girl away and told me she wasn't clean. From what I could see, the skin above her breasts was nice and white, and even her exposed navel was pink; if she wasn't clean, I couldn't tell you who was. Instead of leaving right away, the girl wrapped her arms around my neck and planted her thick lips on mine, nearly suffocating me.

The owner then gave me a girl she considered clean. The girl walked up to me as the others started giggling. The owner took some silver dollars out of my pocket, and said, "This is the price. All my girls have a price."

She took out ten altogether. After counting them, she kept five and put five back. Then she put four into a gilded crimson case and gave the fifth one to the other girls. "My treat," she said. "You girls go to the market and buy yourselves some sweets."

The girls roared with laughter and flitted out like a swarm of agitated bees.

The owner tied the key to her money box around her waist, and said, "The carpenter is putting in the floor, so I'm going to go see how he's doing. If the young master is happy, why not give the girl some loose change for cosmetics."

The fermented fragrance of pine drifted over from where the

house was being built, enhancing the attraction of the girl in my arms.

My manhood was beginning to stir, but in all other respects I was as languid as the weather.

The girl was very good. After undressing me, she told me to just lie there. I didn't have to move; she'd do everything. She did, and it was terrific. I felt wonderful all over, without lifting a finger. Afterward, we lay there naked and talked. That was when I realized that these girls weren't a performing troupe at all, but a group of women who made a living with their bodies. And I was their first client. I asked if she could do something for those old chieftains whose bodies could no longer satisfy their latent desires. She said yes. "Good," I said. "Those old men are rolling in silver. From today on they'll be your clients."

That night, the chieftains took pleasure from women who charged them a fee.

The next day, they looked more energetic than usual when they got together. One of them even asked me why their own women didn't have those kinds of skills.

The female chieftain, on the other hand, slept alone and awoke with dark circles under her eyes. "Just look at the Maichi family," she said to Father resentfully. "Your older son introduced opium and now your idiot son brings women like that."

"And what did you bring?" Chieftain Maichi asked. "What did you bring for us?"

"I think women are all about the same," she said.

The other chieftains told her to shut up. "All women are different."

Chieftain Wangpo didn't join the conversation. He could rest his eyes, but not his hands, on the singing woman upstairs, while the girls in the big tent were both real and beautiful.

The chieftains finally got the answer they were seeking. "The young master of the Maichi family invited us here to enjoy these wonderful girls."

Adviser Huang told us that the girls were prostitutes and that the big tent was a brothel.

"There are two girls reserved for the young master," the madam said to me. "You mustn't touch the others."

342

"Why not?"

"They aren't clean. They're sick."

"What kind of sickness?"

"A sickness that will rot that thing a man has."

I couldn't imagine how that thing of mine could just rot away. So the madam called two girls over and told one of them to lift her skirt. My God, that was no door, it was a cave! Then she showed me the other girl, whose private parts looked like a mushroom and stank like a rotting cow.

That night, when I thought about how someone's private parts could look like that, I lost all interest in women. I stayed home alone while the male chieftains went to the brothel. But I couldn't sleep, so I got up to drink tea with Adviser Huang. I asked about the prostitutes' sickness.

"Syphilis," he said.

"Syphilis?"

"Young Master, I brought you the opium, but not the syphilis."

From the nervous expression on his face I could tell that syphilis presented a real danger.

"My God!" he said. "Even that has shown up here. What next?"

"The chieftains aren't afraid," I said. "The brothel's finished, and now none of them wants to leave."

Each girl had a room upstairs in the brothel. At night, bright lamps lit up the downstairs room. The upstairs was suffused with the girls' fragrance, while the downstairs was redolent with the smells of liquor and meat and bean stew in a cauldron. In the center of the room, a gilded speaker sat next to a wind-up gramophone that played music all day long.

"Let them be," the adviser said. "Their time is over, so let them catch syphilis, let them feel happiness. We need to concentrate on our own situation."

He then told me some stories about syphilis. When he finished, I laughed, and said, "I won't have any appetite for at least three days."

"Money has a terrible effect on people," he said, "but it's not as bad as opium, which in turn pales in comparison with syphilis. But this isn't what I wanted to tell you."

I asked him what he wanted to say.

He raised his voice. "Young Master, they're here."

"They're here?"

"Yes, they're here."

I asked him who *they* were, and he said they were the Han Chinese. I laughed, for it sounded as if he himself weren't a Han, nor my mother, nor the many Han Chinese in the shops in my town. He made it sound as if I'd never seen a Han person before. I was, after all, the son of a Han woman.

But he said earnestly, "What I mean is, the colored Han are here."

Now I understood. The uncolored Han came here merely for money, like the businessmen, or for survival, like the adviser himself. But the colored Han were different – they wanted to dye our land with their own colors. That was what the White Han Chinese wanted. And if the Red Han won the civil war, I heard that they wanted even more to stain every piece of land in that color they revered. We knew they were locked in a mighty struggle in their own place, neither side gaining a clear edge over the other, because every trading caravan from the Han area brought newspapers. My wise adviser was addicted to newspapers, like a smoker to opium. He grew agitated without his newspapers, but sighed when he read them. He was always telling me, "The war is getting worse, much worse."

Adviser Huang, once a provincial representative, had met his downfall by opposing the fight against the Red Han Chinese. But he wasn't happy about the prospect of them winning either.

During that period, there were rumors among the locals that the Han would come soon. The historian had once said that whatever the people believed would happen sooner or later, even if it didn't make much sense. So many people talking about the same thing amounted to chanting the same incantation to express a common wish to heaven.

The adviser had always said that the Han were locked in mortal combat and couldn't break free. Now, all of a sudden, he was saying, "They're here."

I asked him, "Have they come to see me?"

He laughed, saying those were truly the thoughts of a master.

"Fine," I said. "Send them over so we can see which color we like better."

He laughed some more. "The young master sounds like a

woman picking out a piece of silk for a dress." He added, "These people sneak in and don't want to see anyone. Nor will they want people to know about their colors."

I asked how he knew all this.

"I'm your adviser. I'm supposed to know, aren't I?"

I didn't like his tone of voice a bit. Seeing the displeasure on my face, he quickly added, "The young master must have forgotten that your adviser used to be a colored Han too, which is why I can spot them right off."

I asked him what these people planned to do, but he told me to get some rest, since they didn't plan to do anything yet. They would act within permissible bounds, more cautious in their actions than others in town. They had come to look around and see what was what.

I went up to my room to rest.

Before falling asleep, I kept thinking about syphilis and about "them." I'd take a stroll on the street as soon as I got up the next morning to see if I could spot the colored Han.

I slept in late the next day and awoke feeling empty, as if I'd lost something. But I had no idea exactly what that was; I just felt that something was wrong. So I asked the servants what was missing. They looked around, at the ornaments I was wearing and at the valuable objects and utensils around the house, before telling me that nothing was missing.

It was Sonam Tserang who finally announced, "The mistress isn't singing today."

The others agreed: "She sits upstairs and sings every day, but not today."

Yes, Tharna always sat behind the carved railing upstairs and sang as soon as the sun was up.

Lately I'd been feeling that time was passing faster than ever. Consider all that had happened during those days: the chieftains had come, then syphilis had come, and now the colored Han Chinese had come. Only when my wife sang to seduce the young Chieftain Wangpo did I feel time slow down, returning to its unbearable pace.

But that morning, when she stopped singing, time went on a dizzying tear.

None of the chieftains had returned from the brothel in town yet. Servants accompanied me out of the house, under the malevolent, yet victorious gaze of the female chieftain, who had no way of demonstrating her prowess in a brothel. It was quiet all around me, but my heart was thumping as if I were galloping on a horse, with the wind howling past my ears.

The chieftains eventually emerged from the brothel and walked toward us on their way to bed. Time was turned upside down in that big new house in town. After abandoning themselves to the sound of the music and the aroma of liquor and meat, the chieftains were returning, lazily, looking forward to some sleep. The sight of their slothful figures told me that something was about to happen. But then, reminded of my conversation with Adviser Huang, I led the servants up the street. I wanted to see if I could spot the colored Han Chinese who had sneaked into town. When I reached the bridge, I was face-to-face with the chieftains. I saw that many of their noses were redder than before. Yes, I thought, they've contracted syphilis from the girls.

I laughed.

I laughed at their ignorance of what the girls were carrying.

Twelve ∼

46 Colored People ∼

I saw some newly arrived Han Chinese, but couldn't tell which of them were colored, except for two clerks in recently opened shops, who were actually Han dressed in Tibetan clothes.

At the inn I frequented, the owner asked me what I was looking for out on the street. I told him. "Do you think they paint their faces?" he replied. "Their colors are in their hearts."

"Then I can't spot them."

So I sat down to drink. I even joked that now would be the best time to kill Chieftain Maichi for revenge, if only the innkeeper's brother were around. "If he really must have his revenge, this is the time."

With a sigh, the innkeeper told me he didn't know where his brother had run off to.

"Then what about you?"

"If I knew my brother was dead or didn't want to do it anymore, then I'd take over. That's the rule we agreed to follow."

Part of their agreement sent a chill up my spine: if Chieftain Maichi died before they had a chance to act, then the next Chieftain Maichi – me – would automatically become their target. They had to kill the actual Chieftain Maichi to avenge the wrong done to their family.

I was so scared that I thought about sending someone to kill Chieftain Maichi for the two brothers. The innkeeper just laughed, and said, "My friend, you really are an idiot. Why haven't you considered killing me and my brother?"

He was right; the idea hadn't crossed my mind.

"That way you wouldn't have to worry about me killing you someday." As he saw me out the door, he said, "The young

347

master has many things to tend to. Go home and take care of them."

While we were talking, the madam came to invite me to her brothel. Even from the inn I could hear the girls' distant laughter and some scratchy music from the gramophone, while the aroma of stewed meat and beans filled my nostrils.

I took a seat downstairs, but had no interest in eating or in touching the girl in my lap. I could detect the odor of syphilis in the air, even though I wasn't sure if it had a smell. I just sensed something of it in the air. As I sat there with a clean girl in my lap, the madam entertained me with tales of curious incidents involving the chieftains. Even the girls began to giggle as they relived some of the things that had happened to them. But I didn't find any of it all that funny.

I asked the madam about the colored Han. She laughed. "Colored or not, Red or White, they're all the same to us." She spat on the floor. "Men are the same, whatever their color, unless, of course, they're like the young master."

"What about me?"

She picked a sliver of meat from her teeth and flicked it away. "I wouldn't know about someone like the young master, who looks like an idiot but isn't."

She sounded as if she had seen people of all colors. Phooey! A woman who spread syphilis.

I spat angrily on the ground after walking out of that house of loose morals.

A tiny, solitary whirlwind twisted its way over from the distance, sending dust, scrap paper, and grass swirling into the air along the way and making a popping sound like a flag flapping in the wind. Lots of people fled out of its path, stopping only long enough to spit at it. Everyone said that ghosts and demons rode in whirlwinds, and that only human saliva was powerful enough to scare them away. But it kept getting bigger. It fell to earth and broke up only after some of the girls ran out of the big house and lifted their skirts, exposing the syphilis flowers between their legs to the whirlwind.

There was a void in my heart. Maybe that was because I couldn't tell who the colored Han were; spotting them would have filled the empty space.

The servants found me while I was looking for the whirlwind's hiding place.

My wife had run off with Chieftain Wangpo.

Sonam Tserang, leading a party of horsemen, went after them without even waiting for my order. They took off like a whirlwind themselves and headed south. Three days later Sonam Tserang came back empty-handed and ordered that a stake be erected in the yard. Then he told Aryi to tie him to the stake. I wasn't sad or anything, but I couldn't get out of bed. The minute I tried to sleep, Tharna's beautiful face floated before my eyes. Then, from downstairs, the crack of a whip tore through the air. The maid who had once been called Tharna took advantage of the moment to appear before me. She'd stayed away all these years, spending her time with the other maids. Now she was once again speaking to me in her mosquito voice as she circled my bed, urging me not to be sad while she cursed the name Tharna. I felt like slapping her, a woman with tiny arms and legs who could spew pure venom. But I was too lazy to raise a hand, so I told her to get out. "If you don't, I'll give you to a one-eyed shoemaker."

She knelt by my bed, and pleaded, "Please don't do that. I don't want to give birth to a slave."

"Then get out!"

"Please don't give me to any other man," she begged. "I'm your woman. Even when you don't want me anymore, I'll still consider myself yours."

Her words touched my heart. But before I could say anything further, she'd already closed the door behind her and returned to be with the other maids.

Downstairs, Sonam Tserang finally screamed as the whip continued cutting into his flesh.

That gave me the strength to go downstairs and order Aryi to stop.

That was the first time that Aryi had ever punished someone on my behalf; I never expected Sonam Tserang to be the first. As soon as the rope was untied, he slid down the stake to the ground, as the chieftains stood around admiring the refined lashing skills of the Maichi executioner. Chieftain Rongong opened her mouth to say something, but swallowed her words when she saw my face and the menacing whip in Aryi's hand. So did Chieftain Maichi. Among the chieftains, Lha Shopa was now my only true friend. He too was about to say something, but I didn't give him a chance, since it wouldn't have done any good. I said to the chieftains, "You asked why I invited you over. Now you know. I invited you so you could see a woman of the Rongong family betray me." I added, "Those who want to leave may do so tomorrow, since you already have my gift."

They spread their hands, meaning they hadn't received anything. They had no idea that my gift was called syphilis.

Ready to depart, the chieftains took turns coming to say good-bye to their heartbroken host.

"The mother told her daughter to seduce Wangpo," Chieftain Lha Shopa said. "Don't let her off the hook easily, Young Master."

To everyone's surprise, Tharna returned just as the chieftains were departing. She came home swaying back and forth on her horse. The dust on her face was like ash after a blazing fire. Calmly, she said, "I'll be your woman for the rest of my life. You see, I'm back."

It was a repeat performance of when she'd slept with the first young master of the Maichi family. Instead of saying anything, I just stared at her back as she went upstairs.

The chieftains' eyes were fixed on me as I watched Tharna walk quietly upstairs. Her mother should not have shown her face at that particular moment, but the old hag came down to meet her beautiful daughter. Chieftain Rongong discovered that the glow on her pretty daughter's face was gone, as if a fire had seared it off. Even I felt a dull pain in my heart at the sight. Tharna wailed the moment she looked up and saw her mother.

Grief-stricken howls poured from Tharna's mouth as she sat on the stairs and looked up at her mother.

At first the female chieftain appeared despondent, but then her bent back slowly began to straighten and she spat savagely at her beloved daughter in front of everyone. Then, holding herself erect with a hand on her hip, she walked downstairs and came directly to me. "This useless girl is no longer a daughter of the Rongong family. Go say something nice to her, idiot, and tell her not to cry. I'm leaving now."

There's a woman's logic for you. It was as if that single comment divorced her completely from what had just happened. That seemed wrong to me, but I couldn't say why. Just then Father yelled from upstairs that I shouldn't let the woman go. Chieftain Maichi ran down the stairs, gasping for breath, and shouted, "What she just said means you won't be Chieftain Rongong. You won't succeed her in the future."

"The future?" I said foolishly. "How could I be chieftain of both Maichi and Rongong?"

All the other chieftains laughed at that.

But Chieftain Maichi nearly keeled over from anger. He would have fallen if servants hadn't rushed up to catch him. The chieftain's wife ran down, and shouted to her son, "You'll be Chieftain Rongong first, then Chieftain Maichi."

The female chieftain laughed. "Do you think that decrepit old man of yours will outlive me?" she asked the chieftain's wife.

She spat once more toward her daughter before returning to her room to pack.

The other chieftains slowly walked off. Some set out at once, while others wanted to spend one last night at the brothel.

The wind carried Tharna's sobs the way it had delivered her songs a few days earlier.

With his eyes, the historian said, "The show is over."

Meanwhile, Adviser Huang was all in a stew up in his room.

He was worried about the arrival of his colored compatriots. My adviser had lost his job over objections to the White Han fighting the Red Han, but still he hoped that the Whites would prevail. He said he might survive if the White Han won, but had no idea what the Red Han would do if they came. I'd donated money to the White Han for airplanes, so he and I quickly agreed that if the Han, the colored Han, had to come, then let it be the White ones.

As for Tharna, she had been cast aside after Wangpo had flung her into the flames of lust, in which she'd been badly burned.

If everyone wanted something, so did I. But if no one wanted it, I didn't either. That included a woman, even the most beautiful woman in the world, even if I'd never again meet one as beautiful.

Let her slowly grow old in that room of hers.

Chieftain Rongong came to say good-bye.

"Don't you want to take your daughter along?" I asked her.

"No."

"Chieftain Wangpo abandoned her."

"She was your wife first."

"She'll wither away and die in that room."

"Why don't you ask Chieftain Rongong if there's anything she wants to say?" the steward said.

She said, "I want you to promise me, in front of all these chieftains, that you will not send assassins after me."

Everyone heard her. Sonam Tserang, Aryi, and Chieftain Maichi's wife all shook their heads spiritedly, signaling me not to promise that woman anything, while the other chieftains asked me to agree to her request. They knew they weren't in any danger so long as Chieftain Rongong was allowed to return home safely. I had no choice. "All right, you may get on the road with no worries."

After Chieftain Rongong had traveled far down the road, I said to my other invited guests, "You may also get on the road with no worries."

A day later, our guests were gone.

Chieftain Maichi and his wife were the last to leave. As we were saying good-bye, Mother's eyes reddened, but Father and I had nothing to say to each other. Mother bent down from her horse to kiss me on the forehead. "Be patient, son," she whispered. "I'll live to see you become chieftain."

I felt like telling her it was too late, that time was passing faster and faster, but I couldn't. Instead I said, "I'll miss you, Ah-ma."

Tears streamed down her face.

She flicked her reins, and her horse took a step forward. I hadn't heard a sound made by all the other horses, but that first step by Mother's horse thudded in my ears as if it had landed on my heart. I reached out and grabbed her reins. "Ah-ma," I said, "the colored Han are here."

Halting her horse, she stopped a moment, but said nothing. Then her whip landed on the horse's flank, and it began moving again.

And once again her idiot son ran up to her. As the mistress bent down low, I told her not to sleep with Chieftain Maichi anymore, because he'd contracted syphilis. She appeared to know what I was talking about. The land of chieftains may not have known syphilis before, but she came from a place where the disease had been known for a long time.

"Why didn't the young master say something about the throne?" the steward asked.

Adviser Huang said, "There isn't much time left."

Sonam Tserang asked permission to go after Chieftain Rongong, even though he knew I wouldn't give it. That headstrong slave's ultimate goal was to be permitted to kill Chieftain Wangpo. On that score, I had to give in. My only condition was that Wangpo be killed on the road. If he was killed after returning to his estate, then I'd have Aryi snuff out Sonam's dog life.

Without a word, he set out with a pair of pistols. I thought at least he should turn to look back at us one more time, but he didn't. So I just stood there staring at his back until he disappeared from view.

After Sonam Tserang left, I began to count the days he'd been gone; that is to say, my life was measured against the days of his absence. Ten days after he'd left, someone asked to replace him as the head tax collector. I summoned Aryi, who gave the man a good lashing. He had been working under Sonam Tserang, but now was even stripped of his brown uniform. I told the steward to check the roster, and it turned out that he was a freeman. So I made him a slave, who would be free again only if Sonam Tserang returned safely. Now, I wasn't a chieftain, the only person who could determine the numbers of free servants and slaves, so in this case I simply switched their status, slave and free, something Father would not have objected to, had he known.

On the twelfth day, Sangye Dolma's husband, the silversmith, showed up. His wife was not around, since she had gone out to the pastureland by the spring to find the girl with the same name as hers. She knew I hadn't been with Tharna for a long time. I had two Tharnas around me, one of whom had betrayed me, while the other aroused no interest in me.

The silversmith came to see me, but I said I had no need for him at the border.

Knowing what I had in mind where matters like this were concerned, the steward told the man, "Sangye Dolma is the head of all the women here, and you are no longer a good match for her."

The silversmith yelled that he loved his wife.

"Go home," the steward said. "If the chieftain feels like helping you, he can make you a freeman."

Actually, the silversmith could have pleaded his case with me, since I was sitting nearby while he was talking with the steward. But an arrogant smile common among craftsmen spread across his face as he said, "The chieftain will set me free."

Then he slung his tool bag over his shoulder and took a few steps before turning back. "Young Master, you'll have to pay me when I return to make silverware for you."

What he meant was he'd be a freeman, a good match for Dolma, when he returned. So I said, "Fine. I'll pay double for your work."

He turned and walked away. I could see loneliness and pain in his back, and recalled how he had lost his freedom over Sangye Dolma. Watching his receding figure, I once again tasted the same bitterness in my mouth and agony in my heart that I'd felt when he'd first caught the eye of my personal maid. This time he was going to ask for the return of his freedom, also on account of Dolma. I felt there was no hope for him.

The silversmith was bound to be deeply disappointed. But people are all the same, whether they're silversmiths or chieftains or slaves. They think only about what they want, not daring to ask themselves if there is any reason to be hopeful. The historian, Wangpo Yeshi, for example, found nothing interesting, yet he still sought out a comfortable place to sit and meditate.

Not long after the silversmith left, I told Aryi to get on a fast horse and bring him back. When he saw the executioner coming after him, the silversmith broke out in a sweat, thinking he was about to die. But Aryi took him to the brothel, where he nearly keeled over from the earsplitting music and the fragrance of barbecued meat and soup with stewed beans and bones. The girls took him upstairs, where he finished two big plates of food in bed before getting a workout on the girl's belly, belching the whole time. He should not have eaten so much.

Sangye Dolma returned from the pasture empty-handed. The girl she was looking for had been married off to someone far away. As I sat with my one-time personal maid, I found we had nothing to say to each other. Then she asked me softly if I missed the past. I didn't feel like talking. She sighed and said I was a master who valued friendship. That's when I told her the silversmith had come to see me. She sighed again. I knew she loved him, but she was now in an official position and was aware that she'd no longer be a slave once I was chieftain. That is why she had nothing to say regarding the silversmith.

Aryi came in to report that the silversmith was belching the whole time he was riding the girl in the brothel. That sent tears down Dolma's face. "I thank Young Master for giving the silversmith pleasure," she said.

The madam kept the silversmith around, saying that she needed lots of silver objects made.

People who emerged from the brothel after that said they noticed more and more fine silver objects. Sangye Dolma cried a few more times. She refused to sleep with the steward again, but she didn't go back to the silversmith either. And that was how the romance between a maid and a silversmith came to an end.

Sonam Tserang had been gone nearly a month, but there was no news of him. One day I was gazing at the southbound road when Tharna came up behind me, followed by Tharna – what I mean is, the daughter of a chieftain was followed by the daughter of a groom, or my wife was followed by my personal maid. My unfaithful wife had just smoked a heavy dose of opium. She looked haggard, but a crazy glint flickered in her eyes. A gust of wind made her sway. When I reached out to steady her, her hands were as cold as if she'd grown up in a place with icy winds. She said, "Your killer won't be coming back."

I was never someone who tucked everything away in my memory, for that would have made me a smart person, not an idiot. But now she was treating me like a smart person. Nonetheless, she brought back memories of the past, so I went downstairs, leaving her up there. When I reached the ground floor, I called for Tharna, and the groom's daughter came to me, leaving the chieftain's daughter upstairs all alone, standing behind a carved railing, the wind billowing her clothes and making it seem as if she were about to fly away. It would have surprised no one to see a beautiful woman like her fly with the wind. With her beauty, people would believe that she was a fairy from heaven. But she didn't fly. Standing there alone turned her even more icy cold.

That night I dreamed that Tharna, my wife, had turned into jade that sparkled in the moonlight.

The ground was covered by a layer of frost when I awoke the next morning. It was the first frost of the year, which meant that winter would be here soon.

Sonam Tserang finally returned, but he had lost one hand and one of his pistols.

We learned that before Sonam Tserang could catch up with Wangpo, the chieftain had returned to his estate. Sonam Tserang waited for him to leave the estate so he could kill him on the road. But Wangpo stayed inside, going nowhere. Later he heard that Wangpo had contracted a strange disease that kept him in bed. The syphilis he'd acquired at the brothel was taking effect, rotting away his manhood. So Sonam Tserang swaggered onto the estate, where he took out his pistol and fired into the sky. He was immediately seized by Chieftain Wangpo's men, who chopped off one of his hands. Chieftain Wangpo came out to see him. His face glowed, as if he were in perfect health. But Sonam Tserang saw that he had trouble walking, as if he were afraid of losing that thing hanging between his legs. Looking down at his amputated hand, which was already beginning to change color, and at Chieftain Wangpo, Sonam Tserang laughed.

Wangpo laughed too, but his face paled. "Women," he said. "Just look what they've turned us into."

"My master would laugh if he heard you," Sonam Tserang replied.

"Then go home and tell him."

"I'm not begging you to spare me."

Wangpo handed him a letter. "Then think of yourself not as a killer, but as a messenger."

That was how Sonam Tserang returned with a letter from Wangpo. But before he left, Wangpo ordered a small burial mound for the amputated hand, and Sonam Tserang went to see it.

In the letter, Wangpo said, "Women, women, your women have destroyed me." He complained that in my new town the prostitutes had destroyed his body and that his friend's wife had shattered his spirit.

He added that many chieftains had cursed my town. Their bodies, they said, were rotting because of it. Now, who has ever heard of a living person rotting away? In the past, people started to decompose only after their souls left their bodies in death. But now, still alive, these bodies had begun to rot, starting with that thing they had used to continue their family lines and to gain pleasure.

I asked the historian if the town should be cursed. He replied that not everyone who came here was rotting away; only those who were outmatched by the town.

The former monk, my present historian, Wangpo Yeshi, said that new things grow in places where things are rotting.

47 Toilets ∿

The Red Han Chinese defeated the White ones.

The routed White Han Chinese surged into our border town.

At first, they underestimated us, thinking their guns were all they needed to obtain grain and meat. I gave it to them. When they had eaten their fill, they wanted liquor and women, something we had in abundance. But since they had no money, they came to me for silver. That was when they discovered that we had armed ourselves years before, and in the end, they were forced to exchange their guns for silver, which they then used to buy wine and women. In droves they swarmed to the brothel, that place that spread syphilis. They were forever shouting, forever leaving their giant footprints in the snow. With them around, even starving dogs had trouble finding a pristine patch of snow on which to deposit their flowerlike footprints.

Adviser Huang, draped in a fox fur robe, said, "They're too cold to sleep."

I agreed. The wind cut through their tents. Adviser Huang sighed so much that I had no choice but to give those people food and liquor when it snowed.

They spent most of their time in the brothel, but none of them suffered from syphilis. Then I heard that they had a special medicine to prevent contamination. I asked one of the army officers to give me some. I was free of the disease, since the madam had always given me a healthy girl, so I divided the medicine into two portions – one for Tharna, who had contracted the disease from Wangpo, and one for Chieftain Maichi, to show that his idiot son didn't want his own father rotting and stinking in bed.

Deeply moved, Father wrote to say that the estate was lonely in the winter. His letter called out to me, "Come back, my son, and bring us a festive new year with the skills you've used to run the border town."

I asked my servants if they wanted to go back. They said they did, especially the one-handed Sonam Tserang, who missed his mother. I asked Aryi if he missed his old executioner father. He shook his head, but then nodded. "Good," I said. "I miss the chieftain and his wife too."

So Dolma and the servants began packing. For me, it was all the same wherever we were. I don't mean that I was a stranger to loneliness, although I seldom felt lonely. The historian reminded me that they called me an idiot. He said that the advantage of being an idiot was that many things that would hurt a normal person had no effect on me. That made sense.

But now we were going back.

A heavy snow fell on the day of our departure. It was a record snowfall, with thick flakes rushing toward earth like flocks of birds. By noontime, it had caved in the tents of the routed White Chinese soldiers. Tucking their heads between their shoulders and cradling their remaining rifles, they ran straight to our big, warm house. This time they would have fought to the death if I had refused to let them in, since they would surely have frozen outside. I waved off the servants, telling them to put away their guns and let the people come upstairs. Soldiers who were too far gone fell facedown in the snow, as if embarrassed to trouble us. A few of the fallen men were saved; the rest were beyond help.

I told Sangye Dolma to get the survivors something to eat.

At that moment, everyone, me included, realized that we could not leave for the estate. So the soldiers were put up in one half of the house, while we occupied the other. And in the basement was all the silver and treasure we had accumulated over the years. If we left, it would surely fall into the hands of the White Chinese.

Fortunately, there was no strife between us and our uninvited guests. The officers in their beaked caps would stand on the opposite veranda and smile at me, while his soldiers bowed and called me "Master," just like servants. Meanwhile, I gave them grain, meat, oil, and salt. But they were on their own if they had an itch for the liquor and prostitutes in town.

Everyone on both sides took pains to keep a safe distance.

We smiled and greeted one another across that distance, but

never got too close. Distance is necessary for people who don't know one another but must live together. There was one exception, a place where distance seemed to disappear. The toilets. Since we wore long robes, nothing was revealed in the toilet, but the Han Chinese, who wore short jackets, even on bone-chilling winter days, had to stick out their naked rear ends. And those pale rear ends were a source of ridicule by my troops.

And that is why, to tell you what happened, I must begin with the toilets.

But first, we need to see where they were located.

Adviser Huang once said that our house was shaped like a Chinese character. He tore a page from the historian's notebook to write it for me. It had the exact same shape as the house. This is what it looked like: 凵 . The open side faced the town. We lived in one leg of the house, while the Han lived in the other. And the bottom part was the toilet.

I'd heard stories contrasting the Tibetans with the Han. One of them told of a pair of thieves, a Tibetan and a Han, who were caught stealing gold. When their stomachs were cut open, the Tibetan's was half-filled with animal hair, the Han's with iron shavings. Tibetans eat mostly meat, and since it's never very clean, they ingest lots of cow and goat hairs. The Hans, on the other hand, eat mainly greens – leaves, roots, and stems – which they stir-fry with a metal spatula in an iron wok; over time their stomachs fill up with iron shavings.

Where stomachs are concerned, I guess it's a tie. Strictly speaking, that's less a story than a simple contrast. The same holds true for toilets. Now we all know that the Han consider even the British to be barbarians, let alone the Tibetans. Barbarians, that's what they usually call us. But we have our sense of superiority too. Take toilets, for instance. My sister, who was in far-off England, said that the British revile the Han primarily because of those Chinese toilets. My Han mother said that if asked to name her favorite things in the land of the chieftains, toilets would come in second, right after silver.

I'd never been to the Han area, so I had no idea what their toilets were like. I can describe only ours, which are attached to windowless walls behind our houses. A story tells of a high-ranking official from the Han imperial court who mistook one of our toilets for a little house that we Buddha-worshiping Tibetans had built for birds, because only birdhouses hang on walls, and also because large flocks of red-beaked crows and pigeons were always flying around towering houses. The story goes on to say that the official returned to the imperial court with nothing but praise for the chieftains. That's right, Tibetans who live in towering houses hang their toilets in the open air.

We and our guests lived on either leg of that Chinese character, with the toilet sandwiched in between. So it became the one place where the two sides met during that extraordinary winter. The Han soldiers aimed their rear ends at the small wooden house hanging on the wall as unimpeded wintry winds froze their exposed extremities. They could not stop shivering, which my people stubbornly interpreted as a fear of us. I tried to make them understand that the Han people were shivering in the toilet because of the cold wind and a fear of heights.

"It can't do you any harm if they believe that others are weak," Adviser Huang said.

So I let my people go on ridiculing the other men in the toilet.

I had a private toilet.

To reach it, I had to walk through a room where a charcoal fire burned bright in a bronze brazier. Fragrant smoke from an incense burner would be curling up into the rafters when I walked in. Two married women, probably middle-aged, were in charge. When I emerged from the toilet, whoever was on duty would ask me to sit by the fire to warm myself as she fumigated me from head to toe with incense smoke.

I told Adviser Huang to invite the ranking officer of the defeated army to share the toilet with me. Soon after the invitation was sent, I ran into him outside the toilet. I first invited him to sit by the brazier while the women lit incense and we waited for the fragrance to fill the room. I didn't have a thing to say to him, so he broke the ice by asking me to join forces to repel an imminent attack by the Communists. He said that the Communists were the party of the poor and that the chieftains would be finished if they came, not to mention a rich man with guns like myself.

"Let's join forces against them," he said earnestly.

His eyes reddened when he spoke of what the Communists did to the wealthy. Getting to his feet, he clasped my shoulder with one hand and shook my hand forcefully with the other.

I believed everything he said.

I knew that the officer was talking about matters of life and death, but I couldn't hold back any longer. Wrenching free of his hands, I dashed into the toilet. A wind happened to be blowing up from below. When I returned after finishing my business, the women fumigated me, and I saw the officer cover his nose with a silk handkerchief. A look of disgust appeared on his face as if my body stank all the time. Before that, I'd been a rich man like him, but that seemed to change after my visit to the toilet, and I had become a stinking barbarian. Yes, how could an officer discuss important matters in a toilet? I walked out.

"Damn him!" I said to Adviser Huang. "Tell the Han to fight their own battles."

Adviser Huang sighed long and loud. He'd hoped that I'd become an ally of the White Han Chinese. "I guess that means I'll have to bid farewell to the young master," he said.

"Go on, then. You can't forget you're a damned Chinese, so follow whomever you want."

I can't say that the officer's reaction to the toilet was the only reason I decided not to be the White Han ally, but it sure was an important one.

Spring finally arrived.

My people told me that the Han soldiers no longer shivered in the toilet, partly because the wind was warmer and partly because their fear of heights was no longer a problem; they'd gotten used to the midair toilet. I met the ranking officer in the toilet one more time after that. I didn't have anything to say to him, and all he said was, "Spring is here."

"Yes," I agreed. "Spring is here."

That was the extent of our conversation.

As soon as spring arrived, the People's Liberation Army began clearing wide passages with explosives for motor vehicles and artillery for their advance into the chieftains' territory. Some of the chieftains opted to fight the Communists, while others prepared to surrender. My friend Lha Shopa was one of the latter. I heard that a messenger he sent to negotiate with the Communists returned with a complete PLA uniform for him as well as a piece of paper appointing him as some kind of commander. Chieftain Rongong, on the other hand, liquidated the wealth she'd accumulated to buy rifles and artillery pieces, in preparation for a battle with the Communists. All the news that came to me indicated that the woman seemed to be getting younger. Chieftain Wangpo was the most interesting. He said he knew nothing about the Communists or what they'd do to him, but he'd never be on the same side as the Maichi family. In other words, he'd surrender if I resisted the Communists and resist if I surrendered.

The steward and Adviser Huang suggested that I hold one last talk with the White Chinese army. Adviser Huang said, "If you want to fight, then you'll have to make up your mind to work with them. If not, you can tell them to move on, since the weather has warmed up."

The steward said, "And you can't talk in the toilet anymore."

I laughed. "You're right about that."

They laughed with me.

The steward asked Adviser Huang if the stuff that came out of the Han rear ends didn't stink. Adviser Huang said it did. Then the steward asked him which smelled worse, Han Chinese shit or Tibetan shit. That was a tough question, but instead of getting upset or angry, Adviser Huang treated it as a joke. He laughed, and said, "Why doesn't the steward ask the young master, since he's shared the toilet with a Han Chinese."

We all laughed again.

I was preparing to talk to the Nationalist representative about forming an alliance when something happened that caused everything to go up in smoke. One night I was sitting by the lamp with my tongueless historian. We were quiet, because what we faced now went beyond his knowledge, even though it was my habit to summon him whenever something important occurred. As the burning oil popped and crackled, he seemed first puzzled and then lost. Just then Sonam Tserang came in with a sheepish, yet triumphant look on his face, bringing with him a wind that made the lamp flicker.

"I caught her at last," he announced proudly.

For some time he had been telling me that I should keep an eye on Tharna.

By then, I had all but put her out of my life, except that she still lived in my house and was fed and clothed by me. Sonam Tserang was convinced that that alone was reason for me to be concerned.

That, of course, is how servants view relationships; you give someone something, and somehow that binds you together. The Communists were coming, but he focused all his attention on that one woman.

Sonam Tserang had long felt embarrassed over his failure to kill Chieftain Wangpo. Now he had caught Tharna in the act – he had seen a White Han officer come out of her room. He summoned some servants to disarm the officer of his pistol belt before pushing him downstairs, where Aryi tied the offender to a stake. Sonam Tserang dragged me out of my room, but I couldn't see what was going on downstairs; I merely heard the cracks of the executioner's whip and the agonizing screams of the offender. Dogs far and near howled as if crazed.

Tharna had committed adultery – again.

Then the moon rose into the sky, and the sounds of snapping dogs echoed in the moonlight.

48 Artillery Fire ~

The White Chinese soldiers left.

They left in the middle of the night without even saying good-bye.

When I got up in the morning, I saw the man they'd left for me, the officer tied to the stake, a dagger from his own people stuck in his chest. They had cleaned the rooms they'd stayed in, which meant they hadn't left in a hurry. Adviser Huang had gone with them. In his room was a pile of neatly folded newspapers, with a letter for me resting on top. Since it was written in Chinese, no one in the house could read it. The ashes in his incense burner were still warm. My wife had gone with them, but had left her room in a mess. Her blankets, her bed curtain, and lots of silk embroidery had been cut to ribbons. The door and windows were wide open. When the wind blew over, the ribbons flew around the room like butter-flies, then fell to the floor when the wind stopped. Those ribbons, with their metallic luster, were the fragments of a woman's hatred and resentment.

Sonam Tserang again yelled that he'd go after her.

The steward laughed and asked him which direction he'd take. Sonam Tserang shook his head blankly. He may have been a loyal servant, but he looked pretty stupid at that moment. And, since I wasn't feeling so good just then, I gave him a kick and told him to get the hell away from me.

But he flashed me a loyal smile before taking a dagger from his waistband and waving it. Then he ran downstairs, grabbed a horse, jumped into the saddle, and raced off into the distance, leaving a cloud of rolling dust over the dry ground of early spring.

"Let him go," the steward said.

As I watched the yellow dust dissipate in the air, I was suddenly gripped by sadness. "Will he be back?" I asked.

Tears welled up in Aryi's eyes as he said with his usual shyness, "Young Master, let me go help him."

"He'll be back, as long as he's alive," the steward said.

I asked the historian if Sonam Tserang would return.

He shook his head. His eyes told me that Sonam Tserang had made up his mind to die for his master.

I paced the floor upstairs that day, cursing myself for not being able to make him a freeman earlier. In the end, it was my former personal maid, Sangye Dolma, who came to me and took my hands. She touched my forehead with her own, and said, "Young Master, you're a good man! Make those strange ideas that cause you to suffer leave your head. Sonam Tserang is your slave, and he went off to kill that bitch for you."

Tears ran down my face.

Laying her head against my chest, Dolma cried, and said, "Young Master, you are a good man. I just wish I could have continued to wait on you."

I looked up at the sun. How bright it was. It had been a long time since the heart of this idiot had been moistened like that. I heard myself say to Dolma, the first woman in my life, "Go get the silversmith. I want to make you both free."

Dolma laughed with tears still on her cheeks. "Idiot. The old master has yet to make you a chieftain."

She had barely dried her tears before new ones took their place. "Young Master," she said, "the silversmith has gone over to the Red Chinese."

I called Aryi over and told him to take some people with him to the Maichi estate to check on the chieftain.

For the first time, Aryi said without his customary shyness, "What's the use of checking on him? The Red Army will be here soon, and it will do no good for him to make you chieftain now."

"It will help," I said, "because I want to make every slave free."

The words were barely out of my mouth when the slaves began running around, upstairs and downstairs. Some were preparing food for Aryi's trip, some were getting his weapons together, while others were saddling his horse. He couldn't refuse now, even if he wanted to. The Red Army, which was fighting for the rights of the poor, had not yet arrived, and the slaves were acting as if they'd already been liberated.

After I sent Aryi on the road, the steward said, "If this is how things are going to be, the Communists won't have anything to do when they get here."

"Would they turn back if they knew?"

"Stop saying such silly things."

The Communists weren't even here yet, and no one knew what they were like, but everyone believed they were indestructible. The chieftains who were preparing for war were nothing but dying fish ripping the net before their destruction. But I hadn't decided what to do, which made the steward anxious. I told him not to worry, since a decision would be made sooner or later. He laughed. "You're right. It's always me who's worried sick, and it always turns out that you're right."

I wanted to wait for my two servants' return before deciding, so I had nothing to do but drink and sleep.

One night I was awakened by something at my feet. I realized it was the tiny maid Tharna, sobbing at the foot of the bed. I'd long since lost interest in her, but I let her stay there to talk to me. "You'll be free as soon as Aryi returns," I told her.

She didn't say anything, but the sobbing stopped.

"I'll give you a big dowry when the time comes."

The groom's daughter began to cry again.

"Stop crying, will you?"

"The mistress didn't take her jewelry box with her."

I told her she could have it, since she had the same cursed name. The sobs stopped again, and the little slut was now kissing my toes. In the past, she'd kissed many more parts of my body, bringing me such pleasure that I'd screamed like a beast. She had followed her mistress with the same name for so long that I believed she'd picked up some of her wicked ways. We have a saying that some women are like poison. Now the groom's daughter had been tainted by poison. While I was thinking about all this, she fell asleep and was snoring at my feet.

She was gone by the time I awoke the next morning – she never made much noise, no matter what she was doing. I never again saw the groom's daughter named Tharna. Since the chieftain's daughter had run off, the groom's daughter, with no place to go, shut herself up in a room upstairs and held the gilded jewelry box tightly in her arms. The other Tharna, who had run away with the White Chinese, was a nobler woman, and I had to admit that there were fundamental differences between the daughter of a chieftain and the daughter of a groom, even though they were known by the same name and had once shared the same man. But at a critical moment, the chieftain's daughter had left without her jewelry, which was worth tens of thousands. The groom's daughter, on the other hand, refused to let go of the case, having already stashed a fair amount of food and water in the room. She'd had her eyes on that jewelry for a very long time.

All right, enough of that. Let that woman disappear from sight.

We heard the rumble of artillery fire.

The sound, like springtime thunder, first came from Chieftain Rongong's northern border. That was the sound of the Red Army cutting into mountains and building roads. Some also said that a battle raged between the Red Army and the united forces of Chieftain Rongong and the White Chinese army.

Sonam Tserang returned for the second time. My loyal servant had failed again. This time he had lost more than a hand – he'd lost his life. Automatic rifle fire had turned his chest into a sieve. They had killed my servant; they had slain the tax collector of my town. Then they had strapped him faceup on his horse, which knew the way, and sent him home. On the road, birds of prey had pecked his face beyond recognition.

Many people cried.

Fine, I said to myself. If this is how the White Chinese and Chieftain Rongong do things, I'll wait for the Communists to arrive and surrender to them.

Shortly after Sonam Tserang's funeral, noises came from the east, the direction of Chieftain Maichi's estate, and no one could tell whether they were the sounds of road building or of battle. Artillery fire rumbled like spring thunder both to the east and to the north. One clear night, when the starry sky twinkled like gem-studded velvet, the Maichi enemy, my innkeeper friend, came to see me. Carrying a jug of wine, he walked into my room without waiting for the servants to report his arrival. I told the servants to close the window, as I didn't want to gaze at the stars in the sky anymore.

When the servants lit the lamps, I saw that the innkeeper's nose was bright red, and that some sticky stuff was running from it. "So," I said, "you have syphilis too."

He smiled. "The young master needn't worry. My younger brother says he can cure me."

"Your brother? You mean that gutless killer? Didn't he run off?"

"He's back," the innkeeper told me calmly.

"Has he killed Chieftain Maichi?" I asked him. "If he has, then the enmity between our two families is over."

At that moment, with a laugh, his brother surprised me by bursting in through the door like a wronged ghost. "At a time like this," he said, "that matter between our families means nothing."

I didn't know what time he was talking about, or why that meaningful matter between our families would suddenly become meaningless.

The former killer laughed. "I didn't kill your father, and I don't want to kill you."

His brother asked him straight out, "Then why did you come back?"

The former killer told us everything. He had joined the White Chinese army while he was on the run, then had joined the Red Army after they'd captured him. Now he called himself a Red Tibetan. He proudly proclaimed that red was the rarest color among Tibetans, but soon it would burn like wildfire all over the chieftains' land and turn them red. He'd come back as a scout for the Red Army. He came up to me, and said, "That matter between our families means nothing. It will be the time to square accounts with you chieftains when our army arrives." He repeated, "That will be the time to square accounts."

The steward entered, and said humbly, "But our young master is not a chieftain."

"Not a chieftain? He *is* the chieftain of chieftains."

After this Red Tibetan had made an appearance, no one wanted to join the Red Chinese anymore, even though everyone knew they would meet with a bad end if they fought against them. Every chieftain's army had met defeat at the hands of the Red Army. The defeated chieftains then led their armies westward. The west belonged to Wangpo Yeshi's religious sect, which claimed to be the purest of all. The chieftains had always preferred the worldly empire of the east, not the land of western deities. But now those chieftains who were determined to resist had no choice but to move west. They did not believe that the holy palace in the west could shield them from harm, but they went there nevertheless after fighting a losing battle against the Red Army.

I said to the historian, "We'll soon have to escape to the place where you came from."

His eyes said, "That's the place you should have gone to a very long time ago. But you all insisted on going east."

"Will your gods forgive us?"

"You've already been punished."

"My God!" the steward said. "After so many years you're still a stubborn lama, not a historian."

"No, I'm a good historian. I've written down everything. Later generations will know what happened on the land of the chieftains – from the time I arrived, that is."

He told us that he'd kept two copies of everything, one of which was hidden in a cave and would be found eventually. He carried the other copy with him. "My only wish is that my body will be found by a literate person."

I wasn't a chieftain, yet I too wanted to flee west.

The artillery fire was lessening in the north, Chieftain Rongong's land, but was intensifying on the eastern lands of Chieftain Maichi. Some said that the chieftain's Chinese wife had told him to resist, but others said that the White Chinese army had captured the chieftain, who was then forced to join the fight. In a word, it was Han people who told him to fight other Han.

We left town on a misty morning. The steward wanted to set fire to the town before we left, but I stopped him. I looked around and saw that everyone wanted to torch the place and burn down the marketplace, the bank, the shops, the warehouses, the soup kitchen for the passing poor, and the brothel with its gaudily painted walls. It was I, the idiot, who had built all this. Of course I had every right to burn it down, but I didn't. Closing my eyes, I told the servants to throw away their torches. The smoke from the extinguished torches brought tears to my eyes.

The steward recommended that we kill the Red Tibetan, to which I agreed, since he was the one who had forced me into resisting the Red Chinese.

Our men stormed into town on horseback, followed by crisp gunshots that echoed in the mist. I held my reins and stood on a high hill, wanting to take one last look at the town I'd created. But everything was hidden behind the mist. I'd never seen the town as it looked at that moment. Gunfire continued to sound before some horses shot out from the mist. They hadn't found the Red Tibetan, so I spurred my horse and got moving. Some women behind me were sobbing. They were the maids who were following Sangye Dolma. Apparently not knowing that we were fleeing for our lives, they had all put on their colorful holiday best. Every maid was there, except my personal maid. Sangye Dolma told me that Tharna had been clutching the nearly priceless jewelry box, refusing to come downstairs.

We had to travel south for a while before entering the mountains, where we followed a winding path in the valley to the west. That would take us to the foothills of several snowcapped mountains, where we would find the westward path. Originally a path for pilgrims, it was now covered with the scrambled footsteps of refugees.

We hugged the border between Chieftain Maichi's and Lha Shopa's lands, drawing closer to the sounds of battle coming from the southeast. Apparently, my aging father had taken on the Red Chinese.

Hearing the sounds of rapid gunfire, I felt my heart suddenly gripped by a warm longing for my parents, something I hadn't felt for a very long time. I thought I had stopped loving Father and didn't even care for Mother anymore, but now I realized that I still loved them both very much. I couldn't flee to the west and just leave them in the line of fire. I told the historian, the steward, and the women to wait in the valley while the soldiers and I headed back to the Maichi estate. When we reached the mountain pass, I turned to look at the people I was leaving behind along with their white tents in the dark green valley. The women were waving to us. I felt a sudden foreboding that I'd never see them again.

Our eastward journey took three days.

The Red Army had pushed all the way to the edge of the Maichi estate. Red flags flew above the forest in the foothills. Machine-gun emplacements blocked the main road, forcing us to break through to the house under the cover of darkness. Armed soldiers filled the compound; some were Tibetans, but most were White Chinese. Those moving around upstairs were the living; those lying in the yard were the dead. The Maichi family and soldiers had been under siege for nearly two weeks.

I burst into the chieftain's room, where I came face-to-face with my father, Chieftain Maichi. His hair and beard were gray, but he didn't look older; his eyes were lit up with a mad glint. He grabbed me. His hands were still powerful. Now, I'm an idiot, with a slow mind, but three days on the road had given me plenty of time to imagine the scene when father and son met after all this time, tears drenching our faces and our hearts. But I was wrong. He cried out, "Look who's here. It's my idiot son!"

Intentionally raising my voice, I said, "I'm here to fetch Father and Mother!"

But Chieftain Maichi said he was old and dying, and didn't want to go anywhere. "I thought I'd die an uneventful death," he said. "I never imagined that such an opportunity would present itself." He added, "A chieftain, a nobleman, should die in the heat of battle if his death is to be meaningful."

He clapped my shoulder, and said, "Except that my idiot son won't ever be a chieftain." And he shouted, "I'm the last of the Maichi chieftains!"

Alerted by Father's shout, Mother walked in with a smile on her face. She rushed up, held my head to her breast, and rocked it back and forth. "I didn't think I'd ever see my son again," she whispered. Then came the tears, which fell on my ears and neck. She declared that she wanted to die with the chieftain.

The Red Army halted their attack that night. Father said that night and day made no difference to them, that they never rested.

"Those Red Chinese aren't bad," he said. "They probably know that father and son have been reunited."

He asked two White Chinese officers in for a drink.

The chieftain praised their courage. The two brave men suggested that we send out the women and those who no longer wanted to fight while the Communists were taking a breather. But Father said their machine guns would open up as soon as people left the house. So we kept drinking. It was a moonless night. Off in the distance, the Red Chinese lit bonfires, their flames licking the night sky like the flags they fought under.

Aryi came up to me when I went out to look at the fires. I could tell from the look on his face that the old executioner was dead. But he didn't mention his father. Instead, he asked if Sonam Tserang had returned. I told him that a dead Sonam Tserang with holes in his chest had been sent back.

"I thought so," he said softly, shyly. Then he added, "There is no more need for an executioner, and I shall die soon."

Then he slipped away like a ghost.

The moon rose in the middle of the night. With a white flag on the tip of his bayonet, an officer walked in the moonlight toward the Red Chinese camp. Machine guns raked the area around him, and he threw himself to the ground. When the gunfire stopped, he got up and continued walking with his white flag. Machine-gun fire crackled again, raising dust all around him. But when they saw the white flag, they stopped firing. Sometime before dawn he returned with a promise that the Red Army would not fire on noncombatants who wanted to leave the house.

His voice cracking with emotion, the courageous man reported that they were facing a righteous army and lamented the fact that they held different beliefs.

Some White Chinese soldiers were the first to leave. With their hands in the air, they walked toward the enemy camp. Subjects of the chieftain who were afraid to die headed west to places not yet reached by the Chinese. Chieftain Maichi wanted me to go. I looked at Mother, who showed no interest in leaving. Since she didn't want to go, neither could I. Everyone knew that this night would be the last in this world for those who remained in the house. So we started drinking again. Spring had nearly arrived, and a moist wind cleansed the air of the smell of gunpowder. The sweet aroma of decay rose slowly from the underground storeroom and curled around people who were only half awake. Not knowing what the smell was, the Han officers sniffed the air greedily. But we in the Maichi family knew that it was the mixed fragrance of barley, silver, and opium. I fell asleep amid the comforting, ethereal aroma.

I dreamed through the remainder of the night, fragmented dreams that covered all my life experiences. I woke up with the sun flickering in my eyes, and discovered that I was sleeping in my childhood room in the very bed I'd slept in as a boy. It was here that I had first put my hand under the clothes of a maid called Sangye Dolma. It had been a snowy morning marked by the incessant cries of thrushes outside the window. A maidservant's body had awakened the little bit of wisdom in the head of a slumbering idiot. My memories start with that morning, this house, and this bed. My life began the year I was thirteen. Now I didn't know how old I was. Alone in my room, I looked in the mirror. My God, look at that wrinkled forehead! If Mother were sitting in this room, as she had on that morning so many years ago, I'd have asked her how old her idiot son was. Thirty? Forty? Maybe even fifty. So many years had flown by. I walked over to the window. Outside, a heavy fog was lifting slowly, and the birds' calls were crisp and pleasing to the ear, as if time had stood still and life had stopped many, many years ago.

I could hear thrushes, robins, and tiny green-beaked mountain sparrows.

Suddenly, flocks of startled birds flew up from the bushes and the grass. They wheeled in the sky and shrieked, unwilling to land again. In the end, they flapped their wings and flew off into the distance. It was quiet all around, but we sensed danger pressing ever closer. Inside the towering estate house, people were running with guns and taking up positions behind every available window.

The chieftain's wife was the only person who stayed put. She ordered the servants to brew some tea over a small brazier and made a series of opium pellets. Then she washed her face with milk and sprayed herself with perfume before putting on a pink satin robe and lying down on her opium bed. She said, "Come sit for a while, son. Don't stand there like an idiot."

I sat down, my palm sweaty from holding a pistol.

"Let me take a good look at you," she said. "I've already said good-bye to your father."

I sat there like an idiot for her to gaze at me. The tea was boiling on the clay brazier. The chieftain's wife said, "Son, you know my background, don't you?"

I said I did.

She sighed. "I've had the best life of all those who will die today." Then she went on to say how she'd been born a Han, but had become a Tibetan. When she sniffed herself, she could tell she smelled like a Tibetan from head to toe. Of course, she was happiest over the fact that she'd been elevated from the lower class to the aristocracy. She told me to bend down so she could whisper something to me. "From my degrading origins, I became the respected wife of a chieftain."

Mother then revealed a secret she had hidden all those years: she had once been a prostitute. As soon as the words were out of her mouth, I was reminded of the gaudy house in my border town, and could even hear the scratchy songs from the gramophone and smell the warm aroma of barbecued meat and boiled beans. But there was no such smell on the chieftain's wife. She ordered the servants to warm some wine in a teapot, which she used to swallow several of the opium pellets. Then while the servants obediently warmed another cup of wine, she told me to bend forward again, this time to kiss my forehead. "I'll never again have to worry about whether I gave birth to an idiot son," she said softly.

After swallowing some more opium pellets, she lay on her side on the fancy low bed and muttered to herself, "I was strapped for cash when I wanted opium in the past, but I've never had to worry about money as a Maichi. Life has been good to me."

Then she closed her eyes and fell asleep. The maids pushed me out the door. I wanted to turn and take another look when a series of loud shrieks shattered the morning tranquillity and tore through the air toward me.

After a siege of several days, the enemy outside had released all those who were afraid to die. That was the limit of their righteousness and benevolence. Now it was time to fight, but not by sending their soldiers through a hail of gunfire. I'd thought we would be engaged in hand-to-hand combat, but their patience had run out, and they were training their heavy artillery on us.

This first shell landed with a deafening boom and created a huge crater in the yard. The executioner's stake was blown up, the pieces flying out into the field. The next shell landed behind the house. Then the barrage stopped, at least for now. Chieftain Maichi waved me to his side, where we waited for the next shell to land. But it didn't come, which gave me a chance to tell Father that Mother had just swallowed opium pellets with wine.

"My little idiot, your mother has taken her own life." He didn't cry. An ugly smile twisted his face as he continued hoarsely, "Very well then. She no longer has to worry that the dust will soil her clothes."

It wasn't until then that I realized that Mother had committed suicide.

The White Chinese officer threw down his gun and sat on the floor. I thought he was afraid, but he said it was useless to resist, that the enemy's third shell would land right on our heads. But most of the men still held their weapons tightly. The shriek of artillery fire cut through the air again. This time, it wasn't a single shell, but a barrage targeting Chieftain Maichi's house. They landed, and the house shook amid the deafening booms. Shells exploded, one after the other, blinding us with fire, smoke, and dust. It had never occurred to me that one could not see the world before dying. But we couldn't, we really couldn't. Amid the violent explosions, the gigantic stone structure that had been the Maichi estate house finally crumbled, taking us with it. The act of falling was so exquisite that I actually felt as if I were flying.

49 The Dust Settles

I thought the idiot son of the Maichi family must have risen to heaven; otherwise, why would so many bright stars be sparkling before his eyes? It was the heaviness of my body that told me I was still alive. Climbing out of the debris, I choked on dust.

Bending over in the ruins, I was racked by coughing.

My cough traveled out to the field and disappeared. In the past, no matter what kind of sound I made, it would have been blocked by the estate's high walls to create an echo. But this time my voice disappeared as soon as it left my mouth. I cocked my ears to listen, but there wasn't a sound. The artillery crews were gone, it seemed, leaving the Maichi family and those unwilling to surrender buried in the rubble. Quiet, soundless, everyone else seemed to be sleeping in a tomb created by exploded shells.

I started walking under the starlight, heading west, toward the place I'd come from. But I'd barely started when I tripped over something. When I stood up, the cold barrel of a gun was pressed up against my head. I heard myself shout, "Bang!" As soon as I made the sound of a gunshot, I felt darkness descend before my eyes, and I died one more time.

Around daybreak, I woke up to find Chieftain Maichi's third wife, Yangzom, sobbing by my side. As soon as she saw me open my eyes, she said, "The chieftain and mistress are both dead."

At that moment, the bright red sun of another brand-new day was just rising in the east.

Like me, she had climbed out of the debris only to end up in the Red Army camp.

The Red Chinese were happy to have captured two members of Chieftain Maichi's family. They gave us injections and some medicine to take, and sent over a Red Tibetan to talk to us. All the time they were showering us with their hospitality, they kept shelling the house. The Red Tibetan talked on and on, but I didn't feel like speaking. What he said at the end, however, took me by surprise. They had decided that I could inherit Chieftain Maichi's title so long as I threw in my lot with the People's Government.

When I heard that, I said, "Don't you Red Chinese want to eliminate the chieftains?"

He laughed, and said, "You can continue to be chieftain until we eliminate them."

The Red Tibetan said many other things, some of which I understood, some of which I didn't. Actually, what he said can be summed up in a single phrase: in the future I would be different from those who weren't chieftains, even if I were only chieftain for a day. I asked him if that's what he meant.

He cracked a smile, and said, "Now you've got it."

The army was leaving again.

The Red Army unloaded artillery from two horses for the soldiers to carry. Yangzom and I were to ride. The army slowly moved westward. When we were about to cross the mountain, I turned to look at the place where I was born and grew up, the Maichi estate.

Signs of battle were virtually invisible, except for the disappearance of the towering house itself. Spring was turning the orchard and the vast barley fields green, and among the greenery, the chieftain's house was now a pile of rubble. The lower portions lay beneath the shadow cast by the debris, while the upper portions emitted a metallic luster in the sunlight. The sight brought tears to my eyes. A tiny whirlwind rose up from the rubble, stirring up clouds of dust that roiled above the debris. At noon on clear days with a bright sun, such tiny whirlwinds could be seen in the river valleys ruled by the chieftains, rising up suddenly, carrying dust and dead leaves and branches to dance in the sky.

On this day, it signaled the souls of Chieftain Maichi and his wife rising up to heaven, at least to me.

The whirlwind rose higher and higher, and eventually broke up in a very high place: the invisible objects inside went up to heaven, while the visible dust fell from the sky and covered the piles of rocks. Dust is dust, after all; in the end, the dust fell among the rocks, leaving nothing but the silent sun shining on the debris. As the tears in my eyes increased the brightness of the sun, I called out silently to my family.

Ah-pa! Ah-ma!

I also called out, Aryi!

A pain I'd never felt before tore at my heart.

The army transported me over the mountain ridge, and I couldn't see anything anymore.

Those I'd left behind in the valley were still waiting there, and that eased the pain in my heart somewhat. From a distance, I saw the white tents they'd pitched. Then they spotted the Red Army troops. Someone fired at the army still on the hill, and two Red soldiers crumpled to the ground, facedown, with a groan, blood oozing from their backs. Luckily, only one person had fired. The lonely gunshots echoed in the deep valley as my people stood there in a daze until the army charged up to them. It was the steward who had fired. Gun in hand, he was standing on a felled tree trunk, like a hero, but looking somewhat bewildered. Before I could walk up to him, he was knocked to the ground by a gun barrel and tied up. I rode past the tents, as lines of faces glided by, one after another. Everyone was looking at me blankly. After I passed, I heard howls rise up behind me. Quickly the valley was filled with sad wails.

That upset the soldiers, for wherever they went, they had been greeted by loud cheers. They were the army of the poor, who made up the majority of the world's population. The poor people cheered because they had finally gotten an army of their own. But not here, where the slaves opened wide their foolish mouths to cry for their masters.

We kept moving toward the border.

The town appeared before our eyes two days later. The long narrow street that had always been dusty was now as still as the nearby creek. The army marched down the street, as eyes watched from behind boarded-up shops. Even the brothel that had spread syphilis was unusually quiet, a pink curtain draped over the window facing the street.

Several ranking officers moved into my big house, where they could see the whole town from upstairs. They said I had new ideas, and that people like me would never be out of date.

I told them I was going to die soon.

"No, people like you will always be up to date."

But I felt that dying was unrelated to being up to date.

They said, "You'll be a good friend to the Communists. You're doing construction here. We have come to this place to build pretty towns like this everywhere."

The senior officer even patted me on the shoulder, and said, "Of course, there'll be no more opium or brothels. Your town needs some reform and so do you."

I smiled.

He grabbed my hand and shook it enthusiastically as he said, "You'll be Chieftain Maichi. And you'll be our best friend when the revolution spreads and there are no more chieftains."

But I'd never live to see that day. I'd seen Chieftain Maichi's spirit turn into a whirlwind and rise up to heaven. The remaining dust fell and returned to the earth. My time was coming. I'd been an idiot all my life, but now I knew I was neither an idiot nor a smart person. I was just a passerby who came to this wondrous land when the chieftain system was nearing its end.

Yes, heaven had let me see and let me hear, had placed me in the middle of everything while having me remain above it all. It was for this purpose that heaven had made me look like an idiot.

The historian was sitting in his room, his pen a blur as he

recorded everything. The bodhi tree downstairs, planted by this tongueless person, had grown as tall as a two-story building. I told myself that I would recognize only this tree if I returned in a future life.

News of the total destruction of Chieftain Rongong came from the north.

But the news didn't draw much of a reaction from me, because before that happened, even Chieftain Maichi had similarly disappeared like flying ashes and dying smoke. One day, the Red Chinese brought me news of all the other chieftains and asked me to guess what Chieftain Lha Shopa had done. "He surrendered," I said.

"Yes," the friendly officer said. "He set a good example for other chieftains."

But my sense was that Lha Shopa surrendered because he knew he was a small and weak chieftain. Years before, I'd been able to make him bend his knee with little pressure, unlike Chieftain Wangpo, who had fought again and again with no regard for his own life. But surprisingly, even Chieftain Wangpo had surrendered. The funny thing was that he had believed that the chieftain system would last forever and he took the opportunity to seize other chieftains' lands, including lots of land from Chieftain Maichi, who no longer existed.

I couldn't help but laugh when I heard the news. I said, "It would have been more practical if he'd snatched Tharna."

The Red Chinese agreed with me.

"Was that Tharna, the beauty of beauties?" one of the officers asked. You see, the reputation of my beautiful wife had spread far and wide; even the virtuous Red Chinese had heard her name.

"Yes, that pretty woman was my unfaithful wife." These normally serious people laughed.

Tharna would probably have run to Chieftain Wangpo to continue their affair if she'd known he had surrendered, since there was nothing to stop her now. The army that had defeated Chieftain Rongong in the north continued to move from the northern grassland into my town, where they linked up with the army that had vanquished Chieftain Maichi in the southeast. There were no more chieftains to oppose them around here. Chieftain Rongong had waged a determined resistance, so only a handful of her people fell into the enemy's hands. Those taken alive were brought over with their hands tied behind their backs. I spotted Adviser Huang and Tharna among them.

I pointed her out to the Red Army. "That woman is my wife."

They returned Tharna to me, although they found it hard to believe that a woman with such a widespread reputation for beauty could look like that. I told Sangye Dolma to wash the dust, the bloodstains, and traces of tears from Tharna's face, and dress her in fresh, bright clothes. Her glamour immediately lit up the soldiers' eyes. Now we were together again, husband and wife. We stood with the officers, with their booming voices and pistols on their belts, watching the army move into town. The soldiers who had defeated Chieftain Maichi were singing as they lined up to welcome the victors from the north. The town seemed forsaken that spring, with green grass blanketing the street. Now the army stopped and sang as they marched in place. These soldiers, in their khaki uniforms, blotted out the green on the street, staining the spring town with the color of autumn.

I wanted to save Adviser Huang.

As soon as I said so, a Red Army officer smiled, and asked me, "Why?"

"Because he's my adviser."

"No," he said. "These are enemies of the people."

In the end, Adviser Huang was shot on the riverbank. I went to see his body. The bullet had taken off the upper half of his head, leaving only his mouth, which was filled with sand. Beside him lay the bodies of several White Chinese.

Tharna slept with me that night. She asked me when I'd surrendered. When she learned that I'd unceremoniously fallen into their hands, she laughed. But her laughter turned to tears, which fell on my face. "Idiot," she said, "you make me hurt you all the time, but then you make me realize how desirable you are."

Her sincerity touched me, but I lay there motionless. Then she asked if I was really unafraid of dying. Just as I was going to reply, she put her finger to my lips, and said, "Think twice before answering."

I thought hard and thought some more and concluded that I was not afraid to die.

So she whispered to me, "My God, I'm starting to love you again." Her body was warming up. I wanted her that night, wanted her badly. Afterward, I asked her if she had syphilis. She giggled, and replied, "Idiot, didn't I already ask you that question?"

"You only asked if I was afraid of dying."

My beautiful wife said, "If you're not afraid to die, then why be afraid of syphilis?"

We both laughed. I asked if she knew when she'd die. She said she didn't. Then she asked me the same question, and I told her, "Tomorrow."

We were both silent for a while before starting to laugh again.

By that time, morning light had crossed the bars of the window and shone on our bed. She said, "Then you'll have to wait for the sun to rise once more. Let's get some more sleep."

So we lay there with our backs to each other, wrapped tightly in the blanket, and fell asleep. I didn't have a single dream and didn't wake up until noon.

I was leaning against the railing, looking at the deepening spring colors around town, when I spotted the Maichi enemy, the innkeeper, crossing the town, heading my way with a jug of liquor. Apparently, I couldn't wait till tomorrow. I said to my wife, "Tharna, go up to the roof and see what the people in town are doing."

She said, "Idiot, why do you always make such ridiculous requests? But you've never sounded so tender before. All right, I'll go up and take a look for you."

I returned to the room, where I soon heard a knock at the door.

It was my fate knocking.

The knocks were very calm. I guess my innkeeper friend hadn't become arrogant simply because his younger brother had changed from a killer into a Red Tibetan. He was intent on following the rules set up before the arrival of the Red Chinese. The door was ajar, but he kept up his leisurely knocking, obviously in no hurry. He didn't enter with his jug until I told him to. With one hand holding the jug and the other hidden beneath his robe, he said, "Young Master, I've brought you some liquor."

"Put it down," I said. "You didn't come to give me liquor. You're here to kill me."

He let go of the jug, which split open when it hit the floor.

The room quickly filled with the fragrance of liquor. It was very good liquor. I said, "Your brother is a Red Tibetan now. Since they can't just go around killing people, the task of revenge has fallen to you."

"That was my best liquor," he said hoarsely. "I wanted you to drink it."

"We don't have time. My wife will be here soon, so you should act now."

He then took his hand out from under his robe to reveal a shining dagger. Beads of sweat dotted his pale forehead as he pressed forward.

"Wait," I said. I climbed into bed and lay down before saying, "All right."

When he raised his dagger, I said, "Wait."

He asked me what I wanted. I planned to tell him how good the liquor smelled, but what came out of my mouth was, "What's your name? What's your clan name?"

Yes, I knew that the two brothers were the Maichis' enemy, but I'd forgotten their clan name. My question pained him deeply. He hadn't harbored a grudge toward me, but my question kindled the fire of hatred in his eyes. The aroma of liquor permeating the room made me sleepy. A dagger, a sharp dagger, entered my belly like a cube of ice. It didn't hurt; it felt like ice. But the ice quickly turned hot. I could hear my blood dripping to the floor; I also heard my innkeeper friend's hoarse voice say good-bye.

Now, Heaven, you spirits and deities who sent me to this world! My body is slowly splitting into two halves. One half is dry and is rising up, while the blood-drenched half is sinking. At this moment, I hear my wife's footsteps coming down the stairs. I want to call out her name, but I can't find my voice.

Dear God, if our souls can really be reincarnated, please send me back to this place in my next life. I love this beautiful place. Deities and spirits! My soul has finally struggled out of my bleeding body and is flying upward. When the sunlight flickers, the soul will disperse. There will be nothing except a white light.

The blood drips to the floor, forming a pool. As I grow cold on the bed, my blood is slowly turning into the color of a dark night.